2 ?

A Fatal Encounter

The Adventures of John Grey
Book One

Frederick A. Read

A *Guaranteed* Book

First Published in 2007 by
Guaranteed Books

an imprint of Pendragon Press, Po Box 12, Maesteg
Mid Glamorgan, South Wales, CF34 0XG, UK

Large Print Edition 2010

ISBN 978 0 9554452 4 8

Designed and typeset by Christopher Teague

Printed and Bound in Wales by
Print Evolution

www.guaranteedbooks.co.uk

Dedication

This book 'A Fatal Encounter' is dedicated to the memory of my late Uncle John, who served in some of the British Merchant Shipping Lines as a Marine Engineer officer, during the 1950's and '60's.

However, the series is dedicated to all the rest of the seafaring members of my family and all the mariner friends and shipmates whom we've shared sea time together, who are now probably over the seas and far away.

All of whom, like myself had sailed in, over, and even under all the oceans, seas, lakes and most major rivers of the world, and of the countries or islands we had visited in doing so.

Acknowledgement

To my dear wife Anne, who spent many a lonely evening for weeks on end during my creative writing sessions.

To my late Uncle John, and to my fellow author and very good friend Christopher Teague, as both of them encouraged me to continue over the 10 years it took to complete this and other series of novels and short stories.

Foreword

The Adventures of John Grey is a series of 10 fictional maritime novels that was inspired by and written in a style as accredited to C.S. Forrester's celebrated *Hornblower* series.

The series is set between post WW2 and the 1970's, and can be considered as a major new series and the first of its kind to be written in decades.

Each book within the series will take you on a different adventure whilst voyaging to various locations around the world.

"A Fatal Encounter" is the lead novel, which introduces the main character, John Grey, and the start of his rights of passage through life as a Marine Engineering Officer.

He will meet up and form several relationships with fellow shipmates and others ashore, wherever he may find himself at the time.

This is his first adventure and voyage, which is one of self-discovery, full of high drama, and the ways of life on the high seas.

Chapters

Chapter I
Leaving Home

The heavy wooden door shut out the last vestiges of the warm glow of light shining in the now empty hallway, as eighteen year old John Grey stood on the doorstep one early September morning to get his eyes accustomed to the dark.

As he pulled the collar of his overcoat closely around his neck to shut out the cold, he wondered how long it would be for him to return and change his mother's tears of goodbye to joyous ones of welcome home.

Picking up his heavy suitcase, with his footsteps muffled by the thick fog, he scrunched his way down the long narrow cinder path that skirted around the house, and made his way to the garden gate.

On his way down the path, he met his boyhood playmate Bridget coming slowly to meet him, she gave a little yelp and wagged her tail as she recognised her master. John scooped her up into his arms, stroked her muzzle gently and told her to be a good dog whilst he was away. Putting her down again gently, he told her to stay as he went through the gate, locking it behind him. He walked over a little wooden bridge that spanned a brook, through the gap in the hedgerow to a pale yellow street light which also served as a bus stop, and stood at what he thought was the kerb of the main road.

Looking left and right and listening for any signs of traffic, he quickly crossed the wide road to the other side, and walked up a long steep hill to where he knew for certain there was a bus stop and where his new journey in life would begin.

After waiting for a few minutes, stamping his feet to keep warm, he saw a twin yellow eyed monster coming out of the fog and realised that this was his bus to take him to the city.

Before stepping onto the brightly lit bus, John was able to take one last look at his home marked only by a thin column of smoke that pierced its way through the low lying fog and coming from the tall Victorian chimney of his home.

The bus appeared to have its own fog bank inside because of the tobacco smoke coming from several large pipes of other travellers, but John didn't mind and when he too started to smoke, also added to the smell of various brands of tobacco.

When he finally reached his destination stop, he picked up his suitcase and stepped off the bus, bidding the conductor goodbye.

The bus left John and chugged its way back into the thick fog, leaving him isolated, in a dark cobble stoned alley, which he knew would lead him to the docks, in the very heart of BELFAST.

Making his way along the docks, stopping at each ship to read their names on their bows, wondering from whence it came or where it might be going, he came to a space in the line of ships where his should have been.

"That's strange! Now what." John whispered to himself for fear of being heard by some unknown person lurking in the dark. He stood for a few minutes and observed the dock cranes nodding and bowing to each other as they loaded or unloaded the ship next to them.

The deep melancholic foghorns calling in the distance made him realise just how cold and quite alone he was in this seemingly deserted part of the docks.

He remembered seeing and passing a small hut that had people standing around it, drinking from large mugs. He made his way back to it and found a brazier burning merrily away nearby and sat down near to it to keep warm.

"That's better!" he muttered to himself, as he could feel the fire warming his hands and legs.

As he sat there wrapped up in his thoughts, he looked round and watched and marvelled as four large magnificent shire horses appeared out of the icy gloom, pulling with ease the heavily laden wagon that was rattling noisily over the cobble stones. After a short while as they disappeared back into the gloom again, he noticed that it was now taking on a dull silver sheen.

'It must be near daybreak.' he mused as he took out his pocket watch to check the time of day.

"Six Thirty, not a bad guess." he opined to himself as he put his watch back into his breast pocket.

As he was about to re-button his coat again to keep out the cold, he was alarmed and shocked to feel a strong hand gripping his shoulder, accompanied by a gravely voice behind him.

"What's a fine looking specimen like you doing sitting around like a lost tailor's dummy?"

John jumped up and turning around to confront his would be attacker, saw a well built, giant of a man smiling down at him.

"Sorry I startled you, my name is Andy Sinclair and I'm supposed to be meeting a couple of the lads that's joining the *Brooklea*." The stranger said in a broad Scottish accent.

"That's great! My name is John Grey and you must be one of the people I'm supposed to meet at berth seven." he said as he introduced himself.

"I'm frae a fishing village called Fraserburgh in the North East of Scotland. What about you?"

"I am just a local boy from a small village called Dunmurry which is about 8 miles west of here, and this is my first ship since passing my engineering college exams in the local shipyards." John replied modestly.

When he spoke, a soft lilt in his voice told the world that he came from the lovely County of Down. It was polished enough to declare that he was educated, but not that of a *lah-de-dah*.

He had a twinkle in his blue eyes that meant that he was a mischievous enough to share a joke or some banter.

"Well here ye are laddie. Say, aren't you the new bloke joining that's got some bright ideas and supposed to be good with engines and that?"

"What is it you do on board?"

"Me? I'm the ship's coxswain, but known as the Boatswain. Er, take a wee tip, just call me the Bosun when we're aboard. But on occasions like this, just call me Andy when we're ashore together."

"All right, Andy it is." John agreed, as he shook Sinclair's hand that looked as big as a shovel and with a vice like grip to match, compared with his own slim and much tinier one.

'Andy is going to be someone to reckon with, but I'm glad he appears to be on my side,' John mused as they sat down on their own luggage.

"I've just come off yon ferry from Glasgow. Talk about a slow boat to China. That so called Bosun, must have waltzed that ferry all over the Irish Sea before coming here. Why, he couldn't sail a wee wooden boat in a tin bath." Sinclair snorted as he pointed over his shoulder with a large thumb.

John looked up at Sinclair and saw that he was dressed in sea boots, with a less than clean seaman's jersey under a faded blue uniform.

A battered cap hid a mop of black curly hair, which prompted a string of questions that were springing from John's inquisitive mind, "have you been to sea long Andy? What?"

"Whoa! Hold on laddie! I've heard you're a one for asking questions, but try me one at a time." Sinclair replied in a mock chiding manner.

"Right ho! I'll start again." John said sheepishly and

5

started again: "Have you been to sea long?"

"Aye! Served in His Majesty's Navy all through the war, afore joining the *Lea* line. Do you hope to travel the world like me?"

"I hope to sail far and wide but as I've just said, this is my first ship."

"Well never you mind. We'll all be the same when we get to sea. All strangers together until we get to know each others worth on board."

John reflected on what Sinclair had said, which gave him a feeling of knowing he was finally going to see the world, and of trepidation as to what his life was going to be like amongst a gathering of seafarers from God knows where.

"Mmm! Smell that bacon that's reekin from yonder wee hut. I'd give a tot of my best rum for one of those butties they're selling. Only I've no money left on me until I see the Purser." Sinclair moaned as he turned to John appealingly and commenced pulling his pockets inside out, one by one.

John was now getting to like Andy's strange Scottish accent, especially when he rolled his 'R's on every occasion, which seem to accentuate his own soft lilting accent.

"As a matter of fact, that's just what I had in mind when you came along, Andy. You sit there and guard the baggage whilst I get us something to warm ourselves up with." he said with a grin.

"What a canny young man ye are." Sinclair replied

as he licked his lips in tasty anticipation.

John came back bearing two large enamel mugs of steaming hot tea, and two large wheaten farls, that were stuffed with thick slices of gammon and dripping with butter, which they promptly devoured and drunk with great relish.

"That's much better, I feel a bit more civilised now." Sinclair sighed, and gave a loud burp, then started to lick the remains of the melted butter from his large fingers.

When Sinclair had finished licking his fingers, he turned to John.

"Here ye are, have yerself a roll of my baccy. You deserve that at least, but it's all I got the noo." he said, as he presented his tobacco tin to John in a gesture of appreciation.

John looked at the offered tobacco tin and thought of his own pockets that had only about a shilling left and not quite enough to buy a decent packet of cigarettes. He thanked him for his offer but stated that he'd rather try a tailor made one if he had one.

Sinclair looked into John's young fresh face and said.

"That tells me, you've just started out on the Tobacco road. I think I've got one of them left somewhere."

After much fumbling, but like a magician, Sinclair pulled out a crumpled cigarette packet from deep within his jacket pocket and gave it to him.

"Here ye are, that's my last one." He said with surprise as he looked into the empty packet.

"But be careful mind, cause these are real men's fags like what was issued in the Royal Navy. Full strength they are."

They both sat quietly smoking their cigarettes and starting to enjoy each others new found company, when another person came out of the gloom and stopped right by them.

"Well hello me old shipmate Bruce." Sinclair boomed as he stood up and shook the newcomers hand.

"Hello Andy, you old Scotch egg!" Larter replied.

"And who's this with you Andy?" he asked as he looked over and nodded to John.

"Bruce, this is John Grey, one of our new trainee Engineers. John, meet Bruce Larter. Our 2nd Sparker, and a fellow officer of yours." Was the brief introduction to each other.

As John stood up and shook Larter's hand, he noticed that although his hand was clean and soft, the grip was strong which belied Larter's tall slender stature.

Sinclair and Larter started to recall some of the old voyages they shared together for a moment, leaving John marvelling at what a bond they seem to have considering they were two entirely different people from different parts of the country.

"Pardon my ignorance Bruce," John interrupted politely.

"This is my first ship and voyage, and I'm not sure of all the sailors jargon yet, but the question is, what's a Sparker?"

The two men chuckled for a moment until Larter replied.

"Ok! I'm a Radio Officer 2nd class as opposed to an electrician. Andy here is the Chief Bosun and sometimes gets called a Cox'n, depending on the ship and the shipping line. Like him, you too will get called many things from different people, but mostly it'll be your rank like 5th or 2nd until you reach the dizzy heights of a Chief Engineer. Then you can be called 'Mr', or 'Chief', or just plain 'Engines."

"That's sounds nice!" replied John and added solemnly that he had hopes to be the Chief Engineer on some big luxury liner like the *SS Queen Mary*, just like one of his apprenticeship instructors had been.

"And so you shall." the other two said in hearty unison.

It was Larter's turn to weigh up the measure of John, then stated.

"Mind you, you'll have to work very hard. Everybody needs looking after on their first voyage, so if we two are on the same ship as you, then we'll take you under our wing as and when necessary, providing you don't let us down and you prove that you are worth your 'salt' shall we say."

Larter and Sinclair looked at each other then at John.

"Is that a promise or an agreement we've got from you John?" Sinclair asked in a challenging and serious voice.

John thought swiftly and carefully at this exciting new prospect, then studied the weather beaten faces of the two challengers.

After a moment, John cleared his throat nervously and held his hand out to shake on the agreement.

"I agree." he said, and all three shook hands together in a triple hand shake, to seal a promise that was to become a long lasting bond between them.

Sinclair broke the little spell by saying to Larter.

"Young John got me a cuppa and a bite to eat from yon galley over there. Why don't you do the same, as the *'Brook'* won't be in for a while yet due to this infernal fog."

"That's a grand idea Andy, except..." Larter stated as he pulled his pockets inside out indicating that he was just as broke as Andy had been.

Sinclair looked at John very closely and saw that he had already put his hand into his pocket, and then gave Larter some money.

"Here you are Bruce, it's all I've got but you're welcome to it. Now, we are all broke together." John concluded as he handed over the last of his money to this newly found friend.

As John watched Larter making his way towards the hut, he turned to Sinclair and asked him what part of the world or country did Larter come from.

Sinclair laughed and replied.

"Can't you tell the accent? He's a Scouser from Bootle, that's in Liverpool. You'll get used to all the different dialects and accents as you go along, so don't worry too much about it yet."

John had heard of Liverpool as a big shipping port and the Albert docks there, but this was the first time he'd met somebody from there, but thanked Andy for the information anyway.

Moments later, Larter came back cursing as hot tea was spilling out from three overfull mugs and onto his fingers, scalding them in the process.

"Oyah! Ouch! Geez! I wished me Mam gave me asbestos hands. Quick, grab a mug each, they're getting hotter and heavier by the second." Larter muttered and swore as he came right up to the other two.

The two quickly obliged Larter's request and sat huddled together in the gloom, supping this life giving drink.

"Got any fags on ye Bruce?" Sinclair asked as he drained the last drop of his tea from his mug.

"Why yes! And that's just about all." was the reply as Larter fished out from his immaculate tunic pocket a matching cigarette case and lighter, opened it and gave them all a cigarette each to enjoy.

John stopped Larter's hand from putting the case and lighter away by asking him if he could have a look at them.

"Certainly! That way you'll know who they belong to if I ever lose them."

"Which is more than often than not." Sinclair quipped.

John looked carefully at the solid silver matching pair and noticed the initials B.L. inscribed on them.

"Bruce Larter I presume?" John asked politely.

"No. Benjamin Larter. These were given to me by my mother when my father was killed in action in the early part of the last war." Larter replied wistfully.

"I'm sorry to hear that." John said sympathetically and remembered an incident that caused the near loss of one of his brother's in law.

"Thanks." replied Larter, as he seemed to be looking at some far off place. Then added philosophically.

"But I've just about got over it now, so not to worry."

The other two just nodded slowly and they lapsed into a silence as if to give a mark of respect to all those who perished in that recent and dreadful WW2.

Their silence was short lived and their private thoughts disturbed with an announcement from Sinclair.

"There she is! Just look at the state of her!" he exclaimed in amazement.

John and Larter looked round to where Sinclair was staring and pointing.

"That's the '*Brook*' and your new home." Larter advised John.

"Yes. She's looking a wee bit sick. I wonder what's up with her this time?" enquired Sinclair.

"Come on lads! Let's give a hand to tie her up nicely." Larter prompted. Then turned to John and informed him that all ships were always referred to in female terms, such as 'Her' and 'She'.

The three friends carried their belongings and walked swiftly down to the dock-side, stopping by a large black and white cast iron bollard that was sticking out of the cobble stones like a giant mushroom.

Sinclair turned to John and enquired whether he'd ever tied up a ship before.

When John shook his head for no, Sinclair turned to Larter with the suggestion.

"Bruce, go and get the stern rope. Don't forget to go 'through the eye' and I'll see you at that gangway ladder over there."

He then turned to John and explained what Larter was about to do with the 'stern rope'. Sinclair then left John to see to the placement of the two gangways.

John carried out his allotted task as if he was a robot, for he was mesmerised by the spectacle of his new home that was rapidly dwarfing him as the ship came closer to the docking berth.

With his job done, he gathered up all the bags and walked precariously towards his muster point indicated by Sinclair, where he dumped them unceremoniously onto the ground, and waited for the other two to come back.

It was light now, and with the fog lifting steadily, he could see virtually all that took place in front of his very eyes.

The *Brooklea* had a very deep sounding horn that gave a few long resonant blasts, which must have been a signal to the little tugs that were pushing the ship into her place. In turn the little tugs stopped pushing, sounded their little horns that tooted as if to say, "TA TA for NOW," and paddled their way back down the harbour like little ducks.

The ship finally thumped against the harbour wall and took on a distinct list that suggested that it was tired and had to lean on the jetty for support.

John looked down over the side between the dock wall and the ship and discovered with mild shock, the reason for the ship having such a pronounced list.

What he saw was a large gash in the side of the ship, and what appeared to be an attempt at welding, judging by the patch that was put on.

It didn't match the symmetric lines of the rivets that were used in its construction.

"Hmm a riveted ship. Why don't they build ships like submarines, all welded hulls" he said quietly to himself and lapsed into pondering over other ideas in his mind.

John had used his favourite apprentice school Instructor as a role model, and was still in the process of developing a very active and inquisitive mind. Which meant that, just like his mentor, he sometimes spoke his thoughts aloud, or used himself as a sounding board for them.

Those thoughts were suddenly interrupted with a constantly ringing bell that was getting louder and apparently closer to him.

He looked over his shoulder and saw a small convoy of vehicles coming towards then pass him. *'Let's see. An ambulance, a very handsome sleek limousine, and a hearse? What's all this about? I wonder what the hearse is doing here?'* As yet more questions sprang to his mind.

He saw that the gangway had already been lowered into position to allow access to or from the ship as her best boarding point.

A large burly man with a big bushy beard, suddenly appeared and stood at the top of the gangway, dressed in a navy blue uniform, with a chest full of coloured ribbons and four gold rings on the cuffs of each sleeve.

'That must be the ship's Captain,' he thought, as the person swiftly descended the steep gangway and stopped by the sleek limousine.

The Captain appeared to speak quite animatedly for some minutes to some unknown person concealed in the limousine, before he finally stepped back.

The vehicle suddenly roared into life and sped away in a cloud of dust from the ship, leaving the Captain muttering angrily to himself and brushing the dust from his coat sleeves.

"I wouldn't like to cross his bow" John whispered as if to convince himself, and thinking he was still quite alone.

"Make certain ye don't laddie." Sinclair whispered in John's ear, which made him flinch with surprise.

"Are you in the habit of talking to yourself John?" Larter asked gently.

"You two didn't half scare me then." replied John, declining to answer the question.

The three of them stood and watched as two men were carried off the ship on stretchers, with a third draped in the company's House flag that was quickly loaded into the waiting hearse which moved off sedately from the scene.

"Come on." prompted Larter. "As I'm the senior of us, I'd better lead the way over the brow, in true naval tradition." As the trio marched up the gangway, finally to arrive on board.

When John crossed over the brow of the gangway and stepped on board, he noticed Larter shaking hands with another Officer. Likewise Sinclair and another man who was apparently glad to see him.

'Who's here to greet me?' he thought as he witnessed the comings and goings of other men.

He stood quietly behind his new shipmates and looked longingly at some distant point where his home would have been some miles away, and hoped his greeting would be just as his friends had got.

"And what are we, then laddie?" shouted a raucous voice, seemingly coming out of nowhere, that snapped him from his thoughts.

He looked around nervously and saw a squat grey bearded man in spotlessly white overalls, looking very ominously at him.

John felt as if he had been welded to the spot by the glaring eyes and threatening voice of this uncouthly mannered person.

"Yes, you laddie! Has the cat got yer tongue? What's yer name and state your business?" barked the stranger.

John drew himself erect as he nervously blurted out the answers.

"My name is John Grey. Assigned to this ship as a junior Engineer 5th class." then added "Sir".

"My aren't we a fine handsome mannered pup. Well, I'm Mr Cresswell. The *Lea* line Chief Engineer to you, and don't you forget it." was the bullying and surly reply.

The Chief looked at his watch and added.

"Get yer snivelling self and yer belongings below and see me in one hour. Remember, one hour, and don't be adrift." as he held up a large, fat and oily finger to John to emphasise the amount of hours. The chief quickly disappeared down some hatchway muttering something to himself about "schoolboys sent to do a man's job".

Suddenly he sensed the presence of someone standing close by him, and felt someone gripping his elbow.

"Hello John Grey. I'm Henry Obediah Day, the 2nd Engineer. I have been expecting you. You will probably find, and certainly since your last shipping company, this line is run almost on the same lines as the Royal Navy. That is to say, most of the entire fleet is manned by ex-RN from the war on account that most of us Merchantmen were lost during it. Which also means that the company can operate on cheap labour as opposed to the new Merchantile Shipping companies now afloat.

"However as your guide and mentor, you can call me Happy Day. Welcome to the *Brooklea*." Day said soothingly.

John turned and saw a fairly tall but well built man standing there smiling at him.

He shook Days offered hand gratefully in a flood of relief, as he could feel and draw the warmth and a new found strength that appeared to come from it.

"Actually this is my very first ship." John replied almost robotically. His mind had a myriad of questions to ask, like "What to do?" "Were to go?" "What's it like on board?" and started to ask them in quick fire succession.

"In that case, whoa John! Let's get your articles signed on and meet the Captain in the pursers office then take you to your cabin to stow your stuff and change into your working gear. After that, I'll answer those questions that seem to have you in a quandary. Then we'll go and meet Mr Cresswell, er, the 'Chief Engineer' at his commanded time." Day informed him then asked.

"How's about that young man, will that suit you for now?"

"Thanks!" John replied gratefully and followed Day into the ship.

When he arrived at his quarters, he was pleasantly surprised to find he had a nice wood panelled cabin with little red curtains around a shiny brass port-hole to look out of, and the place appeared quite spacious with sumptuous furniture.

"If this is my cabin, then I'd like to see the Captain's" he said with a soft whistle. But was put gently down by Day, when he explained to John that this was in fact a spare passenger cabin, and not the usual standard for the ships' officers let alone the crew.

He changed out of his civilian clothes and stowed them neatly away, to don his brand new white boiler suit. He had his name stencilled in bold letters across his left chest.

His epaulettes had a thin gold stripe on a blue background indicating that he was in fact an Engineering Officer.

A soft knock on his cabin door heralded Day's return and entrance.

"My my! I didn't realise how smart ones uniform can look. That's the trouble of it. Mine hasn't been as clean as that for years. Still never mind John, the greasier it gets the more work you've done." Then with a large grin, he quipped,"the last part at least is our chief's motto."

John looked at Day, with a self-conscious grin and thanked him for his kindness.

"It's nearly time, so let's go down the engine room now to make your grand entrance and meet our big white Chief. But One thing you will realise, is that this ship is still a novelty to other shipping companies, and is used by the owners as a kind of training ship for us engineers. Also, because of whom the skipper is. This means that some of the junior Deck Officers get trained

19

in seamanship as well. Anyway, I'll tell you more about the set-up as we go along. But before we go. Here, this'll save your new one and it's only to protect your hair from dripping oil and grease." Day said, as he handed him a floppy flat cap to wear.

John put the hat on, took a fleeting glimpse of the world outside his porthole and saw that it was going to be a nice day after all. He followed his new mentor down into the depths of this, his new home, to meet the CHIEF and his appointed time. 0900hrs.

CHAPTER II
Old Ship – New Master

Built during the early 1920's as a private yacht for a German Industrial Baron, who used her as a floating home and private Head-office.

It was launched with much ceremony and christened the M.V. *SCHLEZWIG.*

To describe her as the latest in personal yacht design, as was the rage in those days, she had a spoon type stern, a sharp clipper like bow, with raked funnel and masts, and could carry up to 100 passengers in complete luxury and style. She was originally built at 275 feet long with a displacement of 2,200 tonnes, with a beam of 45 feet. The ship was built with futuristic ideas on ship propulsion, which were kept very much a secret for many years, and proved that she was a very sea worthy vessel.

Whereas all ships built in that era were powered by coal, with just a few fuel oil burning steam ships, this one in fact was driven by four powerful diesel engines. Aptly and as befitting the person who invented the engines, designed and owned the ship.

Early in the year of the outbreak of WW2, the ship was taken over by the German Kriegsmarine. They modified and equipped her as a fast Support and Supply ship for the new batch of U boats that were being launched and would eventually be used to deadly effect as the now infamous German U Boat Wolf packs.

The uniqueness of this ship were her multiple diesel engines that gave her a cruising speed of 30 knots which gave a range of several thousand miles without refuelling and an emergency turn of speed of over 35 knots.

Coupled with her armour-plated hull, she had an array of armament that was hidden away from prying eyes. It meant that she had the choice to stay and fight it out, or be able to run away from most British or Allied warships that tried to give her grief.

As the war progressed, her operational role and areas were changed to suit the requirements of the German Navy, ending up in the waters of the South Atlantic.

It was commanded by a daring young German sea captain, Hans Otto Von Meir, with a crew of 150 volunteers to man his vessel.[*]

After the war she was acquired by the present owners, and given another major conversion at the Belfast shipyard. When she was ready to sail again, she was finally re-launched in the early part of 1946 and renamed by Lord and Lady Belverley as the M.V. *Brooklea*.

As a medium passenger/cargo ship the *Brooklea* had been plying trade to and from ports all over the rapidly diminishing 'British Empire', soon to become 'The Commonwealth'. But the ship always had to end its last part of its voyage in its registered homeport of Belfast.

---

[*] See *The Black Rose*.

As in every port, this ship has made people come to look at it for one reason or another, like a freak show in some circus.

Could it be because of her still graceful lines that gave it a handsome silhouette as a reminder to the old seafarers of yesteryear? Perhaps!

Could it be because of memories of her reputation and infamous exploits from the recent war? Maybe!

Or could it be because she's always limping home from one mishap after another for yet another visit to the repair dockyard? Probably!

New Master

The new Master of the *Brooklea* was Captain Michael Trewarthy, one of many sons of a poor Cornish fisherman. His last official appointment and ship was as a Junior Deck Officer on the Triple star liner the S.S. *Southern Star*, of some 20,000 tonnes.

In the latter part of 1942, the ship was on the long but relatively safe voyage from Sydney via Cape town to Liverpool; she was to rendezvous with a large convoy that was to be assembled near the Madagascar Islands. From there, be escorted to Cape town by Royal Navy escort ships, when they arrived.

The ship's Captain was Michael's eldest brother, whose secret orders were to get to fortress Britain with all best possible speed, which was a good one for his ship and no problem to him.

After an agonising twenty-four hour wait for his escort, the Captain had opted for his ships high speed as opposed to safety in numbers, and in what looked to him as a collection of very slow ships that made up the convoy.

Intelligence sources informed them of a wolf pack waiting for them and the possibility that there was a marauding Q ship in the area off the Cape.

Never the less he sailed off alone at high speed early on the following morning.

Shortly after 8 o'clock that morning, and only a few hours from leaving the assembled convoy, they encountered an elegant and fast moving ship coming close and towards them.

As they were passing what appeared to be a friendly ship, to their utter horror they discovered too late that this ship was in fact, none other that the dreaded Q ship everybody was worried about.

Within ten short minutes, Michael Trewarthy was one of only three survivors, who were eventually picked up by Von Meir's crew.

The *Southern Star* succumbed to a vicious torpedo and gun bombardment meted out by the much smaller ship, and sank rapidly to the bottom of the four-mile deep Indian Ocean, taking some 2500 poor souls with it.

In those few minutes Trewarthy had lost his Brother, and his Cousin, the ship's junior Engineer Officer.

He also lost his best pal the ship's Chief Boatswain, not to mention his other friends and colleagues on the ship. Trewarthy swore then that he'd avenge their deaths, as later on at Valparaiso in 1945 he had witnessed Von Meir had been arrested as a war criminal.

Von Meir was found guilty at the Nuremberg war trials and subsequently sentenced to be hanged, for this and other atrocities.

It was reputed that he escaped to South America with other such criminals but nobody could confirm or deny it at the time.

Trewarthy had always maintained that since Von Meir took his family and his ship away from him during that dreadful morning, now as Captain, Trewarthy would keep Von Meir's.

Although Trewarthy would never admit it, but during his enforced service under Von Meir, he learned more seamanship and ship handling than during the entire time he was with the Triple Star fleet. This, with an extremely good weather-eye for ships and their behaviour had stood him in good stead ever since.

So when he brought the *Schlezwig* to the attention of his present shipping line owners, in Punto Arenas, they too had realised what an asset this ship would be.

Better still, a whole fleet of diesel ships, only much bigger.

For his reward, they sent him home for a few months rest, then invited him to re-join the ship in Belfast. This he did, and found himself promoted to a full Captain, but better still, Master of the *Brooklea*.

Since leaving Belfast Lough after its recent conversion, he and the ship had circumnavigated the globe more than once. But as each transit was done from port to port, it had become increasingly more difficult for both of them.

Rumour had it that the ship had become jinxed since the alleged demise of Von Meir, or that the ghosts of the ships sunk by Von Meir on this ship, were still haunting her.

In certain maritime circles they were saying privately that Trewarthy is still living out his wartime traumatic experiences. That his conduct or deeds concerning the *Brooklea* and her crew seemed to be governed by some ghostly spectre, which one could only assume as none other that the infamous Captain Von Meir.

CHAPTER III
Decreasing Circles

At the given hour, John followed Day through a watertight hatch and stood on a small platform above a large room. He looked down in the dim lighting to see some machinery that appeared quite unfamiliar to him. He also saw the white overall clad figure of the Chief Engineer with his back to them. He heard the Chief speak gruffly to a gathering of grubbily dressed engine room crew standing in a semi-circle around him.

John landed heavily with a loud clang onto a loose deck plating at the bottom of the near vertical ladder.

"So you've made it then Grey." Cresswell observed.

"Stand over there." he added, as he pointed to a spot next to where Day was standing.

John did as he was told, then listened to Cresswell rattle out orders that seem to despatch men to all parts of the ship. As each order was given, he noticed the faces and demeanour of the men concerned. Some seemed reluctant to carry out their allotted task, whilst others went away muttering angrily to themselves.

He felt a chill run down his spine at this, even though this big room was still quite hot from when the engines were running.

As he looked sideways at Day's impassive face, *'Is that what people call 'near mutiny',*' he thought to himself and decided not to speak or even dare to move for fear of invoking some terrible wrath from this

27

fearsome character.

After what seemed an eternity, the Chief turned to Day and rattled off a stream of orders to him. John thought he'd be next and steeled himself for it.

But the Chief stormed past him and clattered up the ladder to disappear out of sight.

"Right, 5th Engineer Grey. I have my orders, which include yours. So follow me if you please." ordered Day, but giving him a sly wink.

"Phew! Is he always like this, Happy?" John asked with much relief.

"Yes and No! Yes because he hates junior and especially trainee Engineer Officers. And no because this is what appears to be one of his quieter moments. All you have to do is keep out of his way for a few days. Listen to what I have to tell or show you. You only get told the once, O.K?"

John nodded and followed Day back up the ladder to the small platform from where they came in and stopped for a breather.

"Right then. What you're standing on is the Chief's observation platform, but sometimes gets called the inspection platform.

From here you can oversee all that's going on in this, the engine room." Day commenced, as he pointed around below them and pointed out where they had been standing only moments ago.

He went on by saying, "the compartment in front of the engine room and the other side of that bulkhead there, is the Evaporator room which makes the fresh water. See that bulkhead there behind the diesel engines? Well that is the Motor room where we generate our electricity. We have an Auxiliary machine space in the after ends of the ship, but more about that later." Day stated as he rattled off the areas of the engine room he pointed to.

"What do you know about diesel engines? Have you been given or have you a copy of this ship's layout, its various machinery master manuals and the like?"

"No on all counts. All I was given from the Shipping Office was this book here. I have to fill in and return it at the end of the voyage." John replied as he gave Day his handbook to look at.

"Just as I thought. Most of this is no good on this type of ship. Okay for a steamer but no mention of diesel engines." Day said with a weary sigh.

"The best thing for us to do is get you the proper *'Brooklea'* manual from the ship's office, which incidentally, the Chief keeps under lock and key. Then we'll take a proper guided tour round the engine room."

Day looked into John's face and seeing him looking troubled added quietly.

"Come on John, let's have a cuppa with the lads in the motor room first. Maybe you'll feel better then."

"Thanks Happy. I sure could do with one, but I've no money now." he replied, then wondered where he'd heard that expression before.

Day chuckled and informed him that as he was on board now, for Officers at least, any expenses incurred are put onto his cabin bill and paid at the end of the entire voyage.

"So that's why those two were broke." John whispered to himself with a knowing smile.

They arrived in the motor room and joined five men sitting at a heavy wooden table, each drinking from the now familiar, almost bucket sized enamel mugs and puffing away merrily at their smokes.

John was introduced to the group to find that the tallest one in the scruffiest green overalls amongst them was Dave (Dusty) Miller, the Line's Electrical Officer.

"Hello John" said Miller, as he shook John's hand.

"These are my Welsh electricians. You've got to humour them because from what I gather, unlike the rest of humanity who live in houses, they all live down a hole or up in the trees."

One of the electricians stood up and said.

"You'll have to excuse these ignorant Englishmen, so don't pay any attention to him. What he means is that we all come from mining villages of South Wales, and our villages name starts with TRE.

"That is, I live in Treharris, my butty from school over there is from Trelewis, and Doug comes from Tregarron, then Ken from Treherbert." He announced with annoyance in his voice as he introduced his fellow countrymen.

"And he's a right Herbert too, by all accounts! But each one of them are good electricians which is perhaps their only saving grace." Miller added with a condescending smile, as the men started up a round of banter between them, which was good humoured enough for him to turn back to John.

"Are you here to stay? Only the last junior Engineer was carted away in the hearse this morning. The poor sod, He only lasted one voyage." Miller stated matter of factly.

There was a deathly hush over the group as they waited for a reply.

"For Jeez sakes, stow it Dusty." Day interceded on John's behalf.

"He's got enough on his plate right now without you adding to it."

"My apologies, John. Don't mind me, but I've got a big mouth sometimes." Miller said softly, patting John on his shoulder as he stood up preparing to leave.

The conversation held by the others started back up as if to cover that vacuum in time caused by the embarrassed silence.

"Happy! You'd better do John a favour and give him a blue overall to wear. You know what Cresswell's feelings are on white ones." Miller suggested.

"A good idea." Day agreed, as he nodded to John.

"Don't mention it." said Miller, as he finally left shepherding the electricians out with him like a hen with her chicks.

"Come on 5th! It's our turn now. Let's go and get some work done before lunch." Day prompted as he nodded his head towards the engine room.

***

With a new pair of blue overalls on, a clipboard with notepaper in one hand, a wheel spanner in the other, a torch and a slide rule in his breast pocket; John, like a scholar on his first day at school, was ready for his detailed and conducted tour of the ship.

They crawled behind, under, over and round all sorts of machinery. Through awkward inspection hatches, looking at pipes, valves and places you would never guess existed on a ship.

Up endless ladders, along passageways, tunnels, and even down dark holes or into smelly bilges. All the time John was making notes and asking questions as they went along.

Finally they stopped for a breather on the inspection platform where they had started.

"Right John. Lets clean up and go for lunch now. After our lunch, I'll take you around the forward hold and beyond until secure at 1700 hrs." Day suggested, then asked: "Before I go. Any questions?"

"Er. Just one question for now if you please."

"And what's that?"

"You've lost me. How do I get from here?"

Day laughed and replied, "Yes, we've been going around in ever decreasing circles. It's quite simple John. Just follow me as my cabin is in the same cabin flat as yours."

John smiled meekly and followed Day to the cabin flat, making a mental note of which way he had come.

He washed and changed quickly, then noticed that someone had been in his cabin and left him a large pile of leaflets. On the top of the pile, was a neatly written note, which said, *'Here's some literature about the company, who's who, trade unions and other items that you are expected to know, that you might want to gen up on when you've got a spare moment.'* Signed B.L.

'That's kind of Bruce.' he thought to himself. I'll read them tonight, he promised himself as he stepped out of his cabin meeting Day who was coming towards him.

"Ready then John? The 'mess' as you sometimes call it, is in fact the passenger dining room, just one deck above us.

The Skipper's giving us our pre voyage briefing before lunch, so let's shake a leg and get there early. The Skipper doesn't like people being adrift at his briefings." Day instructed, then as an after thought added, "Adrift means the same as being late. That is a big NO NO in our profession and you'll probably find out why, someday."

"In that case, lead on Boss. I'm right behind you." John quipped.

When they arrived, Day quickly introduced John to the other Officers who were sitting at a large oak table, each with a drink of some sort in front of them. John nodded and smiled at Larter and thanked him for the leaflets, then handed him his lighter that he'd dropped whilst in the cabin.

"See. What did I tell you John?" Larter asked and thanked him for the return of the lighter.

"Right young man. What'll you have John?" asked Day, as he went over to the small cocktail bar.

"I'll have a... a..." He didn't know what to order as he was still officially under age and still getting to know the different alcoholic drinks you can buy, then concluded.

"I'll leave it up to you Happy."

Larter waved John over and pointed to the seat he was to sit in.

He looked down at the neat place setting and saw a card with his name on it.

The protocol of seating was in order of rank starting with the Captain, with the Engineers on one side of the table or room, and the Seamen on the other.

As he sat down, Day arrived and gave him a large whisky and pointed to a soda siphon in front of him.

"Here you are John. Splash some of that soda into it if its too strong, and especially to make it last. We're only allowed one drink during the day, so might as well make it a large one."

John looked round the rosewood and walnut panelled room.

At the brightly coloured curtains surrounding rectangular windows and noticed how cheerful it all was compared with everything else he'd seen so far.

He listened to the buzz of the conversations being carried out by his fellow officers, when all of a sudden there was a deathly hush.

With a reflex action, he was standing up in unison with the others to see the Captain coming through the double doorway, followed closely by the white overall clad Chief Engineer.

When the two took up their positions at the top of the table, the Captain motioned everybody to sit down, leaving the Captain, as the only one standing.

"Good afternoon gentlemen" the Captain said in a deep and condescending voice.

"We have a lot to go through, but first, who's the new officer that joined my ship this morning, that I haven't had the pleasure of meeting yet?"

John froze in his seat, remembering what he saw this morning, but Day was nudging him on to his feet, so he stood up quickly and turned to address the Captain.

As their eyes met, he saw that the Captain's deeply tanned complexion showing above his bushy beard, seemed to go quite pale as if he had seen a ghost.

"I'm here Captain. John Grey, Junior 5th Engineer, sir."

"Another snotty nosed brat too, I'll wager." Sneered Cresswell.

"Stow it, Engines." the Captain hissed, as he stood looking at John as if mesmerised, then very slowly, almost in a whisper announced:

"My name is Captain Trewarthy. Welcome aboard the M.V. *Brooklea,* 5th Engineer Grey. No doubt you've been given your orders." Then, as if suddenly coming out of a trance Trewarthy added, "You may sit down now." Dismissing him and turned to a large pile of papers in front of him.

Trewarthy poured out a full tumbler of whisky from a nearby decanter, drank it all up quickly, then having replenished his glass again he cleared his throat and commenced reciting from a large ream of paper.

He spoke in a deep resonant voice that sometimes gave way to a rich Cornish brogue as he read each document.

He posed several questions, eliciting answers from the officers and snapping orders to all except John. Stopping only for a periodic drink from a seemingly ever-full whisky glass.

After about forty minutes non-stop oration, and giving out orders he finished by saying.

"You have now been notified what's required from you, and your orders have now been officially issued. If you have not taken out the stores items concerning your department within one hour after this meeting... TOUGH!"

Trewarthy paused briefly to make his words seemingly hang in mid air, picked up the now mandatory whisky glass, and drank slowly from it, looking ominously around the room. He then said menacingly, and with belligerence in his voice.

"Any questions?" he asked. Then gave a lengthy pause before speaking again:

"Good! That's what I like to hear. Silence! Because nobody's got one. That will be all gentlemen." He concluded.

Drinking the last drop from his glass with an exaggerated flourish, he slammed it down onto the table, picked up his pile of papers then marched swiftly from the room with Cresswell following closely behind him as if they'd been tied together with a piece of string.

For several minutes, nobody stirred or spoke.

The ship seemed still and hushed, the very loud tick of the ships clock seemed non existent, even the usually noisy dockyard was silent and was as if to recover from the verbal onslaught the Captain had just delivered to his officers.

Then, as if to break that deathly silence, a steward came into the room pushing a noisily squeaking trolley, and in a loud but cheerful Welsh voice announced:

"Here you are gentlemen. Food for the Gods and other Officers. There's lovely it is!"

CHAPTER IV
Humble Abode

Day continued with his forward tour of the ship. He took John through the No2 then No1 holds, tracing this conduit from a drawing, or that pipe from another. They paused for a moment at a small cordoned off area in the No1 cargo hold, where Day pointed to the place where the recent accident had occurred.

He explained the circumstances, the fight to save the cargo, of how two sailors were badly injured and finally of the tragic death of John's predecessor. John looked for several moments at the mangled machinery and the twisted pipes dangling down from the deck head (ceiling), then asked.

"Has this sort of accident happened before Happy?"

"Yes. That makes it about the tenth time this year. In different parts of the ship and virtually with similar results." Day paused as if to remember them, then added philosophically.

"It's either she's jinxed, bad planning, bad training and malpractice by members of the crew, or even a combination of them all."

They stood gazing at the wreckage for a few moments longer, each wrapped in their own thoughts.

Then they started slowly and moved onwards through to the anchor chain locker. On through to the cordage stowage space and then up to an area marked on a brass plate with German writing crossed out and the words 'FORWARD MESS DECK'.

"Hello 5th Engineer! Finding your way around with Mr Day, I see?" greeted Sinclair.

"Hello Bosun! Yes thanks." he said as he spotted Sinclair's big frame coming through a hatchway like a jack in the box.

"So you two have met then." Day observed.

"Yes Mr Day. Young Grey here, is a good 'un, so mind you look after him." Sinclair replied, as he gave John's shoulder a few friendly taps with his shovel sized hand.

John felt a bit shy at this spontaneous show of friendliness and tried to change the subject.

"Is this where you live Bosun?" he asked as he looked round at a large room that had hammocks strung up on a row of hooks looking like large fat sausages.

"Yes. Welcome to my humble abode. In here I'm Bosun Andy." Sinclair replied as he looked proudly around his little domain.

"That smells good. Is it Brazilian and piping hot?" Day asked as he looked over to an overlarge jug bubbling away on a fat bellied stove.

"It certainly is. Grab yourselves a seat, as the lads will be here any minute now for their afternoon cuppa." Sinclair replied swiftly and commenced to pour out a pint-sized mug of hot sweet coffee to each of them.

During their brief break, John met most of the sailors and noticed that Sinclair seemed to be their leader. Also that Sinclair appeared to be held in respect by them.

He also noticed that most of the men were ex Royal Navy men, judging by their mannerisms and that they had brought most of their service traditions with them.

As they were leaving, Sinclair spoke to Day and said, "Mr Day, Able seaman Janner here has something to show you up on the foc'sle deck if you please."

"Very well. Let's have a look." Day replied flatly, as the four of them rattled up a very steep steel ladder and appeared onto the deck.

Janner pointed to the anchor capstan, cursed it and said.

"The *effing* thing keeps jumping gear, or *effing* well stops just when it wants to do Mr Day."

"Yes, and I'm fed up of reporting it. It was like that during our last trip, and especially when we're about to sail for another long voyage." added Sinclair, as if to back up Janner's report.

Day inspected the winch then showed John the problem he'd found, what repairs needed doing and how to test it. Then turning to Janner saying

"Thank you Janner. This time it will be fixed properly even if I have to do it myself."

"Thank you Mr Day. That's good enough for me." Sinclair replied as the two seamen left the deck and went below to their mess again.

Day nodded to them and turned to John and said.

"Right 5th. We're going aft now via the new enclosed bridge." Day went on to explain that there were ships still floating around that still had an open bridge and the basic differences between them.

On the bridge, he was shown all the equipment like the engine telegraphs, the large spoked steering wheel, the newly invented radar and display screen, until they came across a semicircular disc with a brass pointer on it.

"Why, that's an Inclinometer which points to a 12 degrees list to starboard." John declared, then added.

"I noticed a red line at 32 degrees either side of the plumb line."

"Yes. That's the critical point for this ship. Anything over that line then grab a life jacket, as it means the main decks are awash, and moments from capsizing." Day explained, as he walked out to the bridge's port wing that overhung the deck below, pointed his finger over the side and down to the hull, to continue his instructions.

"If you look down there, you'll see that the waterline has moved down towards the keel, due to the list. As a rule of thumb, and for future reference, the first thing you'd see if a ship's been in the water a long time, is a thin line of seaweed growing on the hull slightly below the normal water line. Just below that again about two feet, you'll see a girdle of barnacles that gets thicker as it goes down to the keel.

The larger the expanse of barnacles you see the more the ship is listing, and the crustier looking the barnacles seem, the longer the ship has been in the water."

"Does that happen often Happy? Only I've seen several ships coming in for hull scraping."

"Most British merchantmen have clean hulls." Day responded.

Day finished his small seamanship lecture and went on about the effects different angles of list had, and what it would do to the ship's fuel supply to the engines. Of the drag factors involved between a clean and dirty hull, especially when calculating fuel consumption and other items of note.

John duly noted these salient points and jotted down the answers that had been given him to the questions he had posed.

Finishing the main superstructure tour, the pair of them went down and through the two aft cargo holds to the Auxiliary machine space.

"Ok John. This compartment holds the machinery for the hydraulics, the ships gyro, the fresh water system pump and other machinery not housed in the engine room."

"There are a lot of different types of machinery here then Happy. Am I expected to learn everything about all the machinery straight off or do we just consult the makers manual?"

"No. I'm your Instructor on this ship, so I'll show you how to operate each one and give you notes to write down as we go along. Sufficient to say, the detailed drawings from the manuals should be easy to follow, all you've got to do is learn and recognise the faults as they occur and the repair of them."

"I have managed to see and learn a few different

types of machinery during my dockyard apprentice, so maybe I can learn these just as easy."

"We shall soon see what you are capable of, so not to worry. Anyway, onwards and upwards." Day concluded, as they made their way to the emergency steerage compartments, with John making more notes, asking yet more questions until finally they ended up in the 'AFTER MESS DECK'.

"Here we are John, this is where our lads and the cooks live." Day announced quietly.

"We can have another cuppa if we're lucky, before we wrap this tour up. Ok John?" Day enquired.

That sounds about just right." John replied.

Again he had a chance to meet the rest of the ship's crew and the stokers who would be in his particular watch.

The men expressed a hope that perhaps he could or would help change the hardships and injustices they endured under the present tyrannical regime of Chief Engineer Cresswell.

John replied that he'd do what he could but couldn't promise anything, as he was only a very junior engineer officer after all.

The two left some time later having refreshed themselves made their slow final inspection before going back to their cabins.

Back in his cabin, John threw off his now very dirty boiler suit, washed and changed into his new navy blue uniform then went to discuss his conducted tour with Day in his cabin.

Day answered the myriad of questions John had posed and gained several answers from his own. After ironing out a few problems or difficulties that John had in understanding certain items, he finished the session by saying.

"Well done John. You have certainly impressed me thus far. You appear to have a better quality for an engineer that's required for today's modern ships, than several other junior engineers I have had to train up in the past. If you work hard on this ship then the rest of them will be a doddle, especially if you can get along with a certain Chief engineer who happens to be on board this vessel."

"Thanks, Happy. I'll do my best." John replied shyly.

"By the way." Day continued.

"I don't know if you're aware of it, but we'll be going into a dry dock for the recent hull damage and a few other repairs, tomorrow morning. We'll be in dock for about two to three days or so, before we come back here to load up. We will take on our passengers and whatever else needed for our next voyage."

He paused for a moment to let the statement sink in, then added: "That means that you can have a run ashore tonight if you want to, but you must be back on board before we sail.

You'll find the details from notice board on the gangway, if you're interested."

"What will you be doing to while away your time then Happy?"

"Me? I've got a lot of work to catch up on here." Day replied with a frown on his face, as he pointed his finger to the mass of plans, schedules, almanacs and maintenance books that littered his bunk.

"Me too. You've given me a lot of notes and drawings that I want to gen up on, so I think I'll pass on the offer to go ashore, maybe another night, thanks anyway Happy." John replied as he held his hands apart indicating the thickness of his notes.

Day looked at him for a moment, then stood up and walking towards his cabin door, said:

"Well said that man! I can see you and I are going to get along just fine. Let's go for some supper and maybe a well earned drink in the passenger's lounge afterwards if it's open."

This was also the first opportunity for John to meet the rest of the others who would be under training just like him.

John finally got back to his cabin some hours later, where he made himself comfortable on his bunk and started to wade through the pile of notes he had taken down during his conducted tour.

He studied well into the night, getting buried deeper and deeper under a mounting pile of drawings, plans, and manuals.

Finally falling asleep exhausted, thinking of his predecessor's demise and all the other accidents that occurred through ignorance, bad planning, just plain bad judgement, maybe them all.

CHAPTER V
A Cunning Plan

The next thing John knew was that somebody was shaking him hard, on his shoulder.

"What? That valve there! What's this? Who are you?" he asked disjointedly as he woke up from his troubled sleep.

He raised himself up with paperwork that he fell asleep under cascading from him, looked down in the dim blue lighting that served as safety night lights, and saw a figure wearing a white jacket, looking up at him.

"Who are you?" he enquired.

"Mornin' Mr Grey. I'm one of the ship's stewards, Jimmy Burns."

"What time is it?"

"It's 4 bells of the morning watch. Mr Grey."

"Four bells? What's that?"

"Sorry, it's old Navy talk. That's six o'clock in the morning to you Mr Grey." Burns informed him in his best cockney accent, as he offered him a tray.

"As it's your first morning on board, and ordinarily I don't do cabin service to the crew, but here's a cuppa and some toast for you as you've missed breakfast."

John looked around his cabin and saw the place all neat and tidy and remarked.

"I can't remember putting my books and my uniform away."

"That was me Mr Grey, I tidied up as best I could

without waking you."

"Thank you steward. I'll climb down and have that tea and toast so you can finish off." he said and clambered down to sit in a chair.

"Sorry about the mess." he said apologetically.

"Don't worry yerself Mr Grey. You should see the mess some of the passengers leave. You just enjoy your breakfast whilst it's still hot." Burns confided as he continued folding up and stacking John's books into a neat pile.

Burns finished his work and saw John had finished with the tray so picked it up to leave.

"By the way! Mr Day sends his compliments and says you'll not be required for the dockyard move.

He says that you're to continue with your studies for the entire forenoon. Er! that's all the morning to you."

"Forenoon watch? Until lunch time?" John enquired.

"Yes, that's it Mr Grey. You'll soon get the hang of these sailors phrases." Burns confirmed, as he left shutting the door behind him, leaving John to himself and his thoughts.

He looked out of the porthole and saw the distant street-lights of the city twinkling like stars in the morning mist. He thought of his family in Rathmore Cottage, of his dog for a moment.

Then what he had gone through within the last twenty-four short but extremely hectic hours.

47

His thoughts were suddenly interrupted by the juddering movement of the ship, accompanied by the sounds of tugs tooting to each other.

'We're moving,' he thought, and looked out the porthole to see the harbour lights slip slowly and silently pass him by until they disappeared into the morning mist.

The ship seemed quiet and he guessed that as the engines weren't vibrating or making a noise through the ship's structure to make her feel alive, he therefore decided, that she was under tow from the little tugs he saw yesterday.

'Let's see. It'll take at least an hour to get into the dock, and a further two hours before the docking has been completed and the water drained away. So I'll have time to work on that cunning plan I have concocted.' he thought to himself as he started to study again with renewed vigour.

He poured over the ship's designs, drawings and layouts, making a traced drawing of the various pipes or service systems used on board.

He was putting the finishing touches to his handiwork, when he heard a knock on his cabin door and saw it was Day coming in to see him.

"Hello John! Still stuck into your work? There was another Junior Engineer that joined the ship today, by the name of Jackson, but this will be his second voyage and he will be watch-keeping down the engine room for the whole trip." Day informed him as he greeted him with a nod.

"The docking is going to take a while longer than we thought, so I am taking the opportunity to give you another question and answers sessions. But first let's see what work you've just completed before you put it away."

John showed the tracings, the colour codes and notations and explained exactly what he was about to do, why, the benefits and so on that his plans had to offer.

When he finished he asked Day's opinion about the scheme but requested that he would sanction it, then keep it very much under his hat for now.

Day was wide-eyed and amazed at the simplicity of what he had heard and seen. Then after a few moments, remarked.

"My, you are a dark horse. You do realise that once you have put some of the concepts and theories into practice, you will have achieved more in much less time than all the others I have trained put together, including this new junior, don't you?" he complimented John then added:

"I'll give you a couple of weeks or so watch-keeping alongside Jackson down in the engine room plus, say, another couple of weeks or so to operate the auxiliary machinery and systems. Then you should be ready for an early promotion.

"Mark my words, John. Indeed I think you'll do very nicely providing you do one simple thing, and that is, if you are not sure, don't just stand there, ask!"

John felt himself blush and in a shy but increasingly confident mood replied:

"Thanks very much for your kind words. But I'd need a prompt now and then to make sure that all is well."

"That is fine by me. Remember, you ask to find out." Day replied in earnest, and shook John's hand as if to congratulate him.

"Now let's have a noggin in the mess. It's all on me John."

They walked out of the cabin to the mess and sealed their private pact with several very full noggins.

During the next few days, John busied himself with his plan, with covert aid from Sinclair and three other crewmembers, who volunteered their services.

He even had time to take a discovery trip looking over the ship's hull at dock bottom level.

The fat underbelly of the ship seemed at odds with the sleekness of her water level silhouette, and even her relatively small twin brass propellers shining in the early morning sun seemed to belie the greyhound speed she was capable of.

This was the time to see what was fitted where, discharge, or intake holes, whatever.

Finally when everything was in place, he told his helpers that, and he must have them all to swear secrecy before it was time and right for everything to be revealed.

'Let's hope this plan is well received,' he thought to himself, as he put the last finishing touches to his plan.

John decided to clear away his paperwork so as not for the steward to shuffle them up again for him, then climbed upon his bunk and slept a troubled mans sleep, as he tossed and turned all night with the several questions and problems he had still to remedy.

CHAPTER VI
Mutinous Dogs

The ship had been returned to her berth again, with the crew preparing things and storing ship for the next voyage out into the wild blue yonder.

John was in his cabin reading up on some final notes when Burns burst in through the door, with a very worried look on his face.

"Beggin' yer pardon Mr Grey, but Mr Cresswell wants you in the engine room instantly. He's gone stark raving bonkers and is screaming for your blood." he gasped and panted for breath.

"An I've rushed all the way from my mess-deck to let you know just in case he comes himself, which is not a pretty sight at the best of times, I'll tell ye." Burns advised.

John looked up from his pile of papers at the flustered and sweating steward.

"Thank you steward. Do you know if Mr Day in his cabin?" John asked immediately.

"No. But he'll probably be down in the motor room somewhere."

"Thanks for your tip off. It's okay, so don't worry." John said quietly and reassuringly, and then went calmly down to see what the fuss was about.

He went swiftly down to the engine room and stood on the observation platform where he saw men standing around Cresswell, with their heads bowed, looking nervously around as if to find some place to hide from the mad man in front of them. He saw Jackson hiding behind some ventilation trunking, who signalled him not to give him away.

Cresswell was ranting and raving at them, calling them mutinous dogs and questioning their parentage, then stopped, as he turned round to see John standing above him.

"You! You horrible little man! Come down here Mr 5th Engineer *lah de dah* Grey, and stand there." he bellowed as if he was about to explode, and pointed to some imaginary spot nearby a workbench.

John came quickly down the ladder and stood where he was told.

"Now then Mr 5th Engineer *effing* Grey! What is the meaning of all this?" Creswell cursed and screamed his question as he swept his oil stained hand around the compartment.

"What's all what, chief?" John replied in a puzzled voice.

"What's all what? What's all what he asks?" Cresswell shouted, his voice taking on a rapid crescendo.

"I will show you what's all what, Mr *effing* Grey. This… and this… and that." Cresswell said indignantly as he pointed to specific valves and pipes around the motor room.

"Well," John began timidly.

"Well what?" Cresswell interrupted.

"I am waiting. Who told you to go round swapping pipes over and painting MY ship to making it look like a Christmas tree?" he questioned then continued to harangue John.

"Come on, answer me you 'orrible little man."

Before John had time to answer again, Cresswell interrupted him again.

"You done this, didn't you?" he nodded violently to John, as if to force the correct answer from him.

"What plans did you take from my office? Where did you get the key to my office anyway? It must have taken you ages, so come on. Tell me who helped you?" He snapped, and turned to the stokers asking with equal menace.

He must have seen Jackson pretending to work on a piece of machinery and screamed to him.

"Jackson! You're a miserable excuse for an engineer too. It's no good playing with that until we run main engines. Come down from there and join the others."

Jackson scowled and got a clout behind the ear from Cresswell as he passed to join the rest.

"That's right. You stand there where I can see you." he snarled, then turned to the other men.

"Who among you useless lot helped this excuse of an Engineer?"

John looked sideways at the two stokers who'd helped him, waiting for them to own up, but there was complete silence and nobody stirred.

"Just as I thought. A bunch of lily livered cowards,

that's what you lot are." Cresswell snorted, then turned back to John and said:

"Mr 5th Engineer John Grey, as the Chief Engineer on this ship and of the *LEA* line, I am charging you with sabotage. And that still has the penalty of hanging. Now what do you say to that Mr 'Lah de Grey'?" he emphasised with equal vehemence.

Cresswell was now standing so close to John that he sprayed John's face with spittle every time he spoke then started to cross-examine John.

"Did I ask you to go around painting my ship?"

"No Chief!"

"Did I ask you to re-route pipes and valves at random?"

"No Chief!"

"You obviously incited others to help you. That is what's called a mutinous act. Do you know what mutiny is?"

"Yes chief! But that's only for the Royal Navy."

"Don't get fanciful with me laddie. Do you understand what I'm saying?"

"Yes Chief!"

"Yes Chief, No Chief, No *effing* three bags full Chief."

Cresswell shouted mockingly, like a parrot.

John's usually even temperament was sorely tested, and he started to get angry at this blustering, bug eyed man in front of him.

He reached behind him to get what felt like a heavy

stilson wrench that was digging into his back, just in case he had to use it to defend against an actual assault.

Cresswell then went on and on about John's ancestry and his family so much that John couldn't take any more.

He was about to grab and swing the wrench around to strike this monster who was screaming in his face, when he felt somebody's hand preventing him from doing so, and heard a tiny whisper from somewhere behind him.

"Shhh! It's me. Happy Day. Don't do it John. Be still! He doesn't know I'm here, so play along with this and I'll try to slip away and get some help." Day informed him, hoping not to be discovered as well.

Cresswell didn't see the crouched figure of Day behind the bench, but had seen the stilson in John's hand and that John was about to strike him with it. This made Cresswell's fiery eyes light up even more.

"Did you see that?" he cried triumphantly, and rubbing his hands together ,he turned to the group of men behind him.

"You all saw that, didn't you? I said, didn't you?" he bellowed his question to them to provoke the answer he was looking for.

Nobody stirred or spoke, but just stood looking at this spluttering raving spectacle of a monster in front of them. After a few moments of Cresswell pounding a fist into his hand, cackling to himself, and foaming at the mouth, he stopped and pointed at random to two stokers.

"You two there. Come and stand over there. On the double you lazy pair of blaggards! Jackson! you an' all. Take charge of them." He snarled to the three men as they rushed to do as they were told and stood either side, but slightly behind John.

"Here! Tie him up, and be quick about it. You make sure the rope is tight and secure Jackson." Cresswell snapped as he threw a length of rope at them.

They tied John up quickly whispering their apologies for having to do so, as quietly as they could for fear of being heard.

"Just get on with it you three, and stop snivelling to that excuse for a man." Cresswell growled and threw a greasy rag at them.

John stood quietly, allowing the stokers to tie him up, remembering what Day had whispered to him and in the knowledge that someone would put a stop to this despotic tyrant.

Cresswell was still screaming and shouting at the others, vowing to get even with every man jack of them until he finally paused as if to think of what else to say. He turned to John with a pronounced sneer on his face.

"Right, Mr excuse of an Engineer! You have been charged with sabotage, and now mutiny. You will be clapped in irons for this and that's just for starters. Mark my words." He gloated then turned to Jackson and the two stokers.

"You three! Take him away and meet me on the bridge in ten minutes. If not, then you too will be facing the same punishment as this excuse for a person."

Cresswell then climbed the steep ladder and disappeared out of sight, with John being bundled up the ladder behind him, leaving everybody and the engine room in a deathly hush and a seemingly black cloud hanging over it like a shroud.

The trio arrived on the bridge helping John along, where they found Cresswell whispering to the Captain, who was nodding his head as if in agreement at every word Cresswell spoke.

John saw Larter, standing adjacent to them with a large sheet of paper and a note pad in his hand.

Sinclair was also there, standing by the ship's binnacle with his hands behind his back.

But what surprised him most, was Day's presence. Day was standing by the Radar display screen, as nonchalantly as you please, brushing his shoulder at some imaginary bit of fluff.

John was made to stand a couple of paces away from a raised desk where Cresswell and the Captain were standing, both of them looking daggers at him.

Larter cleared his throat then recited from the sheet of paper: "John Grey, Junior Engineer 5th class of the M.V. *Brooklea*. You have been charged with sabotage of the said ship, also with mutiny on the same vessel in that you did attempt to strike a senior officer." Larter paused for a moment then asked: "Who are the accusers laying these charges? State your name and rank, for the record."

"I am." Cresswell said in belligerent triumph, and stated his name and rank.

Trewarthy stood staring at John just as he did at his briefing, then asked: "Do you understand the charges?"

"Yes sir! But we are in the Merchant navy not the Royal." John protested.

"It's AYE, Captain." Trewarthy bellowed, then started to cross examine him.

"On the charge of sabotage, how do you plead?"

"Not guilty, Captain."

"I see. So a ship painted up like a brothel, using God knows what sort of paint is a figment of my..." Trewarthy corrected himself quickly and continued his tirade. "Our imagination?"

"No Captain. It is real enough. The paint I used was from the ship's own stores."

"AH HAH! So you've stolen company property into the bargain as well. You thieving swine." crowed Cresswell, as he interrupted the cross-examinations.

"You have also been charged with mutinous behaviour, in that you attempted to strike a senior officer. How do you plead to that?" Trewarthy asked as he resumed his questioning.

"Not guilty captain! Besides we're Merchant and not Royal Navy and everybody knows it's only a hanging offence in the Royal and not Merchant." John persisted in his protest, and got ignored every time.

"Don't lie to me GREY. Merchant or Royal it makes no difference in this ship. I'll take the chief's

word against a hundred people like you anytime."
Trewarthy snorted angrily.

The proceedings went on for several minutes, with
Larter writing all that was said, until Trewarthy
beckoned Sinclair over.

"Chief Bosun, take the prisoner to the starboard
bridge wing and wait for my signal, and be silent about
it. Jackson, you and the others can go."

"Aye Aye Captain." Sinclair said curtly as he carried
out the order.

After a short while, John heard the ship's bell ringing
out that it was twelve noon, then heard Trewarthy
bellowing command, "bring in the offender."

John was brought in to stand in front of the desk
again, and saw Cresswell rubbing his hands together
and gloating over what was about to happen.

"As Master of this ship, I have the sole right to
uphold the law and maintain total jurisdiction over all
people on board this vessel. You have now been
charged on three accounts, namely sabotage, mutiny
and now stealing company property." Trewarthy stated
coldly, then added, "I that is WE find you, Engineer 5th
class John Grey, guilt..."

He looked at Trewarthy's gaping mouth and
wondered what made him stop in mid sentence, then
saw four very elegantly dressed men come into the
confines of an otherwise spacious bridge.

"I have come aboard to see you Captain Trewarthy."

said the smallest of the newcomers.

"What is this man tied up for? In fact what's all this, Captain?" demanded this man who spoke in a polished but challenging voice.

"Good afternoon Lord Belverley. How nice to see you, and you gentlemen." Trewarthy nodded as he greeted the men.

"Had I've known that I was going to be visited by the ship owners Board of Governors I would have prepared a suitable welcome." Trewarthy added as he and Cresswell nodded and fawned over the four men.

"Captain Trewarthy, explain yourself! Just exactly what's going on and I want to know right this second the meaning of this outrageous behaviour. The ship is alongside, in harbour, and you are holding a court?" Belverley demanded.

"Well My lord. I, that is Chief Engineer Cresswell and I have found this man guilty of sabotage, inciting mutiny, threatening to kill the Chief Engineer and stealing from my, er, your ship's stores." Trewarthy replied gloatingly.

"Really?" asked Belverley incredulously then turned to John and asked flatly.

"Is this right young man?" he looked at Trewarthy and asking who this young man was, added "5th Engineer John Grey."

"No it is not." John stated in a loud voice.

"So it is your word against that of my most respected and most senior Officers, is it?"

"Yes it is, your Lordship." John replied defiantly.

Lord Beverley ordered Sinclair to release John then turned to Cresswell and in a commanding voice said:

"Chief Engineer Cresswell. It appears that you are the principle accuser, therefore tell us all in your own words, exactly on what basis you have brought these very serious capital charges against Engineer Grey, here."

Cresswell related in a whining voice what he had found, what Grey was going to do with the stilson, and that the proof of Grey's theft from the stores was all over the ship. When he had finished his embellished report, Beverley turned to John and asked if any of what Cresswell had said was true.

Before John had time to collect his thoughts and time to answer, Day stepped forward, clearing his throat as if to announce himself:

"Excuse me my Lord and gentlemen ship owners. I am the ship's 2nd Engineer, Day, and I feel that I can help out in the defence of 5th Engineer Grey."

"And I can your worships." Sinclair chipped in, as he tugged the peak of his cap in salute.

"You appear to have some friends to vouch for you, that I warrant were not given the chance to do so at this so called Tribunal." Belverley said coldly as he saw the two men come forward from where they had been standing.

Trewarthy and Cresswell looked in total disbelief and amazement at Day and Sinclair coming to John's rescue.

"I'll get you both for this." hissed Cresswell as he gave John and his friends a withering look.

First, Day related to the ship owners exactly what John was trying to do, how it worked, his own opinions on John's plans and what exactly what transpired in the engine room.

Then Sinclair related the same, plus how he and three other crewmen had helped John in completing the task for the issue of the paint.

The four ship owners listened intently to the two stories portrayed by Day and Sinclair, nodding their heads and looking at John in increasing admiration, until finally Belverley spoke out.

"So it appears Mr Grey, that this plan of yours is not only going to save the Board of Ship owners a lot of money in ship repairs, but will also help your fellow crew members to stay alive and run my ship properly. That is a tall order even for such a junior Engineering Officer such as you. However, I for one will most definitely want to see this plan of yours work."

Belverley then turned to the other three ship owners and beckoned them to follow him to an empty spot on the bridge away from prying ears, they stood in a small circle, talking quietly amongst themselves, glancing over occasionally at the waiting officers.

John and his three friends stood in a line several feet away from Trewarthy and Cresswell, looking anywhere but at each other. He was feeling a lot happier now that he knew he'd got some true friends and was thinking of what was taking those Ship owners to come to the right conclusion, as far as he was concerned.

Finally, the ship owners came back, led by Belverley, who started to speak in commanding tones.

"It is the decision of the Board of Ship owners which I wholly endorse, that the following is to take place as I speak." Belverley paused for a moment for his statement to take effect. Then continued by addressing Trewarthy and Cresswell.

"In the first instance. This tribunal of yours Messr's Trewarthy and Cresswell, is at an end. This will be the last time you two will ever hold a kangaroo court on this or indeed any other ship afloat. It is therefore proposed that you Mr Cresswell, are to get yourself off this ship and to a suitable doctor. For in about three months you are to join the *Cloverlea* when it goes for its major refit."

"But, but, but" stammered Cresswell as he tried to interrupt Belverley's deliverance.

"No buts, Mr Cresswell. You are lucky you're not beached permanently." Belverley said severely and over the voice of the complaining man.

"Mr Trewarthy, you are a big fish in my shipping company but a mere sprat in any others. So if anything untoward like this should ever happen again then just you remember what I have said." Belverley threatened Trewarthy.

When Trewarthy and Cresswell started to curse and make threats to John and his friends, Belverley turned to Cresswell and said:

"Oh! And another thing Mr Cresswell! You will hand over to 2nd Engineer Day here as your relief on this ship, and you are relieved of your duty as of now."

Cresswell gasped and choked, as if about to have some sort of a fit.

His face went bright red, then he started to scream abuse and threats at John and his friends, but was silenced by the ominous withering looks of the ship owners, and their threats of what they would do if he didn't shut up.

Belverley watched Cresswell for a moment then turned to Day and pronounced, "2nd Engineer Day, thanks to the foul mouthing of Mr Cresswell, you have now been promoted, and are now the chief Engineer of the *Brooklea*. I know you have the capability to do so. You will draw your pay as of today."

Day looked at Belverley with astonishment, but nodded his head in acknowledgement of his newly bestowed rank.

Belverley then turned to Trewarthy.

"Captain Trewarthy! You will arrange with Mr Brooks here, the swap with the *Meadowlea*'s cargo and passengers when it arrives tomorrow. You will also arrange with Mr Lowther, a fifty fifty split between yours and the *Meadowlea* crew but excluding 5th Engineer Grey here."

"Very well your Lordship." Trewarthy grimaced and was visibly cringing in his sea boots.

"Mr Burford. You are to give Engineer Grey twenty guineas for his ordeal, plus five for his run ashore tonight and a further month's pay to be sent to his parents or next of kin.

"That money Mr Burford, will be deducted from Messr's Trewarthy and Cresswells voyage pay and from this months wages."

In unison, Trewarthy and Cresswell started to wail and protest profusely, shaking their fists at John and avowing evil revenge on him.

"Make it double Mr Burford, if you please." shouted Belverley.

Then told the two men that if they uttered another word or offered any more complaints, the sum would be doubled and doubled again each time they protested.

Trewarthy and Cresswell were fighting to subdue their anger, looking daggers at John and his three friends and trying not to make a sound.

"Finally Engineer Grey we come to you." Belverley announced calmly as he approached John.

"On behalf of the Board of Ship owners, we wish to try and dispel any misgivings about joining us for your first voyage, and also offer you some personal restitution. You will become an Acting 4th Engineer and assume your duties as of now. But you will remain on this vessel until you are confirmed at that rank. Congratulations." he said as he shook John's hand to confirm his instant promotion.

John was hit with tremendous elation, and only came to his senses from his euphoric state as Sinclair was guiding him across the bridge, to go down the ladder onto the main deck below.

"Before you go Engineer Grey, don't forget that run ashore, by courtesy of your Captain and Chief Engineer." Belverley said with a beaming smile, as if trying to make light of the grave situation that had transpired earlier.

As John and his friends arrived on the main deck, they were greeted with a loud cheer and whistles from the ship's company who had gathered round like bees to a honey pot.

"What's all this Bosun?" he asked.

"Oh that! Its simple." replied Day with a big grin.

"Bruce Larter had the ship's entire tannoy system switched on for everybody here including the dockyard mateys to hear exactly what went on."

"And that was a gripping story too. We would have loved to been there and to have witnessed everything." a voice from the crowd shouted.

The four friends laughed and joked their way to their cabins to prepare for a celebration run ashore. John's first.

'Judging what I've just gone through, I wonder what else my first voyage will have in store for me' he thought as he stepped over the gangway and off for a night in the city.

CHAPTER VII
The Plan

The ship sailed at high tide early the following morning, carrying its full load of mixed cargo and bound for the wide open ocean of the Atlantic to the sunny climes of the Caribbean. It was going to be the first of many a voyage that would take John across several thousands of miles of liquid landscapes.

The four ship's owners plus some plantation owners and their families were on board, which met the board of trades' maximum of a fifty passenger limit for this type of ship.

This meant that John and all the other junior officers under training had, for the outward voyage, relinquished their cabins. John had doubled up with Jack Cunningham the *Meadowlea*'s 3rd Engineer.

During the trip down the Irish Sea proved yet again, that for a small sea, it can give a rough passage for any ship that sails its waters. John soon discovered the nauseating and inescapable feeling of sea sickness, and no matter what he drank or ate, it was rapidly sent down the nearest toilet again, or, if on the main-deck, over the side. He was not alone there, as he met Jackson and a couple of the others sharing the same stretch of water.

He was glad and took heart that the ship was about to dock in Southampton soon, albeit, for a few short hours.

"Those few blissful hours where nothing moves, will be ideal to get some much needed rest. Still, at least the other trainee officers on board, Deck Officers or not, will probably share the same sentiments as me," he said to himself quietly.

For he knew the ship would be crossing the much bigger, renowned to be more angry, vast open waters of the Atlantic, and hoped to get those sea legs that the others on board were talking about.

He stood in his shared cabin looking out of the porthole, watching the busy scenes of Southampton docks pass by him. The ship made her way slowly up the main seaway of the harbour towards its allocated berth.

He noticed some of the bigger passenger liners in the world slumbering at their own personal piers, as he passed them by.

'That's the one I wouldn't mind being CHIEF on one day.' he thought again to himself, then climbed into his narrow bunk and fell asleep thinking of probably the biggest liner in the world, the S.S. *Queen Mary*.

Someone else some decks above him was also deep in thought as he too looked at the impressive sight of several magnificent liners gathered together.

The *Brooklea* passed the succession of liners, the *Queen Mary*, the *Leviathan*, the *Normandie* and the *Melbourne*, and each one a veritable mountain compared to the *Brooklea*, the proverbial molehill.

'Just look at those Von Meir. I bet you'd sell your

soul to the devil to see those ships over there that probably gross more that half a million tonnes, coming your way. I wonder how long you would take to destroy these beauties, you bastard.' Trewarthy thought to himself angrily as he remembered how Von Meir had sunk his ship the 'Southern Star', and other such poor unfortunates that came his way.

The ship took on more cargo and exchanged a few passengers before she was ready to cast off again to sail along the English Channel.

As they left Southampton behind them, John managed to take his last glimpse of the British Isles. Over the next few days on their downward leg of their voyage, John mastered the rolling gait of the ship as the short choppy seas of the Bay of Biscay gave way to the big but gentle swell of the deep Atlantic Ocean.

He was delighted to discover the secrets of how to walk around the ship without stumbling into or over things, and it was pronounced by most of his pals that he had finally got his sea legs.

The ship had passed the mouth of the Mediterranean Sea, and was off the coast of Morocco by a hundred miles or so when the ship ran into a sandstorm that engulfed them for several hours.

'A sandstorm at sea? That's very odd!' John mused.[†]

The sand seemed to get everywhere, but was a heavenly diversion for the passenger's children as they

---

[†] See *The Lost Legion*.

played sand castles for as long as it lasted and before the sailors washed it all away again.

It took the *Brooklea* a week from leaving Belfast, to arrive at the Spanish islands of the Grand Canarias and tie up alongside the mole in Las Palmas harbour.

Also, that's all it took for John to explain the different coloured markings on all the ship's systems; and for the crew to get a good working knowledge of them. The simple method and plan of recognition as to which valve or pipe was used, be it for the fuel line, or fresh water, pneumatics instead of hydraulics, or even electrical systems, took out the guesswork for the crew.

This in turn, increased their safety and operating efficiency almost one hundred fold.

Lord Belverley and his joint ship owners had, during the transit, monitored closely the effects of the plan, and saw how everything become easier for all concerned. They also realised that most shipping lines had their own set of rules, regulations, ship's drawings, operating procedures and the like.

So if this simple plan had been in place a few years back, then the company would not have paid out several hundred thousands of pounds for ship repairs.

And almost the same in compensations to the ever-growing band of bereaved families as each accident or mishap took place.

The ship arrived at her first destination called the Grand Canarias, which was a collection of volcanic islands in the North Atlantic some 2000 nautical miles south of the United Kingdom but only a few hundred miles from the North African coastal area of Morocco.

The island inhabitants are of Spanish decent and enjoy the balmy weather coming off the deserts of the Spanish Sahara. They enjoy the visits from ships of all nationalities, as it is one of only a few fuelling stops before making their Transatlantic voyage across to the Americas.

The ship was in port for a couple of days, and had already unloaded the cargo for this destination before taking a replacement load on board for the next port of call.

As they had to wait for an oiler, or a fuel barge to arrive the following morning for the ship to refuel herself, virtually all of the ship's crew were living it up in the bars and nightspots that Las Palmas had to offer.

Except that is, for the Officers, who had to remain on board and entertain the local VIPs, dignitaries and any ships officers who wished to come along from other merchant ships that were in the harbour.

This took on the form of a small cocktail party, with a banquet afterwards for the *Brooklea* passengers and her officers.

This party was paid for, directly by the ship owners, who had made John the guest of honour for the night.

After the cocktail party, when the V.I.Ps and other guests had left, everybody was in a happy party mood, relaxing and enjoying each other's company in the passenger lounge.

Trewarthy left his little circle of friends suddenly and came over to where John was standing, then told him to report to his bridge cabin.

John immediately excused himself from his company who looked concerned for him as he left to go where he was told.

"Come in Acting 4th Engineer." Trewarthy barked as he heard John knocking at the cabin door.

"Aye Aye! Captain" he replied as he stepped through the doorway.

"Can I help you Captain?" he asked politely.

"Yes you bloody well can!" Trewarthy snapped.

"Do you see this man here?" Trewarthy demanded as he pointed to a man bleeding from several cuts and writhing painfully on the deck.

"So much for that crackpot scheme of yours Acting 4th. Look what you've done to my, er, the Donkey man Barnes, here."

John knelt down and asked Barnes gently what had happened, as he tried to administer some first aid to him as best as he could.

Barnes told John haltingly what had happened but told him that it wasn't him to blame.

"Not to blame Barnes? Are you insane man? He did this to you and he is going to pay for it." Trewarthy replied as he tried to overhear what Barnes was saying to John.

"Of course he's to blame!" Trewarthy concluded, his voice getting towards a full screaming shout.

Trewarthy abruptly stopped his shouting and left, only to return immediately with the ship's doctor, who had summoned two stretcher-bearers to take Barnes away.

They were followed almost unnoticed into the cabin, and in succession by Cunningham, Day and Mr Brooks, a ship owner of the same shipping line.

"Who asked you lot."Trewarthy started to shout then stopped as he saw Mr Brooks coming in.

"What seems to be the problem Captain Trewarthy?" asked Brooks evenly.

Trewarthy explained what had happened to Barnes and another stoker. Then started to blame it all on John and his so called plan.

"I see. This is the first accident on board this vessel for over a week now, which, taking this ship's past safety record and history into consideration is very good going. Junior Engineer Jackson lost his brother over the last one." Brooks announced to the group of officers, and then turned to John.

"However, if this is a by product of your doing Engineer Grey, you will need to offer a solution to it, and be quick about it."

"To be honest gentlemen, I had not taken the facts into consideration as described by the Captain.

"Therefore one can only assume, it's one of these unfortunate occurrences which some people will have to put up with for the present." he replied with some thought to his answer.

"Do you mean John, that there's room for people like

Barnes in this plan of things?" Cunningham asked, still a bit puzzled.

"Why yes. A few simple adjustments, that is all it takes to make things more fool proof shall we say."

"What is the crux of the matter and your solution to the problem, Grey?" Day asked urgently.

Trewarthy stood there looking amazed at the circle of officers holding this conversation in his cabin with him being an apparent bystander, not wanting to butt in.

Brooks stroked his chin all the while the engineers were talking, as if to formulate a solution, then in an authoritative voice announced:

"Okay gentlemen. Enough! Let the Captain and myself into your secret, so don't keep us in suspense any longer. You must have reached your solution."

"It's quite simple really, Mr Brooks. You see –" Cunningham started to say but was interrupted by John.

"Stoker Barnes is colour blind Mr Brooks."

"Colour blind? Colour blind? He can't be." Trewarthy echoed as he interrupted John, then started mumbling about all these years he didn't know of his friend's condition.

The other men stood and watched in amazement as Trewarthy looked out of a port-hole, pounding a fist into his other open hand, still mumbling to himself as he was in another world.

"Okay then gentlemen. I've discovered the truth about Barnes." announced the ship's doctor as he returned to the cabin.

"Yes. We have just discovered it ourselves." John informed the doctor.

"I had suspected something like this a few months ago on the Cape town trip." Day revealed.

Trewarthy stopped his mumbling and looked at Brooks.

"He's the best donkey-man in your fleet, Mr Brooks and of the others in the company. He knows this ship inside out, inch by inch, and rivet by rivet. So what's happened for it to change all of a sudden?"

"A person who is colour-blind compensates for their disability much the same way as a blind person. A blind person will get to know the exact position and the feel of each piece of furniture in a room. But if somebody moves one piece, even say a few inches, or even changes some furniture, then that blind person would stumble into it or fall over it. In Barnes' case, both pipes he handled appeared to be identical, therefore he chose the wrong one." The doctor informed them.

"So when those pipes in No1 hold had been straightened and routed differently, and colour coded for recognition, Barnes used the wrong valve on the wrong system." Cunningham concluded as he joined in the discussion.

"As I said. I suspected something was up, which is why I had Engineer Jackson to accompany him on this trip." was Days rejoinder.

"Barnes doesn't need anybody to help him. Why he'd probably show you lot a thing or two, I'll wager." snorted Trewarthy in defence of his friend.

"Now, now Captain." Brooks said soothingly to Trewarthy.

"I think Barnes was lucky he had help this time round, especially as Jackson had a vested interest, otherwise he'd be joining Jackson's brother and the others. Besides, I think Barnes should recover from his ordeal, but he's to stay in the sick bay until he does. Right Doc?" he confirmed with a nod to the doctor then added:

"That gentlemen, concludes the affair, and I think we all need a good drink. Anyway, Engineer Grey here has some speeches to prepare and deliver shortly. What do you say Mr Grey?"

"Amen to all that Mr Brooks." Day and Cunningham said in unison and left Trewarthy to pace up and down his cabin, swearing and mumbling to himself.

John sat between the Ship owners and beside Lord Belverley and Mr Brooks in the passenger's lounge, thus placing two people between himself and Trewarthy.

He was feeling a bit nervous at the thought of sitting next to some very powerful and influential people because of his modest and humble background, but looked around the lounge and saw his fellow officers smiling at him in support, and the passengers nodding their approval of him.

He listened to the speeches given by Lord Belverley and other Ship owners that were delivered between several toasts and salutations, but his thoughts were of his family and if only they could see him now.

He thought also of his mistreatment at the hands of Cresswell and Trewarthy. Of his future career, of... of... he felt Belverley's hand gripping his shoulder gently to bring him back into his senses, and who had asked him a point blank question.

"And what do you say to that young Mr Grey?"

"Speech! Speech! Give us a speech John." he heard his friends call to him as they egged him onto his feet, which he did with a shy grin.

"Lord and Lady Belverley, Ladies and Gentlemen of the Ship owners Board, ladies and gentlemen passengers, Captain and fellow officers" he began and spoke for a few minutes with modesty and sincerity and even managed a touch of humour. Then ended by thanking Lord Belverley on behalf of everyone for being such a generous host providing such a magnificent banquet.

"Hear! Hear! Well spoken." said his friends loudly, who then led a brief standing ovation for him, which everybody except Trewarthy took part in, just nodded his head for the sake of appearances.

With the banquet and the speeches over , the guests started to leave to retire to their cabins. All except Day and Larter, who persuaded John to stay a little while longer until all the others had left. They sat in the deep leather upholstered seats that surrounded a table, talking about who said what in their speeches.

They helped themselves to a full magnum of champagne the steward had found, and smoked fat Havana cigars that had been presented to John by the

Ship owners. The chief steward served them tea and coffee before leaving them to talk quietly amongst themselves.

A little time later Sinclair joined them, who had arrived back on board with some of his fellow crewmen.

He told the trio, that for some of the crew, it had been their first run ashore since Cresswell left. And although they were slightly the worse for wear from drinking, they'd promised to take John for a run ashore in the next decent port of call, as their personal thanks to him.

Day echoed what Sinclair had said concerning the stokers. Which meant that Barbados was going to be one lulu of a stop for them all bar none.

John protested his teetotal ways and was promptly given a brief heckling in disbelief by his friends, and given another large drink to celebrate yet another success.

The little private party went into the small hours of the morning, until finally they too went to their cabins to sleep off the effects of the past several emotional hours of wining, dining and speeches.

'I wonder what's in store for me tomorrow' John thought as he passed quickly into the land of nod.

CHAPTER VIII
Promotion

For the next few days in their westerly leg of the voyage from Las Palmas, Day had John working towards his Watch-keeping and Diesel certificate trade papers. All of which kept him occupied in the engine room, as Day had already told him what he had to do to get qualified as an Engineer.

Chief Engineer Day was quietly filling in his personnel report of John Grey, which was to be submitted to the Captain for sanction, and then to the Ship owners before they left the ship at their next port of call, Barbados.

For John to be judged honestly and fairly, Day's own judgement and comments had also to be entered in the same manner, there were a few areas of John's ability still to be assessed.

So without John's knowledge, he had conspired with the other officers to put him through several contrived problems, or situations an engineer would have to normally contend with at sea. To see if he would make the correct responses, all of which he needed to gain the required standard that was a prerequisite to promotion.

The ship's owners were let in on the secret plot and had sanctioned the plan, but were keeping their judgement until last. The scheme was also hatched without Trewarthy's knowledge, sufficient to tell him that they'd decided to play a few games with the ship's crew, so Trewarthy was not to worry about a few hours loss of schedule. *'They were always playing silly games with the different trainees. But then I had to do it for real, not very long ago either,'* Trewarthy thought to himself as he remembered his days with Von Meir.

The so called games that were to be played, were typical of real events and regular frequent occurrences experienced by mariners all over the world, but put down as *"just another bad day at the office."*

For the first exercise on John's behalf, Trewarthy had to pretend that the rudder had been damaged due to an underwater hazard, or a stern collision by another ship. This meant that, for this type of ship with twin propellers, the ship had to be steered by main engines.

So John had to stop or start the engines for various speeds, one side or the other and depending on which way the ship had to turn.

All this without the help or prompt from any other Engineering officer, who had to pretend they were dead, incapacitated or not even on board.

Trewarthy had to pretend to steer the ship by engines only, before now and knew from his friend Cresswell, how hectic and blood racing it could be in the engine room when different speeds were rung down by the engine telegraphs.

So it was with great delight that when he found who the Engineer was in charge of the engine room, he certainly let John have it, by constant turns of the ship, or reversing. In fact the whole gamut of commands

Trewarthy could possibly imagine.

Trewarthy even had some of the Deck Officer trainees test their seamanship using this rare method of steering and giving John an even more arduous time.

Day had let Trewarthy have his fling, knowing full well that his actions would give an added spur to John's workout. Day then called a halt after an hour or two, to do something else.

The next thing was a fire-fighting drill, without the ship's water main or mains pump in action. This was followed by the pretence of shoring up a compartment that had flooded due to yet another collision. The penultimate one was providing steerage from the emergency steering position aft.

The last one would test John's creative skills, by making a new component for the still very dodgy foc'sle capstan, which was to be fitted, inspected and in full working order. This was part of his trade apprenticeship training, as he would be required to make components whilst at sea instead of waiting for proper dockyard facilities, or for the postman to turn up with something the ship needed to keep going.

John's reactions and conduct proved that he was cool, calm, and collected throughout and he acquitted himself well, which made Day's assessment report easier and much more pleasing to write about than any of the others he had to do.

'In my opinion, Acting 4th Engineer John Grey has proved he is very capable of conducting his duties as

required of an Engineer Officer and that he is beginning to show a deep understanding of his trade.

'*He is capable of using his initiative and able to work well under pressure. During his brief stay on board M.V. Brooklea so far, he has built up a good working relationship with all on board. Add to that, he has lifted the morale of his men and has gained a mutual respect between them.*' Day went on to describe other items of note required for his report, and finished off by commenting:

'*He is soft spoken and of a mild mannered nature, never the less was able to motivate all those within his department and beyond.*

'*I therefore do hereby recommend that the aforesaid person be promoted to the full rank of 4th Engineer. Signed on this day.*'

Day looked at what he had just written and signed the report. He also thought of John's future, and wondered if this early success would follow him onwards and upwards, in much the same way as his own meteoric rise to Chief Engineer.

'*Perhaps with another stroke of luck like mine, he might just do that,*' he mused.

He put the report neatly into a brown envelope, and was about to wax seal it prior to handing it to Trewarthy, when he realised that Trewarthy may not grant the promotion.

This Trewarthy could do by stalling until the Ship owners had left the ship.

Or worse still, he thought. Accidentally naturally, but on purpose throw it overboard claiming it flew out of his hand whilst reading it, therefore having to wait until another form could be obtained from headquarters in Belfast.

With those thoughts on his mind, he went to see Mr Burford, Lord Belverley's secretary, and asked him either to make a copy of its contents, or note what was reported, then after that he was to give it to Trewarthy the evening prior to docking in Barbados.

When Burford asked why, Day told him of his suspicions and reasons. Burford was surprised at what he'd just heard, so acquiesced to the request, if only to find out for himself.

As the ship neared her next port of call, everybody on board was getting land happy now. The crew were happily making plans of what they were going to do ashore, drinking the rum barrels dry, buying presents, wenching, or whatever their desires were, then making more plans as their minds changed from ideas to ideas.

John liked fishing and shooting, but decided to see and explore the sights of these far off islands everybody was talking about. His plans and thoughts had been marred by the worry of the bombshell Jack Cunningham had the misfortune to give him.

He was to sit a special Selection & Promotion panel this evening at 1730 hours.

He was to be suitably attired in Officers tropical

uniform, but hadn't been issued with any. He was to bring his task book, duly completed and signed, but still had lots to write up on.

He'd just come off the afternoon watch from the engine room, feeling exhausted and grimy, and his stomach was tied up in knots at the very thought of this panel.

For the first time since this trip had started, his mind was in a turmoil.

His body needed a good wash, he needed to find some tropical gear from somebody about his own size, but that would take time. And what about his course book?

First thing he had was a cool shower, which made him feel a lot better, then as he sat at his desk with just a towel around his waist, furiously writing up his notes, in walked Burns, who was followed closely in by Sinclair then by Larter.

"Right then Mr Grey. You come and stand over here and pay attention." Burns ordered as he pointed to the full-length mirror attached to the wardrobe.

"What? What's this?" he said as he was taken by surprise.

"Here, try these on while Andy helps. Steward, give the Bosun a hand will you." Larter commanded, as he took overall charge of the situation.

Sinclair helped John try out various sizes of tropical wear, with Burns fussing around him seeing that things were tidy or fitting properly.

"How's about that John?" Sinclair finally asked.

"But where did you get all this clothing, Andy?"

"Never you mind Mr Grey. Let's just say they've been borrowed temporary like, ahem, on loan to you." Burns chuckled as he was tugging sleeves or adjusting other garments on John. "Right John. Let me see your book. I will ask or describe a scenario for you, all you've got to do is give me, in your own words, what I'll be writing into your book." Larter said authoritatively.

"Write? You can't write in my book Bruce." John started to protest but in vain.

"Don't you worry about old Brucey! He's the best I know at copy writing." Sinclair revealed gently, to calm John down.

"Aye, and that's a fact." Burns confirmed, with an exaggerated nod of his head.

The task to produce John and his book ready for his panel, was completed with only about ten minutes to spare.

Day made a surprise visit, poking his head through the cabin doorway and seeing that John was in fact ready.

"I'm not supposed to see you before this panel, as I'm one of your adjudicators, but with Jack Cunningham's compliments, get yourself a stiff tot of rum from his locker and calm yourself down to something like a mild panic. And good luck." He informed John as he disappeared from sight.

Sinclair and Burns gave John a final brush down and wished him luck as they too left the cabin.

"Come on Engineer Grey. Obey the last order if you please." Larter said in a serious voice.

"What order?"

"Let's get that drink. And don't forget that book of yours Engineer Grey."

"Aye Aye sir." John replied as he gave Larter a mock salute, and followed meekly behind him.

"Lambs to the slaughter is it Sparks?" Cunningham asked as he gave John a large measure of rum.

"Aye and he's adrift already." Larter stated as he hustled John away to the bridge.

The Selection & Promotion Board was held in Trewarthy's day cabin. It was presided over by Mr Brooks, with the two other Ship owners as advisors, with Captain Trewarthy and Chief Engineer Day comprising the rest of the panel, leaving Lord Belverley as an observer or independent moderator.

The four panellists bombarded him with all sorts of questions with Day putting in technical ones and Trewarthy acting the devil's advocate as per his usual character.

The proceedings took nearly two hours, when John was asked step outside and wait on the bridge for the panel's deliberations and final verdict.

He stood looking out of the rectangular bridge windows, watching the sun go down, and having the same sinking feeling too as he recalled to himself the answers he had given to all the questions he could remember.

The wide open spaces of the ocean appeared as flat as a mill pond but John felt as if he was in a violent storm, such were the knots in his stomach.

In an attempt to relax for the final onslaught of the verdict, he looked around his surroundings to take his mind off things and saw that Sinclair was steering the ship with apparent ease.

"Just imagine if you had an automatic steering device Bosun. You'd be able to put your feet up more." he remarked.

"So you're trying to get rid of us sailors now are ye." Sinclair chided with mock horror on his face.

"No Bosun. But it would leave yourself free, to be able to go or do something else." he replied without taking offence.

"Chance would be a fine thing on these ships I'll wager, despite all the new fangled stuff being dreamed up." Sinclair replied with a pensive sigh.

"Never mind Bosun, some boffin ashore somewhere might be able to apply some thought into it and sort something out for you."

A seaman came onto the bridge and interrupted their little conversation.

"Beggin' yer pardon Mr Grey, but you've to present yerself back to the panel if you please." he informed John quickly.

As John left the bridge, the sailors wished him luck.

"Thank you for waiting patiently for so long Engineer Grey, but we had shall we say, a small hiccup with the Chief Engineer's report. It seemed to have got, shall we say somewhat mislaid." Brooks stated as John came quietly through the cabin doorway.

"However! Let us live in hope what?"

'Oh no! I've fluffed it and will probably get reverted back to 5th engineer or something.' John thought, as his mind started to run riot with pictures of impending disasters and trying to listen to Brooks going on about needing to improve, striving to make inroads to his career; the good of the shipping line. Brooks droned on in a very serious voice for a while with the other ship owners nodding in unison to each statement made, then paused.

Here we go, John groaned inwardly to himself.

"Congratulations Engineer Grey! You are to be confirmed as Engineer 4th class as of now." Brooks concluded with a big beaming smile.

He felt as if a great weight had been lifted off his shoulders but also that his knees had turned to jelly.

'I've done it. I've done it.' he rejoiced inwardly, feeling a great elation creep over his body, as first Belverley, then the others took turns to shake his hand, giving hearty slaps on his back in congratulating him.

John stood in the warmth of their praises and he felt he was floating on a wave of euphoria, but watched closely as Trewarthy stood up, with a face like a thunder cloud, donned his cap and scurried out of the cabin muttering to himself.

'*If the last night in Las Palmas was a very good night, then the last night on this leg of the voyage is going to be much better if it were possible*'. he thought as he made his way to join and celebrate with his pals, who were waiting on the bridge for him. Even the other trainee officers joined in to congratulate him and hoped that his luck might rub off on them.

CHAPTER IX
Black and White

Eastwards of the Windward Islands and farthest to the east of any other West Indian islands of the Caribbean, is the proud island of BARBADOS: about the size of the Isle of Wight on the southern coast of Britain, and with a population of about 100,000 people.

The first British settlers arrived in the early 1600's where it became a British Possession, and now part of the great family called the Commonwealth.

Its mainstay was sugar cane, cotton and fruit, but perhaps the increase of, or the reliance or the tourism trade could be its hopes for the future.

As an Island people, and understandably, it had a considerable fishing industry, with an expanding deep-water harbour, which is used as its principle trading port. The capital of this warmly situated island is that port, Bridgetown, with an estimated population of 15,000.

The inhabitants of today are the latest generation in a long history of the slave trade that pervaded the Caribbean for centuries. Happily, all the folk are free now to pursue their own destiny.

Barbados today is an independent State, with its own Parliament, but still has a very British way of life and its own fair share of colonial buildings.

John had never seen dark skinned or any other coloured people before coming here.

Therefore, on looking out of his cabin porthole, he

saw dark brown or black skinned dock workers toiling away at unloading his ship. He marvelled at their brightly dressed womenfolk who were carrying enormous baskets on their heads, and how gracefully they walked under such heavy loads.

Given this brief background and the era based on post WW2 of the late 1940's, this then is where the *Brooklea* was to make her home for the next few days, and from where John's story of life continues.

Shortly after John had his morning coffee and completed some minor machinery repairs, he was shanghaied into a run ashore by Day, Cunningham, and all egged on by the stokers.

They were chanting 'For he's a jolly good fellow' and stated that they had promised him this treat because of their own excellent run ashore when in Las Palmas. They walked through the dock gates and down into the long fairly wide streets of Bridgetown.

The raised wooden walkways, which were shaded by overhead verandas, proved impossible to walk on due to the throngs of people doing their daily shopping. This left them walking in the busy road, dodging horse and carts or the occasional rickety motor vehicles, constantly honking their horns as they passed by.

"Where are we going, Happy?" John shouted over the noises.

"Search me. I've never been here before. I'm just following the lads." Day replied, equally mystified.

"Here we are lads! I knew it was just past the Excelsior Stores." a stoker proudly exclaimed, as he nodded his head.

"Yeah! That's it! The best pub in town." bragged another.

"Well what are we waiting for? Last one in buys the drinks." someone shouted, which created a stampede and a crush in the doorway of the building as everybody tried to get in at once.

Once inside the building he discovered a giant black man dressed in shorts and a string vest standing behind some upturned beer barrels, which had a long, wide wooden plank over them that served as the bar.

He had a half smoked cheroot drooping from his mouth whilst reverently spitting then polishing each glass as he stacked them up.

Behind him stood a rack of beer barrels, each had wooden taps and cork bungs sticking out of them, and galvanised buckets under the taps to catch any drips from them.

The man came from behind his bar to meet the visitors, and spat out his cigarette stub that landed into a foul smelling spittoon. Then indicated with a sweep of his huge tree trunk like arms where they were going to sit.

Two of the men had been recognised by the landlord and they exchanged noisy greetings with much back-slapping and handshakes all round. All of which bemused John, especially the quick exchange of greetings that he heard next, but could not quite decide as to what they were talking about.

"Well, if it ain't me old black enamelled bugger Harry, the best barman in all the Caribee!" one stoker greeted, pretending to be a pirate.

"Is dat you Banjo? The honkey with the buck teeth?" came the reply.

"An' don't ferget me too!" replied another stoker.

"Well well! So how's the snowflake country these days? Welcome back to these gay shores." The barman said with a big grin as he scooped the two men together and hugged them as one, before letting them go, as they gasped for air.

"'Ow's the missus, er, Matilida? She still up to her old tricks?"

"She gone and got herself dead a few years ago. She got run over by a horse and cart, God rest 'er soul. But never mind, I've got another good red hot Mamma to keep me up at night." He added with a smile as he pointed to a very large bosomed woman that came waddling through a bamboo curtain from the back of the room.

"Meet my new missus Bella! She can out wrestle any of you scrawny snowflakes so she can. So in the interest of your good health, sit down and I'll send my new girls to see to you." He concluded, as the crew meekly did as they were told and under the close eye of the large buxom woman that was ushering them to their tables.

"Hope some of you whiteys are cherry boys so my new girls can practice on! 15 Caribee dollars a short time!" she announced in a gruff voice.

"15 dollars? Blimey, that's bloody expensive! It woz only 5 dollars last time we woz 'ere. What can we get for that now?"

The big woman cackled and said, "Better you go and see Miss Palm, 'cause that's all you'll get nowadays. Now go and sit down so I can keep a good eye on you." She concluded with a toothless grin.

They all sat at a roughly hewn timbered table, using old upturned wine or rum casks as seats, in the cool dark room lit only by the mid morning sunlight streaming in through the glass less windows.

"Okay you lot!" a stoker announced over the building excitement coming from the men.

"We'll 'ave a Yorkshire. Everybody is to chip in, say ten bob, except for Mr Grey. An' you hofficers can make it a pound. So get your shekels out an' put them into this jug here on the table."

Once the money that had been collected, it was put into the middle of the table for everybody to see.

"Sixteen flagons of your coldest beer and a gallon of your finest rum, landlord. And bring your prettiest wenches to serve us." the stoker ordered, as he clapped his hands as if to hurry the barman up.

John watched with amazement at the ritual of the rum as it arrived and was about to be given out.

It was brought across to the table in a stone jar covered in a wicker basket, then its entire contents poured into an ice filled galvanised bucket. A large wooden spoon was produced to stir it all up, and half pint glass tumblers put in a row in front of the tub.

The stoker who was obviously in charge of the proceedings and acting as 'Barman' started to scoop out glasses of rum and hand them to each man at the table.

When that was taking place, John saw three lovely dark skinned girls were each carrying a tray loaded with bamboo jugs, frothing over with beer.

The girls smiled at the wolf whistles, but slapped many a roving hand or admonished the wayward sailor whom they thought got too fresh with them, before they finally extricated themselves and made their escape from an obviously appreciative bunch of woman flesh hungry sailors.

After a little while of bawdy banter the men got up onto their feet, and with their glass of rum in their hands, they all spoke their toast.

"To the KING! God bless him!"

To a man, they completely drained their glasses in one go, then slapped them onto the table indicating that they had downed it all in one drink.

When they had all put their glasses onto the table, and now with flagons of ale in their hands, they gave a toast to John, declaring that he was the best trainee hofficer ever to board the *Brook*. With one loud voice and much whistling, they urged and egged him on to give a short speech.

John felt that his officer friends had probably connived with the men to do something like this. He felt very bashful at the kind attention he was given. So

John meekly complied with their demand, quietly thanking them for their appreciation and hoped that he would enjoy their company for many a voyage to come.

Several flagons of drinks later, when the beer and rum was flowing freely, even across the table, the men started to sing some rather salty shanties, making merry, and having a whale of a time.

It was a lull in the drinking when they all decided to leave for some other equally famous place. When finally they all got up and bade farewell to the landlord, they showered the young waitresses with hugs and kisses and promises of coming back again later. They trooped out of the building and down an alley, which led them directly onto a wooden pier with a thatched roofed hut on the end of it, which turned out to be an alfresco type of pub and restaurant.

John and his officer friends sat in the hut enjoying a fresh lobster salad, whilst the men swigged from stoneware jugs that somehow magically appeared from nowhere.

They listened to the rhythmic and melodic calypso of a steel band, which was playing nearby them. He watched the stokers trying to do a limbo dance on the sandy beach with some dusky maidens who happened to be there.

It appeared there was more falling down in the sand, laughing and joking, and fondling the maiden's obvious attributes than actually trying to dance.

Apart from the light sea breeze, the only thing that

kept him and his friends cool, was the iced rum and coke they sipped from seemingly never empty glasses.

Some of the men left the beach to buy some *rabbits*[‡] for their folk back home. But due to the excessive spending on their drinks, they returned shortly afterwards because they could only afford the odd postcard, wooden toy or gaudily printed scarf.

John and his friends had given some money over to one of the men with specific instructions on what present to buy on their behalf, and a drink for his trouble.

Finally with the party seemingly over, they all got their prized, extremely expensive rabbits and walked or staggered back in the setting sun to their ship to sleep it off. Each one vowing a rerun of the same events tomorrow.

Maybe with the Christmas season looming up, extra money would be needed for that extra special present for the wife or girlfriend back home.

So the men would have to barter or swap something, usually ships cordage or ropes normally found on board, that 'somehow' came into their possession. This was the normal business ritual of sailors the world over. Hence the saying, *'money for old rope'*.

The following day, being a Sunday, John decided to hire a pony and trap and be taken for a leisurely ride to look around and explore the island.

[‡] Naval slang for 'presents'.

He was taken down the little lanes that had the occasional brightly decorated wooden huts with the ever-present corrugated iron for roofs. The children he saw, although poorly dressed and some in little more than rags, seemed very clean and happy, playing at whatever was in their little fairy tale world.

When the pony and trap came round a bend in the road in the middle of a sugar cane plantation, he saw a wooden building painted as white as the driven snow, with a tall spire topped with a small golden cross.

There were neat rows of gravestones and wooden crosses that flanked each side of a white pebbled pathway which led up to the heavy wooden door of the church.

"The Parish of St. Michael," he read to himself from a board hanging over a rustic archway that marked the beginning of the path.

He asked the driver to stop for a moment so that he could take in this very peaceful scene.

Within moments, he saw the worshippers filing out and being shaken by the hand by the black and white robed preacher who seemed to appear from nowhere as if by magic.

"Black and White, or White and Black. The striking contrast is so different as is the colour of the people who emerged from this old, but seemingly well preserved church!" he said softly at this new discovery.

His driver was about to move off with soft clicking noises to his pony but was engulfed by the crowd of sugar cane workers and their families.

The whooping and laughter from the boisterous children startled the animal, which reared up suddenly, and in doing so, kicked and knocked an old lady over until she lay quite still in a ditch by the roadside.

The driver started to calm the pony down, as John leaped out of the trap to render first aid to the stricken woman.

Two black, burly men came swiftly over, shouting at him to get away from her and started to drag him off, demanding angrily for him to leave for his own safety.

John explained that unless the woman got to a hospital immediately, there would be yet another fresh wooden cross in the graveyard.

He was astounded at their arguments and reasons against this, but never the less, he picked the woman up into his arms, took her to the trap and placed her gently into it.

"Quick driver! To the nearest hospital as quick and as safely as you can." he ordered the driver away.

'No treatment because she's black! Couldn't afford treatment! White folk bothering with blacks! Those statements were racing in his mind as the pony and trap finally arrived at the hospital. He carried the woman carefully in his arms, through a barrier of white doctors and nurses, then placed her gently onto an empty trolley bed.

"Now look here! You don't bring *'that'* in here. We can't treat *'that'* in here." protested a stethoscope-garlanded doctor, as he looked down his nose at the patient in undisguised loathing and disgust.

"And why not?" John demanded angrily.

"That, doctor is a *'she'*. *'She'* is a human being just like us." he snapped and gave them all an angry look feeling totally disgusted with these so called medical people.

"Because the blacks and other natives have their own place on the other side of the island from here." was a curt reply.

"Now you look here! I am an Engineer off the M.V. *Brooklea*, with instructions and an order to install your new electricity generator, due tomorrow. Either you treat that woman or I will see to it that your generator goes straight back to England again when we sail. What will it be?" he replied in a quiet but menacing voice conceded in a condescending voice.

"Nurse, take this, er, patient, to the surgery and prepare her for treatment." he ordered, then turned to John and said, "As for you Mr. er, Mr?" he started to enquire.

"Never mind who I am. I'll be back tomorrow to see how that woman is doing. Remember this doctor. No treatment! No generator! That's the deal." John threatened in an icy voice, then made his way back to the pony and trap leaving the doctors to their dilemma.

With his sightseeing tour ruined, he returned to the ship to report the incident to his friends and to his senior officer, Happy Day.

His incident ashore was duly reported and received

Frederick A Read

like a lead balloon by Trewarthy. That evening, after another verbal altercation with Trewarthy, John decided to get turned in for a good night's rest and an early start the following morning.

'*What a disgusting collection of people those doctors are.*' he thought as he climbed into his bunk and slept.

The ancient lorry carrying the equipment, had the stores and a few of the crewmen in the back, with John sitting in the front next to the driver as it rattled and honked its way through the streets.

As the streets were thronged with early morning shoppers, they had to wend their way very slowly through them and out some distance to the hospital.

The hospital was on a hill, which had outbuildings, built onto stilts that making them look much loftier. All overlooking lush green lawns and neatly kept flowerbeds. The main building was a large two-storied wooden building, each storey with its own veranda.

It was painted pure white, with large red crosses painted in prominent places and matching the bright red tiled roof. Thus proclaiming to the world that it was a hospital.

He climbed down from the cab of the rickety old truck, to face a small welcoming committee that greeted him and the long awaited machinery.

John spotted the doctor he spoke to yesterday among the little crowd and spoke directly to him: "Well doctor, how is the lady?"

"Mrs Stock? She's doing fine and should be going home later today. Would you like to see her before you start?"

"Indeed. Why not doctor. Lead on if you please."

He was taken through the pristine clean wards with high ceilings that had large electric fans rotating slowly to keep the place cool, and looking like a giant aeroplane getting ready to take off.

"Here she is Mr, err, Mr." the doctor announced and enquired about whom he was speaking to.

"4th Engineer Grey." John prompted, then asked for the doctor's name.

"Dr Whitcombe." was the reply as they both nodded in brief acknowledgement.

"Here's Mrs Stock." Whitcombe said as he pointed the woman out to him, and John saw that she was sitting up in her bed with a couple of nurses fussing around her.

"Hello Mrs Stock. How are you feeling? Do you remember me?" John greeted politely.

"Hello young man. Gather you is de one what brungs me here. You know us folks ain gonna be allowed in d' white folks places, man. An jus howz am a gonna afford dis' place anyway, man?" she greeted John in a broad Barbadian accent. As she spoke, she displayed a set of gleaming white teeth in an otherwise dark brown and wrinkly face.

"Now don't you fret, it is all taken care of." John replied soothingly to her as he looked at Whitcombe who nodded his head in agreement.

"There you are. See? Even the senior hospital surgeon, Doctor Whitcombe here, said so." he assured the woman.

"I understand you will be discharged this afternoon. Have you got some transport to take you home?" he asked her politely.

"You knows I aint man, and anyway, my boys are working all de day and can't have de' time off to collect me neither." she said sulkily.

"Dr Whitcombe will see to that as well, won't you Doc." he announced and looked over to Whitcombe to see his reactions.

Again Whitcombe nodded his head in agreement for fear of losing his precious generator.

"Hey man! What's you white folks up to eh? I don't take charity from nobody no how, I always work for it, so I'm not about to start now." she said indignantly.

"Now Mrs Stock, don't get yourself upset." John said quietly, trying to calm her down.

"In my family, if we can't help a person in need then we won't hinder them, and if we do help, then it is done without favour or reward." he added.

Mrs Stock stopped her protestations, and looked at John for a moment.

"Apart from de' white folk I look after, you are the beginning of a new breed of people where colour don't matter no how. I'll accept your offer, young man, but I want to pay you back just as soon as I've saved enough to do so. Do you hear?"

"If that pleases you, then so shall it be. I must leave now and put new life into this hospital, just as surely as the Doctor here has put into you. Goodbye Mrs Stock." he said as he bade her farewell and left her being tended to by two nurses, as Whitcombe went with him to show where the machinery was to be installed.

It was late in the afternoon, when he finished his task of installing and testing the new generator, much to the relief and pleasure of the hospital staff.

As he waited in the lorry to leave, he saw Mrs Stock being helped into a pony and trap by the same two burly men he saw yesterday and guessed they were her two sons. When the lorry passed them, they waved and shouted their thanks at him as he left the hospital grounds to return to the ship.

He arrived back on board and found that the *Meadowlea* was tied up alongside and outboard of the *Brooklea* which was busy unloading her cargo or transferring some cargo between them.

The *Meadowlea* was a newer ship and although a copy of *Brooklea* internally, her outward appearance was much different. She was taller, several tens of feet longer and much fatter, thus almost dwarfing her elder sister as they snuggled together in the very congested harbour.

'Two ships tied up together, with the bigger one

using the other one as a dock fender. Can't do much good to the little one.' John thought to himself as he watched the dock cranes, derricks and masts dip and sway in unison, quietly doing their work.

"Hello John. How did the job go? Everything okay?" Day asked as he came up to him.

"Yes Happy. Everything tested and correct and just fine." he reported, as he remembered Whitcombe's face when forced to concede free treatment for Mrs Stock.

"Well done that man. I'm sure the hospital will thank you for helping them." Day answered as he nodded his approval to him.

'If only you knew the reality, Happy.' John thought, as he was quickly trying to change the subject.

They stood talking for a while enjoying a cigarette when they heard a loud screaming voice.

"Those men there! Put those pipes or cigarettes out." a shout came from above them. They both turned round and looked up to see the First mate Tritton and Trewarthy staring down at them menacingly.

"Yes! You two!" commanded Tritton.

"Don't you know there's a highly inflammable cargo being loaded aboard?"

"Our apologies, Mr Tritton." said Day in an appeasing manner, as they stubbed out their cigarettes.

"Very well, Mr Day. Make sure your man knows it as well." Tritton replied arrogantly, and left the bridge wing with Trewarthy still scowling at them.

"There's that look again. I keep getting that kind of

look from Trewarthy. Like as if he's trying to see straight through me. Did you see it Happy?" John remarked.

"Yes I did. The Doc was telling me that since you've come aboard, Trewarthy has been eating tablets like sweets and hitting the bottle very hard. Have you got anything to do with it, bearing in mind what happened in Belfast?"

"No. This is my first ship as you well know. I've never seen the man before coming aboard, believe me Happy." he replied earnestly and looking into Day's face.

"The rumours might be true after all. According to one, his Lordship wanted Trewarthy ashore for a couple of months leave as he hadn't been on leave since joining the ship." Day said pensively.

"How long's that Happy?"

"From stoker Barne's account, Trewarthy has been on board since she was re-launched nearly four years ago."

"Four years? That's a long time on board without leave, and good going by any stretch of the imagination." John marvelled at the feat, and gave a soft whistle.

"I expect that's why his Lordship lets him stay a little longer in port, even though the *Brook* is supposed to be the flagship of the line and Trewarthy is his most experienced seagoing Captain in the entire shipping company."

"Is that what happened to Cresswell?"

"More or less. Cresswell had a bad war too apparently, and is to be quietly pensioned off after his next voyage." Day volunteered.

The two discussed this subject for a while longer then Day decided to change the subject.

"By the way. There's a bash we've got to attend tonight. It's at the Yacht club somewhere near here."

"Bash? Oh you mean a dinner party with loads of highbrow people there?"

"No. Just a cocktail party like we had in Las Palmas, only the ships officers from the other British ships have been invited to attend. Something to do with Royalty." Day informed him.

"I'd much rather go ashore for a quiet drink than all this 'hoity toity' stuff. Just you, Bruce, myself and maybe another friend. One of those *'rabbits'* runs ashore, that steward Burns keeps telling me about." he revealed candidly.

"Anyway, what time does it start, where does it take place, and for how long, Happy?"

"In about two hours time for say a couple of hours, that's all it should take, unless his Lordship has something else planned for us."

"Okay, count me in. But as we are sailing early tomorrow morning, I want a last look round before I come back on board."

"That is fine by me John. And by the way, its best whistle and flute as Burns would say, so get your glad rags on."

"Right, I'll see you on the gangway at about sevenish." he confirmed as they parted company to prepare for this big occasion.

He looked out of the porthole again to see that the sun had almost gone down now, with the sky showing sheets of bright red on a backdrop of deep blue, and with the odd little pink coloured, fluffy cotton wool type of cloud, floating along high above them.

He could feel the light breezes fanning his face, coming into his cabin from the open porthole, and he shivered slightly at the pleasure of such delicious coolness of the evening against the almost overbearing searing heat of the day.

'I wonder if there are black lords and V.I.P's attending tonight's do as well,' he thought as he prepared himself for this bash.

CHAPTER X
An Impostor

It was a lofty, imposing building of the finest Aberdeen granite, topped by a raised dome that sparkled in the light from the mother of pearl shells that completely covered it. The main building was square shaped, with a front facade like a roman temple and pink marble pillars that stood as sentinels at the entrance of the cavernous gothic doorway.

There were several small coloured spotlights strategically placed and used to illuminate the building at night, which gave a breathtaking display.

The entrance to the grounds had a large black and gilt wrought iron gate, ornately decorated with a nautical theme, and with an heraldic crest sitting over the equally finely wrought iron archway above it.

This was the start to a white pebbled drive-way, that circled a very tall but lone palm tree, which itself was surrounded by four smaller, white pampas grass mounds on an island of lush green manicured lawn.

A high privet hedge marked the spacious ground's perimeter with oleander bushes interspersed around it, and re-enforced with spiked iron railings to match the colour of the gateway.

As a yacht club it backed onto the shore-line, therefore it also had its own square shaped pier attached to the back of the building, with a sloping multi-coloured canvas awning as its roof.

It too was lit up with fairy lights and lanterns that adorned the awning supports, and anybody standing in there would have a semi-circular but panoramic view of small bays and sandy beaches each side of the small pier.

There was a tall, graceful mast from some bygone sailing ship, which was securely tied down by four steel ropes at the end of it. During the day it would probably have proudly flown the White Ensign and the clubs pennant from its top. But after dark it stood alone as a white needle that pointed to the stars as if trying to navigate its way to some distant galactic shore.

Inside the main building, the raised dome had several stained glass windows, so that when the light shone through it, it gave the illusion of a cascading waterfall of colour that beamed down and danced across the spacious floor of pure white marble as its centrepiece.

This circular floor was surrounded with shell shaped alcoves painted in shades of blue and green, each alcove having a glass bowl with a candle in it and placed on smoked glass tables. When the candles were lit, they looked like large pearls glowing in a shimmering sea.

Such is the splendour and flamboyance to be found in a jewel of the Caribbean despite its brutal and bloody past of slavery and debauchery.

John took the opportunity during the coach ride to the yacht club, to meet other officers of the *Meadowlea*, each introduced at length by Cunningham, his now ex cabin mate.

He noticed that most of them were not much older than him, and most were ex-Royal Navy men. All were wearing white dinner jackets, with their rank showing on the epaulettes and for the war heroes, their miniature medals which gave a coloured display on their chests.

They were slightly late for the appointed time, but were announced in a booming voice by the doorman as they arrived:

"Officers of the *Brooklea* and *Meadowlea*."

The guests were announced in their groups and were standing in their own little groups of friends, the higher the social rank the closer to the canopied wooden pier you were placed.

Thus the dignitaries, the club's Commodore and friends were on the pier, the captains of the ships and plantation owners in the middle, and last but not least, the shopkeepers and the other ships officers were near the entrance.

Such insidious snobbery and class structure is still very much in evidence today.

There were several elegantly dressed ladies, dripping in jewellery, but others were dressed for the weather. Therefore, the flimsy garments on these, showed their attributes and charms especially well under any bright light, which was often contrived by the women to do so.

There were plenty of extra tables and chairs in the semi-circular alcoves that surrounded the hall, but all were taken up by all the early arrivals. So John and his fellow officers stood in a semi-circle as did most of the groups that had arrived late, bathed in the natural kaleidoscope of light given off by the stained glass windows above them.

Larter gave John a friendly tip, telling him this was the sort of do, you got to know other ships and officers, just in case you're stuck in a port or want to go somewhere else around the world, so as not to repeat his Belfast experiences. This then is the scene set for John's first official 'bash'.

He decided to stay next to Larter, making light conversation, enjoying the free flowing glasses of sherry and smoking large fat cigars, which the club waiters provided and carried in large trays, when he spotted Trewarthy sitting at a table with other ship's captains. "There's the skipper, Bruce. Looks as if he's got company." he said as he indicated with his head instead of pointing.

"Yes. He's celebrating his thirty fifth birthday today, and a reunion with what looks like some old pals, judging by the way they're slapping each other on the back."

"Thirty fifth? He looks more like it should be his sixty fifth." John remarked in astonishment.

"Yes. He had a tough war, as did most of them, judging by their looks and medals. I have heard rumours that there's another one starting or in the making out in the Orient, so I wonder how many of them will be recalled to serve King and Country again." Larter intoned.

Day came over from another circle with another officer and introduced him to John.

"Chief Engineer Jim Gregson, meet my newly promoted 4th Engineer, John Grey." he said, starting the brief introductions.

"And you know our 2nd Sparker of course, don't you?" Day continued.

"Yes. Hello Bruce." Gregson said as he shook Larter's hand then John's.

"Hello John. Gather you're the one that put paid to the partnership of Messrs Cresswell and Trewarthy, by that brilliant plan of yours everyone's talking about."

"I'm sure I don't know what you mean. Er, Jim." he replied shyly.

"Let's put it this way." Gregson said and explain how much easier it appeared to be, according to Jack Cunningham. That he had his own entire crew effecting the same colour coding as John had stipulated. Then finished by saying. "Well done John. This might not sound much, but if you are ever stuck for a voyage or a ride then I'll gladly have you aboard as part of my Engine room staff."

"Thanks Jim, that is good of you. I'll remember that." he replied as Day and Gregson left to rejoin their own circle of friends.

"See what I mean John?" Larter asked, as they watched them go.

"Yes. I think I'll take your advice just as soon as I get a decent drink. This sherry's getting a bit too warm." he replied and started to move towards the bar.

"Mine too. I think I'll join you. I could do with stretching my legs a bit." Replied Larter, and followed John closely behind.

The two friends made their way through the crowds of guests.

'They're seamen talking navigation. They're plantation owners talking about their crops.' John thought as he heard the topics being discussed in the groups he passed as he made his way to the equally crowded bar counter.

They had a couple of large cold drinks each, then armed with another loaded glass in each hand, decided to risk the crushing journey back again, when John accidentally bumped into someone he didn't notice behind him as he turned, the person having his back to John.

"Beg your pardon." he said politely as the man turned round.

"And so..." the person began.

"Hello you two, fancy bumping into you." It was Sinclair.

"Hello Andy! Where've you been hiding since we've arrived?" Larter asked with interest.

"You must be well connected to get in here."

"I've had this leave organised for some time now." Sinclair replied as he winked and tapped his nose. Then introduced the two shipmates to the people he was with.

"Folks! This is Bruce Larter our Radio Officer and this is John Grey, the 4th Engineer I've been telling you about."

"Hello Bruce, hello John." the elderly couple said as they all shook hands.

"Bruce, John, this is my great Aunt and Uncle Jean and Larry. They are one of the very few who own and live on a plantation in the parish of St Michael." Sinclair informed them.

"Ah yes! John Grey. Isn't he the one who saved our Doris?" Jean asked Larry.

"By Doris's description, it certainly looks like him." was the reply.

"Doris? Who's that?" John asked non-plussed.

"Doris was the nanny to me and my two cousins. It's a long and ancient story from the days of Henry Morgan and the LaSalle's, but I'll tell you again later." replied Sinclair, turning to his aunt.

"Why do you ask, Aunt Jean? What has John got to do with Nanny Stock?"

"You were out in the plantation somewhere yesterday, when Nanny Stock was hit by a horse and nearly died, if it wasn't for the quick thinking of young John here." replied Jean sombrely.

'Mrs Stock? Andy's Nanny?' John thought as he cast his mind back to the incident then started to feel a bit embarrassed.

"Yes! That's him. The very same John Grey at the hospital." confirmed Whitcombe, as he butted into their conversation and turning away from his own circle of friends, joined theirs.

"That's the man who, um, blackmailed me, if that's

the right word, into treating Mrs Stock." Whitcombe stated, and carried on to describe what happened.

"That sounds about right, according to Nanny Stock." said Larry, who then related Mrs Stock's version.

"So you see, it was the Doc who did everything. I was merely a bystander." John said quickly and diplomatically as if to dodge the limelight.

"If it weren't for you John Grey, then all hell would have broken loose, as Mrs Stock is well respected and well liked by all on the island." Whitcombe added.

"Come on now, stop blushing and own up, John Grey. You've made us all very happy and if Nanny Stock were here she'd thank you herself." Larry said cheerfully.

"Any time you're in Barbados, with or without Andy, you two come by and see us again, you hear." commanded Jean with a wink and a beaming smile.

"Yes. You do just that." Sinclair confirmed, with a nod of approval.

"Well thank you all. It's very kind of you. We'll certainly do that." Larter replied, as they politely excused themselves and continued their crushing journey back to their other friends.

"Where've you two been? They're passing the champagne round, so get yourself a glass or two." Cunningham informed them, as the two friends finally arrived back at their own circle.

John and Larter downed their now very warm drinks

and swapped glasses for those of bubbling pink champagne in time for an auspicious happening.

A loud bell rang in the hall that hushed the guests to silence.

"My Lords, Ladies and Gentlemen." the M.C. announced in a polished English voice. "You will raise your glasses in a toast to our Commodore, in congratulations to the knighthood bestowed upon him in the new Christmas Honours list, and to be presented by our new Governor General. I give you Commodore Sir Tarquin Friar."

After the cheers and polite clapping, there followed several speeches and many more toasts to this person or that person, almost ad infinitum.

"Now I know how boring it is from this side." John observed as he remembered his last night in Las Palmas and the speech he delivered.

"Yes. I don't think I could stand up and 'witter on' like that. Still, I expect it'll be my turn for it happen one day." Larter replied as he stifled a yawn.

The party atmosphere was well underway when John decided he had to go for a toilet, but asked Sinclair, who had just arrived and joined them, to grab him another drink when he was away.

"I'm busting too, so I'll join you. By the way, my folks had to leave early but send their wishes to you." Sinclair informed him.

They had to go through the guests to a doorway near

the entrance of the hall, which took some time, because some of the intoxicated female guests were flirting with them as they went by.

"If it weren't that I was busting, I'd have taken that freckled filly on, there and then." boasted Sinclair.

"Do you know her?" John asked with surprise in his voice.

"Yes. Her father owns the next plantation to great uncle Larry. The one with that church you'd seen." Sinclair replied, then added.

"If I wasn't a free spirited sailor, I'd gladly settle down with her." he vowed with an emphatic nod of his head.

"There is no answer to that Andy." John replied as they reached their destination, only to join a small queue of equally desperate bodies wanting relief.

John led the way back into the hall and had to pass the area designated as 'Captain's table' where all the ships' captains were seated.

He saw that there were three officers with their backs to him, who were reaching over the table collecting some cards or snapshots that Trewarthy was offering them to the man next to him.

Trewarthy looked up as John was passing and gave a shout.

"That's him. That's whom I mean. See?" as he pointed between John and the snapshots as if in comparison.

Here we go again, moaned John as he tried to hurry his way out of harms way.

The three men facing Trewarthy stood up and turning round to see who he was pointing at, saw John walking quickly past them.

Two of the men dropped their glasses from their hands, their colour went pure white, their eyes almost popping out of their heads, and their mouths agape.

The third man who had a full glass raised to his mouth about to take a drink, spluttered and coughed into it, went red as a beetroot and started to wave his arms around like a windmill.

The man sitting next to Trewarthy stood bolt upright, knocking his chair over with a loud clatter and in equal shock, said in a loud whisper.

"Von Meir! You're dead! You... You... You must be!" he stammered but his voice tailed off into dumb silence.

A woman's shrill voice pierced the now silent and amazed guests: "Michael! You said his name is Grey. But that's Meir! Without his medals, I just know it!" she nodded violently and peered into John's face intently.

The first man finally recovered enough to say in an increasingly indignant and menacing voice:

"That man's an impostor. His name is not Grey, nor any other but Von Meir." As he emphasised the name. "Meir had been sentenced to death for war crimes but somehow escaped, and now apparently dares to turn up here in this cunning disguise."

The second man who began to regain his senses, urgently commanded.

"Quick, you three. Grab him and send for the police." he snapped to three others of the amazed but less affected men.

In a flash, John was pounced upon and roughly seized by the men, who started to manhandle him and pin his hands tightly behind his back.

'What's all this? Von Meir? War crimes?' John thought as he tried desperately to wrestle himself clear from the men, but in vain.

An irate woman rushed forward and slapped John's face so hard that it sounded like a whiplash that reverberated around the high domed hall.

"That's for my husband. See what else you've done to him." She cried as she pointed to a fainted man.

Then shrieked loudly at everybody.

"Someone get a doctor to my husband. I think he's had a heart attack."

She was about to slap John again, when Sinclair leapt over a table and grabbed the woman's arm so hard, she was sent stumbling across the floor, crashing into several tables and chairs, upsetting several drinks. Ending up in a drink-soaked, squawking, gibbering heap on the marble floor.

In the meantime, Trewarthy was mumbling and agreeing with the other men in his company, who started chanting and shouting loudly.

"Impostor! Meir! Hang him!"

Such was the great commotion caused, it attracted the attention of even those on the pier.

Commodore Friar moved swiftly onto the scene, followed closely on his heels by Lord Belverley, Doctor Whitcombe and Commissioner Carlysle, the island's Chief of Police.

Whitcombe bent down to see to and attend the stricken man, meanwhile Friar and Belverley came across to the heart of the disturbance.

"What the deuce is going on here. Who is responsible for all this?" Friar demanded angrily.

"Trewarthy. What has got into you Captain? Is this another one of your kangaroo courts again? Explain yourself man." hissed Belverley as he arrived next to him.

Day, Larter and Cunningham had wrestled John from his captors, and shoved them away into the guests who had gathered round in a large circle to witness such an explosive drama unfolding in front of their disbelieving eyes.

The first man turned to Carlysle and vehemently demanded that this person, "so called" Grey be arrested. That he, Grey, was the man in all the photographs.

"Let's see them." Carlysle growled angrily, as he grabbed the photos, cards, and newspaper clippings that were on the table, including those that were in Trewarthy's fists.

He looked at each one, then handed them to Friar, who in turn handed them to Belverley to look at. Finally he showed them to John, who took each one to see what he was accused of, and just who he was accused of being.

The first one was a picture of a scruffily dressed man in uniform, with his hands in handcuffs, who appeared to be bundled into the back of an open lorry by other uniformed men. He looked up and saw that were the same men now standing by Trewarthy.

The next was of a man standing over other men sitting under some ship's guns, with a long list of names and ships hanging from between the gun barrels.

Reading down the list of 'SHIPS SUNK' and the names of survivors from them, he could decipher most of the names himself and see the faces to tally with them. Trewarthy, Cresswell, Barnes, Johns, Downton, Dolbere, Thompson.

Again he looked up and saw that most of the people at the table in front of him were those in the picture.

He finally came to the last one, which was a picture of a sleek ship bristling with guns, and read the inscription at the bottom of it. M.V. *SCHLEZWIG*.

That ship looks familiar to me, he thought to himself, then froze as if in a shock as he looked at a picture of himself.

It took him several seconds to recover from this shock, then managed to see the name under the picture of 'him'.

'Cruiser Kapitan Hans Otto Von Meir. Knights Cross. No wonder these men were hysterical. Such is the likeness; same hairstyle; same black hair; medium build and height. But he has a higher forehead, his nose is different, and almost baby faced.' he thought,

but was snapped out of them by an insistent question by Carlysle.

"Well? Is that you in these photographs?"

"No. That person is not me. He looks like me but it's definitely not me. I am only eighteen." he replied in flat denial.

John's friends managed a look over his shoulder at the photos and even they gasped at the likeness between John and Von Meir.

"So that what's been troubling Trewarthy." Day whispered as he looked at the photograph and compared it with John's likeness.

"These men have gone raving mad. That's not John Grey." Cunningham stated with an exaggerated sideways shake of his head.

"For a start this was taken in the middle of the 1940's. John Grey was fresh out of the Engineering College at Belfast last month."

"So that's why they wanted to string you up in Belfast. The likeness is so uncanny." Sinclair said quietly into John's ear.

What followed next was a series of questions Carlysle put to Trewarthy, his group of friends, and to John and his group of friends.

Every time John tried to give an answer or could not even give one, Trewarthy and his cronies called him a liar or told everybody that he pretended to have amnesia to escape being trapped and to escape being hung.

While all this was going on, Belverley was talking quietly to his co ship-owners, and with Friar who left the scene discreetly to get something.

When Friar came back, he had a large folder crammed full with newspaper cuttings, files, and photographs.

"Right, Commissioner! I have here, a dossier on all known Naval war criminals from whatever navy, who have been caught and dealt with before, during and after the Nuremberg trials.

Some of the files are still open as the persons concerned haven't been caught yet or have escaped, but perhaps this will clear the matter up." he announced as he waved some of the folder's contents around for people to see.

Belverley, Carlysle and Friar sat at the table and looked through the bulging file for several minutes.

"A HAH!" Friar shouted triumphantly.

"Here it is. It was one of my more intriguing ones. I am very good at finding things, places and people.

Maybe this dossier is partly the reason why I was given my knighthood." he explained as he pulled out some documents and photographs then handed the dossier to Carlysle to scrutinise.

Carlysle sifted through the dossier then began to read the documents out loud for everybody to hear:

"Cruiser Kapitan Hans Otto Von Meir, late of the M.V. *SCHLEZWIG,* who had escaped during his trial. Was re-traced and found in South Africa with other war criminals and along with a huge pile of nazi gold, and not in the Argentinas, as was reported. He was re-apprehended by Commodore Tarquin Friar DSC MC RN.

After a military court martial presided over by Commodore Friar in the September of 1947 he and his friends were summarily executed by a firing squad at police H.Q. in Mardensburg." he announced.

Carlysle then held the evidence with outstretched hands for Trewarthy and his friends to read, who grabbed the paperwork in total disbelief.

When Trewarthy and his cronies had seen enough, the documents were literally thrown back into Carlysle's face, he picked up the scattered paper and held it up for anyone to read, and everybody else to be a witness to.

By then Trewarthy and his friends were slumped in some chairs looking spent, almost lifeless, with their women folk sobbing quietly beside them.

There was a deafening silence of disbelief from the rest of the onlookers for several moments, then a woman's voice sliced through the atmosphere like a hot knife through butter.

"Oh my god! That poor young man's been arrested, beaten up and was nearly hung by these men."

That seemed to be a trigger for them all to bay for blood like a pack of wolves, demanding justice for the young man and retribution to the perpetrators.

Carlysle held his hands up and with great difficulty

quietened everybody down, with Friar restoring his file back together again. Belverley stood menacingly over Trewarthy's group.

"Captain Trewarthy! You and Chief Engineer Cresswell were about to do the same harm to Engineer Grey in Belfast, if I hadn't come along." Belverley growled, then turned to the rest of the audience, and told them exactly what had taken place in Belfast.

Carlysle listened intently to what was being told, then turned to John and said in a clear and concise manner.

"These are very serious offences perpetrated against you and your good name. I am satisfied as to who and what you are, but you will have to remain on the Island as well as the others until you have made a full statement. I will charge these people for attempted murder, for a start." he paused and asked Belverley if his ships were sufficiently manned to account for the absence of Trewarthy and other witnesses.

Belverley replied that his ships were to sail in the morning and couldn't possibly do without his officers.

That no doubt the other shipping companies would be in the same position. Therefore he would seek further time to consider the request.

"Very well Lord Belverley. We will discuss it further, once I have got a statement from Grey." Carlysle replied after a moments pause.

A platoon of the local militia had arrived noisily, heralded by the stamping of their hobnailed boots that echoed in the hall, as they marched menacingly towards the group.

"We have come to escort Trewarthy and his friends away Sir!" said the platoon commander.

Carlyle indicated to Trewarthy and his group, and told the officer to lock them up pending a special court case in the morning.

The platoon soon marched off under a barrage of orders screamed out by their commander, leaving John sitting on a chair and safely surrounded by his close friends.

The party atmosphere had been shattered, but people were standing around talking quietly to each other for some time until Friar blew his sailors whistle and commanded.

"Ladies and Gentlemen, I think we all deserve a stiff drink after this high drama. So the bar will remain open until 2330 hours, then I'm afraid you will all have to go home. That is about an hour from now. Thank you."

John's friends were sitting around guarding him, as he too felt drained of any emotion, his ears still ringing from the slap that woman gave him.

Several of the guests had come up to talk and to offer John some sympathy, but were politely asked by his friends to leave him to recover from his ordeal.

Instead, the guests handed over calling cards and gifts of money for him, and wished him well as they left him.

He felt that he was turning out to be a kind of celebrity, but also like a sideshow in a circus, so he got up and said quietly and forlornly to his pals, "My good friends. I knew I shouldn't have come. All I wanted was a quiet little drink and a last little look at the island before we sailed in the morning. Now look at the mess I'm in. And I've stopped the ship from sailing."

Sinclair put an arm around him as did Larter, and Day stated, "So you shall young friend, but I think we'd better see the Commissioner and Lord Belverley to find out what's happening first."

Immediately, John was gently escorted out of the club to the cheers and claps of the other remaining guests.

The friends found Carlysle, Belverley and Friar slowly pacing round and round the driveway discussing what to do, when Day attracted their attention and managed to stop them. "Excuse me, er, Gentlemen. Is it all right for us to leave now or do you need us again tonight?" he enquired on John's behalf.

Belverley looked at Carlysle with an approving nod of this head.

"Well Angus? I think we can let young Grey go for now. The ships are not going anywhere and he certainly is not. So what do you say?" he asked.

"I'm not sure. It's not Grey I'm worried about, but Trewarthy and his friends. Very well, but keep a good eye on him won't you." Carlysle confirmed with a nod to Day's request.

129

Day thanked the trio and left them to talk over the event as he went and joined his friends to go back on board.

"Come on lads. Let's get back and have a nightcap in the lounge. We've a big day ahead of us tomorrow." Day suggested to his friends, who agreed unanimously.

They arrived on board feeling stone cold sober, and with their adrenaline drained, they just sat quietly chatting in the lounge sipping at their drinks, reflecting on the evening. One by one they left to get turned in, and await tomorrow's aftermath of the night's dramatic events.

'What a waste of a perfectly good evening and what an official 'BASH' that was.' John thought as he tenderly felt his still very sore cheek.

CHAPTER XI
Mistaken Identity

John was woken by the noise created by the cheerful steward bringing his breakfast tray as it rattled and clinked when Burns stepped   through the cabin doorway.

"Good morning Mr Grey. Here's your breakfast. It's a lovely day for it, don't you think? The lads get another final run ashore before going back to Blighty, all thanks to you again Mr Grey." Burns said chirpily.

He sat up and looked down from his bunk at Burns busying himself around the cabin, listening to the happy man flitting from one topic to another.

"What time is it steward?" he asked in a half daze.

"It's 8 bells of the morning watch Mr Grey. Er, sorry. It's eight o'clock and you've got about half an hour to muster on the gangway with Mr Day." Burns replied apologetically as he handed John his breakfast.

"Thank you steward." he replied miserably, as his thoughts flew straight back to last night's debacle, then asked.

"What's going to happen today, steward? I've never experienced such palaver or proceedings before."

"Don't you worry about a thing Mr Grey, you're in the clear. But it's a Court of Enquiry that you'll be attending. Mr Day and Mr Larter will be keeping you company and they'll explain everything as you go on your way there." Burns informed him, then added.

"I've put your best whistle'n flute ready. Er, tropical suit that is, the one you wore in Las Palmas. Finish your breakfast first, then a nice cool shower to make you feel better."

He thanked Burns and did as he was told. When Burns finished fussing around him like a broody hen, he was ready to face the world.

"There you are Mr Grey, you're all shamfered up and ready now. So on behalf of me and all the lads, we wish you all the best, and don't forget to give them hell." Burns said as he finished brushing John's shoes.

"Thank you steward, I need all the luck that can be mustered, I'm sure. But how did you lot get to know about my latest scrape?"

"Ah, that's an easy one. Me, an' some of me mates heard it from the Chief Bosun, and the rest was brought on board by the dockyard mateys. An besides, it's in all the local newspapers, by all accounts." Burns admitted with a big grin.

"Thank you again steward." he replied as he left his cabin.

He made his way to the gangway and met most of the officers who had accompanied him to the club last night.

First mate Tritton who was taking charge of the group of officers waiting for John to arrive, ordered Day, Cunningham and Sinclair to escort John to the court of enquiry, with Larter as his brief, and to inform him of the procedures and customs of what was to take place.

The others had departed in the back of an army lorry, but John and his escort were put in a small coach that had two policemen in attendance with it. As they left the ship's side, the officers and men from both of the ships lined themselves along the inboard one then cheered and whistled as they wished him luck.

"You're very popular with the men John." observed Day.

"Yes, especially as we won't be sailing today, which means that the lads can have another run ashore, courtesy of our Mr Grey here." Sinclair said appreciatively.

John listened to his friends chatting about the whys and wherefores of a missed sailing, whilst he sat in a pensive mood and very mindful as to what was on the immediate agenda.

"Cheer up John. You're the wronged one. It's Trewarthy and the others that should be worried and look out for themselves, especially if this sort of thing has happened before." Larter said with a big smile in an attempt to cheer his fellow officer up.

"Aye, a few years in the pokey for the others I'll warrant. As for the skipper, he'll be beached for good." Day chipped in, with genuine concern for his young Engineer.

"That's a pity, cause he's a bloody good seaman. He certainly knows his ship." Sinclair recalled.

The bus stopped by a tall marble pillared building, which had an inscription in large black lettering above the cavernous hall doorway.

Larter read it aloud and asked if anyone could understand it.

"That means 'Truth and Justice' and so it will be." remarked Larter, as he finally translated the Latin for the benefit to the others.

They were led into a large oak panelled room, with rows of red leather upholstered seats each side of an aisle. John looked at the large ornate throne like seat, which was flanked by four smaller and less ornate ones.

On either side of the room and facing the entrance from where they came in, John noticed there was also a gallery either side of the room.

It was full of people as was the rest of the room, save for those five seats and where he was going to sit.

'So that's what a courtroom looks like,' he thought to himself.

The whispers and buzz of conversation gave way to clapping as he walked down the aisle with his friends a pace behind him, where they all sat by a desk facing the Judges bench as indicated by a court usher.

Very shortly after he sat down, the claps and calls of 'Good luck' turned to hissing and booing as Trewarthy and his friends made their entrance from a side door, escorted by several policemen.

They were shown to a twin row of seats adjacent to

the Judges and opposite the benches a jury would occupy.

"Pray silence in court! All rise." proclaimed the clerk of the court in a commanding voice, as five white wigged, black robed men came through a doorway behind the ornate seats.

'*Black and white, or is it white and black.*' John mused to himself.

"This is a court of enquiry, Lord Justice Dumayne KCB KCVO DSC, presiding." the clerk continued in a dignified voice.

The hall went completely silent as these men took up their positions and sat down.

"You may sit down." ordered the clerk, with a sweep of his hands to the packed courtroom.

"Here we go John." Larter whispered sideways into John's ear.

"This is where the gobble de gook and waffle begins and enough to put you to sleep. But you must keep up with it." He advised.

The judge cleared his throat and with a well polished voice said, "This is a special judicial enquiry into last night's serious breach of the peace at the Barbados yacht club. There are serious matters to be discussed, thus determining further proceedings as pronounced by this court.

It's now 0900 hours, let the proceedings commence." he stated, and gave a nod as the signal to start.

First the prosecutor delivered his opening speech,

followed by Trewarthy's defence counsel, which set the battle of words in motion.

John watched for some time the procession of people go into the witness box, then whispered to Larter in complete puzzlement.

"Why am I not called? All of you, Trewarthy and his friends have been there. It was me they tried to lynch."

"You don't have to go John. Your statement does and says it all. But you'll be asked later on what you'll be wanting to have done on your behalf." Larter whispered his reply.

The photographs, cards, press cuttings and other documents from Friar's folders had been produced in large quantities. Belverley had made his appearance in the witness box, as did Friar, as the enquiry progressed.

"So that's it. That explains it. The strange name on the brass plate welded to the ships keel he had seen whilst the ship was in the Belfast dock. The *Brooklea* and the *Schlezwig* are as one. The same ship!

No wonder it looked familiar. That picture of Von Meir was a mirror image of me. No wonder poor Trewarthy and his friends thought I was that man. What a tragic case of mistaken identity." John whispered again into Larter's ear, as the stark, naked truth started to dawn and have an impact on him.

He looked at Trewarthy and his friends closely, and saw how they were sitting with their heads bowed and looking very subdued.

The men looked unkempt and unshaven, with eyes like black holes sunk into their faces. Their womenfolk were also dishevelled and looked as if they'd been dragged through a hedge backwards.

He felt nothing but pity for these people, although they had wanted to kill him, not once but twice.

But he had to apply his thoughts to natural justice and was formulating in his mind what he must do, not only for his future safety but for the sake of his friends.

The realisation that it was only himself and his say so that would determine the lives and future of these pathetic figures, made him feel all the more uncomfortable. He had to try to put himself in a wiser person's mind, and if he were in their place, what would they do to him?

'Do unto others?' he thought, and felt himself tremble as if he was in a very cold place.

He heard the final words of the defence judge who stood up to say.

"In mitigation M'Lud. The accumulative effect on Trewarthy, is that even several years later, he is still suffering from the trauma of the loss of his kinfolk and the sinking of his first ship, the S.S. *Southern Star*. Von Meir took a terrible revenge on Trewarthy and his friends, 'press-ganging' them into service on the *Schezswig* helping to sink other innocent ships in a similar manner. Finally, Captain Trewarthy had known of Von Meir's escape and Von Meir's explicit revenge on Trewarthy and friends, but not of his recapture and subsequent execution.

"Therefore, we plead a tragic but genuine case of mistaken identity on all accounts. The defence rests."

There followed a brief hush then the judge made a few statements with a bout of questions and answers.

When the court went silent again, John felt everybody's eyes on him, waiting with bated breath to see him stand and hear him speak.

Larter gave John a gentle nudge. "It's all down to you now John. Everybody is waiting on you. They want to hear from you, of what you want to do or take from them, but as I say, it's only you that can take it all from here." Then advised:

"This is your big chance now. I'd stop for a moment and make them sweat for a while if I was you. Remember this, whatever is decided here, becomes the judgement and the full weight of the law, with no further court or trial. So make it a good one, my friend."

John stood up slowly with uncertainty and coughed nervously as if to clear his throat.

"Your lordships." he began. "I am unaccustomed to such procedures of court etiquette, therefore I request your Lordships permission to have a brief consultation with Lord Belverley and the Police Commissioner in private, if I may."

"It will only be at that time, I can deliver my answer to your questions." he concluded.

"Very well Mr Grey." said the judge.

"Providing it will bring us a conclusion to this court's deliberations." he replied, then rapped his gavel and with a loud voice announced: "This court is adjourned for lunch. The court will re-convene at 1400 hours Eastern Standard Time, Mr Clerk of the court if you please."

"Very well your honour. All rise." The clerk said as he nodded his obedience to the Judge.

The judges had left, the defendants were ushered back again under a heavy police escort and people were filing out of the court, nodding and smiling at John as they left.

"You appear to have won a lot of new friends, John." remarked Day, as he came to be next to him.

"Who are they?" he asked in amazement.

"They were at the club last night, and every man jack of them would have stood in the dock for you." Larter replied confidently.

"You seem to know the score on these events Bruce. Why is that? How did you learn about it?"

Larter laughed and revealed that his father was a lawyer before the war, and that he'd go to see his father at work from time to time during his school holidays.

"Yes. That's why Lord Belverley always tries to see that Bruce is present when one of us gets into trouble in foreign ports." Sinclair confirmed, with a nod of his head.

John and his friends went to a room at the side of the courtroom to meet Belverley, the other ship-owners and the Representatives for the other shipping lines.

"Engineer Grey. I will not pretend that you have not had a rough time at the hands of my senior and most respected Captain. But you are also the one that will cost me and my shipping line a lot of time, which means trade, which means money. Unless you agree to let me handle this as I see fit, then you'll find the parting of the way so costly in monetary terms, you'd need to work for the line for the rest of your natural life just to pay off the interest." Belverley started, but Brooks intervened quickly.

"What have you in mind Beverley? We know junior engineers are twelve a penny these days, but this one happens to have come up trumps with that idea of his. If the Ministry of Shipping and Trade finds out that we've taken his patent for ourselves and sacked him in the process, then its *our* parting of the ways would be the costly one."

"And besides, he's still alive and no real harm was done to him." Burford added.

John and his friends stood quietly and listened whilst the arguments and counter proposals of the ship-owners were discussed over their heads.

"Excuse me your lordships. But it is me that has the decision here, not you. It is my name the prosecutor is using not yours.

"Therefore it is me that they are forced to listen to not the other way round." John shouted angrily at the ship owners, which drew sharp gasps of disbelief from them.

"How dare you talk to me in that tone of voice." Belverely responded.

"Look Lord Belverley, I am but a young engineering officer trying to make a living in a profession that I love doing. If you have something suitable to offer from what I have already thought of, then please let me know."

"Aye, let's listen to what he has to say, Belverley. Lets give this increasingly offensive upstart a chance to prove he is what he is." Brooks hissed, which stopped Belverley from uttering another word.

"Go on John! Tell them! Show them we are the ones that make all their money for them." Day urged.

"What I had in mind was. We obviously need somebody to captain the ship, which means that Captain Trewarthy would be needed. As for the rest, they should be kept here until I arrive safely back in Belfast. That way, maybe it would discourage any further such incidents that I experienced both in Belfast and last night."

Belverely took over John's thoughts and stated.

"The others are kept as hostages for your safe passage, thus releasing Captain Trewarthy and my ship to continue. Once you arrive back safely the rest can be released. Is that what you are suggesting Grey?"

"More or less."

The ship-owners huddled round and muttered amongst themselves for a moment before Belverley broke off from them to issue his edict.

"Right then Grey. We have decided to take your suggestion in its simplest terms, but you will leave the rest to us. Chief Engineer Day you have been dismissed and make sure Grey is not late for the start of the second session."

Day nodded and turned to go, grabbing John by the arm and pulling him out through the door.

"Let's get out of here before someone changes their mind," Day hissed in John's ear.

"Phew! That was a near thing Happy. I thought for a moment we'd all end up in the same place as Trewarthy and co." Larter sighed as the friends made their way out of the building to go back to the ship.

Lunch was from a nondescript menu, eaten by John almost trance like, and the return trip back into the court was as if there was a memory lapse.

"Mr Grey?" the presiding judge asked. "Have you formulated your reply? May I remind you, it is your statement now that dictates the outcome of this court."

"I have your honour." John replied as he held a piece of paper up to show the judges.

"Very well. In your own time if you please Mr Grey." the judge commanded.

John looked at Trewarthy and his friends, then handed the piece of paper to the Clerk of the Court who read it slowly before handing it to Belverley.

The defendants looked with horror and a pleading deep within their eyes, first at John then at Belverley, who stood up as John sat down. This action made the defendants squirm and tremble, as they were wringing their hands in fear.

"My Lords, Learned gentlemen, Officers of the court." Belverley commenced. "If it pleases you, I am now conducting the affairs of Mr Grey and wish to make a joint statement on his behalf, in the interest of my shipping line and that of the representatives of the other shipping lines."

Belverley spoke emotively for a while about mutual interests, the consequences of last night's incident, of the future plans concerning the defendants, and of the Police Commissioner's point of view. He ended his oration with.

"If it pleases the court, Mr Grey wishes to reserve the right to suspend his verdicts on the defendants until such time as he finishes his voyage, and is back safely in Belfast.

That they should understand the need for all qualified ships officers on any or all ships in a foreign or far off harbour, including this one. And as they know, I visit these islands on a regular basis.

Therefore it will be in Belfast that he would be notifying you of Mr Grey's decisions on Trewarthy and co. As for the assault perpetrated by one of the woman defendants. We demand that she and the rest of their party should remain in custody here on this island until that time you hear from me. Apart from those provision and in my conclusion, I trust that these arrangements should be amenable to the court and that Mr Grey's statement and instructions remain there."

"Well said, my Lord Belverley." the presiding judge commented, then turned to John and said:

"You have been well advised young man. I commend you for your imagination, your presence of mind and your bearing throughout these proceedings."

He then turned to Trewarthy and the other defendants and explained that Mr Grey was far more lenient to them than they were to him. Had they succeeded in their venture, even in Belfast, then the courts would have meted out the same justice by hanging them forthwith.

To the rest of the court he announced:

"It is the decision of this court to suspend this enquiry until we have heard from Lord Belverley in Belfast and will re-convene at that time.

"The court is now adjourned. The time is 1530hours. Be about your business." The judge rapped his gavel loudly for the last time then left as before, leaving the courtroom in an uproar.

"Silence. Clear the court, clear the court." the flustered clerk shouted over the clapping, the loud cheers and jeers from the packed court of all who witnessed the enquiry.

Some of them came up to John and congratulated him and wished him luck for the future then left him in the protection of his friends.

"That was wicked of you John." remarked Sinclair.

"Very crafty indeed John. It means that they'll all be sweating in fear in case you don't get to Belfast quick enough for them." Day joined in.

"What'll you do when you get home John?" Larter asked swiftly.

Before he had a chance to reply, Belverley had tapped him on his shoulder roughly.

"I wish to have a word in private with you Mr Grey." he said with an authoritative voice.

John left his friends with an inquisitive look on their faces, and noticed that Trewarthy and his friends were still sitting dejectedly and slumped in their stalls.

"That had better be your last stunt. I might not be around to bail you out again do you hear me Grey?" Belverley growled.

"Just as long as I'm not set upon again by any of your other ship's officers, Lord Belverley. Remember that it was I who was the victim not them and certainly not you. What more do you want off me?"

"That will be sufficient for now. Only you'd better have a suitable outcome ready for me when you get back into Belfast. Unless you can offer something right now, that is."

John sensed his anger starting to rise, and decided to take the bull by the horns by standing square to this person who had power of attorney over all in the shipping line, let alone a junior engineer.

"I am just trying to be a good engineer. I do not

know the whys and wherefores of running ships and shipping lines, only valves, engines and the like. As far as I'm concerned Lord Belverely, my arrival back home whenever that is, in one piece, should be the end to the matter. Except for one thing."

"Yes Grey. Go on, what is it." Belverely said slowly as if to bait John.

"You are to get Captain Trewarthy and his cronies ashore for a long spell of leave, or put me on another vessel, or even let me go from my contract with you to join another shipping company."

"You certainly are an upstart Grey. You must have had a strong upbringing to stand up to a Lord of the realm. That may be a good thing, but again it could be your own downfall.

"This Lord of the realm does not take kindly to advice given, especially by someone who has only been to sea a few short weeks.

"However, in view of the current situation, I will accept what you say about Captain Trewarthy, Chief Engineer Cresswell and their wartime friends.

"Maybe they would like to thank you for their concern even if they tried to lynch you not once but twice."

"Then you accept my terms Lord Belverley?"

"Yes Grey. I think that will suffice for now. So be it. I'll tell Captain Trewarthy of this before I leave tomorrow."

"No! Best let the matter stay as the judge has decided.

We will keep a lid on this and offer it as a surprise to Captain Trewarthy and company. That way I can be guaranteed a safe passage back home."

Belverley was taken aback by this last statement, but nodded his head slowly and concluded.

"Grey! Just as well you work for me, and not for one of my competitors. I shall be watching your career very closely from now on. You are dismissed now, so get back on board and do what I am paying you for. Good day!"

By the time John had finished talking to Belverley, and returned to his friends, they were the only other people left in the courtroom.

When John reached his friends, feeling that he had just come from the lion's den, he spoke with a commanding tone in his voice.

"This time gentlemen, we'll have that very quiet run ashore I wanted and that's on Lord Belverley orders. We sail in the morning, so let's go."

'I wonder what's on Trewarthy's agenda tonight' he thought as he left the now very silent courtroom.

The friends walked down the driveway to the main gate of the yacht club, stepped onto the public footpath and commenced what was the original idea and what should have been. A quiet evening, enjoying the atmosphere and flavour of a very Caribbean island and buying that last, all important gift for home.

CHAPTER XII
Like Wings

Due to the lack of a 3rd Engineer Officer and his early promotion, John was given the specific job of the 'Outside Engineer' as his next challenge and career move. This meant that he was to be responsible for the maintenance of all the auxiliary machines. The hydraulics, and other ship systems or machinery that were found outside the engine or motor rooms on the ship, hence the name. Therefore he was expected to conduct his round of inspections prior to the ship's early departure that morning.

Shortly after he had finished his inspection, he decided to remain on deck to enjoy the peace and tranquil coolness in the early morning of yet another typical, scorching Caribbean day.

The ship was virtually silent, as if slumbering peacefully at her berth, as he walked along the upper deck towards the access ladder leading up to the bridge.

All he could hear was his soft footfall on the dew moistened deck and the lapping of the wavelets against the ships steel hull. His chosen place was a vantage point above the bridge by the radar mounting that housed the main navigation radar dish machinery, to have some time to himself and a quiet pre-breakfast cigarette before yet another hectic day began.

He picked a spot that seemed devoid of noise; and sat down on the cold steel deck with his back to the radar mounting and feet dangling over the side of the bridge. Immediately he could feel the cold damp rise through the fabric of his blue shorts that were part of his uniform, with goose bumps creeping up his exposed legs and arms caused by the light sea breezes.

As he looked out beyond the harbour wall to the empty horizon and the vast open stretches of the Atlantic Ocean, he saw that the cobalt blue sea was starting to sparkle.

First in silver then flaming reds and yellows from the sun, as it became a bright orange disc which seemed to balance on its edge and seemingly on the very edge of the world.

Her sister ship the *Meadowlea* had already sailed some hours earlier as had all the other ships, thus leaving the *Brooklea* very much on her own, in the now very empty harbour. Save for a little tug that was silently paddling its way, aimlessly from place to place.

From a nearby ventilation shaft he saw a plume of mist rising from it, that carried the vapours and smells of bacon and eggs and roasting coffee beans, which was the crew's early breakfast being prepared in the galley way below him.

With the smell of the rich tobacco smoke from his cigarette in his nostrils, and the savoury taste of the mist coming up from the galley played on his taste buds. He thought of the freshly baked bread rolls spread thickly with rich creamy butter that he had ordered for his own breakfast, all of which made him decidedly hungry.

But for the moment, he was content just to savour those mouth-watering flavours to whet his appetite even more, and hungrily sucking the last deep draw from his cigarette, that nearly burned his pinched fingers and lips, as the last shred of tobacco was ignited.

The slight almost imperceptible vibration of the ventilation fan and its low humming made the ship feel alive, and the distant but plaintive cry of a lonely seagull slowly circling above the harbour. All this made him realise that his new life could be good one after all.

'This is going to be a very nice day for sailing into the blue yonder and back to the foggy winters of Blighty.' he mused whilst savouring these moments that would be put in his new store of future memories.

This peaceful scene was shattered with the high whooping sound of a ship's horn that sounded familiar to him. Looking round to where the noise was coming from, it caused him to stare at the harbour entrance. He saw the knife edged bows of a powerful looking destroyer poking her way through the narrow gap in the wall that served as the entrance to this sleepy harbour.

The long twin black barrels from each of the two forward gun turrets looked very menacing as they pointed first to him, then swung briefly along the length of his ship as she was manoeuvring her way into the harbour.

He felt his ship shudder and tremble beneath him, and only when the sleek ocean greyhound had slid slowly and quietly past him to tie up on the opposite side of the harbour, did his ship seemed to stop her trembling and resume her peaceful slumbering.

"They must have flashed up the engines, to test them." he whispered, but quickly dismissed the incident from his mind.

John had worked in the Harland & Wolf's shipyard that was famous for many large or famous ships like the SS *TITANIC*, or the famous aircraft carrier *EAGLE*.

So during his apprenticeship and officer training days he'd worked on a couple of these sleek men o' war and wondered if this powerful looking destroyer had been one of them.

The large white painted pennant number of D108 on the grey hull, for the benefit of ship recognition, was easy to read.

'That looks like a Daring class' he thought then tried to read the ship's name painted in tiny red lettering and embossed on the side of it's stern.

'I don't know the number but the writing looks like 'Dainty', he observed with much difficulty.

'A strange name for a warship but she really looks it', as he continued his thoughts of those seemingly far off days of his youth.

After a little while taking in the scenery, he decided to go below and have his breakfast before the hectic day began.

He ate his buttered rolls that tasted just as he anticipated, and washed them down with his cup of Turkish coffee. The whole meal finished off with one more cigarette before he climbed out onto the weather deck to commence his daily tasks.

They left Barbados on the horizon behind them, with the ship sailing through flat calm waters, leaving a silver trail to mark its course and slowly but gently rising and falling in the deep Atlantic swell.

The ship was enjoying her little race with a school of dolphins who were playing hide and seek with her knife like bow for a while, when they met a large ship which was coming fast towards them.

John was on the poop deck enjoying a mid morning cuppa and a cigarette, when he felt the ship start to tremble again.

He looked over the stern to see if there was something wrong with the prop shaft or something that would be indicated by the loss of the white water that was the ships' wake made by the propeller as it turned.

He looked carefully for a while but saw nothing untoward until he looked up and saw to his amazement, a very large warship as big as a skyscraper almost in reaching distance opposite them. 'C09' he said to himself as he read the pennant number on its starboard side.

'I wonder if it's the cruiser BELFAST. She was built there too.' he thought, which triggered his thoughts of

Rathmore Cottage and his family, all of which seemed an eternity ago.

He watched until this big warship disappeared quickly over the blue horizon in a cloud of smoke, which looked like a long black ribbon coming from its funnel.

His ship had stopped her trembling and was busy making its silver line of wake in the blue sea as if nothing had happened. This was the second such occurrence to the ship, which troubled John.

He wanted to know what was causing this phenomena; to try to get to the bottom of it once and for all. He thought that maybe the ship was still fretting about its past escapades, or maybe something else more sinister, so he went to seek Day out to see if he could shed some light on the subject.

Day laughed at John's notions of 'Ghosts from the past' indeed. Then told him not to be daft or he'd go the same way as the skipper and get locked up too.

John wasn't fully convinced with Days' light-hearted approach.

'After all, what about that brass plate on the keel.' He decided to cast it all from his mind and get back to the real world.

During his inspection of the davits, which had the lifeboats lashed against them, and saw a figure sitting over by the base of the squat funnel.

"Hello Bruce. Enjoying a spot of fresh air?"

"Aye. The air conditioning is a bit wonky today, and

it's a bit hot in the radio shack. I've got a radio schedule in half an hour or so, so here I am. Any chance of you looking at it John?"

"Probably, when I've completed my maintenance checks, if that'll do you."

"Aye, that'll do me just fine thanks."

"Any idea, which way we are heading? What's in the weather report for our crossing?"

"We shall most likely be going across via the Azores. That is because according to the recent Met Office synops figure I have just decoded, there's a large fog bank forming in the Sargasso Sea, ahead of us. But nothing more than a light breeze for the next few days or so steaming until we get to the Azores, that is. Then we'll probably hit the gale force winds that usually live there and until we reach Blighty."

"Sargasso Sea? Where's that? I thought we're in the Caribbean."

"Actually, it's an oval shaped part of the ocean that's in the Tropic of Cancer between the mid Atlantic Ridge and Gulf streams." Larter informed, then went on to describe it in greater detail and its mythical legends and other old sea tales.

"You're having me on again Bruce." John replied laughingly, but kept his own inner thoughts to himself, as he was still a bit unsure of seafarers' tales.

"Anyway Bruce enough salty stories for now, I must press on and get my rounds done. See you later to look at your air conditioning or at lunch time."

"Aye s'pose you're right." Larter conceded as he too got up to go back to his radios, brushing his white tropical shorts as he went along.

The ship and her crew settled down to a quiet relaxing voyage home, with the crew recalled their runs ashore, who did what and what happened to whom. Everybody was enjoying the last days of glorious sunshine, sunbathing on the upper decks, before their bodies and minds would be cast to the prospects of the dismal winters that dear old Blighty had to offer.

After lunch on the following day and while still doing some minor repairs on the foc'sle capstan, he looked up ahead of him and was startled to see a large, thick, and very grey bank of fog that the ship was about to enter.

"Do you hear there. All hands off watch, to man extra lookout positions." came a terse metallic warning from the deck tannoy speaker.

"Outside Engineer to rig auxiliary generators for jury lighting to the foc'sle, for'ard derrick, mainmast, after derrick and stern light. Report when completed." was his message that was repeated once more in case it wasn't heard.

He finished the maintenance work that he was doing, then carried out the tannoy orders given him, as fast as he could, in case he was to blame for a collision due to lack of extra lighting.

The ship had slowed almost to a snails pace by the

time John had finished, as the thick billowing fog finally swallowed up yet another unsuspecting ship.

He stumbled and groped through this icy, stinking morass on his way to the foc'sle again to prepare a battery of auxiliary pump in case of some accident or other; and to use the deck phone to report his task was completed.

On his way there, which was very slow and laborious, he literally bumped head to head into someone going in the opposite direction.

"Owch! Who the bloody 'ell is that?" asked a gruff voice as the unknown person's face poked into his.

"Beggin yer pardon Mr Grey, couldn't see you. I've already fell 'lf way down a bleedin' 'atchway some buck stupid person left open." It was Janner who was also groping about trying to get somewhere.

"Are you all right Janner?" John asked as he rubbed his sore head.

The ship's deep foghorn had started up its long, intermittent, ear shattering growling danger signal; that drowned out their voices each time they opened their mouths.

"No I'm, I said I am bleedin well not. I've appeared to hurt my arm and dropped my torch somewhere down, as I've said, some 'atchway that some idiot, I said, some idiot had left open." Janner repeated himself in a shout over the foghorn.

"It's no good, I said, it's no good anyway, cause it only blinds you in this stinkin lot." Janner complained.

"Come on Janner, let's get you to the sick bay and see to your wounds. I have to remain on deck so I'll take your lookout, when I get back." he shouted.

He helped Janner along the deck, through the main superstructure of the ship, then into the sick bay and left him there to go to the bridge and make his report in person.

The bridge was brightly lit up but all you could see through the thick glass windows, was as if someone had painted silvery grey mask over them.

"Hello Bosun!" he greeted as he saw Sinclair standing like a statue with the spokes of the steering wheel in his hands.

"Where's the Captain?"

"He's out on the starboard bridge wing." Sinclair announced flatly.

"Thanks Bosun! I hope us two can have a chat some time when it's quieter.

The foghorn is very loud outside of the bridge at the moment, so you're lucky to be in here." he suggested as he left to see Trewarthy.

He crossed the brightly lit bridge then went out onto the starboard wing and just managed to recognise Trewarthy's large frame in the swirling fog.

"Excuse me Captain."

"Who's there?" Demanded Trewarthy gruffly. "Speak!"

"4th Engineer Grey reporting, Captain." John started.

"Just what do you want of me at this crucial time, Grey?"

"Well Cap'n, it's the bright lights on the bridge and the torches the lookouts are carrying." he continued, despite possibly having to endure another stormy scene with Trewarthy.

"Well? What about them? Speak up man!" Trewarthy interrupted.

"If the main bridge lights were switched off and you used the blue police lights to operate in, and the torches doused, that way the Bosun and the bridge lookouts won't be blinded by their own lights. Instead their eyes would be accustomed to the darkness and would become sharper. The deck lookouts could tie a lanyard to their torches and lower them over the side to help their eyes too, and at the same time help to illuminate the ship's side.

What about getting a lookout hoisted to the top of the foremast in case the fog bank is low, that way he'd be able to see over the top and warn us of any approaching ship?" he said at length, pausing between each blast of the horn.

"Captain?" he asked, uncertain that Trewarthy had heard him in the fog.

"4th Engineer Grey." Trewarthy commenced gruffly.

'Here we go again.' John groaned inwardly and found himself not to be disappointed.

"Are you trying to teach your granny to suck eggs? Who asked you for your opinion. What do you know about seamanship and life at sea? I don't come down your engine room to show you how to run your engines, so I don't expect you to come up here and tell me how to run my ship. Right? Now get on deck for'ard there and lend a hand if you've nothing better to do." Trewarthy hissed, then dismissed John with a deafening shout.

"Do it now!"

"Aye Aye Captain!" John responded calmly and went to carry out his orders.

During a short break from his work, he stood next to a mid ships bollard. He decided on having a quiet smoke as best he could, and tried to look into the swirling fog, before plucking up the courage to go back to the bridge and make his report which he was loth to do but very determined to make.

After a short while he fancied that his surroundings seemed icy and eerie as his thoughts turned to Larter's stories about the Sargasso Sea.

Of how the wooden ships of old seem to get lost in the fog, or be dragged down into the murky depths by the clogging seaweed or unseen alien monsters from the deep.

He could almost see ghostly ships with the skeletons on them that were the remains of the crew. He even imagined that he could hear the cries of anguish from them as if the fog held him in a spell.

"There it is again. Sounds almost real!" he said aloud,

when something caught his eye, which made him stare out to whatever it was he saw.

He ran up the nearby ladder and arrived onto the bridge.

"Cap'n? Cap'n? I thought I heard and saw something over there." he said urgently as he pointed out one of the bridge windows.

"Where away 4th Engineer?" Trewarthy demanded in a gruff manner.

John pointed to the approximate position where he thought he had heard the noise.

"Hmm. Fog tends to bend sound much like a prism does to light." Trewarthy asserted as he peered into the fog with his binoculars, then barked out a series of orders.

"First mate! Prepare for possible collision. Put collision mats and fenders for'ard. Right now if you please! Midships Bosun! Stop engines. Make the announcement 'All hands prepare for possible collision starboard side'. Make it three times. Engineer Grey, inform the engine room."

John rang the engine room as instructed, using the bridge phone, then stood quietly at the back of the bridge waiting for instructions and looking at Trewarthy who was in total control of things like an orchestra conductor.

"Mr Larter. Have you got anything on radar yet?" Trewarthy asked.

"No Cap'n! I've had to stop the radar on active

because it is totally useless in this type of weather, but I've got two faint traces and approximate bearings on passive, and a DF signal in the wireless office." Larter advised urgently.

"Passive? Very well, tell me quickly."

"The relative bearing of about Green 10 which confirms the DF bearing and there's one at Red 5 Cap'n."

Trewarthy and Tritton both swung round looking into the fog with their binoculars at the bearings that were given.

"First Mate! If you haven't already started a running plot since we've entered this area then I suggest that you do it now."

"Wheels amidships Captain." Sinclair advised tersely.

"Slow astern together. Starboard 15 when I give the signal Bosun." Trewarthy snapped.

John appreciated that the ship took a while to stop before going astern; and only then would the propeller finally take them out of danger. Like now, hopefully he thought.

"Both bridge lookouts! Trewarthy snapped.

"Stop sounding your fog warnings and start listening. Bosun, Starboard 15! Messenger! Make the announcement twice, to all deck lookouts.

"All for'ard lookouts on deck muster on the starboard bow with fenders and collision mats. All aft lookouts, on the port side with same.

"4th Engineer Grey?"

"Yes Cap'n?" he answered promptly.

"What is the status of the portable pumps? How many pumps have you got on the for'ard cargo hatchway?"

"I've got two port side and three starboard side ready for use."

"How many aft?"

"The opposite. Three port and two starboard side plus two standbys either side of the bridge ladders, Cap'n."

"Well done Grey." Trewarthy said softly which was a total surprise to John, then added as if absent-mindedly.

"But I might need extra pumps from somewhere in case.'

Trewarthy rang the engine room phone and spoke to Day.

"Chief! The 4th Engineer is with me and has managed to provide all available portapumps on deck. I'll be needing some more immediately on the port side."

The answer he got didn't seem to satisfy Trewarthy as he slammed the receiver down onto its cradle and almost breaking it.

The clatter of the phone was replaced by a loud growling noise of a foghorn that seemed to come from both sides of the bow.

"Cap'n! SHUSH everybody! Listen. The noise has

two tones to it. There's two ships ahead of us, not one." John warned with a shout to overcome the ever-increasing growling noises from the unseen vessels.

"Bleedin' ell. He's right!" Sinclair cursed loudly, as he gripped his steering wheel tight.

"Half astern together!" Trewarthy said quickly then calmly issued a string of orders to various personnel on the bridge.

"Put your wheel amidships for thirty seconds then starboard 20 Bosun. Log recorder, make sure your log is exact in every detail and in your best writing. Mr Tritton, keep a stopwatch on the changes from our base course if you please.

Boson's mate, tell the engine room to prepare extra damage control teams immediately. Signalman, take over Mr Larter now. Mr Larter, take the ship's position, get yourself to the wireless office and start the immediate transmission of an alert on our position now in case."

As each order was given, they were repeated by the recipient, who then carried them out, then reported when that order had been completed.

The ship was starting to go astern judging by the juddering and shuddering of her, but John went down to the deck and looked over the side to see the tell tale signs of the wake rushing forwards to envelope the ship that shows when she actually was going astern.

"Wake passing for'ard Cap'n." he reported as he

rushed back onto the bridge.

"Thank you 4th Engineer." Trewarthy replied and carried on looking out through his binoculars.

Some of the orders given out were now being reported back by each person as having been done, with the phones being answered, adding to the organised chaos and noise on the bridge.

"Keep silence on the bridge!" Trewarthy shouted his command, which had the desired effect to stop the hustle and bustle there and then, as the bridge lapsed into complete silence. Only the growling foghorn now dared to defy the captain.

"Twenty of starboard wheel on Cap'n." Sinclair reported tersely.

"Count 15 seconds then reverse your rudder." was the return command.

Trewarthy had Sinclair reverse the rudder so that the ship wriggled its way backwards like a snake, in trying to get out of the fog bank, which seemed like an eternity.

The silence was suddenly shattered by a shout from Sinclair

"Jeeezus effing Cher-rist!" Sinclair gasped and crossed himself like a preacher would, for his blasphemy.

Everybody looked quickly at Sinclair to see what had caused his outburst, then out of the bridge windows and saw two tall and massively wide bows towering above them. The bows looked like veritable cliffs as they loomed menacingly out of the fog, appearing both sides of the diminutive bow of the *Brooklea.*

The sudden mesmeric appearance of this awesome apparition was quickly overcome by the calm voice of Trewarthy.

"Emergency full astern together. Mid ship your wheel Bosun. First Mate, get all hands on deck aft, on the double if you please. 4th Engineer, tell engine room to brace themselves. Get the 2nd and 3rd Mates to get the lifeboats on standby."

Trewarthy's orders were soothing and calming as the three ships were on the verge of colliding 'Y' shaped, bow onto bow, in a fatal encounter.

The ship on the starboard side was hit just slightly forward of her bridge by the one on the port bow, and was virtually stopped in her tracks, otherwise it would have crushed the bows of the *Brooklea.*

Instead, she gave the *Brooklea* a large bow bending smack that pushed her backwards faster than the engines could ever take her.

The crash and screech of metal on metal from the freighter on the port side as it buried itself like a giant spear, into the tanker on the starboard side, rolled over the retreating *Brooklea* like the rumble of thunder.

This was swiftly followed by an ear shattering bang and a blinding flash of light that sent a massive ball of flame shooting upwards, as it burned its way out of the fog bank.

"Stop engines. Wheel amidships Bosun. Slow

ahead together." Trewarthy shouted as he issued his orders over the terrific clattering noises of tortured metal.

"First Mate, are you still plotting all this?"

"Aye Captain. I've given our amended position to the wireless office." Tritton replied curtly as he marked the chart.

"4th Engineer. Get for'ard and organise a damage control team with the 3rd Mate and tell him to keep an ear on the tannoy for further orders."

"On my way Cap'n." John replied as he ducked to escape another explosion that came from the stricken tanker. As the individual fuel compartments on the tanker overheated, they started to rupture and explode like a miniature volcanoes, sending balls of flame, burning oil and lumps of metal, all over everything in its fall out range.

He had a quick look at the twisted bow of his ship that was starkly illuminated by the great walls of flames burning fiercely up into the sky from the stricken vessels. Then took the immediate decision that the for'ard bulkhead of Sinclair's little home had to be the one to withstand the weight of the ship, as she went ahead in the water.

The work took some time with everybody in his team working flat out. They got it shored up solid then sealed off to the next bulkhead backwards towards the bridge to act as an air bag. He got the men to slip the anchor overboard and removed the anchor cables to the No1 hold, then shored up the remaining forward sections bulkheads. To make doubly sure, he also had as much cargo moved as he could in the No 1 hold and had it stacked up against its forward bulkhead as a last resort.

'If that gives way, then we can all look out.' he thought as he gave a final but cursory look at the repairs.

The hours had slipped by and the men were now slumped on a cargo hatchway, exhausted through their frantic hard work.

The ship was moving very slowly forward again, inching herself towards the orange patch in the ever blackening fog to where the other two stricken vessels were.

The men sat grim faced as they realised that they were about to be committed to another bout of the same punishing work, without respite, and looking to John for their next orders.

During that brief pause as the ships drew nearer, and to their surprise, John and his team heard a cheerful Welsh voice above the noises. "Here you are me Boyos! Come and have some of this, there's lovely it is." It was one of the chefs coming round dishing out cups of tea and handing out thick wedges that were disguised as sandwiches.

The fatigue of the men vanished as they watched, entranced by the apparition they saw, the ghostly figure of the chef suddenly appearing through the voluminous black clouds.

"There it is again, black and white." John said to himself absentmindedly as he too stared at this spectre.

He was amazed at the striking contrast of the fresh, white linen clad chef making his way among the men who were soaked and covered in oil and soot as they lay around looking like cast off rag dolls.

The cheers of "Well done Chef!" from the men snapped him from his trance like stare as the chef made his way around to him.

"Not forgetting Hofficers Lovely boy!" the chef said with a smile.

The very thought of this life giving sustenance made his stomach rumble and groan with hunger, but with a sigh and a shake of his head, he declined the offer of this nourishing banquet.

"Thank you chef, but I'll have mine later. Just see to my men then get below before you set fire to yourself."

John saw that his fire fighters were safe and tucking into their impromptu meal, then left them under the supervision of the 3rd Mate to report to the bridge and to make his all important damage report.

There was to be no respite for him as Trewarthy received his report in silence.

"Get yourself back on deck and get the men armed with fire hoses, heaving lines with life belts attached to them, and put scrambling nets over both sides. Stand by for fire fighting and man overboard rescue.

"Let go a few Carley floats as well in case. Get some of the Deck Officers to help, as we're about to render what assistance we can to those poor bastards over there. So be quick about it. You've got about five minutes, Grey."

John turned to leave feeling hurt at being treated shabbily this way, when Trewarthy conceded sulkily.

"Engineer Grey, I hope this plan of yours works too. I'll get a relief for you as soon as I can. By the way, you've got full mains pressure to fight any major hot spots with, and don't forget to keep ourselves covered under your idea of a water umbrella or we'll end up in smoke as well. Watch out for 'flash backs' or we'll lose good men unnecessarily."

He looked at his Captain and saw that there was a trace of a smile on his craggy, oil stained face as Trewarthy nodded and wished him good luck.

"Aye Aye Captain." he replied slowly, savouring this very rare moment, then went swiftly down the ladder and rejoined his men on the cargo deck.

The icy blanket of fog had started to dissipate being burned off by the massive fire from the two other ships, so John could see much plainer now to send men to their tasks as ordered by Trewarthy.

The *Brooklea* nosed her way slowly and carefully into the searing heat under her umbrella of water, as she tried to get as close to the stern of the tanker as possible.

Her fire hoses crackled and bulged under the strain of water spurting from them like powerful fountains, as the fire fighters strained to hold onto them to direct their jets of water.

He had his men split into teams of primary, secondary and ancillary duties, with life rescue and own ship boundary cooling as the main concern. The paintwork on the ship was starting to blister and peel off in large bubbles, with the main deck getting like the surface of a hot iron, yet infinitely cooler than the glowing metal of the stricken vessels.

The *Brooklea*'s task to attempt a rescue of possible survivors from the ships seemed virtually hopeless in this accidentally man made volcano of destruction, but Trewarthy's past life gave him the sheer guts to try.

He ordered that a Boson's Chair be rigged to assist the transfer of some of the tanker's crew that were trapped on the bridge.

The survivors were brought over with as many as the chair cable could support at a time, slowly and gently in case of dropping someone, then escorted to the passengers lounge and quarters for treatment. This was done until nobody could be seen left behind to perish.

Trewarthy then manoeuvred the ship round to the freighter and did the same for those poor unfortunate beings, and all the time having foam sprayed on the burning ships and survivors to keep the heat down in case they too caught fire.

The cold sea water that was sprayed over the ships

created more problems, because it turned to steam that was spitting and sizzling, which in turn added to the poor visibility, noise and mayhem of the disaster.

Two of the Trainee Deck Officers had got all the lifeboats into the water, searching for survivors but finding precious few. They even had a scramble net and a Jacob's ladder rigged over the side in case someone was near enough to use them. But John clambered halfway down one of them to listen and see if he could help anyone in the water, and called out in case someone would hear and swim towards him.

His efforts were rewarded almost immediately when he heard someone shouting up to him and a blackened, stick-like being started to crawl slowly up the net. He leaned down, quickly grabbed hold of and gently helped this being onto the safety of the deck.

Before anything else could be attempted, he instinctively tried to make sure everything was okay.

As he gently laid the naked being down onto the deck, he noticed that it had two soft balloon-like things for a chest, and as he looked further down the body he saw it had no genitals.

He guessed that this naked person was in fact a woman and felt embarrassed for them both, even in this extremely dangerous place.

He had never seen an undressed woman before, let alone this completely naked one, even though he grew up with several elder sisters.

He stripped off his now very oily overalls and

provided her some modesty and decency, as he would have expected to be treated given the same circumstances.

She was moaning and mumbling something he didn't understand as it was in a foreign tongue, so he wiped the oil from her face very carefully, then tried to make her understand him. In desperation, he pointed to her then counted on his fingers then pointed to the ship and hoped she'd understand what he was asking her.

She looked at him then indicated by touching her breasts in the same manner that there were four other women and six children aboard the freighter.

'That accounts for the tanker, what about the freighter,' he thought as he looked back to the freighter. When he turned back to look down at this woman again, he found that she had passed out.

He picked her up over his shoulders and carried her carefully up to the bridge to get help for her.

"Cap'n! This is only one of possibly five other women and there are six children apparently aboard the tanker.

I don't know yet if there's any off the freighter." he announced quickly as he stepped out of the searing heat and into the cool safety of the bridge.

"Bloody 'ell. Poor bastards." Sinclair said sympathetically.

"Very well, Grey. Take her below to the sick bay immediately then get back to where you're supposed to be. If you find anymore then send a crewman, as I need you on the foc'sle."

"Aye aye Cap'n." John replied with a sigh.

He took her down to the sick bay informing the Doc what he'd discovered and what to expect.

"We've got all the women and children and ten crewmen from both ships. Thankful for small mercies anyway Mr Grey! The freighter had fewer passengers than normal, according to what looks like an officer, over here." the Doc informed him.

"Can I have a word with him Doc?"

"With luck, he should be coming round now. He has a few bumps and bruises and I had to pump his stomach out. Full of oil it was."

"What's his name?"

"I can't make it out for the oil, but his ID tag says Fergusson."

"Thanks Doc!"

He spoke slowly and quietly to the injured man for a few moments, trying to make out what he said, repeating his questions, with the replies given back to him in a hesitant and stammering voice.

When he was finished asking the survivor what he wanted to know, he thanked him softly and left the sick bay to report to the bridge and the Captain, what had been revealed to him.

"Cap'n."

"What? It's you again 4th Engineer." Trewarthy said in amazement.

"I thought I told you to get on deck for'ard."

But John was determined and insisted on telling Trewarthy what Fergusson had told him almost verbatim, then without waiting for another blast from Trewarthy, he started to leave the bridge.

"4th Engineer Grey! Stand still and wait." barked Trewarthy.

Trewarthy turned to Tritton and spoke to him until they seemed to agree on some point or other, then grabbed the bridge telephone to the engine room.

He held a similar brief conversation with the person on the other end of the phone, before he slammed the receiver back down again issuing more orders.

While John was waiting for his further orders, he stood mesmerised at the sight of the two fiercely burning ships fatally locked together, and drowning in an embrace as their bridges got lower and nearer to the burning water. To him watching from the bridge vantage point, compared with his own at deck level, it was like a birds eye view of the whole scene. Trewarthy had seen John's amazement of the overall picture and taking full advantage of it, said:

"Right Grey. We're going to make another pass behind them, to see if we can salvage some of their cargo. So here's what I want you to do."

Trewarthy pointed and explained about the porta-pumps and derricks then after making sure what John had to do, he despatched him promptly, to carry out the orders as given.

Tritton accompanied John to assist him, as did any spare men they could get hold of, then proceeded with what John felt was like grave robbing.

* * *

By the time they'd finished their tasks, the fog was gone and it was now almost sunset. The *Brooklea* was standing off with about a mile of sea room between them and the two stricken ships, which in sea terms, means that you could almost reach out and touch each other.

The sinking ships were giving blasts of explosions before pointing their lifeless tails up into the air, as if in a V salute, then slid to the bottom of the ocean in a cacophony of hissing, bubbling and screeches of metal.

Those who had managed to escape the man-made holocaust heard the death rattles from the two stricken ships, in dumb silence.

John stopped for a moment, to see this spectacle, when suddenly there was one last enormous explosion, whose shock waves were so strong that it knocked him right off his feet.

He managed to raise himself off the deck to see very large bubbles of air rising to the surface of the water.

The splashing bubbles were extinguishing the dancing fingers of candle like flames on the water, then marking the ocean with a large ring of white foam where the two ships had met their deaths.

There was total silence on board the *Brooklea* from those who witnessed such a tragic death of two fine ships, which had sunk agonisingly to the great depths of the ocean floor and their watery graves.

It was John's first encounter of such things that

happen at sea and was to be an unforgettable sight to him.

But to all those others who had witnessed the same thing several times before, making them into hardened seafarers, this was just one more fact in the life of a ship at sea.

'The death of a ship is such a sorrowful and forlorn thing to witness. At least we managed to rescue some sixty souls from the same watery grave,' were his solemn thoughts.

It was several minutes before he managed to get those thoughts and feelings under control and before he started to render what assistance was needed on deck.

From the salvage operation, large bundles of timber and a few container boxes on the forward cargo deck, with several hundred barrels of oil on the after cargo deck, left the *Brooklea* much lower in the water.

She was laden almost to the internationally regarded safety level, called the 'Plimsoll line', which made her look as if one good wave would sink her too.

The 3rd Mate and the trainee Deck officers under the direction of Tritton, appeared to have everything under control now, or taken care of by other seamen, which left John with nothing immediate in engineering terms to do.

He went around gathering up his damage control party together again, thanked them for their brave and sterling work, dismissed them for a well earned rest, watch-keeping permitted.

John felt ravenously hungry, but because he was young, his adrenaline was still pumping hard even after several hours of non-stop drama and extremely hard work. So he decided to go to his cabin to have a good shower and change, but discovered on entering, it was occupied by three of the female survivors.

He politely excused himself to get some fresh clothes from his locker before leaving them, and decided to go and ask Larter if he could share with him.

As he left, a flaxen haired woman wrapped up in a borrowed bathrobe, stopped him and spoke in broken English.

"Excuse me young man, but my friend here thanks you for helping her."

He looked over and saw a young brown haired woman who looked shyly at him and started to speak to him.

But as she spoke she then started to giggle, and he couldn't understand why or what was happening.

The older woman explained to him that the girl was sorry if she embarrassed him, but as he was such a gentleman, she had offered to wash and return his clothing when she felt better.

The third woman gave a big smile too and giggled with the younger one, who was building up to uncontrollable laughter.

'I've been told that these foreigners are crazy,' he thought to himself.

His looks and his puzzled face made the women

shriek and laugh even more, until the flaxen haired woman swung his wardrobe door open that had a full-length mirror on it.

He gazed into the mirror with absolute horror, which made the women shriek again, as he saw that his tropical shirt and shorts were in oily tatters, with his socks round his ankles and his legs blotched in oil and soot.

His once white-topped shoes were broken laced and almost black. Apart from two pink holes where his eyes were and a gash of pink where his mouth was, he was absolutely black all over.

For a full minute he stood there looking into the mirror, trying to tidy himself up, which only added to the mirth, making the women shriek all the more.

"This bloody epaulette won't stay flat." he whispered angrily to himself, as every time he pressed it to his shoulder, it would slowly curl up neatly again and flap the other way just like tiny wings.

He stopped what he was doing, then realised what was happening d how comical he was looking. He felt a big smile come onto his face, and tried to suppress a giggle, but failed as he too started to laugh just as much as the women at this comical vision in the mirror.

"What's all the jollity?" Larter asked as he poked his head through the cabin doorway to see who was laughing and at what, when he spotted John in all his glory.

Larter standing there, dressed immaculately as always

in his tropical gear, made John look even more comical as the women saw what he should have looked like.

"Come on John! Let's get you organised and cleaned up." Larter said as he tried to straighten his face, but in vain, and he too burst into laughter.

John shook his head in hopeless resignation at the situation and followed Larter out of the cabin leaving the now hysterical women to themselves.

The warm shower and the faint smell on the soap replaced the oil and stink of smoke as John took his time to enjoy this brief luxury. With a new shift of clothing, probably borrowed, if Burns had anything to do with it, John made his way to the saloon and sat in his place at dining table ready to satisfy his inner self.

The steward fussed around the new passengers who managed to find their way to the dining room, but made certain that his own officers had the best or the most of what was being served up.

It was good to be alive.

CHAPTER XIII
Damage Control

After a good meal, and with a large whisky and soda in reach, John sat in the passenger lounge feeling quite relaxed and drowsy. His fellow officers and some of the survivors had, despite the differing languages spoken, according to the conversations, experienced just as hectic a time as him, and they too were starting to wind down after such a traumatic day.

The Doc had learned of John's incident in his cabin and his happy ten minutes, and explained to all and sundry that it was a very good sign, as a natural remedy to relieve ones body from the extreme stresses and strains.

"So there you are John." Day greeted him when they met in the lounge.

"Hello Happy. How was your day?" he said with a shy grin at Day as he'd just given an off the cuff word play.

Day smiled at it too and said, "You'll be sharing my cabin as Larter's, yours, and the other Trainee Officers cabins have been taken over for a while. The skipper and I have checked the work you did on the bows and we are happy with it for the present, so well done John."

Day went on to explain to the other Junior Engineers about the stresses and strains what the bulkhead had had to endure; and the effects on the engines. After his little lesson on engineering, Day stated that he had another even larger headache in the engine room, which could cause even more problems for the ship. He finished and turning to John told him that he was to get some sleep as he was needed in the engine room very soon, and never mind the outside machinery for a while.

In fact, it would probably be sooner than was first thought as he needed all engineers available and on hand.

Early the next morning and after snatching a quick breakfast and a smoke, John climbed wearily down to the engine room as the effect of yesterday still ravaging through his body.

He stood on the observation platform looking down at the carnage he saw below him when Day arrived and joined him, and started to explain the problems facing them.

For a Chief Engineer to take the time to explain to even a 4th Engineer, would only be done on a very rare occasion such as this. But Day needed every Engineer Officer to know what their tasks ahead contained.

The starboard forward diesel engine had jumped its resilient mountings when the tanker gave them their massive backwards shove.

That engine had been disengaged and its partner engine behind it couldn't be used for fear of bending the coupled propeller shaft even further that it was already.

They had a port thruster block, which the propeller shaft pushes against to move the ship, which was also suspected as damaged.

The stern glands that stopped the water from leaking into the ship through the propeller shaft holes out through the hull were almost blasted from their casings. These had to be remounted and repacked or even replaced, once the flooding had stopped enough for the men to get at them.

The port engines were only going quarter revs to keep the ship moving. The steering rams that control the rudder had to be locked for starboard use only, until it was fixed. Otherwise the ship would go round in circles. The bent bow was giving a bigger drag than the extra weight on the decks.

The ship had to move crablike to protect the forward bulkheads, because any heavy seas encountered could overload the port thruster blocks all the way down to the propeller.

The ship's nose has bent into the shape of a hairpin. The engines have been disturbed. We have a bent shaft so we can't propel with it. The rudder is damaged and we have leaks everywhere.

"In short John. We're in one hell of a mess. And what you see or what I've just mentioned is only the start." Day explained.

Day continued to list the problems and strategy of how to tackle them. Although John was listening to Day, he was deep in thought, trying to apply his mind to the enormity of the tasks ahead of every engineer and stoker on board.

Day stopped his monologue and asked John what he was thinking.

"OK Happy, how does this sound, and it is just a thought, mind you." John commenced.

"When a ship goes into a dry dock; once she is lined up on her dock bottom cradle, she gets shored up with long pieces of timber to prevent her toppling over sideways. Once the water gets drained away that is, right?

Then, what say we apply the same technique but in reverse and upside down for the engines.

We can use some of the salvaged timber from the after cargo deck, unless you've already got a stock of timber under the catwalk plates. You could put blocks to spread the load to prevent the props piercing the deck plates as well. But any timber to pin down the engines would do the trick. Right Happy?"

"Hmm. Not a bad idea. It could work." Day replied, as he thought further into it.

"In fact we'll make sure it does work. It's a pity old Cresswell's not here. If he'd been around long enough to give you a chance, he would be delighted to find that you take after his own heart. He truly believed in good damage control. We have already used up his generous stock of timbers to shore up the for'ard bulkheads. Some deck cargo will have to be sacrificed and make do, but we need the Captain's permission first."

Day whistled and signalled the other Engineer officers toiling away, to join them so that he could hold a briefing in his cabin.

This early briefing lasted until the mid-morning break time, with various ideas and suggestions about to be carried out, subject to the Captain's permission.

After their briefing and Days conference with Trewarthy and Tritton, the seamen were organised into working parties on the deck, working hard to provide the cut timber to the sizes and shapes the engine room staff needed.

The weather forecast was for good weather, light winds and a calm sea, but Trewarthy knew the area better. He gave them all two or three hours to complete their tasks and plans, and if lucky they might get a further two hours to get things back to as normal as possible.

The engine room looked like a forest by the time they had finished, as the engines were now pinned down by several rows of sturdy props. They had to wait until the bent prop shaft was fan heated enough to be hydraulically jacked back into position, and as straight as they could make it, before it could be used with some safety.

The broken steering ram was removed along with the wrecked auxiliary steering gear, with men working to replace the steering ram. The engine room bilges had been awash with fuel from the now almost empty fuel tank ruptured in the collision.

But as it was now fixed, the spilled fuel was being pumped back into it, making it the last big task to be completed.

Everybody worked like Trojans until they had completed their chores and almost within the time allocated by the Captain.

There was a large gathering of other members of the crew and even some of the survivors who came down to the engine room to watch, when Day attempted to start the engines again.

Day took his time to make sure that all the preliminary checks and start up procedures had been carefully adhered to.

The engines coughed, spluttered, raced and almost stopped before Day teased them back into life and settled them down to their normal rhythmic throbbing.

The stokers crawled all over the engines, slaving over them with grease cans and rags as they tended these mechanical monsters that were the heart of the ship.

Everybody gave a huge cheer and stood in amazement to see that although several lengths of timber now pinned down the engines; all four of them were back in business. The stokers cheered the loudest and with much relief. That meant most of them would now get their much-needed rest. Day gave a bow to his audience and went up the ladder to the bridge to report to Trewarthy.

Once his report was completed Day would be

allowed to get some rest too, for he and his men had been working non-stop since the triple collision yesterday.

Captain Trewarthy was a Master Mariner, who had been in worse situations before on this very same ship, and had to decide very soon, whether or not to risk his very sick ship to the hazards of crossing an unpredictable ocean.

The ship was almost over the Mid Atlantic ridge where they reached the middle of a triangle between Barbados, Bermuda and the Azores. He tried to visualise or think what his erstwhile instructor would have done. Von Meir would have pressed on, he guessed.

With that decision in mind, Trewarthy decided to inform his officers and the survivors off the two sunken ships, but he knew exactly what reaction he would get from them. *'Stuff them all, it's my ship anyway'* he thought and even said so at the end of a very heated debate that emanated from his briefing.

From his past experiences, Trewarthy knew that with double the amount of people on board, the meagre fresh food stores would be drastically depleted long before reaching British landfall.

After that, he would simply put them all on half or even quarter rations, and even put everybody onto the ship's abundant store of war rations that somehow nobody had bothered to eat.

He wasn't too perturbed about the loss of or running

out of fuel from the ruptured fuel tanks.

All he had to do there was to keep in the main flow of the gulf stream that would eventually carry the ship more or less where he was going anyway.

Besides, he could use some of the fuel from the salvaged oil drums to get them safely home but only, *and only* if really necessary.

He wasn't really concerned about the several hundred tonnes of extra cargo the ship was now carrying. His salvage money would come in very handy as their lucrative 'speed money' was, as of now, non-existent.

He wasn't even unduly worried about being in the middle of Hurricane Alley that gives birth to the severe tempests always lashing the American shores. In fact, thanks to the severe training by Von Meir, he could handle his ship through most water hazards.

All of these paled into significance because it was the state of the bow in its present condition that gave him the deepest concern he'd ever felt since joining the ship. If the flimsy bulkheads were to give way in any one of the mountainous waves the Atlantic was more than able to produce; he would be gambling all. All of this, just to get back to Belfast and have Grey's hold over him removed. Such was his dilemma.

John was doing his own rounds on deck, along with Tritton and his junior Deck officers in attendance, checking that everything was lashed and secured properly.

John had stokers busy welding all and any spare sheets of metal together, be it engine room deck plating, or lesser important bulkhead doors, to make two prefabricated bulkheads that were to be welded onto the existing ones for extra strength.

Some sailors were busy sawing up some of the salvaged timber to use as extra props to help re-enforce the shores already in place there.

Some of the container boxes were lowered into the forward hold and placed up against the already fortified bulkhead.

Tritton suggested to John that they erect a kind of air bubble in the for'ard mess so that if the bow dug too deep then it would bob up again like a cork. But for that, he had to create a small pressure in the compartments and at the same time keep the flooding down to a minimum.

John thought for a moment then agreed, as it followed more or less his own ideas he had for the damaged compartment.

"To do that, we would have to remove any loose garments or effects from the compartment in case the suction hoses got clogged, before we finally seal off the entire area. The bulkheads should be able to withstand a certain amount of air pressure." he stated then asked: "Do you agree with that observation Mr Tritton?"

"Yes, sounds about right. We've got a following sea current at the moment that is helping to push us along, but I will speak to the captain to see if we can go astern just long enough to relieve the bulkhead pressure." Tritton replied pensively, then left John to go up onto the bridge.

Tritton came back and rejoined John who was supervising the damage control team. "Okay 4th Engineer. We have got about twenty minutes. The Captain says to get all your team in there and strip the compartment. You are to shut each valve and stop cock except the HP air valves, and if you can, make a hull inspection in each compartment."

John galvanised his men into action with himself making checks and inspections as each phase of the work got finished.

He managed to complete a final inspection thus ensuring that Sinclair's humble abode, which was literally a mess, was able to take the contrived air bubble they were going to make.

He made his report not only to Tritton but also Day, because it was Day's responsibility to ensure that the ship maintained her water tight integrity, more than it was the Captain's.

After supper that evening, John decided to take a stroll on the boat deck, but was surprised to find that it was used as an alfresco dormitory for some of the crew.

'The night air is still warm but what about when we get into the freezing British weather.' he thought as he looked out to the empty wastes of the ocean. After a little while he decided to go into the bridge and have

that chat with Sinclair, whom he knew would be on watch now.

"Hello Andy, er, Bosun." he commenced and having to check his ship protocol. "How are we doing? Do you think we will make Belfast for Christmas?"

"Hello 4th! Naw, we're only going about eight knots and that's with the wind and tide behind us. At this rate, we'll be lucky to reach Blighty by Easter, happen of course the bow drops off then we'll be rowing there even slower." Sinclair said miserably.

"Think positive Bosun, and a good prayer won't go amiss either." breezed John.

"Huh! It'll take more than a prayer in these waters. We just might get halfway and reach the Azores. With no decent port or a dock within a thousand miles of us, like Bermuda for instance, me and the boys think we've got as much chance as a snowball in hell of getting across."

"I'll have none of that talk on this ship." Came a gruff voice from the chart room at the back of the bridge.

"4th Engineer Grey. If you've nothing better to do, then I suggest you get off my bridge and get down to your cabin." It was Trewarthy poking his head out of his night cabin.

"In case you have not been enlightened, Officers on this ship do not fraternise with the crew, so leave them alone Grey, and unless you have a job to do, get off my bridge."

Sinclair looked disdainfully at John, then with a mock salute said.

"Nice talking 4th. Good night."

"Yes Bosun, thank you. See you in the morning." John replied then left the bridge to the watchmen.

On his way down to his shared cabin, he met Larter, who offered to buy him a drink in the saloon.

"That is decent of you Bruce, but I really must get some shut eye. Tomorrow is another battle waiting for me."

"What's the panic? As long as the engines keep going, we'll get there no matter how much you fret otherwise." Larter quipped stoically trying to change John's mind.

"Maybe we'll have one tomorrow when I've sorted out my maintenance schedule Bruce, and decided what to do with your air conditioning plant. Oh and by the way! Here's your lighter again.

You left it in the saloon at lunch time."

"Cheers John, I thought I dropped it overboard earlier on. Been cadging lights all afternoon. We'll have another chance for a glass tomorrow. See you!"

He arrived back into his shared cabin noting that Day was still fully dressed and flat out on his bunk, fast asleep.

"I wonder if this would be a slow boat to Blighty never mind China, Happy?" he whispered to his slumbering chief before he too climbed onto his bunk for a well-earned night's sleep.

CHAPTER XIV
Ten Minutes

In the bright early morning sunlight, John was on the foc'sle inspecting it for further damage that may have occurred overnight.

He noticed that the thick steel plates probably put on in earlier days as armour plating had been stretched on the one side, but were buckled and bent right over onto the other side.

He spotted several more plates were being loosened from their rivets by the constant pounding of the waves when sea meets bow.

The buckled deck plates came almost right up to the foc'sle capstan, some twenty feet from the u bend in the bow. John deduced that Trewarthy was sailing the ship with the damaged side towards the waves, thus giving that section a double thickness for the purpose of protecting the thinner and stretched metal on the starboard side.

John studied the movement of the ship and thought this was crafty, and guessed that it was probably the only way for it. However, the weight of the ship, albeit gliding over the slight swell it met, was giving this bent section such a pounding that it was almost flopping about. He thought of the possibility of lashing it firmly so that it didn't, or having it removed.

The metal taken off, could then be used to make a false nose cap to protect those bulkheads under him.

Since coming on board, he had learned a lot about damage control and how ships were kept afloat.

"Warships were built differently from their merchantmen counterparts, but it was of paramount importance for both types to keep a good watertight integrity in order to stay afloat, even more so the ones that were used in wartime. The more bulkheads and compartments the better the ship had a chance to survive, excluding merchantmen who might have their cavernous cargo holds breached." he muttered to himself.

He needed to see Day to make his morning rounds report and to make his theory known but took his time moving through the ship.

When he arrived and spoke to Day in his cabin, after a lengthy discussion, he was invited to accompany Day to go and see the Captain about this theory of his.

They were asked in and seated at Trewarthy's large table, which was full of charts and ship's drawings, where they discussed the best way to approach the problem of the bows, when Larter interrupted them with an urgent message.

"Captain, I have just intercepted a distress call on the 500Kc/s International Ship Distress frequency, and its from an S.S. *EMPIRE BULLRUSH*.

The S.O.S signal has given a position as well." Larter stated urgently, as he tore off the signal from his large signal pad and handed it quickly over to Trewarthy.

"How far away, Sparks?" Trewarthy promptly asked

and stood up to look over some of the charts on his table.

"I haven't checked the chart yet, but according to my DF they are on a bearing of red 50 and her signal strength is more than good, which means she may be close by.

I have searched all round with the DF and listened out, but have not heard of any transmissions in reply to it."

"What kind of ship is she. Have you looked her up in the Lloyd's Registry?"

"Aye Cap'n. She's listed as a cruise liner, converted from a troop ship, and of some 18,000 tonnes with her registered port down as Liverpool."

"Bloody hell! She's probably overloaded with passengers." Trewarthy mouthed as he checked the chart from the position written down.

"Come with me Sparks. When I've checked our exact position you can reply to the distress call. I'll give you our transit time to reach her as soon as I can work it out." Both men left the cabin leaving the engineers in cliff hanging suspense.

Trewarthy came back some minutes later then announced to the awaiting engineers.

"Right gentlemen. We're going to go to the rescue of that ship, which under normal circumstances of having full power and a proper bow, is only about four hours steaming away.

"However, to make it possible for us, here's what I

want you to do. But first, I need my First mate present."

Trewarthy summoned Tritton to join them, and when he had done so, the four officers hatched an action plan that meant frantic preparations and if possible, a substantial increase of speed.

Once all the plans had been discussed and agreed, Trewarthy reaffirmed his charge of this impromptu meeting by announcing:

"Very well gentlemen, make it so. Lets get this vessel working for some real money." Then dismissed his officers and went to his charts to do his bit to prepare for this latest disaster.

Trewarthy gathered the rescued 'Guest' officers together and told them what he was about, and whether they liked it or not, their crews were needed too. He press-ganged the two ships crews just as he had been some years earlier, and dovetailed them in with his own, to form working parties.

'Why should my crew do all the work when the others were idling about and getting fat from my stores.' he thought.

For two hours the ship was a hive of activity with every man on board busily preparing a crippled, overloaded ship to be ready for the imminent embarkation of probably several hundreds of extra passengers.

Even the female survivors had volunteered to help out in the ship's sickbay. The bow had been reshaped as John had suggested, thus allowing the ship extra strength to push her way through the waves.

The broken steering ram had been rebuilt sufficiently to give extra manoeuvrability, and a strengthening plate attached to the thrusters plates, gave the ship extremely valuable engine power.

The salvaged lumber and all available canvassing and awnings had been fashioned into two large marquees and placed on each cargo waist decks. Some of the fuel from the salvaged oil drums was siphoned off and put into the ship's tanks, with the empty drums flattened and used as further bow re-enforcement panels.

He had most of the oil stains and soot from the collision hosed off and the ship scrubbed as clean as possible, with some fresh paint here and there to smarten her up a bit.

His ship had now taken on a false shape similar to one of Von Meir's many ship disguises he used to sneak past several nosy Allied warships. So Trewarthy knew Meir's psychological factor would be used in that the troubled liner and her passengers would only be too glad to see this ship, as opposed to one obviously over her weight and crippled to boot.

Trewarthy realised that the only way for the ship to try and make her lighter in order to take more weight, was by using up her fuel and the tons of food on board. The extra tonnage gained by the sudden influx of more passengers would more than compensate for that, but the freeboard to the plimsoll line was still getting too dangerously short for his liking, as the ship was built low in the water anyway.

John had finished off his final task on deck when he heard a bridge lookout shout, "There she is. Smoke, fine on the port bow."

He looked out onto the horizon to see a thin black column of smoke slowly rising up from an as yet unseen ship.

The *Brooklea* was riding over the waves in a slight crab-like motion and he felt as if he was on a roller coaster.

'Fortunately, the tide's changed for us to use this speed, otherwise... Good-bye foc'sle, good-bye everybody' he thought, then tried some mental arithmetic.

'So let's see. Three hours at almost fifteen knots and being tide assisted; over laden; a bent prop shaft with a bad rudder and a bad bow for a drag factor.' With a shrug of his shoulders he gave it up as a mind-bending loss and went to get a working party together. He decided to station himself at the bottom of the bridge portside ladder, along with the 2nd Mate, Engineer Fergusson and two stokers from his ship, plus a Dutch Seaman Officer and four seamen from his ship.

Tritton, and a Dutch Engineer with four of his stokers plus Janner and four other sailors that formed the *Brooklea's* after section and were stationed on the after cargo deck.

Their tasks were to man the scramble nets, but to stand by for any fire-fighting or damage control duties.

The derrick winches were manned and ready with other Deck officers in control, awaiting orders from the bridge.

All the lifeboats were swung out on their davits and ready for lowering.

The *Brooklea* was slowly approaching with its port side to and had inched its way almost alongside the starboard side of the liner, which had a severe list on that side.

The stricken ship looked as if some giant brush had swept away most of its deck furnishings; deck ladders, masts, one of its funnels, lifeboats.

What lifeboats had survived were crammed full of people, with as many again in the water, floating or hanging onto pieces of driftwood and other floatable objects.

When the *Brooklea* came close, black dots in the water manifested themselves into screaming human heads that started moving towards them like a swarm of black ants as the people tried to swim towards her.

John and his working party helped the people on board as they clambered up the ladders and nets.

An officer from the stricken liner who managed to clamber on board carrying a small child, shouted to John who ran over to help him.

"What happened? It looks as if someone has washed your ship and forgotten to put everything back, even the

managed to get the cargo holds sealed off and pumped full of air to act as buoyancy bags.

The ship is too top heavy now and the critical angle means it won't be long. So all in all, I'd give it no more than about ten minutes now." the man informed him then asked frantically.

"Where is everybody. We thought there were at least two ships coming. What the bleedin' hell kept you? Why have you been so long getting here?"

"It's a very long story my friend believe you me. For now you'd best be making your way aft along the deck here to the rescue assembly area, and good luck Chief!" John replied soothingly, turning back to urge his working party to work doubly quick to try and beat this ten minute dead line.

But the information given by that engineer prompted John into a different course of action. He ran up to the bridge and saw Day talking to Trewarthy who was flanked by other men he did not recognise.

"Excuse me Chief, and begging your pardon Captain." He shouted at two very surprised men.

"One of the survivors I've just brought on board reckons that the ship has only got two emergency buoyancy bags created in her cargo holds, and will only last for about the next ten minutes." he said urgently to them both.

"Ten minutes?" Day asked.

"Their Captain has just relayed a message by his First mate here, telling me they have a good hour or so."

Trewarthy growled as he turned to John.

"If their Captain says a good hour, then that is what I will act upon. Now get for'ard and see to your work."

"But! But! Captain. It was an Engineer officer who told me." John protested.

"Chief Engineer. Get that man for'ard. Now!" Trewarthy snapped.

Day ushered John off the bridge but listened intently to what he was telling him.

"We're doing all we can John. Even the derricks can't move any faster. They're picking people off the decks by the cargo net full."

"But there's a lot of casualties to come off. The bosuns chairs can't handle more than two at a time. Can't the skipper get us right alongside for us to put a gangway or something across? We've less than ten minutes Happy." John pleaded urgently.

"I'll advise the skipper, just see what you can do your end John. Go quickly before Trewarthy has your guts for garters again." Day whispered soothingly.

"Very well. Just remember. If lives are lost because of this, then don't say didn't warn him." he said then ran back down the ladder again to his station.

He asked the foreign officers to tell their teams and those survivors capable of helping to work as fast as they could, even climb over the side to help people up.

They were to make sure that nobody was left in the water by the time the ship went down or they'd be sucked under with it.

Most of the stricken liner's lifeboats were lost in the waterspout, but those that were left, were picking people out of the sea and almost capsizing with their writhing and screaming human loads.

The *Brooklea* had all her lifeboats out, but they were much smaller and couldn't carry as many as the liner's would, but they too were virtually swamped by the panic stricken passengers who had jumped overboard or fallen into the water.

John watched the stricken liner and saw it give a big lurch before starting to capsize and eventually turn turtle. The *Brooklea* was almost alongside but had to move out of danger and gave a warning on her horn to let the lifeboats know to get away from the now disappearing ship.

Those who had time to witness the scene, noticed that the doomed vessel had a wide diagonal groove running down the right side of its belly and an enormous gash across its middle like an open wound, caused by landing onto the rocks.

Suddenly, with a large explosion, it finally disappeared out of sight, with fountains of water being spouted up. It was exactly ten minutes since his warning.

'*Just like the other two,*' John thought pensively, as he saw bodies and lots of wooden objects and other flotsam being spewed up from the deep, with each successive air bubble that erupted onto the surface.

The smudges of burning oil on the water were leaving wisps of smoke as if to try and hide the tragic scene.

Finally, some twenty minutes later where a large ship should have been, was but a whirlpool carrying its debris, slowly circling the spot where the ship had died.

John forced himself into action again, and got his work party to assist in recovering the debris and dead bodies, then helped to retrieve the lifeboats back on board.

He had heard through the grapevine that there were some 1000 lives on board, with only about 400 of them that were saved.

'Yet another statistic to be recorded in the annals of Lloyd's register of ships.' he thought sadly and mentally noted yet another tragedy, that he had witnessed to tell the world.

Trewarthy found himself in an even bigger dilemma now, what with the extra weight and the nearly eight-fold increase of human beings. He agonised for a long while, but was forced to abandon his plans of an epic Trans Atlantic voyage. Instead he decided to make his precarious way to Bermuda some thousand miles away, both to off load this cargo of human misery and as the nearest place with a ship repair facility.

There were now several ships' captains or senior officers on board, each older and supposedly wiser and more experienced than Treworthy.

Trewarthy, who for the umpteenth time had requested that they stayed off his bridge and stop their interfering suggestions.

This went for the Engineering Officers too, who although they had not seen a diesel-powered ship before, were becoming a nuisance to Chief Day and his men.

By the end of the day of this last rescue by Trewarthy and his ship, tempers were getting rather frayed.

This was especially so, when the guest officers learned that the *Brooklea* wasn't a liner, but some clapped out old tramp steamer only fit for the scrap yard. Trewarthy spoke for all his Officers and men when he told them to get stuffed, and if they wanted something to do, start burying their dead and help create some more space on this so called 'scrap heap' that after all, was their only life raft.

From day one, the *Brooklea* became a floating nightmare with human bodies draped all over the entire ship. It was only licensed to carry fifty passengers, but in fact had survivors from three ships with a live body count totalling almost 750 souls, and several dead ones lined up on the deck in body bags.

There was no upper deck space to walk on, with all cabins or 'tween deck spaces overcrowded especially with the added loss of the forward mess. This included the dining hall and cargo holds. The crew had to give up what bunks or hammocks they had, over to the women and their noisy children.

They too were forced to sleep on the open decks, even in the lifeboats and in shifts to share their spaces with those on watch.

The ship's sanitary system became overwhelmed by the constant use and was shut down until such times as they got back into harbour. Instead, Trewarthy got Tritton to provide specially rigged toilet chutes over the side of the ship for everybody to use, and instead of fresh water for washing, John had to provide low pressure salt water hose pipes rigged up for that purpose.

The fresh water system was shut off, and strict water rationing was in force of half a pint per adult, 1 pint per child and 2 for nursing mothers, with the rest of the days ration piped to the galley for cooking[§].

The galley was in constant use, but the cooking of, or any prepared food was only served up in shifts and in strict rota. All the fresh and frozen food stuff was quickly used up. This, in turn, also proved perilous as people complained about the fact that they had to eat 'war time rations of powdered foods', but never the less created scrums to fight over what was on offer anyway.

Although the sick-bay was fully equipped, it was turned into an operating theatre or for surgical treatment, with the so called 'walking wounded' having to wait until someone appeared on their rounds to attend to them.

There was no privacy on deck and what with the squabble of human noises, the ship was rapidly turned into a miserable incarceration of bedlam.

The *Brooklea's* crew got so desperate, they were volunteering to stay on watch so as to escape the misery

---

[§] See *Fresh Water*.

and overcrowded decks.

Trewarthy even had two sentries posted to keep everybody off his bridge that had no business to be there, so that he could have at least some peace and quiet to command his ship.

Finally, after the fourth agonising day a lookout reported land in sight, and before long they had reached the island of Bermuda, where they entered the commercial port of Hamilton, the island's Capital.

Bermuda is a small group of islands rising up from the great depths of the Atlantic Ocean but bathed in the warm waters of the Gulf stream and located only 700 miles due east off the North American Carolina coastline.

It is an old British colony, which is frequented and used as the rich mans holiday retreat and tax haven. The local inhabitants proudly guard their British way of life and even have their islands named after some of the shire counties of England. It is a friendly place with luxurious flora and fauna, and boasts a cave system that can be rated amongst the wonders of the world.

This was to be the next home for the *Brooklea* over the next few days, as it was almost a second home for her owners, Lord Belverley and Mr Burford.

As the *Brooklea* entered the safety of the harbour, there was a Naval patrol vessel with a Trinity Pilot cutter to escort her in, and a small armada of pleasure launches that gathered around and followed in behind them. She passed each of the ships anchored in the port, they greeted her with long blasts from their foghorns in a gesture of welcoming her back from her heroic deeds.

John was at his usual place on the foc'sle, and saw that a large crowd had gathered on the quay, waving and cheering as he slowly passed them.

"That's handy! The ship is going to tie up alongside the roadway." he muttered to himself as he waved back at the spectators.

Looking down the quayside he noticed another gathering of people, who were standing in front of a military looking band, which was playing with some gusto, tunes he'd never heard before.

"What a heroes welcome. Just what we deserve." John observed.

The warm sun was shining in his face, which made him pull the peak of his cap down further over his eyes so that he could see more of the strange sights as he came nearer to them.

He spotted a large van with somebody standing behind a black box mounted on a tripod.

"We're on the PATHE news. Maybe my parents will see me." he said to himself and started to wave at the camera operator.

Behind the cameraman, there was a column of ambulances and vehicles waiting to take the survivors of the three lost ships off the *Brooklea.*

'Judging by the state of the ship, I bet there's a medical team coming aboard to give them a clean bill

of health, else it will be a period of quarantine for everybody. Maybe we'll be able to stay in port long enough to enjoy a brief respite. Especially in that grand looking hotel overlooking the harbour. I think it is the Hamilton Hotel, whatever. Just give me a thick juicy steak with lashings of mushrooms for my supper, a cool shower of fresh water to wash off this stink and a bed that keeps still and has crisp clean sheets on it. What bliss!' he quietly wished to himself.

The berthing party on the jetty got two gangways lowered onto the ship, one on each cargo deck, and each side of the main superstructure.

Soon, the survivors of the three sunken ships streamed off the after one and were helped into the waiting ambulances, as the captivated crowds cheered them all ashore.

It was the 'chain gang', those golden-chain adorned local dignitaries, and other people full of self-importance that were the Islands' welcoming party, who came streaming up the forward one, each one eager to get a first hand account from the heroic Captain of this equally heroic little ship.

From his vantage point, John observed that Trewarthy was standing at the top of the gangway just as he had in Belfast, but was shaking hands with these dignitaries and being kissed politely by the women that also came on board.

After several camera flashes from the swarms of camera-men and reporters, Trewarthy finally went ashore with the 'chain gang', to be taken away in a large black limousine flanked by several police motorcycle outriders.

'This has the makings of a good story.' he mused again, and thought of what the headline captions would say.

By the time the crew had restored the ship and themselves virtually back to normal again it was almost dusk.

John had completed a few minor repairs on some deck machinery, when the steward informed him that he was finally allowed back in his own cabin.

After spending almost the last week on the open deck, propped up against the funnel, he found that his cabin was neat and tidy and that his female guests had left him a letter on their departure:

'Dear Engineer John! We both sincerely wish to thank you for rescuing us and for lending us your little home. We shall be returning to our own home in Antwerp by aeroplane shortly and are sorry that we were not able to see you before we left. Fond wishes. Helena & Stella.'

He looked at the card and read the address, then noticed a small silver locket on a chain inside the envelope. When he opened it up, it had a picture of each of the two girls on either side of the locket.

"So that's Helena, the one I gave my overalls to." he muttered, with a slight flush of embarrassment as he remembered the incident.

There was to be no banquet or cool sheets for the

officers and men that night, as there had been a fleet of lorries waiting on the quayside to be loaded up with the remains of the salvaged cargoes and anything else that did not belong on board. The ship had to be scrubbed down and disinfected, with the sanitation and bilges flushed out and everywhere made clean and tidy again.

When the job was done, the ship had little tugs fussing around it, pulling it gently away from its berth.

The ship left the gazing crowds of Hamilton and go to the other end of the island where there was a Naval dockyard, and where some decent ship repair facilities could be found. Yet again, one more facility that was sorely needed by this very life-weary ship.

John returned to the now very bare and empty decks for the move, and noticed yet again that when they arrived at the ship repair unit, the ship seemed to tremble as it passed three sleek greyhounds of warships already tied up in the naval base.

'There it is again. Just what causes it.' he wondered.

Before going into a floating dock this time for her own brief rest, the crew had to unload as much cargo and equipment as possible to help lighten the ship sufficiently for the capability of the floating dry dock.

By the time that was done, the ship safely secured in the dock and her rise out of the water completed, it was nearly dawn.

John was to be found sleeping fast in his bunk with the girls' locket in his hand.

CHAPTER XV
The Races

"**G**ood morning Mr Grey. Sleep well did you?"

"Eh! What? What's up now?"

"It's only me, Mr Grey. Here's a nice early morning cuppa for you."

"Oh! It's you, steward. How have you been? I haven't seen you since we left Barbados."

"I'm all right thanks. Mind you, the girls were upset when you didn't come to see them. They kept asking me about you, so I told them."

"Told them what?"

"Oh! This and that." Burns said teasingly.

"Well it couldn't have been much, as I'm still pretty new around here."

"New? New, he says." Burns said in mock surprise.

"Well, new around these parts anyway. You know what I mean, you old rascal." John chided softly, then asked. "Then you know about the letter they left me?"

"Oh the letter? Yes! T'was me what helped to translate for them." Burns replied, then in a wistful voice added. "Lovely girls they were. Make a man happy they would, either of them. Oh to be twenty years younger."

"And still single." John added.

"Cripes, me missus will skin me alive if'n she finds out my shenanigans ashore, she will. No, count me out, thanks all the same." Burns replied with a twitch of his head and a shrug of his shoulders as if trying to shake off an invisible attacker.

"What's the score for today?" John asked as he changed the subject.

"Mr Day's got a conflab with the dockyard Superintendents, I think you call those Navy wallahs. So you'll probably have most of the day off."

"Is that the local paper you've got?" John asked as he saw Burns waving some newspapers around.

"Aye, I brought it in to show you. Look at the headlines, we're all bloomin' famous now."

John took the offered paper and read the banner headlines, and saw a picture of himself waving as the ship came alongside the quay. The paper was full of pictures of the ship; of the rescued people, of Trewarthy with some of his gallant crewmembers and of their rescue work.

"They've covered almost everybody and everything here, except the fact that more lives could have been saved."

"Aye Mr Grey, terrible shame that. But that's not all. Read the second column on the third page. Mr Larter must have been very busy in his radio shack since the first collision."

John read that the two ships never got their S.O.S. calls out due to the so called 'atmospheric conditions' caused by the fog bank, and that they had been classed as missing. He also read that each of those mystery ships were three times bigger that the *Brooklea*, weighing some 65,000 tonnes between them.

He whistled to himself when he thought of the total tonnage of ship losses in less than two days, and in peacetime too.

"It makes you think, doesn't it." he said absent-mindedly.

"Yes. Davy Jones's locker must be pretty full of dead ships since these last ten years or so. If it were salvage, we'd be able to retire, just on the interest of the money we'd be getting from the bank." Burns volunteered.

"Salvage money?"

"Didn't you know? Look at page four Mr Grey."

He did, and sat back in his bunk for a moment, making a quick calculation and thinking of what he'd do with it all.

"You Officers will probably get the most and retire on the proceeds, but us lads will only have the equivalent of about two months pay coming to us, when everything is coughed up by the insurance company." Burns moaned.

"Don't count on it steward. By the time their Lordships, the taxman, and the skipper get their mitts on it, we'll have little chance of even a brass farthing. Besides, according to Mr Larter there is going to be some sort of Admiralty or Board of Trade enquiry into these sinkings.

He said that if the allegations concerning the liner are found to be true, then we'll all be paying out instead of getting money in."

"That's right. Cheer me up why don't you. Those Admiralty enquiries can ruin a man's wallet let alone his life." Burns complained.

"OH! Why is that?"

"I was on contract to another shipping line, on the SS *Bramble*, when the Admiralty found the skipper in breach of doing his duty and of being negligent in giving proper assistance to a stricken vessel. In that case it was the liner *Savannah Princess* with more than 2000 passengers on board. The skipper explained the shipping lines own rules and regulations to that board and they copped it too. The result was that the ship owners were forced to pay millions of pounds to the Lloyd Shipping Insurance Company in London, which eventually made paupers of them and they were forced to sell up. The skipper copped the blame for not doing his best and was beached permanently. He hung himself a few months later leaving his poor wife with seven kids to bring up on her own."

John felt a sharp icy cold tremor go down his spine as he thought of the warnings he gave to Trewarthy who simply ignored him.

"Never mind though, that was in the past. I expect we'll have a free stay here and be toasted by the locals for a while Mr Grey. " Burns said as if to cheer himself up, then left John to get him dressed for the day.

After breakfast, John climbed down the steep ladders and onto the dock bottom to see what other damage might have been done to the ship, and saw a gang of men wearing white boiler suits, standing under the ship's fat belly. As John approached the group, he noticed one of the men was pointing to something on the ship, for the benefit of the upturned faces.

"Superintendent McPhee, this is the man responsible for this, shall we say, handiwork. Meet 4th Engineer Grey." Day stated as John arrived and got briefly introduced to the other members of the dockyard staff.

"It appears Engineer Grey, if you'd gone another foot or so lower down, then apart from cutting off the bits and pieces still remaining, there was nothing more they could do.

"Except maybe put a strengthening spar down the bow and a piece below where you stopped. That should do the trick until you get home again, if you're lucky." McPhee explained.

"Yes, if only I had a diver and his equipment to do so. Mind you, the cargo bulkheads seemed pretty solid and backed up with cargo." John replied.

"Indeed, but we have other problems to consider, such as the stern glands and the hydraulic rams for the rudder, the thruster blocks and a whole host of others not to mention your 'Sherwood Forest'." Day joined in.

The stern glands would have to be replaced, and the hydraulic rams for the rudder fixed to make the ship seaworthy. The affected thruster block would need to be strengthened, apart from that it's either a major dockyard job or the scrap yards."

The survey in the bow compartments amazed them and they had decided to leave well alone. Again as it would take a long time to dismantle, re-construct the bows and do other major jobs such as the ones in the engine room. The consensus of opinion was, that the ship owners wouldn't agree to it, not in this dockyard anyway.

"So it's patch up and get out of here?" John asked in disgust.

"'Fraid so young man. This dock's only for warships and we're expecting one, due in here tomorrow morning." McPhee informed him.

Trewarthy and Tritton, who had finished conducting a brief dock bottom inspection of their own came and joined the main group.

He had agreed with the superintendent's time constraints and consensus with the proviso that the naval staff would give them a signed document stating that the ship was sufficiently seaworthy to return home.

Otherwise, they would have to remain in Bermuda until an ocean going tug came to tow them home.

Before the site meeting had reached its conclusion, and was about to break up, Tritton told Day to inform his department that there was shore leave until tomorrow morning, and for everybody to be on board before the ship undocked and moved under her own steam, back to Hamilton.

With that bit of good news, both Day and John left the group quickly rejoicing in the news as they clambered up out of the dock and back on board to their cabins.

***

During their preparations for a bit of shore leave, they were informed that there was a guest house made available to the Officers for the remainder of their stay in Bermuda, as a small appreciation to them for their brave rescues.

"What about the lads, Happy?" John asked.

"The Seaman's Mission, or the Flying Angel club has their billets. The island can take thousands of visitors, so all our guests will be put up in the hostelries and boarding houses until they're sorted out." Day informed him.

"How long do you think we'll be here? I was hoping to be home for Christmas."

"With a bit of luck John a couple of weeks in this glorious sunshine. But knowing our luck, we'll be sailing tomorrow and docking in Belfast around Christmas Eve, easily.

Remember that the Captain is anxious to get you home again."

"Oh yes. I'd forgotten about that and was hoping that with what we've just been through, so would everybody else."

"Yes, the recent unexpected turn of events have added an extra week onto the voyage, so our expected time of arrival is all down to fate really. But don't kid yourself about Trewarthy. He can be a very nasty piece of work. Anyway, forget it for now." Day added philosophically and with a shrug of his shoulders.

"All this heroics and palaver in the papers and all we get is a measly day out of it? No wonder the lads call the skipper tight fisted, or a 'piso sod' if you like in stokers language." Snorted John

"Now, Now, John. That's no way to repay your Patrons is it? Besides, think of the extra pay we'll be getting from the salvage money." Day replied in mock horror.

"You came aboard as a green, Acting 5th Engineer. If you keep on at this rate, you'll be doing my job next, even before we ever reach the end of this, your very first voyage John. What do you say to that my young friend?" he asked with a grin.

"Maybe not your job Happy, but perhaps on another ship in the not too distant future as I'm fed up with this one already." John replied earnestly.

"That's the ticket. Now let's get ashore before we find something else to fret about or get detailed off for." Day said as he ushered John over the gangway and ashore.

They stepped off the narrow gauge railway carriage, at the quayside where the ship had been the night before in Hamilton and looked around to take their bearings.

"Have you been here before Happy?"

"Once for a couple of days, but three times only for unloading cargo or fuel."

"That's good. Then you can show me the sights. I understand from the steward that there's a lot of fine rich widows looking for a good time sailor or whatever, just like the Caribbean."

"Hah! You can forget all that nonsense John, we're not in the Caribbean any more. This is strictly hoity toity, mega rich people. Still never mind. We should enjoy this visit, if the local papers are anything to go by."

"Thanks Happy. I'm already looking forward to today."

They walked slowly along a broad avenue, up some steps that pointed to and led to St Peter's church, where they turned left and walked along a narrow street until they finally arrived at their lodgings, 'The Plaza Hotel'. It turned out to be a small guest house, yet deceptively spacious and decorated with lots of potted plants. Due to the tourist season they had to share a room that was much like the cabins on board. But these had soft beds, clean white sheets, lashings of hot water and a room service that was boasted to be second to none. Just what John had dreamed of almost an eternity ago, but in fact it was only yesterday.

The two friends sat in the dining hall having their lunch, without having to brace themselves every few seconds as they would on board.

The soft background music was conducive to their ambience, as they each lit up a big fat cigar and armed themselves with a very large glass of whisky each.

"This is the life I wouldn't mind having for a little while, before going back on board, Happy."

"Aye, this suits me just fine." Day started to say when he saw two official looking men with grim faces, who came striding up to their table.

"Excuse me gentlemen. Are you two of the M.V. *Brooklea?*"

"We are!" replied Day as he stood up to face these intruders to their privacy.

"Can we have your names please." asked one of them.

"Why? Who are you, and state your business." Day insisted.

"I am Detective Sergeant Waddle and this is Constable Williams of the Royal Bermuda Constabulary. Now your names if you please sir."

"I'm Chief Engineer Day and this is my 4th Engineer, Engineer Grey. What seems to be the problem officers?"

The other guests had stopped their conversations or their eating, and were looking at the four men inquisitively, wondering what the commotion was, and who was daring to disturb their enjoyment.

"It's a delicate matter, if we could talk in private somewhere." Waddle suggested.

"By all means officers, would our cabin, I mean, our room be sufficient?" Day volunteered.

"That will be just fine." Waddle replied as Day led them to their room.

On their way, they met the landlady coming hastily towards the men.

"What be the problem Mr Grey? Why are the police pestering you?" asked the perplexed manageress.

"Something, maybe nothing, but I feel sure there's nothing for you to be worried about. If there is then we'll tell you later, Mrs Thompson." John replied soothingly.

When the four men got themselves sat down in the bright and breezy room, Waddle explained what they had come to see them about.

They laughed at what the policemen told them, who although seeing the funny side themselves, tried to keep a straight face, almost succeeding in doing so.

"Although motor vehicles are limited on the islands and we encourage people to use mopeds and the like, we've still got very strict traffic laws on these islands gentlemen. If it weren't for the fact that you lot are heralded as heroes we would normally let things go. But you two have been named by the perpetrators as friends to help them, otherwise they may find that they will be banged up for a long while, and with their ships sailing without them to boot." The constable said in an attempt to admonish the two engineers.

"Tell me sergeant, just where will we find these villains of the peace?" Day asked, trying to straighten his face and trying to hold back a burst of laughter.

"We've got them banged up down in the County nick, trying our best to sober them up at the moment, but you'll have to see the station officer if you wish to bail them out." Was the impatient reply.

"Very well, lead on if you please. We can't have non-paying guests in there, now can we. What would the neighbours think." Day managed to reply with an almost serious face.

All four men walked quickly to the police station, not very far from the guest-house, where the engineers were left to be introduced to the officer in charge.

"Good Morning Inspector. I'm Chief Engineer Henry Obediah Day and this is my colleague 4th Engineer John Grey.

I understand you've got some of my men here?" Day said with mock indignance in his voice.

"Ah yes! Good morning gentlemen, I have to read their charges out you understand what they have done, and then sign their release papers. Will you be paying for their fines?"

"Fines? If it is necessary, certainly Inspector." Day agreed assertively.

The six stokers and two seamen were brought out in single file, with their heads bowed but burst out into a loud cheer as they saw their Officers.

"Thanks Mr Grey, thanks Mr Day. You'll sort them out won't you." They called out amongst the whistles and cheers and jibes at the policemen who escorted them out.

"Stow it and stay quiet the lot of you!" Day commanded.

The Inspector looked up from his charge sheet with a frown that pushed his spectacles further down his nose. This gesture started the men laughing again

"You were told to stow it. If not then you really will be in trouble." snapped John.

"These men did break the traffic laws of..." the inspector droned on about laws, bylaws, rules and regulations. Quoting this stoker or that stoker's name, when it came to the crimes of the century:

"1. Was found having three home made devices similar to that of a rickshaw and did hold chariot like races around the streets terrorising the local bazaar owners.

"They knocked into several fruit stalls, which caused the fruit to spill everywhere. The knock on effects were as follows:

"One elderly man slipped on some apples and bounced all the way down a flight of steps, only for these men to go down, pick him up and drag him up the steps in their device to repeat the act. All the while shouting, 'Wheeee, fasten your chastity belt' as the device bounced back down to the bottom of the steps again.

"2. 'Another gentleman driving his moped along the harbour road was passing a steep flight of steps, when an avalanche of coconuts, melons and other such round fruit hit him.

"The ones responsible claimed that they were playing Drake's bowls.

"The problem was that the force with which the fruit hit the man, caused him to swerve off the road, which in turn, made him drive straight over the quay and into the harbour where he and his machine landed in a small motor launch which capsized. The people on the launch were all dressed up to go to a yacht's cocktail party, some of them were catapulted into an oncoming rowing boat, which also sank under the sudden weight of the extra passengers. A lot of expensive jewellery was lost from that one.

"3. 'That another stoker and a sailor have denied this charge, but claim that they accidentally caused a little girl to stumble as she was pushing her little toy pram. This pram raced out of her reach and sped into the path of a man carrying a crate of tomatoes and a crate of eggs.

"The result of that was, as a swim-suited lady hanging out some of her smalls on a line outside her basement flat below was splattered all over with the tomatoes.

"And a tourist living in the apartment opposite had a dozen omelettes at once for his breakfast as the eggs flew through his open kitchen window and landed into his frying pan.

"4. The Reverend Claude Ball, carrying a large posy of ice creams from the café to give to his party of school children, saw a large cat coming running towards him, being chased by a rumbling tide of fruit and vegetables. It jumped up on him and tried to cling onto him, but the weight of the cat was too much for his silk shorts, which were ripped it to shreds as the cat slid down his garment. The result was that the cats' claws caused several scratches to his private parts and he is complaining that people are now spelling his Christian name wrong. Also that the children had heard certain words not usually uttered by a minister. Add to that, the ice cream the Reverend was carrying got thrown up into the air, only to land onto a sleeping man's bald head and several of the cones were seen disappearing down his well endowed wife's cleavage."

The Inspector went on and on until he reached the end of item No 12.

"In all Mr Day, a thoroughly disgusting display by your men, wouldn't you say?" he asked angrily, as he looked down his nose and over his spectacles.

During the tirade the Inspector gave, both officers had to look up to the ceiling and other places and try to look stern enough, even though deep inside they were laughing their socks off.

"Thank you Inspector. I can see your problem, and if you permit me I know just how to deal with these tearaways. I personally shall see to it that these men will be no further trouble to you or the inhabitants of these fair islands. What, or how much are their fines?" Day asked in mock seriousness, his mind s still picturing the scenes.

"Let's see. The cost of the fruit. The motor launch, the moped, the –"

"Never mind all that Inspector. How much are their traffic fines?"

"You only intend paying for their traffic fines? What about the expensive jewellery and the moped and the –"

"No doubt the luckless owners can survive a

handsome pay out from their appropriate insurance agent, Inspector. If you want these so called 'public spirited heroes' gracing your shores off your hands and out by the back door, then accept my offer gracefully. What do you say?" Day stated emphatically.

The Inspector looked pensive for a moment, weighing up his options, then with a sigh he gave up.

"That'll be four pounds two shillings and sixpence three farthings each offence and for each offender" snapped the Inspector.

"You strike a hard bargain Inspector. Bermuda pounds, or Sterling?"

"Bermuda pounds if you please Mr Day." Was the reply.

"Very well Inspector. I haven't had the chance to change any currency, but will 15 guineas Sterling and in cash do?"

"No. I want 20." the inspector demanded as if to regain his own authority.

"Mr. Grey, can you make up the difference?" Day asked aloud to John.

"I think I can just manage that." John replied as he took out his wallet and emptied it into Day's open hand.

"Thank you Mr Grey." Day boomed and turned to the inspector.

"20 guineas Sterling as stipulated, Inspector." Day stated.

"Very well then, sign here Mr Day, if you please. This states that you are now responsible for these men, and you will be held solely responsible should any further incursion of the peace happen again from them. Here is your copy and a receipt for the money."

Day signed the form, handed his money over to the Inspector who gave him his receipt, then turned to the stokers.

"Stoker Dawes, get these men outside and wait for me. You lot are in deep water, that's for sure."

Day thanked the Inspector then walked out with John to see the men lined up outside, then said in a loud menacing voice, for the benefit of anybody inside the building who may be listening.

"Right you shower of misfits." then looked round again to see if any policemen were looking out, but as there was nobody about, he lowered his voice.

"Now you lot, it's our turn. Your punishment will be." then he meted out his own brand of punishment to them.

"But that's daylight robbery, Mr Day." protested one stoker.

"Aye, and what are we supposed to do for a noggin?" questioned another.

"You should have thought about that before you started. Both of us have just saved you lot from missing the ship tomorrow, and you all know what that means." Day said ominously.

"Yes stow it. As the Chief said, it could be worse. We could be rotting in that pokey until the next ship that came along." argued Dawes in a disgruntled manner.

John felt uneasy handing out his cash like that, but he took comfort that he still had a few pounds over to help out just in case Happy had spent all his on the fines.

'Almost like waiting with Bruce and Andy in Belfast,' he thought.

By the end of the afternoon, all the stokers were broke, as they had to buy whatever drink or small 'rabbit' their officers chose to have, no matter wherever they went in the town.

"Right then lads!" Day announced, but winked at John.

"We fancy one more drink before having a nice thick juicy steak for supper. Now whose turn is it this time?"

"Aw c'mon Chief. This is not Las Palmas or Barbados. With these exorbitant prices, we're all broke now and it looks like we'll have to walk all the way back to the ship in the morning." moaned one of the sailors.

"Then you'll just have to enjoy the Missionary supper tonight and make a very early start in the morning won't you." Day teased.

"And don't forget to say your prayers." John added.

"If you say so chief." they all muttered glumly, looking quite downcast and blaming each other for their miserable state, and started to leave for the Missionary Hostel.

"Dawes. Stand fast!" Day shouted to the disappearing crowd of men.

Dawes came back and asked sulkily what was next.

"Here. We've had a good run ashore, the best so far. But we hope that all of you have learned your lesson."

"Yes chief, it was a hair brained idea in the first place anyway, especially after our tot time session.

"There is absolutely no excuse for you and your mates behaviour as it reflects on all of us. But I suppose, and in fairness, as you lot are the finest bunch of stokers I have met in a long while I will take a slight exception to the rule.

So here's a couple of pounds to get yourselves a drink with. Get the men mustered outside our guest house early in the morning and don't be adrift." Day said convincingly but gave Dawes a wink and a nod.

"Oh thanks Mr Day! You're a good 'un after all. And you Mr Grey." Dawes replied gratefully then ran after the men to tell them what he was wanted for.

Day and John went into their guest house, waving to the their stokers as they disappeared somewhere for a drink.

"That was decent of you Happy. I'd have let them stew a little longer." John remarked.

"No, not really. You're just as daft and soft as me, John. I saw you slipping ten bob into Dawes pocket as I was talking to him." Day laughed as he gently slapped John on the back and led the way to their room with their presents to prepare for their evening meal.

After their sumptuous meal occasionally interrupted by

other guests who had heard or read about their rescue deeds, they decided to go for an evening stroll along the promenade.

They needed to walk off their heavy but enjoyable meal and some of the excesses of their afternoon drinks with their men.

The warm evening air was scented from the oleander bushes and passion flowers that were growing in strategic places, it was a favourite time for strollers and promenaders to enjoy the smells and sights.

Soon they met Sinclair, Larter and Burns who were sitting at a French style café, lounging in their chairs and watching the world go by.

"Hello you two. Draw up a pew and join us." Sinclair invited.

"Why not! We don't mind if we do." Day said as he accepted the offer.

"We're the toast of the town, despite today's antics, courtesy of our stokers." Burns exclaimed.

"Yes. We haven't bought a drink all day, no matter where we went. Innit just great?" Sinclair quipped.

"We've been teaching the stokers a lesson today." John informed the others, matter-of-factly.

"A lesson? What for?" Sinclair questioned.

Happy told them all why the stokers were slammed up in jail, and what happened from the time they went to the Police station up to dinner time.

As the story unfolded, the other three were laughing so much that large tears rolled down their faces.

All this mirth, which proved so infectious, was too much for some of the other customers, who started to giggle then laugh when they heard snippets of the stories. In the end everybody in the café was in hysterics, which, somehow and as if by magic, seemed to influence passers-by who wanted to join in. Soon an impromptu street party was born as more and more joined in.

After a long while, the two friends who started it left to go back for a reasonable night's sleep, leaving the party going from strength to strength.

"What a party that was Happy. We started it, and the manager of the restaurant was so pleased, he gave me this to share between us." John said showing Day a Bermudan £20 note.

"Not a bad night's work when you're enjoying yourself. I'll bet that Inspector would do his nut if he found out " Day replied gleefully, as they laughed and joked their way back to their guest-house.

"Good evening Mr Day. Good evening Mr Grey." It was the manageress greeting them as they walked into the foyer.

"Ah, good evening my good lady." Day replied expansively, as he was feeling in a magnanimous mood.

"My friend and I wish to share a little night cap in your lounge, Mrs Thompson. If you care to join us then we'll tell you all that happened earlier, as promised." John invited.

"That's very kind of you, and please, just call me Deborah" she replied as she was chaperoned into the spacious lounge.

There were a few stragglers in the lounge and foyer sipping their last drinks, when the two friends told their story to her as they drank their ale.

Before long, she started to cluck like a chicken, which gave way to a blast of laughter sounding like a braying donkey, which seemed to stir the others up from their drinks. By the time she tried to straighten her face and stop rolling around in fits of laughter, all the onlookers were laughing as well, even more so at her funny laughter and antics.

"This story will be a good after dinner speech any time," Day said with difficulty as he couldn't laugh any more as their sides still ached from the alfresco party.

Finally and with great difficulty, Mrs Thompson got herself under control sufficiently enough to see that the two friends were preparing to retire for the night.

John looked at the woman's mascara smeared face, but suppressing the renewed laughter welling inside him, said to her.

"We have had a lovely time and enjoyed our stay here so far. We came across an appreciative café host who gave us this." Showing her the money.

"We would like you to accept this Bermudan £20 note, or shall we say, we are donating it anonymously, towards any damages our stokers may have caused earlier on today, for it to go to the good people living here.

We request that you see it gets to who needs it most, if you please."

Mrs Thompson looked at the two friends and the money, and with a great effort she struggled to show a bit more decorum as befitting a Proprietor.

"Well John. We don't think that anybody will much care what happened, save maybe a few bruised egos or dignities.

"Your generosity will be put to the best good use, and I recommend it go towards our Orphanage's Christmas fund. Would that suit you?"

"That sounds about right Deborah. Just so that if and when we arrive on our next visit to these islands, we won't be made to feel outcasts." Day explained.

"Very well. I'm sure the gesture will be well received and in the spirit it was given." She assured the two friends.

"Thank you, Deborah. We must be getting some shut eye now as we've a long day ahead of us." John said as they bade everyone good night, then walked out of the bar and up the wooden stairs to their room.

"Hope you didn't mind me doing that Happy?"

"I have no worries with that John, we would have spent more than that amount anyway. And besides, what good is that currency back in Blighty or anywhere else except Bermuda?"

"Oh well, we can put it down as a calling card for the next time we visit this place. Money in the bank so to speak."

"Now you're learning young John" Day concluded as they settled down in their respective beds.

'Oh for a few more days in this lovely place, and today was definitely a Grey Day,' John thought before falling into a deep, trouble free sleep.

CHAPTER XVI
Loud Whispers

John and Day finished their breakfast cup of tea, left the dining room to pick up their overnight things from the foyer, where they met Mrs Thompson again.

"Good morning gentlemen. Everything to your satisfaction?" she asked with a smile on her 'new' face for the day.

"Good morning! Yes, everything is just fine thank you Mrs. Thompson. More's the pity we cannot stay any longer, duty calls and all that. We think we'll be sailing sometime today, and don't know when we'll be back." Day replied courteously.

"Yes, that's the way it is with the world. Still never mind. Maybe next time you visit, you'll come and see us. I'm sure I'll find a room for the both of you."

"That's very kind of you Mrs Thompson. We will remember that, and don't forget our little bargain from last night." John enjoined.

"My name is Deborah, remember boys?" she teased.

"But it's as good as done. Goodbye then John and Happy, must see to my business now." she said with a smile and nod and left them to see to a new intake of visitors.

The two friends stepped out of the hotel foyer onto the ever clean pavement, and saw that the stokers were lined up and waiting for them.

"Morning Dawes! Said your prayers last night?

Only lets hope they were good ones to last you lot until we see Belfast again" Day said cheerfully as Dawes approached him.

"Morning Chief, morning Mr Grey! We've been waiting here 'alf an 'our now just like you ordered yesterday." Dawes said dutifully but smiled at the ribbing he got.

"Right then men. We've got five minutes to catch the train back to the dockyard. I'll see to your passes. Take charge of our baggage's and move out." Day ordered sharply.

The cool of the early morning was welcomed and enjoyed by everybody, as the day would get just as hot as the Caribbean. Everybody was looking and pointing to the scenery as they passed, whilst the little steam engine puffed its way slowly along the narrow gauge railway, tooting its whistle as it went.

The journey took a leisurely twenty minutes and ended in a cloud of steam when the train arrived at the entrance to the naval dockyard, where they found a hive of activity going on all around them. As each man stepped on board the ship it brought him back to reality, and marked the end of yet another memorable run ashore to add to the story of their lives as mariners.

Everybody was busy preparing for sea, with the ship undocked, reloaded and back into Hamilton to embark any passengers who decided to rejoin the ship as it was the first ship due back to British waters.

***

John was on his refurbished foc'sle again, doing nothing in particular except watching the comings and goings of the islanders passing by on the quayside.

"What a nice place for a quiet holiday. Pity about the high prices though. But then it is a rich man's playground. Maybe one day I'll have a longer stay." He said quietly to himself.

"There you are talking to yourself again, mate." John turned round and saw Larter who had somehow appeared unnoticed, by his side.

"Hello Bruce. That was one brilliant run ashore yesterday. How was yours?" he replied with a nod of welcome.

"Got set up with a rich widow, didn't I. Phew! What looks! What style." Larter said boastfully, and made a curvy outline shape with his hands.

"What brings you up on deck then Bruce! Seeing if you can spot her among the passing crowds?"

"No mate. Our sailing has been delayed due to the Admiralty's enquiry into our part in the three rescues, especially the liner, apparently."

"Not another one?" John asked as he remembered first the Belfast enquiry then the Barbados affair.

"But then I expected the one from the liner, as a lot of lives were not saved that could have been. I did warn the Captain." John stated.

"Yes. Funny you said that. I was told about what you said, and I'll wager you'll be prevented by Trewarthy to attend as deemed not required to testify.

In fact, you'll probably be kept on board in case the word gets out." Larter admitted.

"So we've got another stay, delaying our return home Bruce?"

"'Fraid so John. It should take all afternoon from when their Lordships arrive. They're apparently coming by a specially chartered flying boat arriving about now. I expect he'll want us all to meet in the usual briefing room. But it means that we can have an unexpected few hours more ashore, and I know what I'll hope to be doing in that time."

"Good luck to you Bruce. But this meeting, it's in the passenger's dining room, I take it?"

"You've got it. Now where is she?" Larter asked as he changed the subject back again and looked at the people gathered by the gangway.

They heard a car horn beep furiously and both looked down at the offending car.

"There she is." Larter said excitedly, as he waved to the woman driving a pure white open top Rolls Royce.

"I see what you mean, Bruce. How did you ever get to meet her then?"

"Ahh! Now that'll be telling. Lets say it was at the party you started last night." Bruce replied as he tapped the side of his nose.

John started to chuckle again as he remembered how the party came about.

"Now don't start that again, I'm only just recovering from it." Larter stated chuckling with him.

"Listen, John. I'll be on the quay. Give me a shout when Belverley arrives won't you." Larter said hastily as he left hurriedly towards the gangway.

"You'd better be quick Bruce. There's the skipper arriving in that black car." he observed pointing to it. But Larter had already left him and managed to get ashore before Trewarthy got out of the car and onto the gangway.

After their early lunch was over, every officer gathered for the big meeting, with Lord Belverley and two of his Board of Ship-owners.

"Good afternoon gentlemen. I have gathered you all here get an updated briefing, about what Mr Lowther here has been telling me." Belverley commenced.

"But first of all, I must congratulate each and every one of you for the gallant and heroic work in not only saving my ship, but going to the rescue of three others. You will inform your respective departments of this and I'll have a handsome bounty made out to you all, proportionate to activity, and ready when you get back to Belfast."

There followed a brief gloss over each officer's actions, and those of the crew, with Trewarthy just sitting and staring out of a window.

"I'll need you Mr Tritton and you Mr Day to accompany Captain Trewarthy to the Sessions House. There you will join the rescued officers from the other three ships.

Mr Lowther, Brooks and I will meet you there in about half an hour from now." Belverley said as he took the time from his waistcoat watch.

He spotted John and called him over as the other officers left the room.

"Engineer Grey, a word if you please." Belverley called

'The dung must have hit the fan, so stand by John Grey.' John breathed and went over to face the man who promoted him.

"Three things Grey. There are some very loud whispers around, concerning this enquiry into the sinking of the liner, and our part in the rescue of the luckless people on board. From what I gather, you withheld certain vital information that could have saved a lot more people off her than we actually did. I shall need concrete evidence to believe it, and if this is so you are in for the high jump. But for the moment you need to be given something to keep you from further accusations.

"You are not permitted to attend this enquiry, and I shall see to it that you will be required to remain on board until we meet again back in Belfast."

"But that is totally the wrong way round" John protested.

"Silence Grey. Don't interrupt. Secondly, and in case you've forgotten you still have unfinished business to settle, as a fall out from Barbados. But for the moment I will not say any more on that matter."

"But Mr Belverley! I have tried my utmost to do my job and am trying to become a good engineer!" John protested angrily.

"Grey! Damn your eyes man. Do yourself a favour and just listen!" Belverley hissed.

"I was about to say." Belverely continued:

"To be even handed and on a more lighter note, I've had a preliminary report from the naval dockyard here. Mr McPhee has told me about your part in saving my ship. You are still a dark horse, an enigma to me, and trouble with a capital T. I haven't got the time right now to go through it all, but I shall want to speak to you about that too, later when you get back to Belfast. Have you given any though on your part in the *Empire Bullrush* affair?"

"No your Lordship. I simply haven't had the opportunity or the time. Besides I consider it not my responsibility and therefore nothing to do with me."

"Well, innocent or not, you will just have to make the time. Make no bones about this Grey, nobody maligns my shipping line and gets away with it. On top of that, I don't want officers in my shipping line, which cannot maintain their job and the rank I bestow upon them. You really must think hard on these subject's as I will want a full report from you. See you in Belfast and don't forget." Belverley said angrily, as he left the ship to go ashore.

John felt extremely angry but also confused as to know what to make of Belverely.

"He was kind and appreciative one minute but violently angry the next. Yes, he has a temperament like a swing. I wonder who is responsible for accusing me of something totally opposite to what really happened?" he muttered angrily, as he strode out onto the main deck and made his way back to his favourite spot on the foc'sle.

It took several minutes before John managed to calm himself down enough to be able to speak to Janner who had come and sat next to him on the anchor capstan.

"Got the duty as well Mr Grey?" he asked.

"Hello Janner. Yes, something like that" John replied preferring not to commit himself to awkward explanations.

"Where's the rest of your gang. Ashore?"

"Required on board if you like, hence the duty." Janner muttered sullenly.

"Just as well. I've been told that the prices ashore here, are a bit steep for more than one day. Is that right Janner?" John asked innocently.

"A bit steep? A bit steep he asks!" Janner said in disbelief.

"The man asked if it was steep ashore and he's the one wot spent our money like it was going out of fashion."

John looked at Janner and started to chuckle.

"Yes, well it was such a fine day for a crowd of such generous men loaded with money, to lash me and my shipmate up all day with nice cold beers. The 'rabbits' will make super Christmas prezzies too."

Janner started to swear, but realised that he was being bated and ribbed for his affair in yesterdays fete.

"Sore point. Nuff said, eh 4th!" Janner concluded as he made himself a cigarette from a large tobacco tin.

"Ah well. Must go now Janner. Finish off your fag here as we're taking fuel on board aft." John said quietly as he stood up and walked back to the saloon deck.

He noticed a nice relaxed but excited atmosphere in the saloon, now that it was filling up with a new set of passengers. The sound of laughter from some children playing, the buzz of conversation and the clinking of glasses, was to John, a wondrous contrast to the noises of the last set of passengers who recently left the ship.

"I wonder if I will be allowed to enjoy this transformation, and if it will last during this next part of our voyage." He sighed, as he left the saloon to return to his duties.

CHAPTER XVII
Tidal Waves

The *Brooklea* finally left Bermuda with pomp and ceremony and with Belverley waving them off, sailed slowly out of Hamilton harbour for their last and easterly leg to complete their much altered voyage homeward.

The cabin allocation was such that John was able to return to his original one, although a senior Deck Officer had to move out of his and share with someone else. There was no jealousy as that was the luck of the draw, but John received some gentle ribbing from the others about it.

On his first day out of Bermuda, as the weather was fine, John took his time conducting his afternoon rounds on the main weather deck. The passengers had made themselves comfortable sunning themselves on deck chairs, with inquisitive children clambering all over the deck equipment, asking questions of those crew working on deck at the time.

John's main concern during his routine deck inspections was to check the bow thoroughly, to monitor it and see that it was taking the strain of the oncoming Atlantic rollers. Once his rounds were completed and he reported to Day, he had time off to himself.

A chance for a cool shower, change into suitable clothing and mingle with the passengers, or catch up on his long forgotten task book.

After his shower he returned to his cabin, which was in darkness save for the afternoon sun beaming through the open porthole.

To take advantage of the sea breeze coming through the porthole, he lay on his bunk with only a towel over him as he waded into his task book and all the notes he had written up over the past two weeks or so.

All was quiet except for the faint throb of the engines and the sea spraying against the ships hull, when he heard a soft but persistent knocking on his cabin door.

"Who is it?" he whispered as if to match the quiet knock, then felt foolish and asked again in a louder voice.

"Shhh! Me Helena." came a whispered voice as the girl shut the door quietly behind her, then went and put her hand gently over his mouth, shushing him to be quiet.

"Helena? What are you doing on board? What are you doing in my cabin. I'll get shot if anybody finds us together." he whispered.

Helena didn't answer him, instead she climbed onto his bunk and he noticed that she'd left her robe on the cabin floor and was lying next to him, as naked as the day she was born.

"Helena" he whispered softly, but realised it was useless to speak to her, as neither of them understood each other's language.

Instead, he laid quite still, not knowing what to do as he felt her hands stroking him all over his equally naked body, then she started to softly caress his manhood. She stopped after a little while then taking hold of his hands and guided them all over the contours of her body.

After what seemed an eternity for both of them, enjoying their delicate teasing touches, he found that he was over her and with her gentle guiding hand, he entered her soft yielding body. The rhythm of his body merged into the same movement as that of the gentle sway of the ship giving them both exquisite pleasure as the tidal waves of passion swept over them.

The cup of pleasure was drunk from deeply once more before they finally fell asleep with their bodies closely entwined.

It was another gentle knock and her disentangling body that woke him, to find Stella standing at the foot of his bunk, looking at his nakedness and whispering to her sister.

"Hello John. We were given free passage on this ship to continue our trip. We are glad to find you are still on board. Hope you liked our photos" Stella explained.

"Hello Stella!" John said gently as he covered himself with his towel.

"Yes! It is a lovely present you gave me, but I was only doing my duty. I shall treasure it forever. But what are you doing in here?"

Helena whispered to Stella for a moment who turned back to him.

"Helena says that she is glad that you and her have

shared your first times together. And thanks to you, she is feeling alive and all woman now. Maybe later when the night comes you can share a moment with me too."

John felt himself blushing and tried to keep himself from losing out on an offer he probably would never be able to get again.

"If you wish to, but I don't want to get you into any trouble. I'm in enough trouble as it is." John said defensively.

"John, from what I've seen, you just try and stop me. See you later." Stella replied huskily, then leaving him to rest, left with Helena shutting the cabin door quietly behind them.

'That was the best Thank you present I've ever been given. I wonder what Stella has in mind?' he thought as he finally yielded to his sudden tiredness.

The ship, apart from the usual open ocean swell, met too few weather conditions to mention and made better progress than had been planned or even hoped for, as she was ploughed her way at a steady speed and course across the empty wastes of the Atlantic.

Over the next few days John's routine settled down to a cycle of inspections during certain parts of the day, and receiving visitors in his cabin during the quiet afternoons. It was during these long afternoon sessions that John got to know the two girls better both sexually and socially.

On the afternoon of the fifth day out, the magic of

the voyage was broken when it was announced that the *Brooklea* reached her UK landfall and was on her way to dock in Southampton.

John and the girls were sitting quietly talking in the saloon, when the steward came around announcing to the passengers that they would be docking within two hours and for them to get ready to disembark.

"That is my cue to get on deck, so it looks as if we had better say goodbye now girls." John said quietly, feeling quite reluctant to leave them.

"Oh John, must you? Can't you come ashore with us?" Helena asked.

"Now you know John must stay." Stella said gently, as she led Helena away towards the passengers' cabins with John following along behind them.

"Well Engineer John. We hate goodbyes, so write to us soon won't you." Stella whispered as she kissed John on both cheeks.

"Yes. I will even try to visit you both some day on the first ship that goes there." John vowed and returned the kisses the girls gave him.

"I will keep your locket safe with me at all times." he concluded as he left to go up onto the main deck.

The ship came slowly alongside the jetty and was secured to it before receiving her two gangways.

John watched from his spot on the foc'sle to see cargo being offloaded and the passengers disembarking. With great speed and agility he was on the brow of the gangway to see the girls leave and to walk down the gangway with them.

John promised the girls again that he'd come and visit them some day, so with a tearful goodbye from the sisters he waved them off, their taxi sped away from him into the gloom of a typically British winter's eve.

"Stella is off to her fiance and possibly a wedding soon. But I wonder how long it will be for us to meet again my lovely Helena?" John said quietly as he walked slowly up the gangway and back into the warmth of the ship.

CHAPTER XVIII
Brown Envelopes

Within the hour and when all their passengers had disembarked the *Brooklea* sailed for her home-port of Belfast on the last lap of her present voyage.

Messrs Brooks, Burford and Lowther, had ensconced themselves in the now empty passenger's lounge taking advantage of a few glasses of port and their free ride back to Belfast.

During that short passage, the ship owners had sorted and paid out the salvage, bounty, and voyage pay to the crew, and instructed those crew men who would be on board for the ship's next voyage after Christmas and yet one more brief stay in dock.

"See! I was right." Burns moaned, as he was busy tidying up John's cabin.

"What's right?" he asked.

"Here's my brown envelope. I mean just look at it. We've ended up with only two months bounty. Look at yours. You gentlemen got nearly a year's worth, and yet we did all the grafting."

John took his brown envelope out of his jacket pocket, examined it closely then compared it with the steward's.

"Never mind steward. It's more than most crews get, from what I've been told." John replied to console the man.

"Aye s'pose you're right. Maybe next voyage we'll be luckier." The steward conceded grudgingly.

"You've been a steward for a long time. Surely with your experience you'd do a lot better on some posh liner with all those tips from the rich passengers?"

"Not me, mush! I 'ate screaming or stroppy kids, especially when they're not me own. I came to sea to get away from them thanks very much."

"How many have you got then?"

"Let's see.. At the last count, me missus had five. Knowing my luck, she'll have another one on the go by the time I get another ship."

"What? That surprises me. I thought you were *the* steward on board here. I mean, wherever she goes, you go, surely?"

"It doesn't work out like that somehow. I like a change of scenery and anyway, this was my third voyage that I'd signed up for with his lordship."

"Then what'll you do now steward?"

"After this voyage, I don't think I'll go to sea until my bounty is spent, then who knows. But what about yourself then Mr Grey?"

"As I'm under contract, I've got one more voyage aboard this vessel providing it doesn't sink before then. But then again, if things don't change on board here I'll be looking for a transfer to another ship of the line or group. After that, then I'm ashore just like you steward."

"Ah well. All good things come to an end as they say. Yours ended up in Southampton, you dirty lucky young man." Burns said with a knowing wink and a smile.

John blushed deeply as the steward teased him about his visitations from the sisters.

"Never you mind Mr Grey. Your secret's quite safe with me." Burns said and ran a finger over his lips as if to seal them.

"Right then Mr Grey. Your cabin was my last job, so I'm going now to prepare to go ashore, as we'll be docking in about half an hour or so." Burns informed him and left the cabin, shutting the door quietly behind him.

'Half an hour, I'd better get a move on, and I've got to meet Belverley.' he thought to himself then started to prepare and get packed for home.

Shortly afterwards, he shut his cabin door and left to make his way down and onto the foc'sle, leaving his overfull suitcase at the ready for him to grab later on.

Belfast Lough was still a bit choppy, but he didn't mind the odd sea spray that sprinkled his best uniform as he stood at his customary place by the anchor capstan.

He watched the harbour lights get closer until the ship slowly came alongside and stopped.

"Yes. That's the unique smell of Belfast!" he said as he took a deep breath as if to savour the life of the city.

There was a slight bump as the ship hit the quayside.

"We've arrived at last!" he murmured again to himself.

"Aye, and if they hurry up, I'll be able to catch the night ferry over there."

John looked round and saw Sinclair standing there with a broad grin on his face.

"Hello Andy. It's Christmas Eve tomorrow, will you get home in time before the transport stops?" he asked.

"Me cousin will meet me off the ferry, so I expect I'll stay a few days I would think, before getting up to Mam's for Hogmanay." Sinclair said quietly

"I have got about ten days leave, will you be back next trip Andy?"

"Och aye! Bruce and me have signed for another trip. What about you John?"

"Yes. I've another voyage to go, unless…"

"Oh aye. I'd forgotten about that. What'll you do?" Sinclair asked, as they both remembered the Barbados affair, and John's meeting with Belverley in Bermuda, which was the talk of the ships crew.

"The Barbados saga had all been sorted before we left. But I had Bruce send a signal about my decision concerning Barbados. The Bermuda one is a bit more of a political animal for me, Andy." he revealed.

"You what? Do you mean you've kept this under your hat since then? Well! You crafty devil! Fancy that." Sinclair said incredulously.

"Yes. But don't forget that I'm supposed to see the skipper and Lord Belverley before I get ashore. So I hope they hurry up or I'll miss my last bus."

"'Fraid I can't stop and talk now, have a nice leave and I'll see you again. Same time, same place as last time. Is that a deal John?" asked Sinclair as he held his hand out.

"It's a deal, and its your turn to buy the farls." John smiled as he shook Sinclair's hand.

John stood on the gangway, watching the crew going ashore and wishing them all good luck, which was cheerfully returned by the men as they went over the gangway.

After a little while when the last of the crew had gone leaving him to his thoughts, he saw and recognised a sleek car stop by the gangway, from which emerged Belverley.

"Hello Engineer Grey. Have a good voyage home?" Belverley greeted him in a jovial manner.

"Yes thank you Lord Belverley. Did you get my signal?" he replied politely and with a nod of recognition.

"Yes I did. And what's all this Lordship business. Mr Belverley to you from now on O.K?" Belverley said with a smile, then added.

"You'd better come with me to see the captain and put him out of his misery, don't you think?"

"But the inquest in Bermuda. You had me kept on board for fear of some accusation or another." John said tersely.

Belverley's smile and jovial manner was replaced by a snarling retort.

"Now look here Grey! I've told you before, I pay your wages and you do exactly what I or my senior officers tell you to do." Belverley started.

"But I!" John, tried to interrupt.

"Damn you Grey! Anything that happens in my shipping line comes directly to me to deal with. I take all the flak as the buck stops with me. But look out all those who cause it because I'll have them thrown to the fishes."

"But I had a witness to state the opposite of what I was accused of Lord Belverley. Apart from Trewarthy there must be someone else who has an axe to grind." John snapped back.

"Exactly! And I intend finding out just who it is." Belverley revealed, which took John by surprise.

"This was my first voyage. So if I had gone to that tribunal in Bermuda, both of us would have been vindicated?"

"Let me put it this way Grey. You are still a rookie engineer, a 4th at that. If it hadn't been for the character witnesses given by some of my officers, and by some of the other rescued officers then you'd be in Davey Jones's locker by now.

For my part, Lloyds Insurance will be more inclined to settle my ship repair bills from now on, thanks to the excellent officers I keep in my line."

John felt his anger dissipate at this candid revelation by Belverley.

"Does that mean that my contract with your shipping company remains intact and that my services are still required?"

Belverley managed a brief smile and replied with a slight nod of his head.

"And I still get to call you Mr Belverley?"

Belverley laughed. "Yes Grey! But don't push it too far. You've got the makings of a good ambassador for the *Lea line*. Make sure you earn your promotions, as I shall be watching your every step from now on. Now lets go and put your captain out of his misery."

"The sooner the better Mr Belverley."

They climbed the steep ladder up to the bridge then into Trewarthy's cabin and found him sitting down, having a drink with the other ship-owners.

Trewarthy stood up, then scowled and looked a bit uneasy as he saw the two enter his cabin. This was to be his revelation from Grey, and his decision carried over from Barbados.

"Good evening gentlemen. I think it is time we had a few Christmas presents dished out around here. Don't you think captain?' Belverley greeted as he nodded to Trewarthy and gave a smile to the other ship-owners.

"Begging your pardon my Lord?" Trewarthy asked non-plussed.

"Sit down if you please captain. I'm here with 4th Engineer Grey, to conclude unfinished business from Barbados. Is that right Mr Grey?'

"That's correct Mr Belverley." he replied and saw that Trewarthy was standing up slowly with a thinly disguised sneer on his face.

The other ship-owners commenced topping up all their glasses and passing fresh ones to the newcomers.

"But first, we have to make an understanding concerning the loss of the *Empire Bullrush*." Belverley started, then went on to reveal the findings of the Ministry for Shipping, the Lloyds Insurance Investigations into ship losses, also the consequences of not making full use of equipment in saving the lives of people at sea.

Belverley spoke at length, with interventions from the other ship-owners and liberal amounts of sherry. He concluded by saying.

"Captain Trewarthy. It was you who failed to act upon fresh information, even though you had been given so called expert advice earlier. It saddens me to have to say this to my most experienced captain. It does not matter where or from whom your fresh information comes, as you represent the rescue ship, you become the Senior Rescue Officer with the sole responsibility for acting upon that information.

In this case it was 4th Engineer Grey, who was given this information to pass on, which I might add, was far and above his supposed knowledge, and whom you have already tried to destroy twice before. On the face of it, you were responsible for the loss of life of several scores of people from that ship."

"Now wait a minute. I didn't have to attempt any rescue as my vessel was almost unseaworthy. Besides, she couldn't manage any more tonnage, and if we had taken a few more on we would have sunk along with the others." Trewarthy protested.

"Yes Captain. Granted that your own ship was in great peril and your act of bravery sat well with the Board of enquiry. And granted you did save Lloyds Shipping Insurance several millions. But to pin the loss of those liner passengers onto a junior engineer far removed from responsibility, that was something else and totally despicable."

"What do you say to that Captain?" Lowther asked testily.

"Yes Captain. You've had it in for this junior engineer from the word go. I wonder what really did happen to Chief Engineer Day's promotion recommendation report for Grey?" Burford asked, which made Trewarthy scowl and look down towards his cap on the table.

"What do you mean?" He whispered.

"What is all this about Lord Belverley?"

Belverley watched Trewarthy closely for a moment.

"You have been sailing too close to the wind lately, Captain.

It is about time we sorted you out and got you back onto a proper course again. You will be pleased to know therefore, that we the management here in this cabin, have managed to turn things around and at a very crucial time. It is however the last time we shall be covering up for anybody within our line again. Next time, it's a beach party with only one outcome. Do I make myself clear Captain?" Belverley snapped.

"If you say so!" Trewarthy muttered.

"As for you Grey. With regard to two incidents recorded in the Captain's log. You left your post on two different crucial times, and you also have fallen short of the behaviour required of my officers. No Captain, especially one of mine, would tolerate such behaviour from his officers, especially from a low ranking Engineering Officer such as you.

"On this subject, both of you had better buck your ideas up. But I had expected better from you Trewarthy."

Trewarthy and John looked at each other as if to mutually agree on what had just been said.

"So I take it that both myself and Grey can consider ourselves lucky that we managed to save a hefty amount of cargo and people, has that been taken into account?" Trewarthy asked boldly.

"You can say that." Brooks said soothingly.

"And we can now forget it, that it never comes back?" asked John as he enlarged on Trewarthy's question.

"Yes. You have both made us a pile of money, and for that we can bottom line this *Bullrush* affair." Mr Lowther stated as he joined in.

"The matter is now closed and I do not want to repeat myself over it." Belverley announced as he helped himself to another drink from the decanter.

"The next thing on the agenda is Barbados" Belverley announced.

"Ah yes! Captain Trewarthy!" began Brooks.

"Engineer Grey has to tell you something which you should have been told before leaving Barbados. But due to the events at the time wasn't able to, so you'd best sit down."

Trewarthy looked around the room belligerently as if to reclaim his rightful position as Captain of his ship, and in his own cabin.

"No thank you. Anything Engineer Grey has to tell me, then I'd prefer to stand." Trewarthy said spitefully and started to go pale.

Belverley looked over and nodded to John, who began:

"Very well captain!" he opened, then proceeded to recall his chapter of misery since coming on board the vessel, saying that he hoped his next voyage or ship would be entirely different. He noticed that during his speech Trewarthy was flinching and clenching his fists, as John played on the man's emotions. He went on to say.

"You are obviously a very able captain and a very stern one.

"I hope my next captain's a little more lenient with his men. It is therefore my decision that you'll do three things immediately and without question."

John paused to see Trewarthy writhing uncomfortably under the stares of the ship-owners.

"One. Remove all the ghosts of the past from your ship and especially from your cabin." he paused again and pointed to a picture of the *Black Rose*, on the cabin wall.

"That picture there is what I mean." He said, then waited as Trewarthy silently complied with the order.

"Two. It appears that you have not had any decent shore leave since you joined this ship. You are to have 2 weeks rest at home or in a hospice near here until you sail again. That is so you can rehabilitate your memory, as Von Meir is definitely dead. He's kaput, gone, and no impostors or anything. In fact, nothing left."

"That's a good idea." Brooks pronounced cheerily.

"Don't forget to tell all your friends too."

Trewarthy scowled and muttered something nobody could understand.

"I still have number three Captain. So beware of what you say." John advised, and waited yet again to see Trewarthy's reactions. Making him sweat.

"Three. Mr Belverley will send a signal to Barbados for the release of your friends. Apart from the fact that they will have to find their own way home, and have missed Christmas in the bosom of their families that is all. Except" John paused again to see the bug-eyed look Trewarthy was giving him.

"Have a drink captain, and merry Christmas. Let this be the end of an era for both our sakes." John finished with a flourish as he gave Trewarthy a full glass of his favourite whisky.

Trewarthy looked at everybody with total shock written all over his face, then sat down heavily in his chair with a resounding thump, mechanically accepting the drink from John's hand.

"What do you say to that Michael Trewarthy?" Belverley asked with a laugh and a gentle slap on Trewarthy's large shoulder.

"I... I... I don't know what to say." Trewarthy stammered, then as he gained his composure, he turned to John and said quietly but full of venom.

"You bastard! You knew all along! Why didn't you tell me?"

"Ahh captain! That would have spoiled the surprise." Burford spoke quietly.

"And besides, we had to make sure you didn't throw another wobbly on young Grey here." contributed Lowther.

"Do you agree with the conditions Mr Trewarthy? Bear in mind that there are other people in Barbados waiting for your answer?" asked Belverley in a persuasive manner.

"I don't have any options, so I must." Trewarthy sighed and handed John the picture.

"Thank you captain." John said evenly, passing the picture to Belverley, saying.

"This belongs on a wall in the Captains home or in your offices somewhere, as good museum material."

"Well said Grey." Belverley cooed as he took hold of Trewarthy's prized photos.

"Don't despair too much, and besides Michael., I need a good captain for my next voyage, so you'll need as much rest as you can." Belverley said soothingly and nodded to Trewarthy.

"Young Grey here's on board for the *Brooklea's* next voyage. So maybe you'll start it on a different footing, as should have been on this his very first one. I'm sure you two will eventually get along. What do you say to that?'

"I suppose so. I'll see you in two weeks then 4th." Trewarthy conceded.

John stated his business has been concluded and unless he was required further he would rather be on his way home.

"Yes! Run along Grey. No doubt you'll be glad to get ashore again." Belverley said with a smile.

"But before you go, there is a special envelope for you. Mr Burford, if you please."

"What is it Mr Belverley?" John asked on taking the brown envelope from Burford.

"It is your orders for your leave, shall we say. Your Captain gets one too." Burford said pleasantly as he handed an even fatter envelope to Trewarthy.

"You will not open it until you reach home, Grey, and that's an order." Burford smiled, but with a forefinger crossing his lips as if to indicate silence.

"Well whatever it is, I'm sure it might be of some use to me. Thank you." John replied as he stuffed the fat envelope inside his jacket pocket where he kept his wallet.

John bade them all farewell then went swiftly to his cabin for his suitcase and almost ran over the gangway and ashore to catch his bus.

'Phew! I thought I'd have to start all over again. Saving ships and people from a watery grave is definitely a thankless task.' He mused as he climbed onto the green and white bus that would take him to Dunmurry and Rathmore Cottage.

His bus journey home was spent wrapped up in his thoughts and reflecting on what his recent life had been these last few months.

'Still, all in all, what a way to finish a decade. I wonder what the 1950's will bring everybody'. he thought, as he picked up his suitcase overfull with souvenirs and stepped off the bus at his final destination.

Bridget yelped and ran down the path to meet her master as he walked over the little wooden bridge. He picked her up gently and had his face washed by her as she licked him noisily in a happy reunion.

His mother's tears of happiness, and his father's booming voice of welcome made him realise he was home at last for a well earned leave, and how much he had grown up.

CHAPTER XIX
All Change

New Year's day heralded the start of another decade, which the world hoped would be a peaceful one and a time to rebuild itself from the holocausts of its devastating 2nd World War.

John started to prepare himself for his return to his ship, by gathering up and packing his uniforms and personal effects, when he discovered the brown envelope Burford gave him.

'Must have forgotten about this. Hope I haven't missed anything,' he thought, as he pulled out the envelope it ripped open and spilled its contents at his feet.

To his amazement, as he looked at the bits of paper he discovered that several of them were five and ten pound notes, with a separate envelope tied up in blue ribbon and wax sealed.

John knelt down and counting the money as he collected it put it on his dresser, making a mental note of its value. But it was the other sealed item that really intrigued him and he sat on his bed looking at it, not daring to open it.

His mother came into the room carrying some of his clean laundry and saw the money and John looking at the envelope in his hand.

"Goodness me!" she declared. "Where has all that money come from Son?"

"It came in a large brown envelope that I was given by one of the ship- owners as I left the ship, Mam." John replied as if in a far away place.

His mother looked at the item in his hand and said, "Whatever that is you're holding, I suggest you read it now. It looks very important especially with a seal on it. Probably your orders or something."

He did not need any further prompting, but carefully untied the ribbon, broke the wax seal and unfolded the paper.

"Well John!" his mother asked in anticipation. "What does it say?"

John quickly read the two parchment pages then looked over to the pile of money.

"It looks as if I have been given a special bounty for my part in keeping the *Brooklea* afloat. But I will need most of it to live off for a while, whilst the line completes its merger with two other ones.

"The thing is Mam, it appears that another war is looming in the Orient. Something to do with North Korea and something called the United Nations." John said quietly.

"A war in the Orient? But that's miles away. What's that got to do with us?"

"Maybe they need ships or something. The thing is, I should have reported back two days ago, and was to phone a number before doing so."

"Two days ago? But you're on your leave John. Besides, the nearest phone is up by the bus stop."

"Yes, and I had better use it before I get into more trouble" he replied as he scrambled off the bed and left the house in a hurry.

"4th Engineer Grey reporting. What are my instructions?" he stated clearly into the phone, and waited for his reply, before ringing off and returning home.

"Well son? What did they say?" his mother asked anxiously.

"Oh nothing much! Just that the recall was not needed as the *Brooklea* has had her next trip cancelled, but I'm to report to head office first thing in the morning anyway." He replied softly to allay his mother's fears, then returned to his room to continue his packing again.

'Brooklea in for scrap!. New shipping line! New start with new job?' Was his headline news given him, which made him apprehensive but more resolute to meet the challenges that lay ahead of him.

'The bus is just as foggy with the tobacco smoke, but the bus fare is fourpence more.' he remembered with a smile the last time he left, which to him seemed a life time away.

John got off the bus and walked across the wide city street.

He had to dodge the trams and the trolley buses that clanked or buzzed along either side of him.

He walked past a plinth with a large black stone statue of a man standing on it, then down a side lane until he came upon the impressive granite buildings that housed the headquarters of the shipping line.

There was a large crowd standing around on the short flight of stone steps leading up to the cavernous doorway, which John had to squeeze past in his effort to get into the building.

"What's the buzz on all this 4th. What's happening?"

"Hello Dawes. What are you lot milling around here for?" John replied with his own question.

"Hello 4th. Yeah, what's the score? We've been told to come here instead of the *Brooklea*." Janner asked, as more of the ship's crew recognised him and started to crowd around him.

"What's happening to the *Brooklea*. Are we getting paid to stand around here?" asked another in the crowd.

"I'm afraid there's nothing I can tell you, men. I'm just as much in the dark as you are. I have my orders to report here the same as you. Kindly let me pass." John shouted over the hubbub.

The men quietened down, with Dawes shouting to the men to let him pass.

"Thank you Dawes. See you in a bit." John said as he passed the stoker and went swiftly into the large hallway where he met a few other officers standing around in groups.

"There you are 4th. No tea and soda farls today I'm afraid. Have a good Christmas?"

"Hello Bruce! Yes, and you?" he responded.

"Just great! You know that widow you saw me with in Bermuda? Well she only turned up on my doorstep as large as life. My mouth must have looked like the Mersey Tunnel from the surprise she gave me." Larter replied, as he grinned like the proverbial Cheshire cat.

"Maybe your bounty came in handy after all then."

"Just enough to get us a pint later. But tell me about your meeting with Belverley and Trewarthy John. Everybody is dying to know."

"It's a bit complicated Bruce, but after we finish here, we'll go for a wet and talk about it then. What I want to know is what's happening to the *Brooklea.*"

"You and me both and I daresay so do all the men waiting outside. We're supposed to have a lecture in the conference room down the corridor there.

"Knowing the last time, the men will be given a notice to read whereas we will get verbal and written instructions before we leave." Larter explained.

A man with a megaphone appeared and announced that all officers were to assemble in the conference room immediately.

"All pipes and cigarettes are to be put out before entering the hall."

"There! See what I mean? Just like the last time when Belverley bought the line outright, some four years ago. Come on John, let's get a back seat so we can be out first."

On their way into the room they met Day Gregson

and Cunningham sitting along the back row, and John decided to join them.

"Bruce, I'm going to sit with Happy and the others. Are you coming or are you going to sit with your fellow sparkers?"

"Okay then. I've got to see Johnny Rae, my senior Sparker anyway, so I'll catch up with you later. See you!" Larter said as he left John to go down to the front of the room.

Day re-introduced John to the others sitting nearby and he was warmly received by all who had met him in Barbados.

"What is all this about Happy? I've never seen so many officers and of different types before. I hadn't realised we had so many, considering the size of the shipping line."

"From what I can gather from Jim here, and his brother who is down the front there with the other deck officers and some from another line, it looks like another merger of some sort, if Belverley has anything to do with it." Day explained as he waved to various men whom he recognised.

"Bruce Larter said something similar. So you must be right Happy. Time will tell anyway."

"You know John, there's something about you I definitely like. Maybe it's because you remind me of myself when I was your rank." Day said candidly and with a pat on John's back.

"Silence in the room. All stand. Silence in the room!

All stand." Came the loud order from a man standing on a raised platform holding a microphone.

The room fell silent as each man stood up to watch several well dressed men led by Belverly, enter onto the stage in single file, only to sit down at a long table in front of them.

Once everybody sat down there was a brief pause before Belverley stood up to make his speech, with nodded approval from the other men who flanked him.

"Good morning gentlemen! Hope you all had a good Christmas." Belverley commenced, and went on to introduce the other men with him.

He spoke about the future needs of the old and even new trading nations around the world. Of the future commerce gained from it, the need for more competitive shipping companies and for newer and faster ships to operate with. And eventually of the prosperity of the people who sail in them. The oration lasted for a good two hours, before Belverley announced a welcome ten-minute tea and cigarette break.

"You may smoke out in the hallway. And those who wish to partake, can get a mug of tea from the galley. Free of course." Came an announcement that was met with a loud cheer at the prospects of getting something free, but with few takers.

"What a load of blarney! Why can't Belverley just come out with what he really has to say and let's get on with it." Cunningham said irritably.

"We're getting paid to be here, so lets be grateful we're not in a force eight at the moment." Gregson said casually.

The officers finished their cigarettes and as they were re-entering the hall were given a small pamphlet with glossy pictures, special features, and names printed throughout it.

"So that's it! A triple merger! But what for?" Gregson whistled quietly as he glanced down at his copy.

"Right then gentlemen. Let's continue!" Belverley announced, then went on about the merits of mergers, integration and partnerships being for the good of everybody in the room. He referred to the pamphlet as he got other speakers onto their feet to divulge who they were and what they would be doing, each time handing the microphone back to Belverley when they had finished.

"Gentlemen! This conference will be repeated in two other places. However, all you based here in Belfast are the first to be invited to join with me; with Lords InverGarron, Laxenby and Collingforth, not forgetting Sir Alensdale. We intend to form the new shipping company called the Triple Coronet Line, henceforth known as the Tricorn Shipping Group."

Everybody in the room gave a standing ovation for several minutes before Belverley signalled to sit down again.

"We of the Tricorn Shipping Group have a combined fleet of some 70 ships and other craft.

"I shall continue with the administration for the entire group, docking facilities, and my end of the Trans-Oceanic cargo/passenger services;

"Lord Invergarron will have his ocean going freighters from his old *Inver* line; Lord Laxenby will have his ocean going tankers of his old *Bay* line; Collingforth will provide coastal shipping and inland water barges;

"Sir Allensdale providing his tugs, other support vessels, and all ship repair facilities to be based in foreign waters. What that means gentlemen is that each of you will be able to transfer onto any type of craft within our new fleet wherever they may go or be found, without leaving the parent shipping company."

Each announcement drew more cheers and clapping from the audience as each revelation was made. The biggest one was the pay and conditions, but the last one drew complete silence.

"We have been selected by the Admiralty Board in Whitehall, to provide certain ships for their exclusive use. Although we shall be manning them, we shall be sailing under Admiralty orders with the specific duty of supplying any or all of His Majesty's ships and troops wherever they may be. As our shipping line is manned mostly by ex RN personnel anyway, it should not be too difficult for us to be able to blend in with their requirements."

The silence was deafening for several minutes, before a voice from the front asked the question on everybody's lips.

"According to the press and radio, there is a war looming out in Korea. Does that mean that if we go to yet another war, it's only our shipping line that will be used? And if so, will we get special compensation or danger money whilst we're there?"

This drew a large crescendo of catcalls and heckling from the rest of the audience, which Belverley waited to abate before standing up to give his answer.

"The answer to question one is. Yes, our ships will be used, but only volunteers will go to sea on those vessels that sail into dangerous waters or theatres of war. In answer to your second one, yes! You will be paid at a special premium above normal rates. Plus a bonus on return to base port."

This seemed to placate the audience enough to keep the noise down for Belverley to conclude his speech.

"Gentlemen. If you have any more questions, then address them to your respective ships Captains. As I have said, we the ship-owners have two more such meetings to give to other ships crews, before we complete our task. Therefore I draw this meeting to a close, and I wish you all God speed."

Everybody stood up again and clapped the departing ship owners, then they too left the room in a buzz of excitement and eager anticipation at the prospect of earning good wages never before earned in a British shipping company.

The building disgorged its human occupants out onto

the street where there was a scrum of press reporters, and a huge battery of radio and television cameramen, all waiting for them.

"C'mon lads, lets get to the nearest bar and hear ourselves waffling on, on the radio." Day prompted to his close circle of friends, as they struggled through the throng of officers and pressmen.

"In here Happy!" John shouted as he darted into a glass fronted pub extolling the virtues of XX Porters and stouts.

There were several other officers lined against the bar waiting for their pint to settle, before leaving the bar to sit down.

"Here you are lads! Get your mitts around these. You can get the next ones in." shouted Larter, as he called John and his friends over to a table laden with glasses of beer and a bottle of whisky towering above them.

"Cheers Bruce! That saved us from this thirsty queue." Gregson said quickly as each friend came over took their glasses and started to slake their thirst before anybody spoke.

There was only one main topic that dominated their conversation, which constantly referred to the facts quoted in the pamphlets everybody had.

John wanted to know about the *Brooklea* and the second contracts some of the crew still had.

"It's quite simple John. This new merger has superceded all previous instructions and orders, and as of this week we are supposed to get new ones. The *Brooklea's* fate is still in the balance, as their lordships don't know whether to save or scrap her. If she is saved, then your contract still remains valid and you would remain part of the *Lea* line operations. But if she is scrapped then anyone with an open contract would be re-assigned, or leave for another line. Those still at sea or out of home port, have been recalled and will have their implementation then.

"In the meantime, the *Brook* is being used for a few days as an accommodation ship for this big conference we just attended." Larter explained.

"Stay until relieved is the catch-phrase, John" Day added to support Larter's analogy.

"In that case John, mine is a double whisky and soda." Larter teased as he held out his empty glass.

"I don't mind getting the wets in, but I'm hoping to catch my last bus." John protested meekly.

"Never mind going home! Lets have a party and celebrate our good news. We can always go back on board the *Brook* to get our heads down. What do you say lads?"

"Four pints of XX porter, two double whisky and sodas and two double rums, please barman" John requested as he handed his money over the bar.

The evening was wearing on, with the drinks still flowing, when someone suggested that they all went back on board ship to continue their private party in the passenger saloon.

Their slow walk back through the streets down to the dock where the ship was tied up, was a sobering up time for the friends, and they arrived on board raring to go for another session.

When they arrived in the dimly lit saloon the friends discovered that their idea was also thought of by some of the other officers, so they merely joined in.

The same conversation was still fresh in their minds and everyone talked openly about it, until they started to get fewer and fewer as the men filtered back to their allocated cabins to sleep it off.

All except Day, Cunningham, Larter and John, who were sat in a close nest of chairs at the side of the bar obscured from the open doorway.

After a little while during a lull in their conversation, they saw a shadowy figure come through the saloon doorway.

"What the! Just look at all this mess!"

"Hello steward. Back so soon?" Day asked quietly, startling the man

"Whoa! Who said that? Come out whoever you are so I can see you" Burns said angrily, as he looked around at the empty tables.

"We're over here by the bar, steward. Come and join us." Day invited.

Burns dumped his bag onto a chair and walked over to the men.

"There you are! What happened here, some sort of a

party?" he asked.

"You can say that steward. But why are you back on board, we thought your contract was complete." John replied.

"Something to do with that big conflab that was held today. The line I was supposed to join turns out to be part of this one now. So I've been ordered to come back and rejoin the *Brook* for a while. Fat chance and according to the rumours that is." Burns moaned.

"Yes, but why are you off leave so soon? Don't tell me your missus spent all your money already?" Day asked teasingly.

"Flippin' mugged me more like. She skinned me like a flea then threw me out."

"What have you done this time? Last time she threw you out was because you had something belonging to another woman" Gregson prompted.

"More the same. She found that I'd caught a dose and threw me out of the house wearing only my long johns. It must 'ave been that wench back in Barbados, she said she was clean and even charged me five bob extra on top.

"Just wait 'till I get my 'ands on 'er, preferably by the throat." Burns said miserably, which made the others laugh at him.

"That's right, go on, laugh! See if I care."

"C'mon steward. You should know by now, playing away and especially catching the galloping knob rot[**] is

---

[**] A term used to describe VD (veneral disease).

definitely not the done thing." Cunningham said with almost a straight face, and started the others off again with his choice of words.

"Let's stow that. Change the flippin' subject. Any chance of sampling some of that beer? Only, I haven't tasted the stuff since the other day, and no money to buy it." Burns pleaded.

"Why certainly steward. But you'll have to clear up all this mess before you get below to your cabin. We don't want a trash heap for a ship now do we." Day said, as he handed Burns a full glass of ale.

"That's a deal Chief." Burns replied swiftly and drank the full glass down without stopping, before looking for another one.

"You must have been thirsty and ready for that, steward. Here's half a bottle of whisky and some soda." John laughed as he passed them over to the grateful man.

The friends did not mind Burns in their company as he looked after them during their sea trips, and included him in their all-encompassing conversation of the day's conference.

As they talked into the small hours of the morning with their supply of drinks almost depleted and everyone feeling peckish.

"Steward. Can you get or find out where the keys to the galley are, because we'd like something to eat, if it's possible?" Gregson asked.

"I have my own set of keys. For most places on

board this and several other vessels, including the skippers bridge cabin." Burns boasted as his words began to slur.

"Does that include the spirit cupboard behind the bar?" Larter asked

"That'n all." Burns bragged, then added, "I tell you what. If I go down the galley and make us some sarnies, maybe one of you can get us some more drinks from the bar."

"You've got a deal steward. Where's the key?" Gregson asked.

Burns thrust his hands inside his coat pocket and pulled out a large bunch of keys, and threw them onto the table in front of them.

"How's about that then. Didn't I tell you?" Burns said with a large grin on his face, and extracting one of them off the key ring and gave it to Gregson.

"You've got a deal steward. Make plenty of sarnies, we're all ruddy starving here." Gregson quipped as he patted his stomach.

The steward left the friends to go down the galley whilst Gregson opened the bar locker.

"But that's stealing company property Happy. Isn't it Bruce?" John protested mildly but wanting food inside him.

"Not really John. We have paid for all this out of our mess bill when we arrived. Anything left over behind the bar or in the galley is usually kept for the start up of the next voyage.

The other officers you saw here tonight are only accommodated on board *just* for tonight and had to pay across the bar, even though they are our guests. But as there aren't any around now we can have it all to ourselves." Bruce explained.

"Not this time you don't!" Came a shout from behind them.

"First Mate Tritton. What are you doing on board, I thought you left to join daddy's yacht. Lost your way?" Day asked sarcastically.

"You are not entitled to anything behind that bar. The ship got de-stored, which included the mess victuals, the galley and the passenger lounge bar. This saloon is now shut and you lot had better get turned in. Better still, as none of you are registered for overnight accommodation you had better get off my ship." Tritton said with annoyance.

"Your ship Tritton? What do you mean, your ship?" Day asked sharply.

"I am the Senior Executive Officer and temporarily in command until relieved or whilst the Captain is ashore. Therefore I demand that you all leave immediately."

"Says who! You are only a jumped up cabin boy who can't tell his port from his starboard."

"Now look here Day! If you don't get off my ship I will have to report this incident to the ship-owners."

John had not experienced such an altercation between two senior officers and was getting anxious about what might follow.

"Bruce, what's the score here? I have a bad feeling about all this, so why can't we go just like the First mate said." John whispered.

Bruce put his hand on John's arm and whispered back.

"Hold on a minute and enjoy something that's been coming for a while now. Happy and Tritton have been at each others throats ever since we left Las Palmas.

Tritton is way out of his depth and Happy will have him by the short and curlies, you just watch."

"I represent the senior officer here. In case you have forgotten, Tritton, this ship is under Dockyard and under Engineering control until it either gets scrapped or completes its refit and repairs.

Now unless you have been promoted Captain of this vessel, I suggest you take your rotten carcass out of here and leave us all alone." Day said with conviction that made Tritton turn bright red with anger.

"Now look here Day! I've been told to take over from Captain Trewarthy for the duration of his leave. That makes me..." Tritton replied but was cut short by Day.

"You take over from Trewarthy! Not even in a million years. He might be bit of an ogre who rules his ship with an iron fist. And there are several people on board including me, who personally don't care for the man one way or the other, but you'll not get close enough to lick his boots.

In this or any other case, you are still the First Mate. Whereas I am the Chief Engineer, in equal rank as any ships Captain. Therefore Tritton I outrank, you full stop. So I suggest you push off under your own steam now, or you'll live to regret it." Day snarled.

Tritton went as red as beetroot and started to rant on about Executive Officers taking precedence over any other departments.

Day sighed, swore loudly, then picked up a chair and hurled it at Tritton, who ducked as it clattered and broke at his feet.

"Get out Tritton! Or you'll definitely wear the next one." Day shouted.

Tritton turned and ran out of the saloon mouthing off obscenities and threats of getting even with Day.

Day turned to his friends and after a moment whilst he collected his thoughts, spoke.

"I'm very sorry about all this, but that man gets right up my nose. And just for that, we'll have as much as we can sup now." Day apologised.

"Tritton always was a bit of a woofter, trying to suck his way up the ladder. Maybe he lacks enough real backbone to make it on his own!" Cunningham observed.

"He was the one that put the spoke in for John, just in time for the Bermuda enquiry. That was why Belverley prevented John from attending and possibly ending up taking action against Tritton for it." Larter admitted.

"So that's who it was. I thought it was Trewarthy!" John said with surprise.

"Yet Trewarthy took all the blame."

"According to Burns, that's Trewarthy's Achilles heel. He always takes the blame for others, and puts it down to bad Captainship or whatever you might call it. That is until that person does something wrong on board, then he jumps on them from a great height. Then they can ruddy well look out." Cunningham advised.

"Now we're getting down to the real man, John. It seems that Burns here is the only one amongst us that has got the measure of Trewarthy." Larter quipped.

"I suppose this incident will be put on the ship's log. But this time round Happy is right. Happy is the one in charge, engineer or not." Gregson added.

"Well never mind him. I'm going to have a good drink now. Where the hell is the steward, I'm ruddy starving." Day stated as if to close the incident.

The friends were supping their drinks when the steward came back with a tray loaded with sandwiches, cheese and pickles and other edible morsels.

As the food was being shared out, Trewarthy came into the saloon and walked straight up to their table.

"Who's trying to wreck the furniture in my ship?"

"Captain Trewarthy! We thought you were on leave. You're just in time for a noggin and a sarnie." Day offered, and handed Tritton a large whisky.

"That's kind of you Chief. On my way in, I bumped into Tritton. Was it you who upset my First Mate?" Trewarthy asked.

"I'm afraid Tritton has delusions of grandeur, and had forgotten his manners, Captain." Day retorted.

"From what I heard, which was everything chief, thank you for your kind words. Only next time either be careful you don't damage the furniture, or make sure that next time you don't miss. Tritton always was a person to stab you in the back and an arse licker. I'll be glad to get shot of him as and when." Trewarthy said with a smile, as he took the offered drink.

Trewarthy sat down opposite the friends and nodded to each one as he recognised them, but spoke to John.

"Hello 4th. So much for your recommendation for me to go on sick leave, it was much appreciated, I don't think. I was poked and prodded by quacks

This ship has been my home for some time now and I don't like leaving home for anybody. I've come back to face, and to share whatever fate she is about to endure."

Everybody nodded their heads slowly in acknowledgement, as there was no answer to Trewarthy's philosophical statement.

"Yes Captain. Let's hope your leave has done you some good. We did not expect to see you much before the decision is made on the *Brook*." Day commented, but was interrupted by Larter who queried: "When will we know Captain?"

"Probably sometime this forenoon, Sparks. If she's being saved then she'll go into dry dock today, if not then she will be towed to the breakers yard tomorrow." Trewarthy said sadly as he looked around his old and familiar surroundings.

"They'd probably strip her engines out and use them elsewhere, I should imagine." Gregson said tiredly and stifled his yawn.

"Speaking of which Captain. What do you think of the new shipping line, and where do you fit into the overall picture of it?" John asked.

"Yes Captain. As you are the senior Captain of our old line, how will the new set up affect us all?" Cunningham asked.

"Whoa you lot. One at a time!" Trewarthy chuckled, as he finished his drink.

"First off 4th." Trewarthy started, and he went on to answer all the questions posed, with detailed explanations to each one as he went along.

The friends wined and dined and talked all through the night, with Burns clearing and tidying up the whole room as was his bargain.

"Right then gentlemen, it's just gone 0400hrs. I don't know about you lot but I'm knackered and it's time you lot should get turned in." Burns announced quietly, as he held onto a chair to steady himself.

"Yes gentlemen, I agree with the man. We had better be going, as the ship leaves at noon. And you know what that means." Trewarthy suggested.

"If my cabin is still free, then that's the place for me. But it means that I have to nip home to get my sea bag." John said to Day.

"Okay John. Be off the ship by 12 noon today, and stay ashore until tomorrow morning. But you will need to report back to head office by 0900hrs." Day agreed

"Yes that's about right. See you then, John." Larter added, as all the friends left for their respective cabins and a booze-laden sleep.

"Mornin' 4th!" Burns said cheerfully as he came into the cabin.

"Oh it's you! What's happening steward?" John replied sleepily.

"It's nearly 1000hrs. If you want to miss the cold move down to the dry-dock, then you've got about half an hour before the gangway is taken off." Burns explained as he offered John a large mug of tea.

"Here, get this drink down your neck. It will do you until you get home wherever Rathmore Cottage is."

"Cheers steward, much appreciated." John responded as he tried to gulp down the hot tea and straighten up his bunk bedding at the same time.

"Never mind the cabin. It will give me something to do during the docking. Before you go 4th, Chief Day asked me to tell you that after you have reported to HQ, he will see you later probably down at the ship repair facility."

"Again thanks for the info steward. You are

certainly a mine of information to me. But must dash now. See you anon." John smiled, picked up his cap and left hurriedly.

He just managed to get ashore before the gangway was hoisted up and off the ship, and stood for a while watching the proceedings of a ship being untied and towed away.

"Quite the reverse from my first encounter with her" He murmured, as he made his way for his brief return visit home.

CHAPTER XX
Old Habits

The HQ building was quiet and almost empty of the humans that normally turned the place into a hive of activity, as John made his way around and through the massive revolving door.

He spotted an elderly man in a blue serge uniform standing behind a large desk with the word 'RECEPTION' written on a board hanging down just above his head.

"I'm 4th Engineer Grey off the *Brooklea*. I have to report here this morning, but my orders are not clear as to which office or to whom I am to see." John said as he introduced himself.

The elderly man stopped writing in the large book in front of him, and looked up at John.

"The *Brooklea* you said? I have a note here that says, 'all officers and crew off the MV *Brooklea* are to report to Room 301.' That's on the third floor just up those stairs." the man said as he pointed towards the wooden staircase at the back of the hallway.

John thanked him and started to move off when he was called back.

"Hold on a minute. I haven't finished yet! The man shouted indignantly.

"I was about to tell you that in your case as an Engineering Officer, and this will apply to all ships' engineers., the note also states that ' all Engineers must go down to the Ship Repair Yard and report to the yard's 'Chief Engineer'. That will be Mr Cresswell." The man concluded.

John was taken aback at the name of Cresswell, as his last meeting with that man was still fresh and unsavoury in his mind.

"Did you say Chief Cresswell?"

"Yes! A fine man too. He's been put in charge of the entire yard and over all engineering personnel based here at Belfast. Why you ask?"

"Oh no reason!" John lied, as he didn't want to go into any details.

"It's just that I heard through the grapevine that he was pensioned off or got beached or something. Anyway it doesn't matter."

"Well the grapevine was wrong. He's the best engineer this shipping line will ever have, and is just the man to sort out these new fangled, so called Engineering officers the line seems to be hell bent in taking on." the man snapped.

"By your answer, I take it you used to be in engineering with that man too!"

"None of your business! Anyway, do you know where the Ship Repair Facility is situated?" the man asked after a moment.

"Unless it's just down past the *'Caroline'* and the first basin, you're about to tell me then." John rebuffed the man.

"No that's where you're wrong. The *Caroline's*

been moved further down from where she used to be before the war, and is now part of the new Naval Reserve area." the man replied sarcastically.

John just sighed loudly, shook his head, then quickly picked up his suitcase and walked away from the pompous man saying that he'd find it for himself.

"What's wrong with these people. They must belong to a secret gang or organisation or something to defend the names of the likes of Cresswell and co." he muttered to himself as he left the building.

Unlike most cities and ports on the British mainland that were bombed flat by the Hitler war machine, Belfast was virtually untouched. The only bombings and damage done to that lovely city, were by the hands of the faceless members of the IRA, be it a bandstand of innocent musicians, a train carrying several hundred wounded soldiers that had just recently returned from battle. With them living in the community to do the damage for Hitler, the Nazis just didn't bother to turn up.

However, some of its magnificent stone buildings, local landmarks and streets were in still in place to help John to find his way to the SRF, which did not take him long.

John arrived at a long, two-storey building with large letters painted on wooden panels on the roof that declared what it was.

As he stepped through into the main entrance to the building, he met Day on his way out.

"Morning Happy! Didn't expect to meet you here so soon." He greeted with a smile.

"Morning 4th! You've made it here then." Day responded heartily.

"Be on your guard John. Cresswell seemed to have grown some more horns since we last saw him. His promotion to the SRF Chief Engineer job has certainly gone to his head. So be warned." Day said quietly.

"Thanks Happy, just what I needed. But then as I'm still with the *Brook* don't you still remain my Chief, therefore my boss?"

"Yes John, but only on board, not here. It's a different ball game now that we belong to a shipping conglomerate as opposed to a sole trader line.

If in fact you do get any grief from Cresswell, John, just contact me on board at any time."

"Thanks chief! The man can't do any more to me than he tried to do before. Besides, just remember Barbados!"

"Ah yes! That's one trip we all had better not forget in a hurry. It might be our only weapon against him." Day said knowingly.

Before the two friends could say more, there was a loud bellowing shout that came seemingly out of nowhere.

"You two over there, this is not a mothers meeting place." came the roar as Cresswell started his foul-mouthed tirade.

"Well if it ain't the 'lah de dah', snotty nosed,

jumped up so called engineer, Grey. What the hell are you doing in my building?

"Trying to take over this place as well are we? Who asked you to come here anyway?"

John rolled his eyes, sighed slowly and nodded to Day.

"Here we go again chief, isn't this where I came in?"

"Remember what I said. Keep your cool and don't let him rile you. Just think of Barbados" Day whispered as he left John and walked out of the building.

"Good morning Chief!" John said with forced pleasantness and a lot of hope.

"Good morning chief!" mimicked Cresswell.

"You're just the man I want to see anyway! You're adrift! You should have been here half an hour ago and you're holding up my proceedings.

Now get your arse into that room down there, and tell the others I'll be there in five minutes." Cresswell shouted, as he pointed to a room at the other end of a long dimly lit corridor adjacent to where he was standing.

John walked slowly down the corridor and entered what looked like a cinema, with lots of men sitting in seats that banked up high at the back, but was in fact a large lecture room.

He managed to recognise Cunningham and one or two others of the men in the smoke filled room and nodded to them, but paused at Cresswell's desk, which was facing the audience.

"Listen up Gentlemen!" John shouted above the hubbub of the room, which hushed everybody up.

"I'm 4th Engineer Grey off the *Brooklea*. I've just met Chief Cresswell who has instructed me to inform you all that he'll be back in five minutes." He announced.

The sullen quiet gave way instantly to cheering and clapping from the men who had recognised John's name, along with some of the nicknames people have dubbed him with.

"It's the Barbados Kid! The Cresswell Crusher!" all of which made him feel a bit embarrassed and he decided to take a seat next to Cunningham.

"Morning John, we heard the shouting you got even from way back here." Cunningham said as he stood up and shook John's hand.

"Hello Jack! Slight detour around the *Caroline*, that's all." John responded as he sat down.

"What's all the fuss Jack? It seems like an Engineers convention, what's the agenda?"

"Yes! We have every Belfast based naval engineer in here this morning. Something is up but Cresswell is keeping us all guessing.

"The word has it, its something to do with a new ship repair policy. Cresswell has gone to get some film we're going to watch that should put us in the picture!"

"No pun intended I'm sure." John chuckled, which made Cunningham smile in realisation of what he said.

Cresswell came back on the dot as stated, and held up a large film reel announcing that what they were about to see was confidential and any questions anyone had would be addressed by their own ship's Chief Engineer.

Everybody quietened down and studied the films contents, with hushed comments now and again at the revelation of some of the pictures. John was swiftly drawing diagrams and taking notes, that he put question marks against for future references.

Once the film was over, and the lights back on, Cresswell told everybody to follow him down to the SRF dry-dock where the second part of the instructions would take place.

When they arrived, everyone was amazed by the craft being built in the dock. Cresswell pointed out several items and areas of interest then directed everybody back to the lecture room.

"Right you men! As you can see, modern technology means that we can deliver these beasts to wherever we want them to go. Just load up, add a couple of tugs and away you go. I shall allow a short period of questioning. One question per row and at random."

There was complete silence from the men until Cresswell prompted them.

"Surely there must be someone more intelligent than two short planks and with the balls to have a question for me."

John stood up with a myriad of questions on his mind but decided on just the one.

"I might have known you'd be the one to stand up Grey!" Cresswell sneered, then added:

"In case you lot don't know, this is the 'Know it all but really knows nothing, so called Engineer Grey! What stupid question does a 4th engineer dare to ask the Chief?"

John sighed to himself and whispered to Cunningham.

"Old habits die hard they say Jack!"

Then turning to Cresswell put his best question that would demand exact answers to satisfy John's newly found analytical mind.

"This question is in two parts and inter-linked. Given that the critical measurements of this new Super Floating Dock." John started, and went on to phrase his question so as to extract a specific answer from Cresswell.

Cresswell, stood open mouthed at such a complicated question, and took several moments to answer.

This delay created an uneasy pause, which the men quickly seized upon and started a slow handclap, demanding an immediate answer to satisfy them, with the chants.

"Answer the question! Answer the question!"

Cresswell tried to answer the question put to him, but quickly found out that his answers were not the answers to quench the thirsty knowledge of John or to satisfy of the others. In the end, Cresswell just bluffed his way out of the situation by telling everybody to "look at the film again in their own time, and to find their own answers".

"For them to see their own Chief Engineers for any answers, and that that was all he was prepared to tell them." then promptly dismissed everybody telling them to come back tomorrow for a further briefing from the new Commodore of the shipping consortium.

"Remember. 0900 hours and don't be…" Cresswell started to say. But the departing men shouting the word finished off his sentence in unison:

"ADRIFT".

Over the next few days of conferences and other planned instructional meetings, it was clear to John that there was a shift of emphasis from pre-war shipping and their engineering needs, to a more modern approach to the possibilities of newer, faster, and much bigger vessels. The wind of change was blowing now, just as it had when the maritime world embraced the changes from sail to steam, discarding all the old traditional methods for more modern and more predictable mode of plying the oceans of the world. Except in this case, it was the natural progression from coal powered steamships to oil burning, steam turbine ships, and would mean that the next generation of ships would need fewer officers and crew to man and sail them much further and faster than before.

As John was leaving the SRF's dry dock bottom,

after an afternoon trying to satisfy his own curiosity concerning the strange vessel being constructed before his very eyes, he saw Trewarthy talking to a group of Seamen officers who had gathered around him.

He made his way over to the group of men and waited until there was a pause in the instructions Trewarthy was issuing to them, before he coughed politely to indicate that he wished to speak to Trewarthy.

"Gentlemen. We have the dubious privilege of having 4th Engineer Grey in our midst, who is obviously in need or wanting to offer us some words of wisdom." Trewarthy said sarcastically.

"4th Engineer Grey! What the hell is it you want from me this time?" he demanded angrily.

"First, I would like to congratulate you on your promotion to Commodore." John started to say but was cut short by Trewarthy.

"Yes! Yes man! Cut the drivel. Don't tell me you've interrupted me for something trivial. Get on with it man!"

John took a deep breath and showed Trewarthy a drawing with critical dimensions, and formulae and notations.

"I was hoping to see you at a more convenient time and as you are the only person I know suitable to approach concerning these drawings and the ideas behind them, I was hoping you'd spare me the time to discuss them." John replied, defensively, as he handed Trewarthy his sketchbook.

Trewarthy looked slowly over the drawings, comparing them with the SFD behind him.

"Am I right in saying, that you'd put a false 'V' shaped construction on each end, and a temporary decking over the top so you could make this into a temporary barge to carry all its own equipment. Why?" He asked at length.

"The SFD would dispense with the need for a second vessel to carry her equipment to the destination SRF port. On arrival, she could be returned to normal usage apart from the 3rd diagram sheet." John responded enthusiastically, and nodded to some of the other officers who were trying to look over Trewarthy's shoulder.

Trewarthy stroked his beard and turning to the third diagram page, examined it with darting glances to the object in question.

"So what you're saying is, that all we have to do is just couple up and bolt on as many lengths as we need to fit the size of the ship. Something like a train if you like, Grey?"

"Yes! That way we can accommodate the bigger ships that might need docking, and in places where there's no full sized dry dock for thousands of miles away."

"It doesn't follow that if two are needed to lift one ship they can give double lifting power. What about the extra lifting power, have you given thought about that?"

"Yes Captain! I mean Commodore! For instance,

just as a submarine has saddle tanks to help keep its buoyancy, so we could have some of them bolted all the way round to provide the same added lift. That would increase the lifting power by about 90 percent, per each added section. Put it another way," John continued to explain his theory while the other officers just looked at him with a glazed stare.

"The modern freighters and tankers being built are now twice and sometimes three times the size of the pre war ones. If that continues, we'll be talking about future ships over 1000 feet long and grossing 100,000 tonnes. I am not able to substantiate my figures but at least it would be something to get on with and think about, especially about the production of several new SFD vessels that might be needed."

These statistics made the other officers murmur and look at each other in astonishment as they were shown the diagrams and sketches.

"Do you see what I mean gentlemen! This is the very person I have been telling you all about. Who among you would rid me of him?" Trewarthy challenged.

"Engineer Grey. I've never heard such drivel: Ships carrying 100,000 tonnes! Why they'd sink or collapse due to the weight!" A grey headed man with several rows of war medal ribbons adorning his chest, scoffed. Which was the general opinion of the rest of the officers.

"Hold on a minute though. He might be just a 4th Engineer, and that may not be entirely his own fault, but he has a point concerning the temporary usage of a super barge he mentioned." Trewarthy said quickly in John's defence, and much to John's amazement.

"Tell you what Grey. I'll keep these drawings of yours and show them to Mr Cresswell. If there is any merit in what you have shown me then we'll send for you. As far as I'm concerned it's none of your business what we do here, and you should only be concerned about your duties aboard the *Brooklea*. Have you got my drift?"

The other officers were getting disgruntled and making derogatory remarks about John to Trewarthy, enough so that John realised he was not welcome and for him to escape from them. He just nodded his head in acknowledgement to Trewarthy's suggestion and walked swiftly away from his tormentors.

"Ungrateful lot! All my uncles who worked in the H&W shipyards over the past several decades taught me many things in ship design, building and repairs. Those men think that because I'm just starting out and only a 4th Engineer, and they are all sea Captains, they know it all.

"One day I will take that side up and prove them wrong, once I've proved my capabilities as an Engineer." He muttered angrily as he picked his way past the busy dockyard workers, to go back up to land level again.

Two days later, when John was having a quiet smoke in the SRF's Officers canteen he was joined at his table by his colleagues Day and Gregson.

"Hello Jim, nice to see you again. Hello Happy, I was hoping to see you yesterday about some drawings I made of the SFD." John greeted the men as they sat opposite him and commenced drinking their beverage.

"Morning 4th!" Gregson replied with a smile.

"Ah yes John. Glad you mentioned that. Bit of a problem though." Day nodded.

"Anything to do with what I've just said Happy?" John asked, with raised eyebrows.

"It seems John, that our illustrious chief, Cresswell, is accusing you of copying some of his new designs that you somehow managed to purloin; just as he accused you of doing to get the plans of the *Brooklea*." Day said tersely.

"But that is a lie!" John protested loudly.

"Whoa, hold on a minute John." Gregson said calmly as he prevented John from standing up in anger at Day's announcement.

"The thing is, nobody below a Chief Engineer is supposed to come up with such radical thinking or sets of drawings, let alone your good self. Even though you were the one who introduced the colour code for ships pipe systems." Gregson added.

"Yes John. It appears that Cresswell and Trewarthy have laid first claim on your drawings, by virtue of the fact that you must have seen something resembling them during your walkabout in the SRF lately. They have been re-drawn in blue print and were presented to the Board of Trade for patenting yesterday.

It also appears that the lords of the Tricorn have sanctioned them and given instructions for the new designs to be implemented even as we speak. We have a suspicion of the real truth of the matter, but it looks for all the world as if those two men have got off to a good start in their promotions." Day explained quietly.

"But that's daylight robbery. What do you call it? Industrial espionage, or patent thieving? They were my own drawings on my own sketch pad with my own name written on each piece of paper." John said, extremely angrily as he stood up and kicked his chair from behind him, which skidded into the path of another engineer officer on his way past them.

"What's your problem pal! You're asking for a fourpenny one if you're not careful." the man said as the chair slammed into him.

Gregson stood up swiftly and apologising to the man for John's outburst, assured him that no harm was meant his way. This placated the man who just growled at them and walked slowly away from the incident.

"If there is one thing you must learn quickly John, it is that any drawings or notations pertaining to your duty as an engineer, or the ship, and especially anything that would make the ship-owners a lot of money from them; the company has sole rights to them.

That is to say, you are an employee and anything you invent or have ideas on, they own both them and you, not you." Day said slowly as Gregson nodded his agreement.

"I see. So I do all the hard work, they get all the glory."

"That's about the size of it John." Day conceded.

"All right then, try this. Say I find myself in a sticky or dangerous situation whereby I need to invent or do something to get out of that scenario, if I fail to do so, given that the ship owners would end up with that knowledge. What would happen then?"

"Simple, John! You get it in the neck, and probably go to jail for not carrying out your duties that you are employed for." said a new voice John recognised that came into the conversation.

"Hello Bruce! Glad you're here to sort out what Happy and Jim have told me." John said swiftly as he nodded to Larter who sat next to him.

"The only thing you can look forward to is being the first one to try out these ideas. If they go wrong, then you get the fault.

If all is well then the company gets all the glory, and you just might be lucky enough to get a few extra quid onto your voyage pay." Day said knowingly, as he related a similar incidence that happened to him whilst he too was a lowly 4th engineer.

"Which brings me to the point of why I came looking for you John. You're being transferred off the *Brooklea* and onto the SFD2 for a temporary loan period. Once you've completed your stint, you'll be rejoining the *Brooklea* to finish your contract." Larter stated.

"Yes, I've heard that too. It seems that you'll be sailing on the SFD2 that's been assigned to the Falkland Islands, where hopefully the *Brooklea* will follow you down once she's been repaired and re-converted." Day revealed.

"How long will that take then Happy?"

"The last time a vessel of that size was taken under tow for that distance, it took a couple of decent ocean-going tug about forty five days. Mind you, there have been at least three refuelling stops for the tugs." Gregson volunteered, and agreed upon with nods from Day and Larter.

"Remember you're sailing against the wind and tide half the time, and don't forget to pay respects to King Neptune on your way down." Larter teased.

"Yes! And by the way, in case you didn't know. The water goes round anti clockwise down under in the Southern hemisphere. So you'll have to make sure all your bolts are fastened the other way round or they'll undo in the water." Day quipped, as he caught onto Larter's wind up.

John looked at his friends, not knowing whether to believe them or not, but laughed it off and reminded Larter of his attempted wind up about the Sargasso Sea. All of which made the men chuckle and smile, and for John to realise that this is what the name 'SHIPMATES' was all about.

"Joking apart John. You'll have your official orders in the post and will be invited to join me in attending

Trewarthy's pre-voyage briefing." Gregson stated.

Larter nodded slowly and pointed to himself, indicating that he too would be coming along.

"What's happening to the *Brook*, Happy? It appears you're still in charge there." John asked an expressionless Day.

"She's being re-converted back to her days as a fast supply and support vessel. As you know, Trewarthy got promoted and is being replaced by Captain Macintosh off the *Waterlea*. The thing is John, you've got to learn and handle all the onboard machinery of the SFD2, which is where Jim comes in. Any problems, or points of view, then you see him not me."

This seemed to be the closing statement between the friends, so they got up and made their way out of the canteen.

"You mentioned that you're going as well, Bruce. On the SFD2 or what?"

"I've been promoted too John, and will be taking charge of the radio watch for the SFD convoy. But I'll be on board one of the big ocean-going tugs, probably the *Cossack* or the *Nubian;* with a Signalman on each SFD to relay messages to and from us. Anyway, you'll soon see when the pre-voyage briefing comes up in about two weeks time.

In case I don't see you, take care John!" Larter concluded as he held out his hand and shook Johns in farewell.

"See you then, Bruce. If you see Andy Sinclair on

your travels, tell him I said hello. Bye for now." John replied, and both men went their own separate ways.

The next ten days passed quickly for John, as he was taken around the SFD and instructed on how to operate and repair the multitude of machinery it needed to function as a floating dry dock.

During that period, John was particularly upset when he witnessed the transformation of the SFD just as his drawings and sketches portrayed, except for certain details that were vital in his own drawings but found to be missing, at least as far as his own drawings were concerned.

These differences he showed and explained to chief Day and Gregson, who agreed with the logic behind them, but advised that all three of them should keep a lid on them until the time was ripe.

That moment came during the pre-voyage briefing in the lecture room when John finally identified whom his fellow crew-members were to be.

As this meeting was of significant importance, there were several Board members present, including the three lords, who were taking a back seat in the proceedings but voicing opinions as and when they felt it was needed.

It was during the question and answering session that John played his trump card showing that it was in fact he, not Cresswell and Trewarthy who invented the 'SUPER BARGE'.

"4th Engineer Grey. What is your question?" Cresswell asked gruffly.

John produced a large folder containing several drawings giving all the relevant technical details that were suitable to them.

"If your lordships' permit, I have a set of diagrams here, that includes their specifications with regard to the SFD. More to the point, they're for the SFD's temporary conversion to a so-called 'Super Barge'.

"As you know, the blueprints for it came late in its production even though the vessel was almost complete in its construction; these drawings are copies of the ones the Commodore took from me about two weeks ago.

"For you to understand what my concerns area. Although the drawings you have in your hand look similar to the current blue prints, mine represents the true picture of what is required drawn some several days before these blueprints were commissioned." John said, taking several minutes to complete his theory.

The prolonged silence was deafening and lasted for several agonising minutes, as Trewarthy and Cresswell struggled to find an answer.

"Well come on then Commodore! Surely you can answer these possibilities posed by a lowly 4th Engineer." Invergarron snapped.

"But there's nothing to answer to. The vessel is longer than the Atlantic sea swell distance, such problems are unlikely to occur." Cresswell snarled.

"Your answer is not acceptable. I will not loose a multi-million pound project on that type of response." Belverley retorted.

"Can you give us a real answer or not?"

Trewarthy and Cresswell looked at each other quickly.

"It appears that we have a joker in our midst, aren't you Grey." Cresswell spouted, as if to bluff his way out of this predicament.

Gregson stood up and demanded that John be given an answer, which prompted the rest of the audience to do the same, starting a slow but pronounced hand clap, until Belverley stood up and quietened them all down.

"It appears that you posed a question which our Chief Engineer is not familiar with, nor can he understand what you are asking, Engineer Grey. Unless you have something we do not know about, which is highly unlikely, then it must be for you to offer us a solution and an answer."

John resumed his monologue by stating:

"I refuse to sail on that vessel, and any others of its construction, on the grounds that it is mechanically unsafe and dare I say un-seaworthy, unlikely to remain afloat past the harbour wall. Should the Lloyds' Shipping Registry get hold of its current seaworthiness on the basis of your drawings and not mine, then the new consortium's future would be short lived."

"That is definitely a bold and brash statement coming from such a Junior Engineer. But from what we can gather from your drawings, I take it that they constitute an improvement or a modification to the original ones, you really must convince us you are right." Belverley said impassively, but looked questioningly towards the other gentlemen of the board.

John spoke of his deep concern, and the differences between the two sets of diagrams, even giving several examples of past events to emphasise his theories, before Belverley finally called a halt to his lengthy monologue.

"It appears yet again that we have someone in our midst, who has the gall to stand against the status quo rather than just do his duty." Belverley commenced.

Then went on to question the validity of the blueprint drawings, and with other pertinent questions had both Trewarthy and Cresswell squirming in their seats , and through lack of knowledge or the where-with-all, unable to answer their tormentors.

The carefully stage-managed meeting ended up in such a furore, that the room had to be cleared by the local constabulary to prevent an ugly scene turning into a full-blown riot.

"Everything I said was engineering logic, Jim." John said as he was hustled out of the lecture room along with his two colleagues.

"Yes John. The trouble is that what you proved was too much for the management to swallow, and by doing so, means that somebody somewhere is in for the high jump for allowing someone like you to prove them wrong." Gregson muttered, and the three men eased themselves quietly out through a side door thus preventing being caught up in the melee.

"John, you're an utter and complete bloody fool! Why didn't you hold your tongue and keep quiet. You've got the whole bloody group on your back now, let alone Cresswell and Company. Neither the Barbados nor Bermuda affair will save you this time, so you'd better start eating humble pie or whatever it takes to gratify their lordships. You've managed to rub them up the wrong way, despite us telling you about the copyright laws and company perks over employees." Day said angrily.

"But at least what I tried to prove was logical and within the Apprenticeship College tutelage. My maths may not have been spot on, nor my drawings to exact measurements, but at least they were more to the mark than the others on the blueprints!" John protested loudly.

"Look here John, for crying out loud. You are only a mere 4th Engineer. You are not paid to think beyond your remit of a 4th. So for God's sake, just act like one and be thankful you have others above you to do your thinking for you such as us Chief Engineers, and that's exactly what we're here for." Gregson said, as his angry looks backed his statement.

John felt as if he was being betrayed by his superiors, and could not understand why there was such politics or back-biting amongst the engineering fraternity as he had just experienced.

"My original statement stands, Chief. If what you're telling me is correct, then if I was in a position to save lives or company property, it seems that I'm damned if I do make a decision be it right or wrong, and also equally damned if I don't make one." John said angrily, towards his senior colleagues.

"Now you're learning John. That's exactly how it is, and it's called Sod's Law! From now on just take your time and use the system as we have been doing. But for God's sake, use the Engineers Bible as your good book and your guide, that way you won't go wrong.

"Anything outside that, then you're out on a limb waiting for the Hangman's noose, to be strung up from the nearest yardarm.

"Do us all a favour, and promise me you'll do what we've just said. If not then we'll not be able to help you any further. Do you understand?" Day retorted

This was John's first real admonition from not one, but two of his Chief Engineers cum friends. Which made him feel a mixture of emotions, both sad at the thought of losing their valuable support, and glad at the thought that at least he was getting real hands on experiences of Officer-ship just like his favourite Tutor from the Engineering college had warned him about.

Before any of them was able to say another word, Lord Invergarron and Belverley appeared in their midst, and demanded an apology for the furore John had created.

Day and Gregson looked at John appealingly with

their eyes, and turned to yield to the Lords wishes, offering their own humble apologies for the debacle created in the lecture room.

"I hear nothing from you Grey, you do not follow your superiors lead. We demand an apology, especially from you, and we want it now without quibble. You are proving to be as such, that we can sack you in a way that you'll never be able to sail on any ship afloat." Belverley snorted.

"I have nothing to apologise for Mr Belverley. I spoke the truth and stand by my observations." John said truculently.

"Very well Grey. It forces us to dictate that you will be made to sail on the SFD2 as ordered, but you will be the only engineer on it. Any mechanical breakdown or loss of company property because of it will be entirely down to you. Do you understand?" Invergarron said menacingly.

"I will be glad to sail on that craft providing you allow me to make certain alterations to its present construction, and prior to its undocking next week." John said evenly and without looking at his protagonists.

"You sir, are either a total fool and may be proven to be as thick as two short planks, or a madcap genius. Either way, we'll bring you to heel, make no bones about that." Belverley threatened, then added:

"You've got three days to do what you think is necessary, but that vessel will undergo its trials before she sails for the Falklands on the day allocated."

Gregson and Day sucked in their breath at the enormity of the task to be done in such a short time and by someone seemingly ill equipped to do so.

"The *Brooklea* will be ready to sail and hopefully meet up with the SFD prior to her arrival in Port Stanley. If any problems are encountered on the SFD's we can assist, therefore fulfilling our role as a ship support and supply vessel" Day said calmly as if to offer some mitigation towards John.

"That is a very good idea Chief Day!" Belverley said abruptly.

"See Grey! That is what it takes to be a Chief. Lots of diplomacy and plenty of gumption. Look listen and learn from your superiors and may be you might get somewhere." Invergarron agreed.

John said nothing, but turned on his heel and left the two lords with their mouths agape at his sudden departure.

'*It appears that kowtow-ing and mutual ego massages are the only way to succeed in this mans outfit. And here's me thinking that it was all down to just being bloody good at your job.*' John conceded to his inner self, as he left the building to prepare his newly acquired responsibility.

CHAPTER XXI
Non-Stop

The SFD2 rode the choppy Irish Sea with ease, as John watched the two big tugs pulling their charge along some several hundred yards ahead of him. To him it was the final testing area before they met the deeper and much more unpredictable open waters of the Atlantic Ocean.

He was glad to be able to watch and gauge the reactions of his craft in comparison to the behavioural character of the other SFDs that was to accompany them on their long voyage to the other end of the world.

'Apart from a possible cargo shift to prevent an uneven trim, we should be okay. That is of course, unless we hit something dangerous to shipping, or have another vessel ram us. But then that's the sailors pigeon not mine.' John reflected as he wrote some observational notes into his sea diary.

The craft settled into a slow corkscrew motion as it rode the now much bigger waves the Atlantic was creating in their path, which was good news to John, as his decision to add the extra ballast tanks all around the vessel became more apparent in their usefulness.

The temporary Bridge and Accommodation superstructure he devised suspended between the two flanks of the dock were solid, and provided a good safe haven for the small crew of volunteers on board.

Under that were the criss-crossed wires, which

suspended the heavy tarpaulins that spanned over the dock to keep off the sea spray and rain, thus, keeping the cargo relatively dry and safe. The craft looked like a true super barge, as it carried several thousand tons of its own equipment, harbour tugs and other craft that would be needed at their destination port.

His only worry was that the construction of the front V section that constituted its false bow seemed too flimsy for his peace of mind as it had not been altered or strengthened as he had requested.

On the third day out, his worry started to become a reality when he was doing his dock bottom inspection along with the vessel's Captain, Tomlinson.

"Captain, it appears that unless we create a lattice work of scaffolding or support struts to shore up this bulkhead, it would be just like a dam bursting, and nothing will stop the force of water sweeping the deck clear of all small craft and other loose cargo we have." John stated calmly, but full of trepidation as to what this new officer might throw back at him.

"How thick is this bow plating 4th?"

"I recommended at least a full inch, but it's more likely a third of that."

"In that case, if we use some of the dockside crane rail lines, and weld them onto the bulkhead as ribbing; then we can use some of the spare decking plates welded on to create a kind of double hull. If necessary, we can also support that again by winching one of the tugs to nestle at the bottom of the 'vee' as extra security. Mind you, what we do with the rear one is anybody's guess." Tomlinson suggested.

John looked at Tomlinson for a moment, then made some quick calculations of his own before he spoke:

"That sounds feasible to me Captain, but I'm not sure on the shift of cargo. My air compressors are running non-stop to maintain the trim for the air cushion under the vessel, as it is. I have insufficient welding equipment to do the job, not enough even to burn or cut the metal back off again when we arrive in Port Stanley."

"That's not a problem 4th. The tugs will be refuelled in Gibraltar whilst we lay off. But we'll be getting our mail and other supplies during that time, so let me know what you need and I'll get a signal off for it to be delivered at the same time."

"Off Gib? Does that mean we are on a non-stop voyage? How long will that take us?"

"Fortunately for you Grey, these things don't concern you. But seeing as you've asked, yes.

All the tugs will refuel again down at the Ascension Islands and bring our provisions to us then. It should take about forty days at this rate. There is one thing that I'm glad you agree with me on, and that is the crucial re-enforcement of that dodgy looking bow. Whoever designed it should be shot."

John bit his lip and remained silent at Tomlinson's last statement, then concluded the brief conversation by informing Tomlinson that he needed to complete his own part of the inspection and see that his Stokers were all right, and left Tomlinson to do his.

'Just like the Brook and her bows, only we are on a non-stop voyage this time.' John reflected, as he made his way up into the temporary bridge and accommodation platform.

Apart from the four tugboat crew-members who stayed on board their own separate little vessels, which were lashed to the dock bottom, the rest of the twelve men on board the SFD were only volunteers, except for John as its Engineer, and Tomlinson its Captain.

Also from having a separate cabin, which the two officers shared, the rest of the crew were put into one big room, with the galley in between them. The heads (toilets) and bathroom was a short walk across the open gantry towards one side of the SFD.

The stokers kept a watch on the compressor pumps, and John managed to persuade the tugboat engineers to lend a hand keeping a maintenance check on all the other SFD machinery not required until they arrived in the Falklands.

Luxham, the Signalman, was only required to signal the tugs every four hours or in an emergency, using the special telephone cable strung between the leading tug and the dock.

The two cooks and a steward were busy providing all the men with plenty of hot nourishing food and drink.

But it was the sailors, including the tugboat skippers that most of the work fell upon. They had to keep a constant look-out on all four corners of the dock, making sure no other vessel would collide with them, and an eye on the tow ropes to checking they were securely fastened.

Then ensure that the heavy tarpaulin tent over the cargo was not leaking, and the cargo to be lashed securely to prevent cargo shift that might do severe damage to the dock walls. This was a routine that was quickly entered into by the dock crew, so they knew that once they reached south of Gibraltar and the deep swells of the Atlantic, they would be able to handle any reasonable emergency or situation they might encounter.

John found that Tomlinson was not so easy to get along with at the beginning, due to Tomlinson's mood swings, but he managed a professional understanding when it came to the SFD.

"We'll be entering the Straits of Gib tomorrow morning and be laying off for a few hours. That is when we'll have to get that bow seen to." Tomlinson started, then went on to discuss how he wanted it to be done.

"We can use the SFD cranes to lift the rails and sheets of metal whilst my men are welding, but we'll have to remove some of the tarpaulin sheeting to provide ventilation for them. Judging by the pile of spare decking plates, we have enough for the rear section, but not enough angle iron or whatever, suitable for the ribbing." John observed.

"Ah well Engines! At least we can double the thickness of that section if nothing else. Anyway, as we are pulled through the water at a decent speed, the front section will meet any wave action. Whereas the rear section is only to keep us dry and maintain our buoyancy."

"That will exhaust the stock of welding bottles."

"How many do you need? More to the point, how long will it take your men?"

"I need about fourteen to do both end sections and I've only got nine. I only have two qualified welders and even then they're from the harbour craft cargo. You'd have to ask the Gib Dockyard to send us at least six more if you want both jobs done in time." John replied, then scratched his head and added, "If we're doing all this to our SFD, what are the other crews doing about their SFD's?"

"I don't give a monkeys about the other ones, my concern is this vessel, nothing else, Engines. Just you remember that for any future occasions." Tomlinson replied vehemently.

John was taken by surprise at this sudden outburst.

"Well Captain, at least we'll have dry feet to step ashore with when we finally get to Port Stanley." he replied softly and changed the subject.

"Will there be a launch at Gib to take us ashore? Only this will be my second time of passing it without stepping ashore. I heard it's a rock stuffed with bazaars full of all kinds of rabbits."

"No, Engines. We're to remain on board, ready to receive more stores and the like. There's supposed to be a convoy going due south to Cape Town, with a naval escort keeping them company."

"We're going to Cape Town. What's the occasion for all that then?"

"No, we're not going, they are. There's a squadron of destroyers on their way to the Orient without using the Suez Canal. Although I cannot see why, considering the panic that's caused out there. Something to do with Korea I heard. But then what do I know?" Tomlinson said with a shrug of his shoulders.

"Never mind Captain! We're better off on this tub going at 10knots, than tearing through the water at some 35 knots and towards a load of dynamite that's going to be thrown around." John said stoically, which broke up their impromptu meeting

It was evening time when they arrived off Gibraltar and were met by a boat-load of men and several barges of equipment and stores that was hoisted on board.

"Captain Tomlinson! My name is McPhee. I'm the Dockyard's Superintendent. I have brought your extra welders, but I need to see the job you're about to do. In the meantime I need to speak to your Engineer."

Tomlinson shook the hand of McPhee and turned to John, who was standing behind him.

"This is my Engineer, 4th Engineer Grey." He stated.

McPhee looked over Tomlinson and saw John.

"Engineer Grey off the *Brooklea!*" McPhee said with

delight as he took John's hand and pumped it heartily.

"Pleased to meet you again. It's a small world. How are you!"

"Hello Mr McPhee! We have a similar problem as the *Brooklea,* but on a much larger scale." John greeted as his head rocked with the force of McPhee's handshake.

McPhee turned to Tomlinson and looked into his face.

"I know you too. Why you're Tommy Tomlinson's son Joe! I thought I recognised you. You've filled out somewhat since I seen you last. How are you young man?"

Tomlinson looked nonplussed at this revelation and peered back at the man.

"Your old man 'n me were dockyard mateys out in Singapore before the war. You were the deck hand responsible for sailing some rusty bucket to safety from the NIPS at the time they captured Singapore.

That's it! It was you who managed to reach some island with over two hundred survivors. Shame about your father though." McPhee reminisced for a while before Tomlinson managed to recognise the man, but diplomatically reminded McPhee to the purpose of his visit.

"Well said Captain Joe!" McPhee said with satisfaction and turned to the three men standing behind him as onlookers to this chance meeting of 'old friends'.

"Men, we've got two of the best up and coming officers the Triple Crown or Coronet or whatever they call themselves, will ever produce in my book." McPhee commenced, then went on to apportion job lots to each of them, referring to Tomlinson and John's own strategy from time to time.

"Come Joe, let us have a noggin in your cabin. You too John   Let my men earn their keep for a while. Besides, you've got to get ready to meet the Navy soon, who will be sailing with you."

Tomlinson and John looked at each other, grinned and escorted this dynamo to their cabin.

"This is our humble abode Mr McPhee." John said as they arrived.

"Mr McPhee? Come now, its Fergus from now on. You of all people should have remembered, young Joe." McPhee chided softly, as he looked around at the spartan surroundings.

"Hmm! Just as I suspected! Not a cheer anywhere. Still, I came prepared." McPhee said cheerfully as he pulled out a large bottle of whisky.

"Get the glasses and we'll while away the time afore these starch fronted naval wallahs come marching on board. Which, by my watch." he said as he fished out a fob watch from his waistcoat pocket.

"Will be in about one hour from now, mark my words!" he concluded.

The three men sat drinking from their glasses, talking

mainly about the task in hand but slipping back to mutual experiences, until there was a knock on the door as two immaculately dressed naval officers stepped inside the cabin and saluted.

"Good evening gentlemen! I'm Engineer Lieutenant Commander Richardson, and this is Diving officer Sub Lieutenant Morris."

Tomlinson said as he stood up, donned his cap, returned the salute and introduced the other two with him.

"Come in and find a pew somewhere, gentlemen. As you can see, we're a bit pushed for space. Care for a whisky and soda?" Tomlinson invited.

"Why yes thank you. We've brought some goodies along with us starting with this magnum of champagne. We've got to drink it soon as it doesn't seem to travel very well." Richardson said in a well educated and polished voice.

After a little while, McPhee announced that it was time for him and his men to leave.

"Well gentlemen." he said as he turned to the two RN officers.

"You two naval wallahs are advised to take a lead from Grey and Tomlinson, and keep them in constant touch with any naval ideas that you or your boss might come up with. This is their vessel, so just enjoy the cruise such as it is."

Richardson stiffened at the term 'naval wallahs' but smiled and shook McPhee's hand.

The five men finally filed out of the cabin and made their way over to the ladder leading down to the outside of the dock, where there was a launch tied up and waiting to take McPhee away again. "So long Fergus! Thanks for everything. Hope you've not left anybody behind as it's a long swim back again." Tomlinson called out as McPhee stepped onto the launch, took his cap off and waved it.

"Have a good voyage Joe. Tell John to keep his eye on the starboard saddle tank, and keep it pumped up at all times." McPhee shouted back.

John was standing alongside Tomlinson and heard the advice.

"Thanks Fergus, I'll do just that. See you again some time." John replied

John watched as the powerful launch roared off and skimmed its way over the waves towards the harbour, leaving John with an anti-climax feeling as he turned to the world facing him.

"It looks as if we're in for a rough time Captain, with these navy men breathing down our necks. Where are they going to be billeted for a start?"

"You're right Engines. We'll just have to try and find them sort of billet."

When they got back to their cabin they discovered that the two officers were starting to make themselves at home, re-arranging the cabin to suit themselves.

"Thank you for re arranging my cabin in such naval

fashion gentlemen, but the quarters for you and your men will be on dock bottom, starboard side aft. There are several timber staves and heavy tarpaulins there for your men to make your temporary home. However, in your case, if you go and speak to the tugboat skipper off the *Boxer*, it's the front one in the cradle, he'll offer a billet for you both."

Richardson started to protest but was given short shrift by Tomlinson. "In case you have forgotten your naval protocol, you are on my vessel such as it is. This is a merchant vessel and, I am its Captain. Whilst I'm at it, Engineer Grey is my Chief Engineer who is responsible only to me, as are the volunteer men who make up this vessel's crew. Do I make myself clear?"

Richardson and Morris meekly nodded their heads, grabbed their stuff and left.

"You've not heard the end of this Tomlinson." Richardson retorted.

"It's Captain Tomlinson to you, Richardson. I out rank you, and don't you forget it." Tomlinson snarled as he slammed the cabin door on the two departing men.

John was busy re-assembling the room, acting nonchalantly, pretending he didn't care.

"The bloody cheek of them. Just because they're in the Senior Service they think they can take over and get away with it. Well it ain't happening on my ship."

"Have you seen the size of the convoy Captain?" John asked, to change the subject.

"What a good idea Engines! Lets go out and count the ships shall we?" Tomlinson replied sarcastically, which made John sigh quietly.

"I really did not ask for that remark Captain. I was only pointing out the close proximity of other vessels nearing us judging by all the coloured lights I've seen."

Tomlinson grabbed his binoculars and stormed out of the cabin, saying, "Well Engines, don't just stand there, it was your idea to look at the pretty lights, come with me" he commanded.

Both men crossed the gantry and made their way along the deck to where they found a lookout having a smoke but counting the different ships with different sets of lights showing.

"Look-out? This is the Captain. Get the signalman here, on the double." Tomlinson barked.

"Aye Captain!" the lookout answered swiftly as he flicked his cigarette butt out into the blackness.

Tomlinson scanned the darkness, remarking on the lights he saw through his binoculars, offering John a quick look through them now and again, until Luxham arrived puffing and panting.

"You want to see me Captain?" he gasped.

"Signalman, I want you to find out what ship that is and tell her to stand off." he said as he pointed his finger.

"Also tell the lookouts to be extra vigilant astern of us as the two tugs behind us are getting to get too close.

We're moving a lot quicker now we've got our bow re-enforced, but it doesn't excuse these navy wallahs practicing their night time manoeuvres on us, trying to scare us into the bargain. It would only take some idiot to try and cross between us and our tugs to put us into grave danger."

Luxham flashed his aldis lamp at the offending warship and drew its reply, which he spelt out for the Captain.

'It's the destroyer Zephyr. Sorry old Boy. Dodgy steering ram! Fixed now. Hang on tight! See you in the morning.' Tomlinson thought for a moment and said, "Make to them. Sorry we can't help as we've already got four ducklings on board. Keep my tow nylons straight."

Luxham flashed the reply and told the captain that the ship was increasing speed to get ahead of the convoy.

"I have the convoy signal here for you Captain. I only received it just as you sent for me.

Luxham held out the signal and shone his torch for Tomlinson to read:

'From : Tug 'Cossack'. Convoy Commodore.
To : All Ships.
You are formed into four columns of six tows per column. There will be six warships as escort down to the Ascension Islands. From there, we will be joined by two tankers and two supply ships which will stay with

us as far as Cape Town, where the columns will be split for each destination. Up-dated schedules as necessary. All navigation and hazard lights are to be used at all times. Weather forecast will follow on next schedule'

"Thank you signalman. Put it on the clipboard on my table. As soon as you get the weather report, let me have it. Send the lookout back again".

Luxham acknowledged his orders and left to carry them out.

"It looks as if our naval wallahs have got a tough time ahead of them, Captain. But it's nice to know you've got friends around in case of trouble."

"You're darn right there Engines. I'm whacked now and ready for turning in. But we'd better ensure our guests are settled in before we hit the sack ourselves."

Both men completed their final 'late night' inspection before they managed to reach the solitary comfort of their bunks.

John was first to rise, not through choice, but from being roughly shaken by the steward.

"Engineer Grey. Here's an early morning cuppa for you both. The signalman's got the weather forecast and it looks pretty scary."

"Thanks steward. I'll see the Captain is told."

"Told what, Engines?" Tomlinson whispered hoarsely.

"Morning Captain. The steward's brought us a cuppa and the weather forecast has just arrived."

John was already dressed and drinking his tea when Tomlinson climbed down off his bunk, slipped into his trousers and started to gulp down his tea, before he put his shirt and tie on.

"Looks as if we'll be having a late breakfast again Engines!" Tomlinson said quietly placing his empty mug back onto the table, as the officers heard a loud knock on the door.

Tomlinson invited the person in, who turned out to be Luxham followed closely by Richardson.

"Morning Luxham. Are those the latest signals, and weather report?" Tomlinson asked politely, and asked Richardson to wait, before reading the signals slowly one by one.

After a brief while he looked at the weather report and showed it to John, who read it and handed it back.

"It appears Engines, that our naval guests have special work to do.

Especially whilst we are at the mercy of the imminent storm we are heading towards." Tomlinson announced, as he handed a signal over to Richardson.

"This appears to be addressed to you Richardson, and here's the weather forecast for the next few days, as we pass to the east of the Cape Verde Islands."

Richardson took the signals off Tomlinson and read them carefully, asking if he could see a chart for him to follow, Tomlinson obliged by unfolding one onto the table.

"According to my instructions and our current position,

we'll have just the one crack at it. That is unless we hit more that one storm." Richardson stated.

"Okay then Richardson, we'll talk about it after we've done our rounds and had our breakfast. Incidentally, did you get you and your men sorted out? Only I don't want dissatisfied holiday makers on this cruise." Tomlinson replied with a big smile.

"Yes, we're okay, no complaints so far. Only we've got a lot to prepare in such a short space of time Captain."

"Very well Richardson. You and your men carry on until we come back to you again. But don't start anything before we get there, is that clear?"

"That's fine by me!" Richardson conceded as he left the cabin.

"We've got exactly four hours to prepare this vessel, and whatever Richardson is up to. We have to muster the men to tell them what the score is. Care to join me for the forenoon inspection Engines?" Tomlinson asked, but was in fact was a foregone conclusion.

Both officers completed their inspections, had their breakfast and asked the steward to get the men assembled on the dock bottom.

"Okay men, gather round! That includes you navy wallahs!" Tomlinson shouted over the booming noise of the waves hitting the forward bow, as he went on to explain what he wanted them to do.

There were a few questions from the men, and a few additions made by Richardson, before everybody dispersed to their allocated jobs.

Tomlinson called the two navy officers over to join him and John in their cabin to discuss their own plans in more detail.

"What you have to appreciate Richardson, is this is a twin hulled vessel that has only got an eighteen foot beam each, that stands sixty feet above water level, and that's joined together with a deck only a few feet thick but over a hundred foot wide.

"The mean draught of the twin hulls is only twelve feet and the main deck has only got about four feet free board. In normal circumstances, as the deck was open to sea, it would give a much more stable craft to tow, but must sail empty as the waves would wash right over the dock bottom.

"In our case, we're loaded up with supplies, hence our specially constructed 'V' sections forward and aft, to make it an experimental super barge cum floating dock. Yet you want us to trim the dock down a further twenty feet. Do you know how high some of these waves can get. Do you?"

Richardson shook his head, but went on to explain the value of the experiments in view of what these SFD's were really needed for.

"I don't care if the King wants to know, I'm not jeopardising my vessel, let alone the souls on board just for idle curiosity. The average wave can reach a good forty to fifty feet, and some rogue waves much bigger than that. If we trimmed down to the forty- foot free board from the top of the hulls, and those waves start washing over us, we'd sink. This craft is loaded with over 5,000 tons of cargo, which this vessel normally would lift anyway.

"But that is only when it is stable and still, not floating around the oceans like this." Tomlinson said angrily.

"Maybe if you'd consider the same experiment whilst the SFD is in harbour, Richardson. That way if anything should happen, it would only sink to a known depth of feet of approx sixty feet as opposed to some 30,000 feet and no way back." John suggested.

"The whole point of the experiment is for the benefit of Morris and his divers. They need to be able to repair or cut ships hulls open in much rougher conditions than when moored in a harbour. That way, if the vessel sank, the divers would not be trapped underneath it." Richardson admitted, then added.

"This is an ideal craft to be able to carry out these trials. Anyway, I have my Admiralty orders to do so, and it's for you to comply."

"What I don't understand is, why can't you do these experiments on the Mulberrys being towed behind us, Richardson? I mean, they're meant to be purposefully sunk into a permanent position, whereas these are supposed to float back up again giving a piggy back to some ship or another." John asked with a shake of his head.

Tomlinson asked Richardson to show him the orders and instructions that were issued. "It appears Richardson, that according to your instructions, Engines here could be right, and that all you have to do is transfer yourself over to one of the Mulberrys to comply with your orders.

"Other than that, as Captain of this vessel, I will over-rule your orders as it would place my vessel into unwarranted or unnecessary danger or jeopardy." Tomlinson concluded, as Richardson started to stammer and protest.

"There is no accommodation or anything on those Mulberry's, and anyway we can't get to them without a launch to take us there." Morris protested in unison.

"I will compromise with you Richardson. If one of my 'V' sections starts to come apart, then you'll have my permission, and my blessings to go and repair it.

Think of it as a bit like the little Dutch boy and the dyke maybe, but there you have it." Tomlinson offered, as John nodded his head in total agreement.

"Oh very well then Captain. The first sign of a crack or a hole then we take over." Richardson conceded, as he picked up his cap and left the cabin with Morris at his heels.

"It appears that you and me think on the same wave-length. Me with seamanship, and you with obvious damage control and engineering skills." Tomlinson acknowledged with a grin.

The storm hit them with a vengeance and rocked the vessel like a see-saw as the waves made loud booming noises on the front 'V' section and along the side hulls of the dock as if to try and smash their way through a flimsy man made object.

All eyes and binoculars were scanning the bow for the slightest hint of a hole. All except John, who was busy with his stokers keeping a constant watch on the compressors and the saddle ballast-tanks. He saw a small column of water come out of the starboard one which meant that it had sprung a leak and needed patching up. Time to tell the Captain, and maybe get Morris and his merry men to work.

"Captain. Our mother tugs have reported that they have lengthened their cables and slowed right down. They have asked if everything is all right." Luxham said to Tomlinson as he handed the signal over to him.

"Make to him. Bobbing along. Bows holding nicely."

"Aye Captain.' Luxham said as he finished writing down the reply and left.

"Captain, we've sprung a leak on the starboard saddle tank. Maybe we can get these gung- ho navy divers over the side to fix it." John announced as he re-entered the cabin

Tomlinson leaned over the chart table, looked over the drawings of his vessel and stroked his chin.

"According to your drawings, you've got a main air chamber with smaller ones inside that. So if one is punctured then it's only that one and not the entire tank, is that right?"

"Yes. I've done that with all the ballast tanks and even got a spare set below the top ones. But we need all the air we can get as the air cushion under us gets depleted every time we're caught between each trough." John said slowly as he traced over the drawings with his finger.

Tomlinson looked out the cabin window for little while then shouted into the galley for someone to send for the signalman.

"You sent for me Captain?" Luxham asked in puzzlement.

"Ah signalman. Have you sent that signal yet? Only I need to speak to the mother tug, urgently."

"No Captain. The phone line is dead, and I'm trying to flash him up with my Aldis[††]." Luxham admitted.

"The line is dead! How long has this been?" Tomlinson asked angrily.

"Why wasn't I told of this?"

"Just as I went to send your signal off Captain." Luxham replied defensively.

"Why can't we use one of the ducklings radios to speak to the mother tug." John suggested.

"There you are Signalman. If it takes an engineer to tell you, why didn't you think of it?"

"I'm not trained in radio, only visual Captain." Luxham stated: "You don't have to be. The harbour tugs are fitted with a voice radio." Tomlinson retorted.

"Get below and get it sorted. Ask those two naval

[††] An Aldis is a signal lamp and used as a visual communications aid.

officers to come and see me, then report back when you've done that."

"Aye Captain." Luxham mumbled and raced out of the cabin.

"Now we can put the cheer back into our navy wallahs John! Kindly get those officers for me!"

John looked at Tomlinson for a brief moment, realising that at last there was a chink showing through Tomlinson's armour, for him to offer a first name back again.

"On my way Joe. But wait until I get back before you signal the mother tug, if you would."

John explained briefly to the two naval officers what they were needed for, which seemed to brighten their otherwise glum faces.

"Here we are gentlemen! We've an opportunity that's presented itself for you and your men. Mind you, it will be pretty dangerous stuff." Tomlinson stated, as the four officers made themselves relatively comfortable on John's bunk that served as a settee.

They went through all the snags and complications that could be thought of, and eventually agreed on the best plan they could design.

Luxham came in during the meeting, telling Tomlinson that a radio link was now made and for him to use it. This made a natural interlude for the meeting until Tomlinson came back with his news.

"The mother tugs will tow us at an angle so that the

starboard side will be on the lee. The sea swell is still pretty high, and it means that each man over the side will have to wear double safety harnesses and life jackets. The men and the equipment would be lowered or raised by the dock cranes and other hoists, so all they had to do is cut and weld."

"We can get the men to check the rest of the ballast tanks on both sides, once the repair is done." Morris added enthusiastically.

Tomlinson went back to speak to the tug as the others got prepared to do their own thing.

The divers worked hard and furiously at the same time being totally immersed in water for what seemed hours, until they signalled that they could be hoisted back up onto the deck again.

"We discovered a slit in that tank that was larger than we thought. Also one of the internal chambers was ruptured and leaking, so we had to open the main one to fix the inner one. We've sealed the chambers now and are ready for the rest of the inspection." Morris said calmly as he took off his divers face-mask.

"But we've used up too many oxygen bottles and won't be able to do much more."

"We can always use a reducer valve on one of our smaller compressors to recharge your bottles, what do you say Richardson?" John prompted.

"That could work, only we'd have to filter the air otherwise the men would have their lungs contaminated

with God knows what. Yes, lets give it a try."
Richardson agreed.

The divers were given hot drinks to warm
themselves up again, whilst the bottles were re-charged
and tested before they commenced their laborious and
dangerous work.

"Right men. Over the side and use your magnetic
clamps in case you get swept away. Take notice of the
swell, we don't want any of you attempting to swim
back to Blighty." Richardson joked as the men
swarmed down the ladders and onto the tanks.

"Joe, it looks as we've got nosey neighbours!" John
shouted over the howling winds.

The four officers looked up in time to see a destroyer
coming close, with several men on the open bridge of
the destroyer watching them through binoculars.

Luxham was called to answer the flashing aldis from
the destroyer as it slowly passed them.

"From the *Zambesi.* If you're short on soap, let me
know." Luxham said as he read out the signal to
Tomlinson.

"Friends from Atlantis arriving to prepare for
Neptune's visit."

Luxham sent his message, which ended the brief
meeting between the two ships.

The divers completed their exhaustive inspection and
gave their report to Richardson, who in turn, reported it
to John and Tomlinson.

"We've had a full day going the wrong way for you

Richardson. We hope that now you and Morris are satisfied, at least partly anyway. Maybe we can get back on course again."

"Yes Captain. It is better than nothing. You'll be interested to know that the new welding equipment the men were using, are special ones designed to operate in these adverse conditions and for future use on submarine rescues." Richardson said with satisfaction.

"Who designed them? " John asked politely.

"I did. And I've even got a new type of jet nozzle patented for it." Richardson said modestly.

"Maybe you'd let me have a look at one of them before you leave. It seems pretty impressive. I'm partial to innovations too. This experimental craft and its saddle tanks for instance." John revealed, and left to see to his machinery.

The storm blew itself out after three miserable days for the entire crew, who were getting more short-tempered as each hour passed. As the storm vanished so did their tempers.

The convoy was now in calmer and warmer waters as they neared the magical and psychological barrier of the equator.

The men knew that during the time they were in that part of the world, they could enjoy warmth instead of the freezing weather up in the northern waters before re-entering the equally freezing cold southern waters of the Antarctic Ocean.

It also meant that the oppressive tarpaulin canopy could be rolled up to let the sunlight onto the dock bottom. Soon little games of football or cricket were organised between the different groups of men.

It did not matter what it was, as everybody joined in and took it all in good fun.

The day for the old age tradition of 'CROSSING THE LINE' ceremony at the equator, was upon them. Where all landlubbers who had not done so before, had to meet King Neptune and pay their respects to him and his followers. It was a day for jollity, partying and yet one more good excuse, not only for the men to let off steam but to have a few glasses of the alcoholic stuff. Nobody was excused except those who have already partaken in Neptune's hospitality.

Tomlinson was dressed in a false beard, loin cloth, and a dummy trident as Neptune, with two large hairy chested men, dressed up in pretend grass skirts, false bosoms, hooped earrings, and gaudy colours painted onto their faces pretending to be pretty mermaids.

John and the two naval officers along with other men, were duly found guilty of being landlubbers who had perpetrated fiendish and heinous trumped up charges and who dared to sail into King Neptune's waters without his permission. The penalty was to be covered in foam, "shaved" with a giant cardboard razor, dunked into a makeshift swimming pool and made to drink a glass of the most foulest of concoctions the cook could dream up. All washed down with a large flagon of ale just to make it more palatable. Much to the delight of the onlookers who already had their turn.

The days were longer and the vast ocean seemed almost like a mill-pond, as the two mother tugs pulled them along.

This was also the time for the naval officers and their divers to do more experiments, without being washed off the ballast tanks.

In all, the men enjoyed ten days of peace and quiet before the convoy met up with the supply ships at its next supply rendezvous at the Ascension Islands. These are a group of warm, but breezy islands, about 10 degrees below the equator. Slap bang in the middle of the top end of the South Atlantic Ocean, and almost 3,000 miles from the nearest continent.

They were colonised by British settlers during the mid 16th Century and governed by the Mandarins of Whitehall. Due to their location, they are the first or last chance for ships to refuel before continuing long Trans Atlantic voyages.

This is where the rendezvous for the convoy was to take place, and several ships converged on each other throughout the day.

The stores and mail was winched on board off the supply ship, as the mother tugs sucked at the tankers fuel pipes to quench their thirst.

"Look at that Joe. It looks as if two columns have lost an SFD each. That explains why there's four tugs missing. I wonder what happened there." John observed.

"According to this signal here John, during the storm the convoy was spread out to some fifty square miles. The tugs had to rescue the crews of the two sunken vessels and take them back to Gib that is why they're missing. It says that the forward bows just caved in like a dam and swept all the cargo away through the stern section.

"It also states that all of the other converted SFDs have had their bows severely damaged and have been leaking like a sieve. The convoy has to remain here until they have all been repaired and made seaworthy again." Tomlinson narrated the lengthy report then handed it to John.

"I was right after all! Now the shit will really hit the proverbial fan for Trewarthy and Cresswell. But then according to them, what do I Know? I'm only a 4thrate engineer after all." John muttered quietly to himself, with a feeling of vindication on what had transpired in Belfast.

"It seems like we've got the Commodore coming to pay us a visit. He'll be coming over from the supply vessel by launch. It will take off our navy wallahs when it leaves again. Pity because I was getting to like those officers."

"Yes, me too. Those divers have shown me a few things that I know could be useful one day. What do you suppose the convoy Commodore wants with us?"

"Probably want to know how we look in such good shape compared with the other SFD's, John. We'll soon know, because his launch has just left the supply vessel." Tomlinson said as he removed his glasses and gave them to John to look with.

"Do you see the taller of the two men. Well that's everybody's friend Trewarthy and the other is our Fergus McPhee. Not much we can tell those two, as they're all seeing all knowing with eyes that can see through solid steel."

John gave a little groan at the prospects of meeting Trewarthy again, which Tomlinson heard.

"You and me both John." he whispered as they were joined by Richardson and Morris.

"Thank you for the cruise Captain! Remind me to recommend I go first class next time. We've been ordered to join the Ceylon convoy until we complete all the navy wants of us." Richardson announced.

"Yes, you have worked well during the last ten days, shame about the sinking of sister craft. " John replied.

"Two sunk! How?" Morris asked open mouthed.

"They didn't have their bows reinforced nor have the extra ballast tanks that we've got." Tomlinson growled, but added on a more civil note.

"Besides, we had the Royal Navy on board to keep us safe."

"Yes, it was certainly a good inter service experience for me" John added.

"Well gentlemen. If you want a return voyage just

call our number anytime. When you get on the other SFD, have a look at it and remember what this one was like. I feel sure you'll be able to modify it somewhat if only to ensure your survival to Ceylon."

"Thanks for the tip Captain. See you Engines! Must get the men and all the gear ready for the transfer. Goodbye gentlemen." Richardson said politely, as he and Morris saluted and left.

Trewarthy and McPhee walked along the dock bottom, stopping to observe various items that caught their attention, then made their way up the steep ladder onto the starboard hull gantry where Tomlinson and John were there to meet them.

John took a deep breath and waited for McPhee and saluted Trewarthy, who gave a brief salute back.

"Captain Tomlinson, Engineer Grey. No wonder your vessel is in good shape. Your vessel has, shall we say, certain modifications that depart from the existing blueprints. Need I ask who was responsible, or was it a joint effort?" Trewarthy said with surprising civility.

"You see Trewarthy, it was just as I described. Pity the others weren't adapted. Now we've got a hefty repair bill and whatnot to contend with." McPhee said bumptiously, before he greeted the two officers politely.

"Come into the cabin gentlemen." Tomlinson invited with a wave of his hand.

"To what do we owe the pleasure of your visit Commodore? I feel that what you're about to say is more than just chit chat, after having come all this way." Tomlinson asked fearlessly.

"As it happens Captain, I've seen all that I need to know, except for the plans you used to adapt the vessel with." Trewarthy continued in a civil manner.

"Plans? Drawings? We've none of them, only the set we were issued with before undocking in Belfast." Tomlinson lied, which made John prick his ears up and prepare for his own defence. He did not like lying but decided that if needs must, then so be it.

"That's a pity Captain, because I was hoping to have them duplicated so that the consortium could make them legal and used to adapt the other poor unfortunate SFD's in this convoy." Trewarthy said and turned to John.

"All this was probably at your instigation Grey. Haven't you got any notes or improvised drawings I could look at? Pity to waste all this good work don't you think Mr McPhee?"

"As a matter of fact, I did have a drawing, but it somehow got blown out of my hands when I was on deck during the storm. That was why I had to enlist the services of the two naval officers that we had on board." John said convincingly, which made Trewarthy scowl, but just nodded in response.

"It seems to me Commodore, that all we've got to do is get one of my Scribes over from the supply tanker, to make as many drawings as you wish. We'll be here for a few days anyway, so you might as well have a good

look now and start copying the work in the meantime."
McPhee said appeasingly.

"That's not a bad idea McPhee. Anyway, its about
time these two officers showed some hospitality and
offered us a cool drink. Preferably a large scotch and
soda." Trewarthy said with a smile as if to dismiss the
subject.

McPhee pulled out a large bottle of whisky and
planked it on the table.

"There you are gentlemen, compliments from the
Gibraltar Dockyard. Now where is the soda?"

The frosty atmosphere created by Trewarthy's
inquisition got spirited away as the spirit in the bottle
disappeared, but John knew he still had to keep up his
pretence in case Trewarthy beguiled the truth out of him.

It was a knock on the door from Luxham that
brought the session to an abrupt halt.

"Captain. We've got a signal from one of our
mother tugs, the *Cossack*. It seems that both of them
will be taking in and recovering their towing gear. The
two replacement tugs, *Eskimo* and *Tartar* will take us
for our final leg south. She has a spare radio to give us,
before she leaves."

"Radio? What do you want with that?" Trewarthy
said, full of surprise.

"Our phone cable snapped during the storm, and
we've been using the *Boxer's* radio to communicate
between us." Tomlinson replied as he left the cabin
momentarily.

"Now that is also a good idea, don't you think Commodore? It means that apart from an engine, this is a true vessel that can weather any storm now and still keep in touch with the world." Mc Phee chuckled, much to Trewarthys wry amusement.

"Yes. I've got to yield to ingenuity McPhee, and these two officers are full of it I must admit."

"That's the ticket! Anyway, its time we made a move and let these officers get on with their duties."

"Leaving so soon gentlemen?" Tomlinson asked courteously, as he re -entered the cabin.

"We've a lot of work to organise, so we'll let you two get on with your duties but I need to see your log book tomorrow before you sail." Trewarthy replied.

"I'll need to come with you, but from what I've seen so far I'm satisfied with it for the moment" Mc Phee stated with a sly wink aimed at the two officers.

The cabin was in silence for a moment as both men sat reflecting on that verbal exchange.

"It looks as if we've got away with it Joe. I mentioned the plans being blown away, because that's what Trewarthy claimed happened to my promotion board recommendation." John smiled, and took another sip of his unfinished drink.

"He doesn't remember me too well. He did the dirty on me too, a while back and it's thanks to Fergus who managed to uncover his scam. This is the first opportunity or time I can get even with him, but I'm glad you backed me up the way you did. So it means that we are now partners in crime John." Tomlinson admitted and raised his glass as a toast to them both.

"Here's to Fergus McPhee."

The night was warm and the sea calm, as the different crews of the battered convoy worked hard to get their vessels repaired and ready to be re-assembled into their columns again in the morning light.

John was making his usual morning inspection when a sailor called him to meet the Captain on the starboard gangway.

"Morning Captain, what a fine morning again." John breezed as he met up with Tomlinson.

"Morning Engines! Yes, we're about to be hitched up to our new tugs and placed as leader in the column again. I've asked you to see me because Trewarthy and Fergus are due over soon, and I want to know what we're going to do with those drawings of yours."

"That's a point." John said as he gazed over towards the rapidly approaching launch.

"Trewarthy wants to see your logbook that's our diversion. When he's doing that, I'll take Fergus down to the dock bottom and show him some fictitious engineering problem I've found, then slip him my drawings and any other items you might have for him."

"Right, let's get our stuff together. I've got a few things I want Fergus to look after until we get back. I've already drafted a letter to him with instructions concerning our documents, and everything is sealed in a mailbag for him. I'll let you read my copy later, so not to worry John." Tomlinson said as both men made their way quickly back to their cabin.

"I've got the drawings and your bag. Is there anything else such as a spare logbook, or something? Only Trewarthy seems to have a habit of altering things to suit his own ends." John asked.

"Yes, here's my diary, put it with yours, but tell Fergus it's amongst your stuff."

"I'll stow them somewhere on the way out Joe, but we'd better get back to the gangway again in time to meet them." John responded as both men looked at each other and nodded at their secretive plan.

"Morning Commodore, Mr McPhee. Looks like a good day for the regatta!" Tomlinson quipped, as he greeted his visitors.

"Morning Captain, Grey! I've come to see your logbook, among other things. Engineer Grey! The Captain and I will be busy for a while, may I suggest that you conduct Mr McPhee, and his scribe here around the vessel during that time." Trewarthy said gruffly.

"Come this way Mr McPhee." John invited as he indicated that they were to descend the steep ladders towards the dock bottom.

Once the three men arrived the scribe opened his drawing book and commenced to sketch his surroundings.

"We'll let the scribe do his work Fergus, as I've got a

particular engineering problem I wish to show you. So of you care to come over to the cradle that the floating crane is lashed to, we can start from there." John nodded and gave McPhee a meaningful look.

"What a good idea John." McPhee said but turned to the scribe and pointed towards one of the cradled tugs.

"See how they have solved the problem of piggy-backing smaller cargoes Mr Jones. You start on that first and make your way around the rest of the dock bottom."

"Very well Mr McPhee, the hull won't take me long anyway." was the reply from the departing scribe.

When John felt they were quite alone and out of sight he held out the mailbag to McPhee.

"We are putting our trust in your hands Fergus. Here's my full set of drawings that I don't want Trewarthy nor his henchman Cresswell to get hold of, as the original drawings were taken from me by the both of them. But they don't show the modifications I have made. Nor does it show the items Joe Tomlinson had suggested we do.

He has a letter in the mailbag for you, and I've got his diary in amongst my stuff." John whispered as he handed all his papers over.

"I was wondering about you two. I had a sneaky feeling that you were up to something, and I fear so does Trewarthy. That's why he wants to see Joe's logbook."

"Well he won't find anything worth bothering about

in there, as it's all in his diary and on my drawings. All we're asking you to do is keep them safe until we get back to Gib or Belfast again.

In the meantime you know what to do. The other thing is this. Trewarthy is hoping that your scribe can provide the modifications from the drawings he's making, which makes our efforts a waste of time."

"The crafty devil!" McPhee exclaimed as he realised what John had just said was obvious.

"I'll get Mr Jones to use his artistic impressions and creative drawings so that what he's drawn is a long way off the real thing, especially when it comes to facts and figures."

"The thing is Fergus, and as I've told you. Some day I hope to join the Naval Architectural College, and these drawings, just like the ones I gave you in Bermuda will come in very handy. But they must remain secret and that is the great burden we have placed upon you, and we are sorry if it places you in an awkward position."‡‡

"Och! Never you mind that John. I'm near to my last promotion which keeps me deskbound, that's why they gave me this last sea trip down here to sort things out for them."

"It's all explained in Joe's letter. No doubt when the time comes, you'll be able to share some of our fame from it. A good after dinner speech somewhere perhaps Fergus."

---

‡‡ See *Future Homes*.

"I've so many of those, it'd take me another lifetime just to waffle on about them. Anyway John! Sufficient to say that everything is under control so don't worry about it. Trewarthy is only a jumped up sea captain, whereas I hold the King's Badge of Office for his naval dockyards no matter where they may be around the world." McPhee said as he pointed to himself.

"Anyway, what's this problem with this floating crane, apart from the fact that it's not floating, John?" Mc Phee added to change the subject.

John showed the problem and offered a solution that McPhee was delighted to listen to.

"I knew Joe's father. He was a very fine man and I'd promised him that if I survived the Jap P.o.W. camps I'd keep an eye on Joe. I was fortunate I managed to survive, but his father didn't make it. His mother was in the Singapore dockyard hospital at the time the Japs arrived. She and all the other females got raped then got bayoneted to death by them, and all the men there had their genitals chopped off and stuffed into their mouths before their heads were also chopped off." McPhee spoke candidly for a while and added.

"I've taken a shine to you John because you're proving to be as good as me when I was your age. So you see, I'll do what you ask without question. One thing though, make sure this vessel gets to the Falklands in one piece."

John promised the man and thanked him for his kindness before they heard footsteps approaching them.

"Ah Captain, Commodore. Engineer Grey has pointed out a problem with this floating crane barge." McPhee said aloud, pointing to the problem.

"Before it can be used down in the Falklands, I suggest that you remove this section and replace it with a fabricated one." McPhee continued as he distracted Trewarthy long enough for John to smile and nod to Tomlinson.

"Captain, have you the necessary equipment and material to have it done, or do you need me to send it over for you?" Trewarthy asked coldly.

Tomlinson shook his head and requested that when the supplies were sent over, they make sure that he had enough welding and cutting equipment sent over for when the vessel was to be dismantled for its real use as a SFD.

"Your scribe is taking his time Mc Phee. Hope he's done a good job, as I've got to use them for future super barge constructions planned for later on this year." Trewarthy scowled as he nodded his agreement to Tomlinson's request.

The four men made their way back up to the cabin and concluded their business, before Trewarthy announced that it was time to get back.

"So long Captain, Engineer Grey. Have a good voyage. Next time you're in Gib, call by my office and visit me, won't you!" Mc Phee requested as he shook their hands bidding them farewell.

"You have your orders Captain. Take care of the

cargo won't you." Trewarthy said in an unaccustomed civil tone, as he nodded to Tomlinson and John, before climbing down the ladder into the waiting launch.

"Let's hope Fergus can swing it for us Joe! Trewarthy is truly an ominous person to be around."

"Fergus is a tough old bird. Trewarthy is no match for him! In fact Fergus is way out of his league. We're safe now until we get back." Tomlinson said quietly as both of them watch the launch speed away.

"Anyway John. We've got some fresh supplies in the cabin, including fresh orders. Let's go and see what we've got."

That evening was spent reading private and official mail and going through various details of the new orders, until both men decided it was time to call it a day and turned in for the night.

It was a loud clanging and thwacking noise that rudely awoke everybody up on the SFD.

Tomlinson was out of the cabin like a bat out of hell, followed closely by John who was hopping along trying to put his trousers on again. They were met by one of the lookouts running towards them and pointing to a long thick piece of rope.

"Captain. We were being moved to our new position in the convoy when one of the tow ropes snapped. It snaked over the bow, between the two hulls and hit the deck of the front cradled harbour tug." The lookout shouted

John heard the lookout and raced down the ladders to where the rope was laying.

He saw there was a lot of blood on the rope and when he finally got onto the deck of the tug, he found the tugboat skipper and some of his crew picking up two objects.

"What's happened skipper?"

"It's our engineer. He was on deck fixing a winch when he got sliced in two by this tow-rope. It must have snapped taking the strain. This happens all the time in our profession." the skipper said philosophically.

Tomlinson arrived on the scene and quickly assessing what was to follow, issued a string of orders and instructions, including to John.

"Engines! check the bow for slash damage. Some tow-ropes can cut through steel as well. Although we're lucky as this one is hemp, not wire."

The flurry of activity soon abated but was the talk of the men for the rest of the morning, as was the removal of the dead man. He was taken away by a launch to the supply ship for return to his next of kin.

The convoy finally restarted its voyage due south, leaving the shelter of the Ascension Islands far behind, and getting back into the slow but steady rhythm of the Atlantic swell.

"As long as we don't do things by halves during this next stage." John muttered to himself as he restarted his series of rounds again.

CHAPTER XXII
Over

The next two weeks passed off without incident, with everybody enjoying the lazy days. The stores were more plentiful which allowed them to eat and drink their fill; to sleep and even sunbathe, until the convoy started to reach colder climes, when it was time for the tarpaulin to be rigged again and for everybody to start wearing their warm clothing again.

"Captain, message from tug *Eskimo!*" Luxham announced as he knocked the open cabin door.

"What is it signalman? Read it out."

'*Due to our better speed and capability, we've been ordered to increase our towing speed and proceed independently from our convoy column and pass to the west of Tristan De Cunha. We are to rendezvous with the supply ship Brooklea who will meet us off the Falklands. In order for our transit time to be cut, we intend streaming a second tow line, in one hour from now, for you to lash onto your hull's forward bollards. Suggest you weld a Panama Plate on to it. When done so, we'll give a two hour strain/speed test to ensure we don't lose another tow line. You are requested to monitor the tow lines and the increased wave activity on your bows during that time.*'

"Thank you signalman, put it on the table. Ask the *Eskimo* to commence." Tomlinson replied as he dismissed Luxham.

"Did you hear that John? I think we'd better do what the man says."

"Let's go! I'll get my end organised and ready when you are. Although you'd better stand by with sharp axes to cut these tow lines if something happens." John observed, with Tomlinson nodding in agreement as both men scrambled into action.

"We've cracked it John. All we've got to do now is hope this works, although I'm not too happy with the increased bow wave."

Tomlinson said as both men watched the water creep further up the bow. I'll need to speak to the Eskimo's skipper about it. Any comments you want to make or are you happy?"

'Now there's a thought! Fancy me being Happy. But then I wonder what he would have done.' John mused, but indicated to Tomlinson that he was.

The change of course, the increase of speed and the whole behaviour of the vessel's movement must have agreed with it and especially the men on board. As everybody realised that they'd be getting off this nightmare sooner than they thought.

The two officers were up on the port hull taking a breather from their inspection when they saw Luxham operating his aldis.

"Who have you got there, signalman? Is it the *Brooklea?*" Tomlinson asked.

Luxham carried on flashing his message until he finished before turning to reply.

"Captain. It's a merchantman bound for Durban, who has broken down. He's spotted our tugs but cannot raise them by radio, as they've got no power. They've asked us for help, and I was just telling them to wait until I came back to them again."

Tomlinson took Luxham's binoculars and looked over to the distant ship, then asked John to come with him to speak to the Eskimo.

"*Eskimo* this is SFD2, Captain Tomlinson speaking. Do you read? Over!"

"*Eskimo* here. Captain speaking. What can I do for you? Over."

Tomlinson explained the situation and talked briefly about what they could possibly do for the ship.

The radio discussion lasted several minutes before it was decided that they would heave to and go to the stricken vessel.

"Signalman. Make to the ship. Will close you, have your motor launch ready. Intend sending personnel on board to assist you." Tomlinson ordered.

Luxham sent his signal and got a reply, which he spelt out for Tomlinson again.

"It appears John, we both need to go over and help out. We'll find out what's needed, when we get there, so lets hope they're fully equipped. Otherwise we'll be lending the ship one of our tugs to bring back into port again."

"That is exactly what we have been sent down here for Joe. To help Merchantmen! But making as much salvage money as possible for the consortium. The tugs bring them in, the SFD lifts them out of the water, for Fergus and friends to fix them back up again."

"A very cunning plan that is, don't you think John?" Tomlinson replied as they saw the two mother tugs swing round in a large arc and head towards the ship.

The SFD stopped almost alongside the freighter, which demonstrated the skill of the British Mariner.

Tomlinson shouted across to them to get fenders over the side to protect the ballast tanks, and get some lines secured so that they remained alongside each other.

"Ahoy there! I'm Captain Sandford, My ship is the SS. *San Juan* out of Puerto Madryn bound for Durban. This my Chief Engineer Jackson, glad to see you. Not very often a floating dock comes out to meet a ship mind you." Came a loud voice from above them.

John looked up towards the bridge and saw two men looking at them.

"I'm Captain Tomlinson, this the SFD2 on tow, out of Belfast bound for Port Stanley. This is my Engineer. What can we do for you Captain?" Tomlinson replied back in the same manner.

"I need you to come aboard with your Engineer, if you would Captain. There's no need to climb over the side, I'll put a gangway over to you."

Tomlinson stood back and saw the neatly kept gangway lowered gently onto their starboard hull, before they scrambled over it and onto the ship, and were met by the two officers.

"Pleased you could come gentlemen." Sandford said as he and Jackson shook hands with them, but showed their surprise when they discovered that John was only a 4th Engineering Officer and not as Jackson, a full Chief Engineer.

Tomlinson saw the look the men gave each other and quickly dispelled their doubts when he explained that the SFD designer was John.

"In that case, how well do you know triple expansion steam engines, 4th?" Jackson asked as he led John into the ship and down towards the engine room. It was John's turn to be surprised when he realised that Jackson was the only British Engineer on board.

John was taken around the boiler room and through to the steam turbine room before he was taken to the problem that caused the ship to break down.

'*I wonder what Happy Day or Jim Gregson would do?*' John thought to himself as he weighed up some careful answers.

After several minutes of meaningful discussion with Jackson, John told him all he could do was connect up a compressor and blow through the pipes to unblock them, then try the salt water suction pump.

"Suck and blow, suck and blow, Chief!"

Jackson got some of his stokers to fetch a compressor from the SFD and started to operate it between himself and John.

"That's the trouble with foreign crews, Grey. You've got to watch them like a hawk in case they operate the wrong valve or whatever. This is only a steam engine, think what it would be like on a diesel powered one."

John did not answer, merely continued with his task.

It took the two engineers several attempts before they succeeded in unblocking the system.

John opened a valve and found that a powder like substance cascaded all over him.

"That's your problem chief. Your system has choked itself, so you must have problems with your desalination filters. This is pure salt all over me."

Jackson took a pinch of the stuff to confirm it was, and started to shout obscenities at the stokers who were standing around. John couldn't understand the foreign language, but understood the English expletives that punctuated his tirade.

When Jackson finished shouting he calmed himself down enough to speak civilly to John.

"I would gladly swap every man jack of those stokers for just one British one, even a 4th. How about it?" Jackson offered.

"That's the problem of recruiting locals Chief. Especially to man the size of this vessel, she must be at least 20,000 tons." John replied diplomatically.

"Aye, 15,000 tons of useless scrap. The cargo is worth more than that." Jackson swore and wiped his sweaty forehead with a dirty handkerchief.

"I think it's time I saw the Captain now Chief, if that's all right with you. It will only take a few moments to restore power once you've got a head of steam." John stated.

Jackson nodded and led the way up out of the boiler room taking John to the bridge where Tomlinson was chatting away merrily with Sandford.

"Have I got power now Chief? Everything sorted?" Sandford asked excitedly, as John looked at Tomlinson and smiled.

"You'll have steerage in about twenty minutes and be able to get underway in about forty Captain." Jackson replied.

"Well let's get a move on Chief, can't sit around cluttering up the oceans now can we." Sandford said breezily as he turned to Tomlinson.

"It was good of you to stop by Captain. No doubt your engineer was a great help to my Chief. Here's a case of good old Scottish Malt whisky for your troubles. And another one for your Tug master! I'll give a full report to your company HQ when I reach port again.

Once again thank you for your help." Sandford said gratefully as he waved his arm towards the bridge doorway.

Tomlinson and John carried their case of whisky gently back over to the SFD and waved to Sandford as the gangway was lifted back off the hull.

"They haven't returned my compressor Joe." John whispered, but Tomlinson was talking to Luxham indicating that the tugs could pull away now.

Everybody on the SFD waved to the crewmen of the freighter as the gap between the vessels got wider and went their separate ways.

"Joe, they've got my compressor." John reiterated.

"Yes John, I know. I didn't recognise him at first, but Sandford is an old friend of mine, and I owed him one."

"What do you mean, from all the places in the world you end up meeting him here?"

"That is a common thing for many a mariner. It's even more exquisite each time it happens, as you never know when or where it will happen again." Tomlinson said wistfully and explained his reason why Sandford was to keep the compressor.

"In that case, I'm able to write it off, that's no problem Joe. I'm without one for the rest of this voyage that's all." John said with a grin.

"That's the spirit John. Speaking of which, we've got some of the liquid type to sample in these cases. Care to join me?"

The weather was getting much colder and the water much lumpier, which kept the men more vigilant about the state of the SFD, which in turn made them more anxious to get into harbour.

The *Brooklea* met up with them only a few miles to go off the Falkland Islands, with an angry Captain demanding where the hell they were two days ago.

"Sorry we missed you. Went to the assistance of the freighter SS *San Juan*. Over."

"I expect to see your log when we get in. In the meantime, have your tugs follow us into harbour. Over and out."

"That sounded like our illustrious Commodore Trewarthy on the other end John." then spoke to the mother tugs.

"When you come alongside, we've got a present for you off the *San Juan*. Tell your companion. See you later, Out."

"It looks as if our little voyage is over once we anchor and get ashore Joe. But what I would like to know is; are we to stay here or go back with the *Brooklea?*"

"You'll be rejoining the *Brooklea*. I've got to stay here and help set up the Harbour Master's office. That is of course, unless our friend the Commodore has sussed us both out and we're on our way to an early beach party."

"No chance. Wait until you meet my pals Chief Engineers Day and Gregson." John said with conviction.

"Chief Engineer Day, as in Henry Obediah Day? The last time I met him, which was only about three years ago, he was only a 3rd." Tomlinson said with surprise.

"And he's on board the *Brooklea?* Now do you see what I mean about chance meetings! But how did you come to meet him?"

"It's a long story that you've probably heard several

times before. Remind me to tell you about it sometime." John sighed as he remembered his first meeting with Day.

The tugs pulled the SFD slowly and carefully as the procession of vessels entered Port Stanley, led by a tiny launch with the word PILOT written along it in big white lettering.

They passed the *Brooklea*, which was nestled against a short harbour wall, until they finally arrived at their new anchorage, some 9,000 miles away from whence it came.

"Thank God this voyage is over." John mused as the SFD slowed to a stop in the middle of the harbour.

'I hope for a safer return and on a decent vessel this time,' he thought, as he took in the sights of the islands around him

CHAPTER XXIII
Return Ticket

The Falklands are a collection of islands on top of a rocky plateau that rises up from the great depths of the Southern part of the Atlantic and are about 500 miles off the southern tip of the South American coast. They have two main islands side by side, but cover an overall area of approx 1000 square miles.

They were taken from the Spanish Empire area of Argentina in the late 16th Century, and colonised by the British people since then. These head a string of volcanic islands that stretch right down to the tip of the white continent of Antarctica, where many an explorer dared to venture, or whaling fleets operated for the valuable whale meat and oil. There are still some traces of them left, including some of the wrecked ships they left behind.

Today, the Falklands are still occupied by the British, mostly by sheep farmers, and enjoy the passing trade of ships. Just like the Ascension Islands, the Falklands are ideally situated for ships to satisfy their need to refuel before making their way up the whole length of the Atlantic, or round the Cape Horn and into the even vaster expanse of the Pacific Ocean.

Port Stanley is the capital and has a Governor General to govern the sparse population and to exercise the sovereignty of and for the British people.

During WW2 the Falklands maintained the presence

of a Royal Naval Task Force there, a naval base was to be built for that purpose, with special underground ammunition and oil bunkers hewn out of the solid granite.

Since then, the harbour had undergone major construction changes and was now in the process of completing its re-development by the Triple Coronet consortium.

This idea was to provide the extra needs of the merchant shipping which were being built much bigger and several times heavier than those of the sleek men o' war who frequent the port.

This then is the temporary home for John and the sole purpose for the collection of various vessels in his convoy to end up here.

Tomlinson and John stood on the starboard hull by the gangway, and watched the two mother tugs push the SFD end on to a stone and concrete constructed harbour breakwater.

"John, how long do you think it will take to strip the SFD down for its primary role?"

"They have to unload the dockside cranes, re-assemble them onto their rail tracks; and remove the rest of the loose cargo and the false bridge. Then the SFD will have to be moored securely before she dips down to float off the harbour craft. I'd say about four days, providing the weather holds."

"That seems about right. Ready about the time the

rest of the convoy arrives then." Tomlinson observed.

"In the meantime what're we going to do for accommodation Joe?"

"According to my orders and the plans of the dock complex, our bridge structure will be lifted off first, and placed dockside over there, by tonight." Tomlinson replied as he pointed to an empty space.

"Then when the second SFD arrives its bridge structure will also be brought ashore, and put on top of ours. They will eventually form the Harbour Masters Office and admin block. Do you see those warehouses down the bottom end? Well they're workshops and spare parts storage sheds.

The others up on that side are transit sheds for use by the guest ship whilst it's in dock. My office block will eventually be like an arrival / departure area for passengers and crew. The main accommodation spaces will be used for that, whereas our little cabin will house the Customs and Immigration Units. I will have a special bridge-like structure as a control tower on top fitted with radar and radios."

"Sounds as if you're going to have a nice cosy little home down here Joe. Maybe you'll decide to get yourself a little croft built somewhere, settle down with some local lass, and stuff the likes of Trewarthy and co."

"Haven't thought of it that way John. But then I can think of far nicer places to settle down, than this draughty bleak old place."

"I haven't travelled far and wide enough to settle down Joe. Besides I don't want to be just a 4th Engineer."

"Yes I've gathered that much John. Maybe if you stay here with me, you'll eventually become your own boss, with the pick of the ships coming here in need of your services.

"That's what old Fergus did, after he got back from the war. He made his name in Bermuda and Gibraltar, and was able to alternate between the two of them.

"He's due to pick up his knighthood and is thinking of retiring early with a King's pension in his back pocket."

"I wonder which place he'll choose to stay Joe. Let's hope it's Gib."

"Amen to that John." Tomlinson replied as if to conclude the conversation.

"Captain. I've got a message from the *Brooklea* to SFD2. It's an R.S.V.P. All officers are requested to come aboard at 1600hrs to meet the Island's Governor and attend the cocktail party afterwards." Luxham announced as he held the signal out to Tomlinson.

"Thank you Luxham. Acknowledge that, and inform the skippers off our four harbour tugs too. When you've done that, arrange some suitable transport for us all to arrive together. A launch would be appropriate Luxham. Once that's done, tell the steward to come and see me."

"Aye Captain" Luxham responded.

"Best bib and tucker, or as my old steward on the *Brooklea* would say, best whistle and flute."

"Yes, that's why I've sent for the steward. This is one occasion when one has to turn up in uniform. I need mine spruced up somewhat, what about yours John?"

"Mine's hanging up on the back of the cabin door under yours, and thanks Joe."

John stepped into the launch with Tomlinson and observed there were several other officers on board as well as the four harbour tugboat skippers, each of them bedecked with war medals.

John noticed the coloured sash with an adorned cross hanging under it around Joe's neck to garland him, which enhanced the medals he wore on his chest, but was ignorant as to what it was, and dared not ask. Instead he just looked around at the weather beaten faces and the demeanour of the passengers, to try and fathom out the similarities of an earlier occasion.

"The last time I went to one of these, I got beaten up and ended up in court. Let's hope sense will prevail this time." John muttered to himself.

The launch arrived alongside the *Brooklea* and stopping at the bottom of the 'Medway' ladder disgorged its passengers who happily climbed it, to find a sailor waiting to announce their arrival.

"The SFD2 Captain and Engineer. The Captains and Engineers off the harbour tugs." the sailor shouted over the hubbub of earlier arrivals.

Tomlinson was swiftly taken away from John and whisked away towards the 'top table' which left John standing, he looked around to see if he could spot any fellow *Brooklea* shipmates to say hello to.

"This is my return, but with nobody I know to greet me again." John said to himself, and feeling the same loneliness as he did way back in Belfast some thousand years ago.

"Hello John, welcome back."

John spun around and saw Happy Day with a big grin on his face.

"Happy! Ahem, Chief Day. Nice to meet you again!" John said with a hint of glee in his voice as he grasped hold of Day's hand, and shook it vigorously.

"Whoa John! It's nice to see you once more but I want to use my hand again thank you very much." Day laughed.

"Am I pleased to see you Happy! I've had quite an outing with the voyage here, and I've helped with sorting out a triple expansion engine into the bargain."

"Yes, it looks as if you have certainly won your spurs yet again John. Mind you, you were in the exclusive company of the famous Captain Tomlinson."

"Do you mean Joe Tomlinson?"

"You are obviously still very much learning who is who and who does what. Tomlinson has the highest medal for valour, called the Victoria Cross and is also a knight of the realm. Only he keeps it secret from most people so that he can do his own personal sailor thing, without fuss. Otherwise he'd be inundated with the likes of certain arsehole scrapers that you and I are familiar with, who get their promotions without due merit, Tritton for example. The only thing is, and will prove to be a big problem, we've got too many 'prima donnas' in the new consortium, fighting over every little scrap of evidence to prove that they are the ones to keep the 'sea lanes open' so to speak.

"That includes your friends Trewarthy and Cresswell. Their trouble is that the world is moving on in leaps and bounds since the war, leaving them behind. Not a pretty sight by any means, but at least there has been an open challenge within the maritime world to take up the baton when these famous 'old salts' are finally beached."

"So in other words Happy, it's to people like you and me to keep the tradition going, but to invent, adapt or improve our trade to meet the shipping industry of the future."

"You've got it in one John. Anyway, to put it succinctly, your first captain was Trewarthy, your recent one was Tomlinson. Your dilemma is this. Who would you place your trust in, Trewarthy or Tomlinson? But I don't expect an answer from you just yet. Think it over carefully before giving me your answer."

"Bloody hell! He's asking me to choose between Joe and Trewarthy. It's like asking the proverbial mob to choose between the saving of Barrabas or Jesus." John exclaimed softly, but was overheard by somebody that spoke with a familiar voice.

"Engineer Grey. I thought I recognised your voice. How was your trip?' Burns asked as he offered John a glass of liquid from his tray.

John turned and saw Burns smiling at him.

"Hello Burns, you old rascal. Glad to see you again. As you've been everywhere, what do you know about this place?" John replied with surprise as he took a glass from the tray.

"I'm all right so far. This is where I was picked up by a Norwegian whale factory ship and worked my way back to Bergen, before getting home again." Burns revealed and changed the subject.

"Never mind that 4th, just to let you know, this cock and arse party is a re-run of Barbados. So take two glasses of this funny stuff and I'll be back soon with something much more, shall we say, celebratory. Don't forget, mum's the word." Burns whispered, as he looked around in case somebody was listening.

John nodded and tapped the side of his nose just like Burns often did when things confidential were spoken about, and nobody else to know about.

"Hello 4th! Fancy meeting you down in the bottom drawer of the world"

John turned round and saw Jack Cunningham grinning at him, as he offered John a drink.

"Jack Cunningham. How was your voyage? The *Brook* must have flown down here to be tied up before we did. How did you manage that?"

"Not as bad as the convoy, apparently. The ship was able to fulfil her primary role of a support vessel to keep the convoys afloat. But it was your unplanned disappearance with our rendezvous point that threw the wobbly that lost us.

Macintosh went spare when we finally caught up with you. Ask the Bosun when you meet him again."

"You mean, Trewarthy is not on board? But I thought it was his voice, according to our last radio message we received. So who is in charge now?" John asked in total amazement.

"For Trewarthy, read Macintosh." Cunningham chuckled, then informed John of the change of personnel since Gibraltar and the Ascension Islands, ending up with the teasing prospect that John might be able to come back to the *Brooklea* as a second 3rd Engineer, subject to the Board's decision. Otherwise, he'd be assigned to dockyard duties for the next few years.

John froze at the prospect of spending the rest of his natural life down in these almost God forsaken islands.

"Jack! I have come to the conclusion that it doesn't matter what you do on board, there is always some hierarchy that dictates your life, from a cabin boy right up to Admiral."

"That's about the size of it John. But you must keep a track of your 'knockers' or enemies, or they'll do for you quicker than that. My advice to you is to listen to your own calling, never mind all the trappings around you." Cunningham replied swiftly and left him.

"Joe!" John exclaimed, when he saw Tomlinson standing full square in front of him, taking him unawares.

"I fully endorse what Cunningham has just said. So before we finally part company, and strictly as a friend, what you must realise John is this. Throughout your own career and life at sea, you will meet up with many a seafarer, hopefully most of them to be good shipmates, but often you will find that there are some you must steer clear of.

"Because they are the ones that will take you into confidence, then having done so, shit on you from a great height. Classical examples are Trewarthy, Cressswell and their ilk, even though they may appear to be on your side and nurturing your cause." Tomlinson confided, and went on to explain about the perils of placing faith in people whom he had just met, and expecting them to stick up for him when the going got tough.

"But Joe, it sounds as if the perilous voyage all of us on the SFD suffered, and the joint decisions we made together to ensure our safety, in your opinion, counts for nought. I really don't understand what you're saying."

"It's really quite simple John. Make friends with as many as you can whilst on board whatever ship you might sail on, and it really doesn't matter what rank or job they do on board. Keep in touch with those you feel you can trust, but keep a close watch on those who you don't. As you have witnessed on the *San Juan*, good friends turn up when you least expect them to, but there'll always be the bad ones lurking in the shadows just to trip you up."

John thought for a moment to digest this deep and meaningful statement Tomlinson had made, and decided to address this later on when he had a quiet moment to himself.

"Many thanks for your advice Joe, I will think hard on what you said, as it will probably solve my dilemma where personal loyalties are concerned. Insofar as the *Brooklea* is concerned, Trewarthy was my first captain, you my second.

"Whereas I was treated abysmally by him, I have found you totally the opposite, even though you both have had a tough time during the war, albeit in different ways." John spoke with total and open frankness.

"Yes John. I'd already gauged the worth and manner of you almost from day one, and especially when you were highly regarded by my so-called 'Uncle' Fergus. For what it's worth what you must remember is this.

"I am a seaman Officer with knowledge of all things up on deck and how to navigate or handle a ship whatever the situation, but who understands certain points of your profession enough to survive in certain circumstances. Whereas in your profession as an Engineer, your knowledge is normally, purely on the engineering or mechanical side of things."

John nodded his agreement to that fundamental statement, and decided that for once a Deck Officer was speaking to him 'man to man'.

"I thank you for your frankness Joe. Now I know the reason behind the thinking between the two major forces on board. Seamanship V Engineering."

Before Tomlinson had the chance to respond, a tall woman dressed in fine couture, which was designed to accentuated her curvaceous figure, tapped him gently on the shoulder.

"Good evening Captain, may I have a light?" she asked, as she held up a coloured cigarette on the end of a very long cigarette holder.

Tomlinson turned round, and automatically felt for his matches, which he fumbled with before he finally struck a match to ignite the cigarette.

"Thank you Captain!" she purred as she blew a ring of smoke at him, which made him cough slightly.

"That's no problem ma'am" Tomlinson said as he watched the woman smoke, but forgot to drop the burning match, until it burnt his fingers.

The woman just smiled, blew another smoke ring at him and left the two men looking at each other in amazement.

"What the hell was all that about?" Tomlinson stammered.

"It appears that Miss Wren has spotted you and it looks as if you are going to be her next victim." said a voice from behind them.

John turned sharply to see a steward standing there holding a tray of snacks in one hand and a bottle of champagne in the other.

"Explain yourself steward!" Tomlinson hissed, which made the steward bow his head.

"Beggin' your pardon Captain. I'm the Governor's butler, but it seems that his daughter has taken a shine to you, and she normally gets what she wants on these islands, no matter what it is. Especially the young single males of the ship's Captain variety. She tries to have a different one for breakfast." the butler stated without a flinch.

"Thank you butler for your warning. Have you met the *Brooklea* steward here this evening? His name is Mr Burns." John replied casually.

"Mr Burns on the Brooklea, did you say sir?"

"That's the name of the old scoundrel! Unless that Miss Tweety pie whatever you call her has got hold of him." John replied sarcastically.

"It's Miss Wren if you don't mind" the butler answered stuffily, but whispered aside.

"Old knobbly knees Burns still on board the *Brook*? Thanks for the tip 4th, only he and I are cousins, so to speak. If you see him tell him Albie is asking for him."

"Fair enough Albie, but in the meantime, keep miss vampire off our backs. Deal?" John whispered back, which the butler nodded his agreement, and waddled off to plague somebody else with his wares.

"Thanks John. I'm not used to high-class females

like that one. It appears she is trawling for some poor sucker to indulge her flights of fancy." Tomlinson said quietly.

"It looks as if you're first on the menu tonight, or should I say, for breakfast then Joe." John said teasingly, and chuckled when Tomlinson's response was a quick nudge in his ribs.

"Ladies and gentlemen. I give you the governor of the Falklands Lord and Lady Wren KCB DSC." The MC shouted, which brought the proceedings to a silence.

The Governor spoke at length about the new era of opportunity for the Islands, then announced that his co-host would give his response.

John was totally surprised when he heard the voices of Belverley and Invergarron, and indicated to Tomlinson his surprise.

"Typical of these lordships, John. But for god sake don't get too close to them. Just do your job, and forget the social climbing. They have their own ways of weeding out the genuine people from the arse lickers and social hangers on. They'd suck you in and spit you out in little bubbles quicker than batting an eye, they would."

"So you're not interested in Miss Tit or, whatever." John smiled as he teased Tomlinson again.

"Nah! She's like an icicle, cold and skinny. Give me an oriental girl any time. Small but perfectly formed, they really know how to please a man."§§

---

§§ See *Perfumed Dragons.*

The protocol and proceedings came to an abrupt end as the VIP's filed out of the *Brooklea's* passenger lounge, in strict pecking order, leaving the lesser guests to finish off the dregs of the party.

John and Tomlinson decided to take their first stroll ashore on the Island from the Brooklea, as their first land-fall since leaving Belfast almost six weeks ago.

"Makes a change to have solid earth under your feet Joe, what do you say?"

"Make's no difference to me John, although it is nice to stretch your legs a bit without tripping over something. Lets walk back to the SFD shall we?"

"Suits me fine Joe." John replied, and they both walked slowly along the poorly lit roadway towards the dockyard complex.

They arrived to find that the SFD's bridge was in its designed area, fully lit.

"Smell that Joe! That's coming from the galley! Someone's having a good feed. let's go and join them." John said quietly as he could almost taste the smell of the food as it wafted out of the galley windows.

"I wonder if there's enough to reach around to us, because it's made me ruddy starving."

"If not, then its spam sarnies again Joe!" John replied as both men entered their cabin.

"Evening Captain. Engines." the steward acknowledged them.

"We'd been expecting you sooner, so here's a bowl

of mutton stew to share between you." the steward replied, as he handed them a large bowl and two spoons and left the cabin.

When they finished eating and had smoked their after meal cigarette, both men decided it was time to turn in, to be ready for a new day in another new place.

"Captain. Here is the mail, and a few signals for you." Luxham announced, as the two officers emerged from their cabin the next morning.

"Hello signalman!" Tomlinson replied when they met up.

"What's the signal orders for today?"

"The first one is that you and Engineer Grey are requested to attend a briefing on the *Brooklea* at 0930 hours, in the Captain's day cabin.

The second one is to do with harbour movements and the positioning of the two Mulberrys outboard of the SFD. The next two signals and the mail concerns stores etc. I have a jeep coming to pick you both up in about five minutes." Luxham stated.

"Thank you signalman. You'll make a good Personal Secretary to some lucky officer." Tomlinson said warmly, as he heaped praise on the man.

"Good morning Captain Tomlinson, 4th Engineer Grey. We met last night informally, but now this is business. You know everybody here I take it, so lets get down to business." Mackintosh said civilly.

"Come in and take a seat."

John looked around the cabin and noticed a total

change in the character and the ambience of the cabin to when Trewarthy had it.

'Maybe this is what the ship needed?' He thought as he nodded his acknowledgement to the other officers sitting around the large chart table.

Mackintosh unfolded a large scroll of paper, and unwrapped a bundle of sealed documents and commenced to inform them of what was in store for each of them and what the Tricorn shipping group policies surrounding them were.

The session lasted several hours, but was interspersed with refreshment breaks, and continued again after the lunch break.

During the afternoon session Belverley and Invergarron, who answered any pertinent questions that arose from the documents joined them. With Mackintosh answering the practical side of things.

John and Tomlinson walked off the *Brooklea* with their minds full of fresh knowledge and information, so much so that neither of them spoke a word until they arrived back at their cabin again.

"It seems that I'm to stay here and set up the Harbour Master position, then return to Belfast on completion. That will take about two months, give or take a few days, and providing all the equipment arrives on schedule." Joe reflected as he drank from his whisky glass.

"And I'm to join the SS *Invermoriston* when she arrives from Cape town. I was hoping to rejoin the

Brooklea as my return ticket home again." John responded.

"A good ship, if I remember. If it's the same captain on board, then it's Captain Sandford's cousin. I forget his name off hand, but you should be okay there. Mind you, I can't comment on the engine room officers, but no doubt you'll get on."

The next couple of days the two officers were kept fully occupied with their tasks in hand, preparing the SFD for its first customer.

The place was bustling and full of noise, and the growing excitement of the imminent arrival of the rest of the convoy.

Despite the cold and blustery weather they had to endure, everybody was in good spirits and did their tasks well.

When the convoy finally arrived, there was a feeling of satisfaction of a job well done, and a rest was due to everyone once the rest of the pieces of the jigsaw were put into place.

It was a happy time for John, as he got to install or learn different machinery or mechanical devices as required by his temporary Chief Engineer Jim Gregson, and wrote copious notes on them for future references.

But more importantly he read up on the *Invermoriston*'s propulsion, so as to be prepared when he got on board her.

His bubble finally burst when he saw his next home

sail slowly into the harbour and tie up alongside the breakwater jetty, which meant that John was to pack his belongings and report to his new Chief Engineer.

"Look at the state of her. Must have been in some rough weather judging by the lack of paint on her hull. She's got engine troubles too judging by the black smoke coming out of her funnel. Still, as long as she is still floating, that's the main thing" John muttered to himself as he gave the ship a once over.

John packed his things and because Tomlinson was not there at the time, he put a letter on his bunk and left his old cabin, shutting the door quietly, before marching down the dockyard road towards his new home.

"Are you the Quartermaster? If so, I'm 4th Engineer Grey and I'm to report to your Chief Engineer, whoever that is." John said quietly to a man standing at the top of the gangway.

"No, I'm the Bosun on my way ashore. But if you go through the doorway behind that deck ladder there." The Bosun replied, and gave instructions on how to find the Chief's cabin.

"Thank you Bosun. I'll find it." John acknowledged, as he followed those instructions.

"Come in!" Came the invite from inside the cabin.

"Chief engineer. I'm 4th Engineer Grey reporting." John replied as he stepped into the cluttered cabin.

"Why aye man! Welcome aboard 4th. I'm Chief Engineer Baker." the man said as he shook John's hand.

"Set yersel doon man, whilst I sort this drawing out."

Baker said in a broad Geordie accent, as he folded up the large paper into a small neat parcel.

"There, that's done it!" he added with a smile on his face.

"It looks as if you've got plenty of homework to be getting along with Chief!" John observed.

"That's not the half of it. Anyway 4th! Let's get you sorted out like! Now that we've docked, I can give you about an hour to show you around. After that then we'll have a bite to eat! But first, I'll show you to your cabin, which is only about two down and opposite mine."

John looked around his new cabin and saw that it was better quality and bigger than the *Brooklea's*, and certainly much bigger than the SFD.

"A person can get used to such luxury. But there must be some sort of drawback with two bunks in it." John said quietly, but was heard by Baker.

"Did you say something 4th?"

"Just making a mental note on the difference between my cabin on the *Brooklea* and here, that's all Chief." John admitted.

"No comparison 4th. The *'Inver'* ships are either a bulk cargo carrier or general passenger cargo freighters, of about 100 foot longer, 10 foot wider and about 8,000 displacement tons heavier than the *Lea* ships, even more so for the *Brooklea.* Our horsepower is nearly three times more than that of the *Brooklea* even though we can't go as fast. You will also find that the *'Bay'* ships are much bigger than us again." Baker stated, and continued his conducted tour around the ship, via the Pursers Office, saloon, engine room, ending back up in the dining room.

"After dinner, you come and see me again and we'll discuss what job you'll be doing on board. See you later 4th!" Baker ordered and left John to his own devices in the crowded compartment.

"Sit over here 4th!" A steward said as he appeared by John's side.

"You'll be joined by a couple more of your fellow officers shortly. But here's the menu, let me know what you want!"

John did as he was told, feeling a bit self-conscious, but sat down and started to read the mouth-watering descriptions of the food on the menu.

Soon he was joined by the Radio Officer, a 3rd Deck Officer and the 2nd Engineer, who introduced themselves as they gathered around him and started to make him feel welcome.

"Off the *Brooklea?* Then you've met Chief Cresswell! I was the same as you when I first met him about three years ago. Some has it that he's mad, but thanks to him I'm now a 2nd." Holdsworthy bragged.

John decided not to counterclaim the character of Cresswell, and decided to change the subject, and asked about the ship.

Each of them had their own story to tell, which John found fascinating, until he announced that he was to see Baker again.

"I've got to see him as well. I'll show you the way." Holdsworthy offered.

Both men entered Baker's cabin, and to John's surprise, he met Day, who was sitting and having a drink.

"2nd! This is Chief Engineer Day, an old friend of mine. 4th I take it you already know him." Baker said as he introduced his guest.

"Hello 2nd, pleased to meet you! Hello 4th how are you!" Day nodded as he greeted them.

"It seems that Chief Day here has a problem that maybe one of you could help him with" Baker invited. Then asked Day to tell them what it was.

"I have been ordered to change half my engine room staff with this ship, for the return trip back to Belfast.

But as it has double the amount of engineers it can afford to lend me a couple more for that voyage, I need an extra 2nd and another 3rd. or a senior 4th. Your chief has suggested that one if not both of you can be spared as the *Invermoriston* will not be sailing for quite a while yet." Day explained evenly.

"But I've just come aboard Chief Baker!" John protested.

"And I wish to remain on here." Holdsworthy added.

"Yes, yes I know all that. But from the looks of things, this ship's going nowhere until she completes her repairs in that twin floating dock over there." Baker said pointing to the SFD from his port-hole.

"John. You can have your old job back as Outside Engineer, and even get the promotion to go with it.

What do you say?" Day asked, soothingly to entice John to accept.

"You mean I get temporarily promoted to 3rd, then revert back again when I leave, Happy?"

"No. Once you pass your exam for 3rd that's it. Nobody can take it away from you."

"What about Jack Cunningham?"

"He's now my 2nd. You can be my 3rd, as you've already proved that you can do the job, and even more according to what the Dockyard Engineer's been telling me. The exam would be a doddle for you, John. Besides, you're on a promotion roll as it stands, why stop now at 4th." Day said silkily as he poured more enticement onto John's decision making thoughts.

John stood up and walked over to the porthole that had a full view of the two SFDs' that were being joined together just as he had designed them to be, and said nothing whilst the others were talking.

"If Grey is to become a 3rd fills one place. I'm already a 2nd therefore you don't need me. It seems that you'll be taking two of our Junior Engineers." Holdsworthy said smugly.

"You've got a point there 2nd. That's unless Grey wishes to remain here." Baker replied.

"Okay then Chief Baker. I'll accept the challenge of Chief Day, but it means that if I come back and re-join the *Brooklea,* I return as the Outside Engineer." John said finally, as he nodded to Day.

"Good man! I knew you'd accept!" Day whooped

shaking John's hand, which made Baker stare at the two of them.

"Hold on a minute! I smell a rat here. Is there something I've missed that I should know about Happy?" Baker asked with incredulity.

"Nothing for you to worry about old mate. It's just that John Grey here was only on temporary loan to the SFD anyway, and got mixed up with some other 4th who should be joining you when he gets over his sea sickness fever." Happy said magnanimously as he put his arm around Baker's shoulder in sympathy.

"Oh no! Not another 'namby pamby'!" Holdsworthy groaned, which was echoed by Baker.

"C'mon John. Lets get back to real engines and we'll have a welcome home party in my cabin." Day said jubilantly as he ushered John out of Baker's cabin.

"Hello John! Welcome back on board!" Cunningham greeted as John arrived into the saloon.

"Congrats on your promotion Jack! You deserve it!" John responded with his own kindness.

For the following two days, John was in the dockyard taking his trade test for 3rd. He was able to answer any question and complete his task to the complete satisfaction of the examining officers; Tomlinson, Day, and John's temporary boss, the Dockyards' Chief Engineer Gregson.

The *Brooklea* finally sailed out of the cold waters of

Port Stanley to make its 8,000 mile long, sometimes quiet and easy, but mostly turbulent voyage north and back to Belfast.

"Let's hope we get a run ashore in Gib on the way back!" John mused as he continued his familiar rounds on deck, and smiled at his good fortune of returning home, with yet another step up the promotion ladder under his belt, his return ticket stamped '3rd Engineer'.

AFE

A Fatal Encounter is the first book within the epic *Adventures of John Grey* series, which comprises of:

A Fatal Encounter
The Black Rose
The Lost Legion
Fresh Water
A Beach Party
Ice Mountains
Perfumed Dragons (late 2010)
The Repulse Bay (published 2011)
Silver Oak leaves (published 2011)
Future Homes (published 2012)

All published by www.guaranteedbooks.net

Also by the same author
Moreland and Other Stories

Coming Soon
We Come Unseen